MAUREEN KURR

NORTHWARD THE HEART

LEISURE BOOKS   **NEW YORK CITY**

A LEISURE BOOK

Published by

Dorchester Publishing Co., Inc.
6 East 39th Street
New York, NY 10016

Copyright © 1985 by Maureen Kurr

All rights reserved. No part of this book may be reproduced or transmitted in any form or by any electronic or mechanical means, including photocopying, recording, or by any information storage and retrieval system, without the written permission of the Publisher, except where permitted by law.

Printed in the United States of America

For Donna, my friend and most reassuring critic, the first person to call me a writer.

And for my fellow workshop members, especially Jan and Anne, for all their help and encouragement.

And of course for my husband, Jerry, who made it all possible.

Prologue

January, A.D. 919

Wessex

In the distance, the pounding of hooves disturbed the quiet night. From her vantage on higher ground, Ambyre of Athelney could see the horsemen swiftly approaching the palace gates. Flaming torches lit their way, looking like huge fireflies floating through the air.

As they drew near, entering the palace grounds, Ambyre had no doubt that the mission of the night had succeeded. There was jubilance in the movements of those below, triumph in the voices which found their way to Ambyre's ears.

But she did not gaze at them for long; she hurried to carry out her own part in the evening's activities. A path led her to a separate building, its newness apparent by the unworn timber of which it was built. Inside, she lit several candles and stoked the fire in the hearth, and the winter damp succumbed to the heightened flames. She moved a tray of food

NORTHWARD THE HEART

nearby to warm the bread and honey, meats and nuts, and apple cider. On such a cold winter night a warm meal would be welcome.

With a glance, Ambyre assured herself the room was pleasing to the eye. Flowery rushes matched the sweet scent of the bed's mattress and covers. A multi-colored tapestry hung from the room's only drafty wall, and beside it was a finely carved table holding a variety of stitchery material awaiting idle hands. Aye, she thought with an approving smile, this room is suitable for AElfwyn of Mercia.

But when the door opened to its new occupant, Ambyre knew her efforts had been spent in vain. As the weeping woman entered, Ambyre realized none of the comforts within this room would be heeded.

Compassion made her forget her wasted efforts and Ambyre stepped forward, gently touching the slumped and defeated shoulders. The guest looked up, seeing Ambyre for the first time, but abruptly turned away from the kindness she found in those eyes.

Unwavering, the girl took the woman's cloak, placing it near the fire to dry its winter dampness. When Ambyre looked again she saw the gown was wet as well, and went to a chest for dry, warm clothing.

Neither said a word as the one discarded her soiled garments, while Ambyre brought forth the tray of food. There was wariness in their silence, one filled with charity, the other with mistrust. The food was not accepted.

"The fire is warm," said Ambyre at last. " 'Twill take away your chill."

The woman remained still, her eyes now clear and flashing with anger. "Do you know who I am? Why I have been brought here?"

"Aye, milady," she answered. "You are AElfwyn of Mercia, niece to King Edward."

"And why I have been brought here?" AElfwyn persisted.

Ambyre dropped her eyes momentarily. "You know the reason, milady."

"Aye, so I do. But do *you*? Do you offer me my uncle's false hospitality when he has just stolen my kingdom from me?"

" 'Tis not false, milady. Your uncle wishes only for your comfort."

AElfwyn moaned aloud at the comment, going to the fire as formerly invited. "My comfort!" she scoffed. " 'Twas my comfort to remain home in Mercia. Edward has resorted to the tactics of a barbarian, to kidnap his own niece in order to set himself upon my throne."

" 'Twas your throne for such a short time—" began the other, only to be interrupted by AElfwyn's sharp query.

"And what, pray, do you know about my throne?"

"I know that when your mother sat upon it, she was very close to your uncle King Edward. I cannot see why it should be any different for you."

"My mother was allowed to keep her throne."

"And she ruled admirably for many years

after your father died. But she must have known the throne would go to Edward after her death, not to her daughter. 'Twas what Edward planned all along."

"Who are *you*?" AElfwyn asked, for the moment forgetting her anger in curiosity.

"My name is Ambyre of Athelney. I am the ward of your uncle, King Edward."

"You protect his name more like a lover than a ward," AElfwyn taunted. "I should have known 'twas something like that. You're far too pretty to be a serving wench."

Color heightened in Ambyre's cheeks, and she spoke indignantly. "I assure you, 'tis not as you imply. My father was Dunstan of Athelney, close friend to both Edward and his father Alfred. When my parents died—"

"My uncle graciously invited you to his home," AElfwyn finished.

" 'Tis true, and nothing more. My brother is here as well, and we are both in the King's keeping."

AElfwyn laughed. "My uncle always has enjoyed a full house. How many of his own children now live here in Wessex? Nine—or is it ten? And to think I was given the great privilege to be raised with yet another of his children, Athelstan."

"And Athelstan will be the next King," Ambyre reminded her. "Accepted by both Wessex and your loyal Mercians."

Perhaps her tone had been too harsh to use toward the King's niece, but it was in defense of that King, so Ambyre felt no remorse. And the princess, knowing the truth behind those words, let her laughter die and the anger and malice fade away. Left behind was only the weariness of the night and a residue of fear.

"I knew my mother's wishes," AElfwyn softly admitted. "I knew them better than all of those Mercian loyalists who claimed to love her so. 'Twas not her they loved, nor I; they loved their ancient kingdom, and wanted a ruler of their own, not a Wessex King. But my mother accepted fate. She accepted a Wessex King... Edward."

Ambyre went to AElfwyn's side. "Do not resist him, milady," she pleaded gently. " 'Twas your mother's wish."

Near the coast of Yorkshire, a group of men met at the base of a cliff. Some were standing, others sitting. They all faced the solitary old man who stood with his back to the rocky height, addressing one who was not far from him. His voice, though not young and boisterous, was not yet feeble. It echoed off the wall of rock behind him, so that all who gathered had no trouble hearing.

" 'Tis agreed; you shall be permitted your own group of willing men, and sail forth to enact this plan. But understand this: you are my son, my heir, the next of a long line of chieftains for our noble warriors. Even this will not free you from the consequence of this plan. This maiden will be under your guard. She shall be your duty, whether burden or asset. We shall abide by your plan. But if it fails, or if you should die in its course, she will be returned unharmed to her people, to her uncle in Wessex or back to her kingdom in Mercia, if she so desires. I need not add that all such penalties shall fall upon you, or any of your men, as would in the treatment of a freeborn woman. She will not be known as a captive of war; this maiden AElfwyn will be held in the esteem of the nobility to which she belongs by birth."

The man to whom he had spoken stepped forward. Tall, muscular, his features rugged and handsome, he was, like many of those others nearby, blond-haired, blue-eyed. Only the determination of his gaze set him apart. He bowed slightly to his father.

"Let it be witnessed: your words shall be abided. I sail when the sun is seanorth."

I

Wessex

"Beware the Northern scourge! They roam the earth to hunt the gentle Christian, to slaughter and to kill!"

Viewing the twelve-year-old boy from her seat upon a massive oak bench, Ambyre laughed at the sight of her brother Cuthbert, dressed in his own image of the Norsemen. His sturdy young body was wrapped in fur, with a shield before him which had undoubtedly come from the palace discard. A leather hat perched atop reddish-brown hair served as helmet. One hand held the shield, the other waved a wooden stick as though it were an axe.

"Dare not, crazed maiden, to laugh upon such a sight!" her brother continued in as fierce a voice as he could muster. "Know that I strike to kill and remain without regret!"

Caught up in the fantasy, Ambyre jumped from her bench in a sudden mood of childish frolic. Holding out her cloak as a shield, she stood valiantly undaunted by the savage threat facing her.

"I have conquered you before, you heathen dragon!" she stated with exuberance. "Have you dared return to be put back once again?"

The boy's dark eyes could not hide his pleasure in having his older sister join the game, and he continued with inspired relish.

"No one has conquered the Danish spirit!"

"I, King Alfred the Great, have battled and won, and Wessex stands firm against any bloodseeking onslaught." She held out her hand and pointed toward the sea. "So go from here, like the mewling beasts you are, and try for other lands less courageous than mine."

A loud clap prevented the would-be Norseman from replying, but the applause was far from praise. It was a firm, sharp sound, and both turned from each other to view the dissatisfied countenance of their tutor, the Scholar Fauntley. As he neared them, Ambyre's eyes fell upon Fauntley with amusement, for that was what he inspired in her when he attempted to sound gruff and authoritative. Perhaps his size had something to do with it, Ambyre thought. Fauntley had a thin face and a thin body; his shoulders were by no measurement any wider than his slim hips and narrow waist, and overall he looked more like an undeveloped adolescent than a man of twenty-six years.

Now those soft features frowned in displeasure and his brows drew into a scowl. The fawn-like eyes which normally held only affection warned them a lecture was on its way. And the maiden, Ambyre of Athelney, could not but listen to his outpouring, despite the fact that he was a mere six years older than herself. Hardly an imposing elder, as both were fully aware.

"We can be proud that our good King's father, Alfred the Great, kept the pagans from conquering Wessex," Fauntley was saying, "but despite his victory and the victories King Edward now claims, the Danes remain a true threat to all the world. If not here in Wessex, praise be to God, those in other places still suffer their savagery. Certainly we owe those besieged Christians the respect of our prayers rather than the playing of such games."

Had Fauntley but seen the exchange of one glance, he would have assessed the ill-concealed mirth in their eyes. But he continued his lecture, and both seemed to listen with properly bowed heads of chastisement. He did not know his words were hardly taken seriously.

When finished with his somewhat lengthy dissertation on the horrors they had been spared through the fortitude of their King, Cuthbert was dismissed, but Ambyre was requested to remain. The boy left with a knowing glance toward his sister, who grimaced at his amusement. She watched as he tramped the palace greensward toward the building that housed the kitchen, no doubt in search of his favorite treat.

"Forgive me if my speech was too harsh,

milady," Fauntley said immediately, his air of authority gone now that he and Ambyre were alone. "I did not mean to include the horror of battle."

"If you refer to your quotation of the number of lives lost in battle, I hardly count that as being descriptive enough to warrant the title of horror."

She turned away, returning to her seat on the oak bench. Fauntley sat beside her.

"I suppose your father told you many a tale of battle," Fauntley said, not without a slight hint of disapproval.

"Of course he did," she admitted. "And why not? 'Tis nothing I should swoon over."

" 'Tis hardly befitting a young maid's ears," Fauntley said stiffly.

"And what, pray, is the difference between my ears and yours?"

" 'Tis not proper for a maiden to know such horrors as can happen in battle."

Ambyre laughed. "Proper, foo! My proper Fauntley, why must that word be so highly valued and so often used among the many words of your vocabulary? I tell you truthfully, I could easily take care of my own life, even those of others, in any such battle."

Fauntley sometimes shuddered to think of the truth in her words. Her father, a respected but somewhat eccentric man, and in Fauntley's estimation even mad, had not been blessed with the sons he had so desired throughout his life. It was Ambyre whom Dunstan had loved beyond anything but battle itself, and Ambyre whom he had taught all of his warlike skills. Only when learning of an illegitimate son, Cuthbert, did Dunstan of Athelney have hope, apart from his daughter, that these skills could be passed on for future battles and wars. But his vital years Dunstan had given to Ambyre. She had learned to ride with the consent of both her parents, though beyond that her mother closed her eyes in abhorrence as Ambyre was taught to wield a sword, to pitch a dagger and to shoot an arrow. With her young, burgeoning body, thankfully not allowed by her father to become muscular, she nonetheless grew quite strong for a maiden, undeniably lithe, and without a feather's weight of unnecessary proportion.

While Fauntley admitted this training had given Ambyre grace that came with such control over one's body, he could not bring himself to approve of the method by which it had been attained. So from the time he had been there, just a few months after Ambyre and Cuthbert had come to Wessex as wards of the King, Fauntley had sought to undo all that Dunstan had so lovingly given her as his legacy.

"I have duties I must attend to," Ambyre said, tugging Fauntley's thoughts to attention. She stood to leave without further excuse.

Fauntley stood as well, detaining her momentarily. "Do not forget our lessons this afternoon, milady. Will you come to my chambers?"

"I will come to the chancery, as always," Ambyre replied. "You know as well as I that to hold lessons in your chambers would be improper—you, Fauntley, who can think only of what is proper, should have snatched the opportunity to use your favorite word, if even to chastise yourself."

Fauntley flushed under her admonition. "I often hold lessons in my chambers. 'Tis roomy and bright, and many of my books are there. I have more than only my sleeping chamber, you know."

"You may hold your lessons with the children in any building of the palace you wish," she said flippantly, "but I am hardly a child, or hadn't you been aware of that?"

Fauntley swallowed hard.

How could he *not* be aware? Her skin was as smooth as oriental silk, a shade which remained fawn-colored throughout the seasons, even in the winter months. Her eyes were the shape of almonds, their color as dark as a raven's wing. Her nose was thin and straight, at a sharp angle from her large eyes that seemed to bring yet more attention to them. And her mouth . . . her mouth was something which should be kissed, if it was not blessing onlookers with a smile.

Fauntley knew he was not alone in his thoughts, but he, unlike all those others at court who sought her company, knew so much more about her. He knew she had a mind as swift as a bird's flight, as eager as a baby's cry for milk, and as strong and restless as rushing waterfalls. Nothing passed without her taking note, nothing escaped her without being studied. And he admired this in her as much as her beauty.

But it was painfully evident that Ambyre did not seek his admiration. When in her company, Fauntley knew the only excitement she felt for him was from the wonders of his education, though even that was better than naught. In King Edward's Great Hall, there were many men more handsome than Fauntley, and still it was only with himself that she shared her friendship. As of yet, she had shown no interest even in those who were obviously enamoured of her, and Fauntley had patience enough to wait until her sensibility might see a future for them together.

Now, as he watched her walking toward the Great Hall, he scolded himself silently. What had possessed him to ask her to come to his chambers? He certainly had no wish to take her to his bed before they were married—at least no wish he admitted to. He only wanted to be alone with her, in some amount of comfort. The chancery was hardly private, and offered little apart from the stiff official furniture. He wanted to sit near Ambyre, as on a couch near a warm hearth, not across the room behind massive wood tables. But with a sigh he conceded that was precisely what he must settle for, at least until Ambyre came to her senses and behaved like the true woman she was.

"Fauntley says your mind has wandered of late," Ambyre said to Cuthbert. It was much later than she had expected to visit her half-brother's chamber, and he was already abed. The day had passed quickly, the King's court astir with the process of moving on to the Hunt at Cheddar. Edward had left earlier with the entire hunting staff, some twenty sergeants, four hornblowers, a variety of dogs and horses and their keepers, not to mention scores of other huntsmen and their servants. In the excitement, supper had been delayed. It was already well after sunset.

But for now, Ambyre's thoughts were on Cuthbert's grimacing face. "Aren't you interested in all Fauntley has to teach?"

Cuthbert shifted under his sister's scrutiny, glancing away from her. "I'd rather be elsewhere than in a schoolroom."

"Where?" she asked, though she knew him well enough to surmise the truth.

"With you, Ambyre, riding or parrying with swords. Or off on the hunt with Edward! *That* is the type of learning our father wished for his children. Even more so for me because I am a boy. Yet I must spend more hours a day with my wax tablet writing the Roman alphabet than doing that which both my father and myself would wish. Is it fair, Ambyre?"

Ambyre smiled sympathetically. "We are under King Edward's guidance now, Cuddy. We must do as he thinks best, and we should be honored at his concern. Our father loved him dearly, you know, and so must we."

"I could love him more if he would allow me time for what I would like. 'Tis well enough for the other children here—they don't want to grow up to be great soldiers. But *I* do, and ciphering and singing won't help me at all. Couldn't you speak to Fauntley, and ask him to give me more time with you? Fauntley always listens to you."

"Fauntley would hardly concern himself with my wishes regarding your education. He is the master in such regard, and he said just today that you have not paid attention to your lessons recently."

Cuthbert sighed in annoyed resignation at his sister's diligence. "Spring will be here in only three months, Ambyre. Spring and battle!"

"There will be fewer battles now that Edward has taken back much of the land stolen by the Danes."

"But I've heard from the palace guards that there is a new threat to England, from the North, but not the Danes. There will *always* be a battle for me to fight, Ambyre."

Ambyre's first response was to smile at the boy's eagerness, and the foresight of one so young. But a curious frown replaced that smile, for she had not heard of this new threat to the land.

"What news is this you have heard, Cuthbert? The guards speak of renewed battle?"

"In the North country, Ambyre, along Mercia and Yorkshire. Norsemen again, stronger than those that have been with us these past years."

"Will these Northern beasts never stop?" Ambyre whispered, more to herself. But Cuddy heard, and sat upright among his covers.

"Let them come!" he announced. "We'll bury them below the Saxon White Horse itself!"

"Hush now, Cuddy," she softly cooed. "The time for battle is not tonight. 'Tis time for sleep. Perhaps tomorrow we shall go riding—*after* your lessons."

He lay down at her request, but before leaving she gave Cuthbert one final admonition about his study habits, and then quietly closed the door behind her.

She pulled her cloak closer as she stepped outside. On her brow was a ruffle of worry, for both Edward and AElfwyn. She had thought, at long last, Edward could live in peace and enjoy those sports he so loved. And AElfwyn . . . how she would dread to hear her land was threatened yet again.

As unwelcome as this news would be, Ambyre nevertheless hastened to AElfwyn's bower. Certainly AElfwyn preferred to know the truth than to remain unaware of the danger her former kingdom faced.

Despite the hour, AElfwyn was still fully dressed in a plain gray gunna and kirtle, though her head dress was already discarded for the simple linen head covering she slept in. Firelight and candles brightened the room, yet AElfwyn held her embroidery hoop very close to her eyes. Her back was not straight as it would certainly have been had she been aware she was being viewed, and her eyes squinted, creating wrinkles which normally were only shadows of deeper ones to come along the thin, long face. At that moment she looked far older than her thirty years, a mere decade older than Ambyre herself. When Ambyre spoke, making her presence known, the embroidery lowered to her lap, and the back stiffened to a disciplined erectness. She did not look in Ambyre's direction; instead, she waited for Ambyre to stand before her.

" 'Tis late for you to visit, Ambyre," AEflwyn greeted her. "Am I now to be allowed your company without the permission of my uncle? My guard tells me he is off on a hunt."

Familiar bitterness tinted AElfwyn's tone, bitterness which always seemed present when she referred to the King. Ambyre had heard it often enough, but in spite of that she had come to care for this proud former Queen.

"I need no permission to visit you—except perhaps your own."

AElfwyn smiled, and the bitterness disappeared. "That, my dear Ambyre, you shall always have. You have been my only friend in this place."

" 'Tis not only friendship that has brought me here tonight," Ambyre began. She spoke slowly, choosing her words carefully. "I have come with unpleasant news. I have learned there is a new threat of war, not here in Wessex, but northward, near Yorkshire ... and Mercia."

"Surely you've heard that before?" was AElfwyn's surprising reply.

"I've heard of many a war ... between the

Northerners themselves, and between some Norsemen and the Scots. But Mercia, I thought, was safe."

"No kingdom is safe—and most certainly not one that has so recently changed hands. 'Tis no news, Ambyre, that should trouble you. There will always be war."

Ambyre grimaced at the repetition of Cuddy's very words. "I, who pride myself on being knowledgeable in politics, find that I am ignorant of the latest news. I was fearful this would upset you."

"To hear Mercia is threatened yet again? Aye, 'tis nothing to scoff at. But what can I do? Edward now rules, and as you know, *he* does not seek my counsel. He is off hunting, content to wait for spring's battle unperturbed. So shall I."

Ambyre was suddenly laughing, not at the proverbial merry-making before doom, but at her own worries. Of course Edward had nothing to fear! He was King, not only of Wessex, but Mercia as well, and a goodly portion of the Danish-held territory in East Anglia. And that rule would expand yet further; she was as assured of that as Edward must be. He had beaten the Northmen before; he would do so again.

"Edward isn't such a tyrant, you know," Ambyre said, taking a seat on the footstool before her friend. They had come to know the vast difference in their opinions of King Edward, affectionately surnamed The Elder, and the topic had been exhausted to the point of acceptance by them both—almost.

"I'm well aware that it was your beloved father who instilled in you this reverent admiration for my mother's brother," AElfwyn said, her tone no longer filled with a fire to convert Ambyre to her own way of thinking. "You've idolized Edward and his father Alfred till I'm certain you dream of them in a way young maidens dream of their heroes. But do not forget, Edward is devoted to one purpose—uniting all of England. The entire house of Alfred, all of his subjects, all of his children, and all of his children's children, should be devoted to this one cause. But I am not—I cannot be. And you know me well enough now to believe my words."

Ambyre gave a wry smile. "I feel I've known you for so long, AElfwyn, yet 'twas just days ago that you were brought here."

"I've been counting each and every one," AElfwyn said, adding softly, "wondering what is to become of me."

Ambyre heard the words and did not let them pass. She spoke up excitedly. "Why do you say such a thing? Surely you don't believe Edward would harm you?"

AElfwyn calmed her young friend with a smile. "Nay, that much I do not believe of him. But certainly I cannot stay here, hidden away and guarded as if I were some sort of enemy."

Ambyre held up a hand to take in their luxurious surroundings. "Are these the accommodations of a prisoner?"

"True, my uncle has been generous to a point, but how can I forget that I should be ruling my mother's kingdom—a kingdom Edward stole from me by taking me captive? How he must have welcomed the death of my mother!"

"AElfwyn!" Ambyre scolded, sitting bolt upright after the slanderous words against her King. "You cannot believe that! Your mother and King Edward were brother and sister—they worked together for many years to recapture the lands the Danes stole from English rule. Edward loved your mother—he respected her, he even needed her, so how can you think—"

AElfwyn interrupted with a disgusted sigh. "Oh, I didn't say he murdered her, for heaven's sake! I merely said he welcomed the chance to take Mercia into his own hands—at my expense. I admit I've not the military mind my mother had. I'm not ruthless, determined, skilled in the strategies of warfare. But Mercia was *mine*, an ancient kingdom with a right to be its own master, not governed by a Wessex King. Edward gave me a grace period of merely six months to be ruler, perhaps out of the so-called respect you say he had for my mother. He let me be the intermediary between Mercia and Wessex that all of my loyalists wished—but when those six months were over he acted as if on some sort of schedule—stealing me away to this place. And he took over Mercia as if he'd planned it all along."

"Don't you see that he did, AElfwyn?" Ambyre asked earnestly. "Don't you see those plans—perhaps not your kidnapping, but at least Edward's eventual rule—were plans made long ago, plans your mother probably even knew? Why has Edward's eldest son, the heir to his Wessex throne, been raised in your home in Mercia? Because Edward wanted him to be accepted when his rule begins! Accepted by both Wessex and Mercia alike. And why have *you* never married? Why did your mother never set up some important alliance through your matrimony? Because it would have strenghened the loyalty of the Mercians toward you as Queen! Yet your mother never allowed this. For that matter, why did your mother not strive to have more children, a son to carry on—"

AElfwyn stood, dropping her embroidery and turning away from Ambyre. When she spoke over her shoulder, her tone was far harsher than Ambyre had recently heard. "Do not speak of this any further."

Ambyre stood as well.

"I meant no insult, milady. I was merely arguing a point."

"Aye, a point we have argued before. Why must we always talk of this as if we were of some royal importance? We're not, you know; whatever political value I may once have had is now gone . . . and you, you, my dear Ambyre of Athelney, have much value, but only in the hearts of the King and his family. In reality, you are as politically worthless as I myself."

NORTHWARD THE HEART

Ambyre laughed, and AElfwyn delighted in it, for that was the reason Ambyre had found her way so quickly into AElfwyn's heart. She could laugh even when faced with the dour fact of being no more important than a mere peasant. She was good natured and sweet, with a kind word for everyone—everyone but the enemies of her King. On that subject, Ambyre revealed her steadfast loyalty and almost blind devotion to Edward. Nothing could deter that allegiance. AElfwyn knew all of this about Ambyre, knew why she had argued for her point just moments ago, and found herself regretting the harsh tone she had used in return.

"Forgive my unfriendliness, Ambyre," the former Queen said humbly. " 'Tis only that I tire of hearing the truth—the truth that my mother resigned her kingdom to its own oblivion. She loved her people, Ambyre, and they loved her. Yet she was willing that they be brought under Wessex rule. I cannot doubt that now."

" 'Twill not be so bad, will it, to have our land united?"

AElfwyn's smile was not a happy one. " 'Tis easy to say from a Wessex mouth. But for the Mercians? Are they no longer Mercians now that they have no ruler of their own?"

"They have Edward," Ambyre stated firmly. And to her, Edward was the finest ruler one could have. AElfwyn did not need to see the conviction in Ambyre's eyes, she heard it in her voice.

"I'm sorry if my visit tonight has upset you, milady," Ambyre whispered, when AElfwyn remained quiet. "I should have learned already that such topics are best forgotten."

AElfwyn's sigh was long, but the relief from tension was contagious.

" 'Tis not your fault, my friend," AElfwyn told her as she resumed her needlework. "My own thoughts have burdened my spirit today. I will be relieved when I learn what Edward intends for me."

"Then you needn't worry; he is your uncle and cares for your happiness."

AElfwyn nodded, but the younger girl knew there was no agreement.

It was some time before Ambyre prepared to leave. Their conversation became animated and lively, regardless of the hour. They left behind the more serious talk of war, going from childhood stories to grown-up studies, to dowry matters and on to fashion. AElfwyn pulled out a gold silk headrail for Ambyre to have, for it complemented far better her tawny golden skin than it did AElfwyn's pallor. They were adding a finely-wrought yellow circlet atop Ambyre's forehead when they heard a commotion outside the door. Both women turned toward the sound. Ambyre stepped forward, but the door was opened before she reached it, and she was not alone in her initial confusion at the sight.

AElfwyn's guard, nowhere to be seen, had been replaced by four of the tallest and surliest monks Ambyre had ever beheld. The open door behind the intruders let in little moonlight, and in the dim fire's glow they looked huge and menacing, hardly typical of the slim monks so common on palace grounds. Certainly these were too broad of shoulder to live so sedate a life as one devoted to learning. And what could they be doing at AElfwyn's bower, so late at night? Their faces were hidden, but the direction of their eyes remained fixed upon her.

AElfwyn reached for Ambyre, finding her wrist and clutching it tightly. She had vivid recollections of her recent kidnapping, and the scene was far too familiar. Ambyre was barely aware of the movement, for the men who had entered so suddenly and silently were stepping aside to let another pass. Each man was tall, but the last to enter was taller still, and his hood was pulled back to reveal a warrior's helmet, metal glistening in the obscure light. His eyes were barely visible behind the nazal, but Ambyre could see the quickness of his glance between herself and AElfwyn.

"You will not be harmed," he announced in a surprisingly clear dialect.

Ambyre spoke boldly. "Who are you?"

"It will be explained to you in detail and at leisure when we have departed. We have come on a peaceful mission; there is nothing for you to fear."

"How did you get past the guard if all is peaceful? No one—not even clerics—are allowed here."

Her question was left unanswered. "You are AElfwyn of Mercia?"

Ambyre glanced at AElfwyn, seeing her stand stoically still, and the choice was immediately clear. As the queen proudly hid her fear, Ambyre knew she could not allow these Danes to harm her. She was the niece of King Edward! Ambyre knew her duty.

Moving in front of her friend, Ambyre said firmly, "I am AElfwyn. What do you want of me?" And in truth she looked more like a queen than the other, who stood silently, dressed in plain garments. The golden headrail and circlet atop Ambyre's head resembled a crown.

She barely heard the Dane's order to take her before the two at his side stepped closer and pulled her away from the real AElfwyn of Mercia. They dropped a monk's robe like their own over her head, covering her as thoroughly as it covered them.

As they left the room, Ambyre heard the leader command one of his men to see to the servant. Ambyre's eyes flew to AElfwyn, and, suppressing her own fear, she exclaimed, "You have said this is a peaceful mission. Do not harm my maid!"

The Dane paused, staring at her for what seemed an interminable moment. But when he spoke, his voice was not harsh. "I do not kill unless necessary, milady. And certainly not defenseless women. Your servant will merely be kept quiet until we are well on our way. Do not fear for her life."

NORTHWARD THE HEART

Comforted that her deception at least would save AElfwyn's life, Ambyre followed the intruders from the bower. She might have struggled had she not seen the guard outside AElfwyn's door, blood spattered around him. At that sight, Ambyre halted in fear, but one of the men behind nudged her along. The guard's lifeless form was warning enough for her to follow as silently as their example showed.

The palace grounds were desolately quiet. Ambyre merely allowed herself to be led, aware of the danger if she resisted, yet angry that these invaders enacted this plot so simply. Where were the palace guards? Carousing in the Great Hall or off on the hunt with Edward? Whichever it was, the answer infuriated her. These Danes, these Northern pagan beasts, were able to enter the King's own home as though they were invited guests and take a hostage with no more resistance than AElfwyn's single guard. How dare these barbaric warriors do this so easily!

They passed the stables and empty Royal Pack houses, the inhabitants of which were already gone, waiting with the hunting staff upon Edward's pleasure. The smithy, the storerooms, the kitchens, buttery and cellars were all quiet, and even the guardhouse through which they took her outside the palace gates was ominously empty. They left the palace without detection or resistance.

Horses waited among the thick forest trees, and once the party reached their mounts, their monk's clothing was discarded, though Ambyre was allowed to keep hers for warmth.

Now she had her first view of warriors in full battle armor, and, by their banner of Odin's raven, she knew without doubt that her captors were Northmen Danes. Mail chains covered massive chests, swords hung from one hip, daggers from the other. Tunics showed under the mail, and close, unencumbering breeks clung to strong limbs which would undoubtedly give even the horses they rode a good race if tried. Their shields had waited for them near the horses, and now they took them up. With their helmets of metal they looked more monstrous than human, nazal and cheek guards covering most of the face.

The man who had spoken seemed to be their leader, and it was with him that Ambyre was forced to share a steed. Pulled up in front of him, she was suddenly so close that the linked chains of mail dug into her skin. The horse bolted forward, and she was forced ever closer, clinging to him for balance.

"Do you think you will succeed in this with your small handful of men?" Ambyre asked with bravery. She was unsure, sincere. "King Edward will catch the lot of you and have you put to death for it!"

Instead of a response, the Dane merely smiled, for below the dark metal of face guards she could see the whiteness of his teeth. His complete confidence and lack of concern fueled further anger within Ambyre, and she struggled against his firm hold, but to no avail. To look at him, the man sharing this horse with her could have been on a frivolous hunt, off to enjoy a harmless sport. He held her against him as easily as one would hold a small child, and only laughed at her protests.

"You pagan devil!" she spat. "If you'll not return me to the palace I'll make certain you won't keep me so easily!"

With a swift movement, her hand clutched the dagger at his side, pulling it from its sheath. Had he not been so quick, Ambyre might have pierced through the mail and into the Dane's heart. Instead, he took hold of the weapon and pried it away from her. Without losing the reins or loosening his hold of her, he replaced the dagger, then recaptured her hands in his.

Despite the apparent ease with which he had disarmed her, he said, "Do all of you Saxon women possess the strength of men?"

"Nay—you Danes are simply as weak as our women!"

At that he guffawed, but when Ambyre broke free of his grip to claw at the only exposed flesh of his face, he lost his smile and once again seized her hands.

"Do not struggle, milady," he said in an ominous voice. "I said you would not be harmed, and I wish to keep my word."

"The word of a Dane means nothing to me."

"You may soon wish it did," he told her, and pressed her closer against him, making even speech an uncomfortable effort.

They did not take a direct course to the sea, and Ambyre had no hope that King Edward's small fleet stationed outside Wessex would come to her aid. Though it took them well into the night to reach the coast, no one, not even Ambyre, showed fatigue. Two boats waited, hidden in so shallow an inlet that she was amazed the hulls had not been scraped away.

Only the ship Ambyre was taken to was being readied to sail. It was unlike those King Edward had ordered built for his Royal fleet; while his were large and sluggish, this was sleek and narrow. Made of hard oak, there was room for twenty pairs of oarsmen to power it through the water. A mammoth black raven covered the single sail, wings spread as if in flight, as the rigging caught the wind. Horses and men alike jumped aboard the rolling ship, and within minutes, Ambyre, seated at the stern, watched the men row rapidly out to the open sea. Behind her, Wessex swiftly receded from view.

"You *must* tell me where they have taken her! *Why* have they taken her?"

The Northman who was left to guard AElfwyn pretended not to understand, though she knew the Norse language was very similar to her own. There was no doubt that those who had taken Ambyre were Northmen Danes.

At last she stood, past fear. The man had sat with her for over an hour, refusing to let her leave and looking fierce enough that AElfwyn had little desire to cross him. But finally her worry outweighed all, and to her surprise, when she went to the door, the warrior did not try to stop her. Instead, he followed silently, and as she hurried along the pathway toward her uncle's chambers, she did not notice him disappear.

A voice greeted AElfwyn before she had even called for help. Turning, she saw Fauntley coming behind her in his night robe.

"Milady, what has distressed you so?" he asked with concern. "I heard you pass by in such haste that I came out to see if I could be of assistance."

She clutched his arms, her face ashen and her eyes wide. "They've taken her! They've kidnapped Ambyre!"

At the name, Fauntley, too, became agitated. "Why, madam? Who has kidnapped Ambyre?"

"The Danes! They entered my bower dressed as monks—they killed my guard! They—they asked which of us was AElfwyn, and my dear Ambyre took my place. I can never forgive myself for allowing her to do this! I let them take her—I did nothing!"

It was now Fauntley who took AElfwyn's arms urgently. "Are they still within the palace grounds?"

AElfwyn shook her head. "I was held more than an hour in my chamber. They've gone without notice."

"An hour passed..." Fauntley said in disbelief.

"I must inform my uncle," AElfwyn began.

"Perhaps his soldiers can catch the Dane who held me in my bower." But Fauntley was shaking his head.

"Edward is in Cheddar, at the Hunt. Along with most of the guard."

The anxiety in her face turned to a look of desolate futility as AElfwyn realized Ambyre's plight. With Edward gone, it was not surprising that the Northmen had penetrated the palace in disguise. A cunning enemy would have waited for just such a moment. And in the confusion of the evening, they had found their chance. Now AElfwyn had no one to whom she could go for immediate help.

"I must see the King's chamberlain," she said, more to herself than Fauntley, but he had thoughts of his own and was barely listening. As AElfwyn left his side, she did not notice the determination glinting in his eye.

The chamberlain was plainly the only one left who might help. Closest to the King in all matters pertaining to his kingdom, and in many matters otherwise, the chamberlain, left behind when Edward was absent, was the most powerful man in the palace. His quarters were in a building opposite to AElfwyn's, just behind the chancery and very near the King's own chambers. He was astonished to see the King's niece, up and about and unescorted at so late an hour, but her excitement turned his bewilderment to concern. He listened to her tale without interruption.

Hesistant, uncertain how to respond to the

news of Ambyre's capture, the chamberlain let a long, awkward moment pass after AElfwyn finished. How could he take responsibility regarding a member of the household who was in fact no blood relation to the King? Honored she might be, and loved by the family, but how could he risk action for her?

"We must send someone after them immediately," AElfwyn said firmly. "They *killed* my guard! They could do the same to dear Ambyre."

"Milady, how can you expect me to dispatch Edward's fleet over this matter? The palace itself would be defenseless. There is no assurance that this is not exactly what they intended."

"Must I remind you that Ambyre is a ward of the King and greatly loved by all his family?"

"The family, aye," he said slowly, "but politically . . . We cannot risk the whole navy by sending it directly into Danish-held territory for someone so. . ." he did not finish, his search for a subtle word failing him.

"So politically worthless?" AElfwyn asked, her anger barely controlled amidst the tumult of emotions within her. "And if it had been I, as intended? Am I too politically worthless now that I no longer control Mercia?"

The chamberlain could not answer her question. He breathed deeply, tightening the girdle which bound his night robe.

"I will send a message to Edward, to inform him what has taken place. He will act with due haste."

"Something must be done *now*! Ambyre is in danger. She saved *me* from whatever she suffers this very moment."

"I will have a boat sent toward the North Country, where they must surely have taken her. But I cannot risk further warfare without Edward's full consent. You do not understand the implications here, milady. This peace between our people and the Danes is precarious, at best. They have given us allegiance, but as you can see by their actions, 'twas more from the lip, than from the heart. Please, lady AElfwyn, return to your chamber and let me take on this worry. I will send a man with you to assure your safety."

AElfwyn did not know that someone was at that moment doing all she could have asked of one individual alone. Fauntley had left AElfwyn for his own chambers, flinging off his nightclothes and stumbling into his tunic and mantle, almost forgetting his shoes in his urgency. He grabbed only what lay conveniently nearby, extra clothing for warmth, and a sword which he did not realize was more a showpiece than a battle tool. He rushed from his room to the stables, and in his haste and ignorance of animals, chose whatever horse was closest to the entry. He was halted before he even got to the palace gates.

"Fauntley! Fauntley, wait!"

In his urgency, Fauntley would have preferred to ignore the call, and had he not recognized the voice, he might have chosen to do just that. But it was Cuthbert, Ambyre's brother.

"I can't find Ambyre anywhere, Fauntley!" Cuthbert cried to him, and Fauntley knew the boy already had fearful suspicions about his sister's whereabouts. "I thought I heard a commotion and came looking for her—"

"I'm going after her now, Cuddy," Fauntley said with as much convincing boldness as he could stir.

"But where has she gone so late at night? Why didn't she tell me she was going somewhere?"

"It was too sudden. Go back to your room. I'm going for her before it gets any later."

Fauntley again turned his attention to the horse, but Cuthbert detained him once more.

"Fauntley, you can't go after Ambyre on *that* horse!" he announced, and Fauntley could not doubt the assurance of his tone. "She's a brood mare carrying a foal, and won't take you anywhere very fast."

Fauntley was too agitated to be embarrassed. Jumping to the ground, he first noticed the horse's swelled middle, and knew speed would have been impossible. In exasperation, he led the animal back to the stable. Cuthbert took him to a tall stallion who whinnied and snorted at being disturbed at so unusual an hour. Seeing the size and strength of him, Fauntley found his gaze going once more back to the gentle mare. But it was this stallion who could take him to Ambyre quickly, so he braved the animals's wrath and jumped on his back, not noticing that Cuthbert did likewise with another powerful steed.

Outside, however, he heard the hoofbeats behind him.

"Nay, Cuddy!" Fauntley said, more angry at the further delay than at the boy's intentions.

"You can't go without me, Fauntley! You need me—else you would be urging a heavy mare this very moment and getting nowhere!"

"Thank you for your help, but I am going alone."

"If *my* sister is in danger, then I it will be who sees her home safely," Cuthbert said stubbornly.

"I forbid you beyond these palace gates, Cuthbert."

"Why? Has something happened to my sister?"

"Cuddy, trust *me* to bring her home safely."

"Then she is in danger?"

Fauntley breathed deeply. "Aye, but I promise you I shall see her home. Now you must let me go, and promise you'll not follow."

Fauntley spurred his horse forward before receiving Cuthbert's word. Not only had Cuddy been slow to give it, but the horse beneath Fauntley was more responsive than any he had ever ridden, and he found himself clinging to its back as they galloped away.

Cuthbert watched Fauntley leave, his face set, refusing to yield even to his respected tutor. He gave Fauntley a marginal lead, and then went after him.

Those around Ambyre seemed to become more relaxed with each pull of the oars. They were soon laughing and conversing, singing in rhythm to their steady rowing which took them farther and faster from Wessex. The leader was at the side of the ship, holding on, she surmised, to some sort of steering mechanism, for when he moved it right and left, the craft responded by changing course. Ambyre did not doubt that these were indeed the masters of the sea.

No one spoke to her for several hours; there was no attempt at the promised explanation. Ambyre remained still, uncertain of her footing in such a vessel. She watched the strong arms with firm muscles of the men in front of her who urged the ship onward.

She was not surprised at sailing northward toward those remaining Danish strongholds off the eastern coast of England. As the hours passed, the warriors continued relentlessly and tirelessly on course. She'd never been north of London, though she had often wished to see far-off lands. But certainly not under such circumstances! She gazed at the Danes, but none of them, not even the leader, paid her any attention.

It was not until after dawn, without rest or sleep for either herself or the men, that the leader approached. He left the navigation to another and came to sit beside Ambyre. For the first time he took off his helmet and Ambyre could not help but stare at his features. Thick, bluntly cut blond hair topped a fair skinned face, with a slightly darker moustache above his mouth. Blue eyes seemed as bright as the morning sky, yet the effect was not much softer than the unyielding metal of his discarded helmet. A straight, strong nose, high set cheekbones and jutting jaws formed a rugged face, more accustomed to the fierceness of battle than to the smile with which he now attempted to greet her. Ambyre found herself a bit more than pleased at this gesture, though she did not smile in return.

"My name is Rathulfr Olafsson. My father's home is in Yorkshire, where we are taking you. I hope you can forgive us our bold invitation, but I could devise no other plan if I was to succeed in presenting myself to a maiden so close to the King's heart."

Ambyre was astounded by his words. He spoke smoothly, without hesitation or uncertainty. It was as if his actions, though unorthodox, were not by any standards shocking.

"Do you mean you merely wanted to . . . to invite me to your home? For a visit?"

He smiled again, and this time he seemed genuinely amused at her discomposure and surprise.

"I would agree my method was somewhat . . . unusual, but you must admit I would have been refused entrance had I called upon you politely.

At least I have been successful, if not mannerly."

"But *why*?"

"You are AElfwyn of Mercia, are you not?" he questioned, and Ambyre quickly nodded. "I have heard of the unfortunate way you lost your throne to your uncle, King Edward of Wessex. I have heard also that many Mercians remain loyal to you alone."

Ambyre spoke with confusion. "I can hardly imagine very many of them remaining loyal specifically to me. I ruled for only six months."

"But you are your mother's daughter, and that alone is reason enough for many to give you their loyalty. Perhaps news travels biased to you in your guarded walls at Wessex, but there are many in your country who resist your uncle and wish to have an intermediary replaced between themselves and him. You are that choice, milady."

"But you are Danes, not Mercians, are you not?" she asked. "Of what interest is it to you?"

"Very great interest, since we both have a mutual enemy. 'Tis my desire to unite the Mercians with my fellow Danes."

Ambyre's eyes widened. "Englishmen and Danes—fight together?"

The Dane hesitated for the first time. "The Mercian loyalists hardly consider themselves Englishmen, milady. You of all people should realize that their first allegiance is as Mercians."

Ambyre had not realized her mistake before

he spoke. Of course the real AElfwyn would know the hearts and moods of her people. She must tread more carefully, and try to recall just what was said in those conversations with AElfwyn.

"And this enemy you speak of. What threat is it to you?"

"Norwegians, milady. They've come from their settlements in Ireland, looking for new land. There is a man by the name of Ragnold; he is a Norwegian who is now based in Ireland, where he and his men have raided and conquered. Already he has fought with the Scots of this isle, and he has his eye on York, which is under Danish rule." He smiled, adding, "I'm sure even your uncle the King would agree that one tribe from the North is enough."

Ambyre could not restrain her words. "And *I* am sure he would state that one tribe is too many."

A burst of laughter startled Ambyre, not only from the Northman beside her, but also from several of the others seated at the oars nearby. She had not realized they were being overheard.

"Perhaps that is why we have resorted to these tactics," said the leader, the smile still evident upon his face.

She was thinking how unlikely these captors were. Strong, undeniably, but fierce? She had forgotten her fear, even being the only female aboard a ship of alleged barbarians.

The man continued. "We realize to seek Edward's help would be fruitless, and Athelstan his son would be as hopeless. But you, milady, could stir the heart of many a Mercian. With your guidance, they would surely rally to help a just cause—a cause they must believe in if they wish to save Mercia from the Norwegians, as we wish to save York and the remaining Danish holdings."

"Then you wish to set me upon the throne of Mercia—against the wish of Edward?"

He shook his head. "We could not risk the total wrath of King Edward, as they would surely do. We have no wish to resume our fighting with the Saxons while we are intent upon putting the Norwegians at bay."

"But how can I help in getting the Mercians to fight alongside you, then?"

Blue eyes held Ambyre's dark ones, with a gaze so steady she could not turn away. "If there was an alliance between the two groups, Mercian and Dane, a common bond giving reason for cooperation, then the combined forces would have no trouble resisting the single threat of the Norwegians."

"What sort of bond?" Ambyre asked, genuinely interested.

"A political marriage," the Dane said steadily. "If the leader of each race was to be joined, there could only follow an alliance."

Ambyre was thoughtful as the words took meaning. A political marriage...

"You refer to myself, do you not?" she asked without looking up at him.

He put a hand over hers, gently. "I do, AElfwyn. Yourself, and one who will be the next chieftain among my people. Myself."

Ambyre felt herself redden, much to her disconcertment. Here she was, she thought, for once able to prove herself for her King, and it came to the fact of her womanhood! How disillusioned her father would have been!

"I respect the surprise my words have caused you," the Dane was saying as he pulled his hand away. "I expect of you only to dwell on my words, not only of the marriage, but also the reasoning behind such a union. The Norwegian forces can muster as great an invasion as the Danish once did. If we could curtail such a happening before many lives are lost, this marriage could be as noble as any political alliance. You have nothing to fear. For the present, I ask only that you consider this plan. I vow that I'll not hurt you in any way—either in marriage, should you agree, or now. You may seem a captive, milady, but I promise neither I nor my men will harm you."

He stood, moving toward a bundle not far away. "We will be slowing our speed; some of us will be taking rest. There is a fur covering here, if you wish to use it. The air is not warm, and many men prefer to share such covering for warmth. I will be resting now also. Do not take offense that I offer you the warmth of my body as well as the fur."

Ambyre was unsure at first to what he referred, until he unfolded the bundle before them. It looked to her like a large sack with two or more skins sewn together, fur on the outside. He instructed her to slip within the warm folds, and she did so for comfort as much as in obedience. She suddenly realized she had been cold for a long while. However, when the Dane joined her between the skins, she sat up stiffly.

"I cannot sleep in such close quarters," she announced firmly, noticing one of the oarsmen venture a glance in their direction.

The Dane was lying beside her, pulling the covering downward with his weight inside the sack-like confines.

"Sleep will come if you are tired. The added warmth will only aid you in the effort."

"I cannot lie with. . ."

"A Dane?" he asked, amused.

"A man," she countered with a steady gaze.

He held up a hand in motion. "If you look around, there are no women for you to share this with."

"Then I would prefer to sleep alone."

He shook his head. "You are unused to sleeping out of doors. The air is cold and damp. You will be thankful for my warmth."

She did not reply and he added, somewhat more softly, "I said I will not harm you, milady. My word is honorable; I offer you only what little comfort I can."

A gusty wind gave Ambyre her decision, and she lay down beside him in one swift movement, as if the speed with which she encountered this closeness could somehow ease the fact of it. But when his arms went around her, she felt herself stiffen once again.

"Is this the manner in which your warriors share these bags?" she asked tartly.

He only laughed, shifting his position closer. "I assure you, it would be, if any of my warriors were women as beautiful as you."

With such contact, Ambyre expected sleep would never come. But it seemed only moments until her breathing steadied and a dream filled her mind, a dream about warriors and AElfwyn, of her own desire to keep the King's niece safe.

There was no longer any fear in Ambyre, but in her dream rose contorted images of her captors. She imagined herself fighting the battle for which her father had trained her, not conscious that the enemy she faced in her mind was the same she clung to with her body.

II

Fauntley tired long before his horse did, but he kept astride, fear for Ambyre driving him to greater endurance than he would have believed possible of himself. Cuthbert overtook him when they were well away from the palace, and though Fauntley knew that what lay ahead would be dangerous, he thought it equally so to let the boy travel back alone.

As they rode together, Fauntley told all he knew about Ambyre's abduction, and though Cuthbert worried over his sister's welfare, he reveled in his determination to conquer the Danes who had taken her. He would conquer them as Alfred the Great had done, and Edward after him. Cuthbert would show the pagans not to deal with Saxons in such a manner.

He carried a small dagger, a gift from his father with which Cuthbert never parted, not even in sleep. It had been a prize of war; Dunstan had taken the dagger from a Dane he had killed in combat. And now it belonged to his son. How pleased Cuddy would be to thrust a Danish blade into a Danish heart!

He did not tell his tutor that the ornate sword *he* carried would break if pressed into service. Cuthbert had no intention of letting this concerned but somewhat inept scholar into battle. He himself would take care of that.

Fauntley, though painfully lacking in any soldiering abilities, was nonetheless useful to Cuthbert. His mind, as always, was quick. From the palace, he had seen Edward's fleet still peacefully patroling the coast, and quickly assessed the Danes' inland escape. The two then followed fresh tracks Fauntley was certain belonged to the raiding party, which would no doubt lead directly to Ambyre.

They had traveled a good distance when Cuthbert's eye spotted movement ahead. Cautiously, they slowed their pace to see what lay before them, finally dismounting and leaving their horses behind.

It was a black, starless night, but by then their eyes were well accustomed to darkness. They crept behind some bushes, to view the enemy before deciding how best to act.

By a circuitous route they had reached the sea, and in the shallows lay a single Danish ship. Fauntley did not doubt its mariners had waited for the group whose tracks he had followed, for it was just now being prepared to sail.

Many of the Danes were still on shore, and it was the sight of them in their full weaponry which gave Fauntley concern. Though never having imagined himself in actual battle, he knew the odds were hopelessly against him. He scanned the area for sight of Ambyre, hoping he could devise some plan merely to free her and steal away, without having a sword lifted on either side. But she was nowhere, and this only added to his concern.

"She may be aboard already," Fauntley whispered to Cuthbert, whose eyes, too, were skimming the area.

"She must be somewhere," the lad replied.

"We'll wait until she appears, and then we will free her and run for the horses."

"*Run* from Danes?" Cuthbert repeated, though even his confidence was giving way at the sight of such opposition.

But as time went by they began to fear that Ambyre was not there. The vessel was small, and from where they crouched on a slight incline, they saw that only a few oarsmen were on board. Having more than an hour's lead, Fauntley deduced she had been taken ahead in a separate longship. In defeat, they could only return to Wessex in hope of getting help to penetrate Danish-held territory. They could not follow the Danes to sea without going back for a boat.

As the warriors began to board, the two who watched felt the last of their hopes slipping away.

Fauntley turned back to the horses before the Danes had finished breaking camp on the beach. Cuthbert soon followed. But Fauntley, exhausted and disheartened, momentarily forgot his fear of the mount he had ridden all the way from Wessex. Anger welled up, at himself for being unable to bring Ambyre home, at the Danes for taking her, even at AElfwyn for allowing this to happen to his beloved Ambyre, and in this anger he yanked on the bridle, unmindful of the sensitivity of the horse. The stallion whinnied loudly and reared, throwing Fauntley to the ground with a thud. Cuthbert ran to his side.

The Danes, hearing the commotion, halted their departure. They began returning to shore, prepared for battle.

Fauntley, somewhat dazed and holding his head, was trying to soothe Cuthbert's fear as to his welfare, when he saw four Danes, each holding sword and shield, standing and staring at them. His reassurances to Cuthbert ended abruptly when the boy heard the rattle of mail behind him. In a moment he was on his feet, shielding Fauntley and poising his dagger to strike.

Laughter was the only response Cuthbert received, much to his own anger and shame. Then, surprisingly, they turned their backs, ready to leave these unlikely two unharmed and be on their way. Fauntley now stood also, and called after them boldly.

"You have taken the maid AElfwyn!" Cuthbert watched with wide eyes, wondering if perhaps Fauntley had hit his head in the fall. Was he mad to confront these Danes? "I demand you return her to me, before Edward sends his army and destroys the lot of you."

Again, laughter was heard, but Fauntley revealed no sign of shame.

"An army the likes of you?" one Dane scoffed, and there was more laughter.

Fauntley breathed deeply. "If you'll not return her to me, than I demand to be taken to her."

The laughter stopped and Fauntley was regarded curiously.

"Go home, little man," one Dane said, and they all began to turn away once again.

But Fauntley was determined.

"I am her husband," he informed them, and even he did not anticipate the response. The Danes turned to him; one even reached for his dagger, but another stopped all movement with a command.

He stepped closer to Fauntley, towering over him and perusing him closely. Fauntley stood still, as Cuthbert watched in amazement.

"AElfwyn of Mercia is unwed, so it is told throughout Mercia."

Fauntley lifted his chin as he lied so convincingly even Cuthbert would have believed him, had it not been for the ludicrous tale he knew it to be. "We were wed secretly years ago. This boy, Cuthbert, is our son. That is why we risked our lives in search of her."

The Dane's eyes went to the youth, but returned again to Fauntley before speaking with a commanding tone which both were quick to obey. "You will come with us."

They were taken to the ship still waiting off shore. Fauntley, though his heart pumped rapidly, did not reveal his fear. He knew his story had been believed, and tried to take courage from that. If he could not overpower these Danes, perhaps he could outwit them.

Cuthbert shivered at his side, watching Fauntley, who stared at the Danes with distrust and hate. It was a long while before he ventured to speak, so odd was his tutor's behavior.

"Fauntley, you were hurt in the fall," Cuthbert whispered. "You do not seem at all yourself."

"Then 'twas to my own good that I fell," Fauntley replied.

"But are you well? Do you know what you have done?"

Fauntley let his eyes meet Cuthbert's, but only momentarily. He continued to watch the Danes. "I deeply regret putting you in this position, and I pray your sister forgives me for endangering you so."

"*I* am not afraid," Cuthbert said, perhaps a bit too loudly. One of the oarsmen turned to them.

"Nor am I," Fauntley whispered in response. "I have a plan, Cuthbert, a plan which did not occur to me until I saw those Danes staring down at us. These barbarians, as pagan and savage as they are, are not above orders of their own. They do what they wish to those of the lands they plunder and spoil, but among themselves they abide by rules which even the fiercest of them does not break, for fear of the punishment. They have taken Ambyre believing her to be AElfwyn. AElfwyn would be no ordinary captive, whom I pray would be treated kindly, and not as a slave. If so, and I cannot imagine these fox-like creatures handling such an important captive otherwise, then my announcement of being her husband will save her from at least one shame these beasts could inflict upon her. They will not force attentions upon a married woman who is not a slave, for if they do, their own code says they must die."

Cuthbert was unsure whether to be grateful or worried over Fauntley's words. He had not imagined *that* type of jeopardy for his dear sister. He only hoped they reached her in time to save her from this terrible possibility.

"We will have a much better chance of freeing her if we are taken directly to her," Fauntley continued in low tones. "They are saving us weeks of searching, and perhaps we alone can achieve what Edward's army would risk many lives to do. We must save her before there are any battles fought, Cuddy."

Cuthbert nodded eagerly, these thoughts more welcome than those of Ambyre being ravished by bestial Danes.

Ambyre woke when the sun was high. Disoriented at first, she wondered at the strange sensation of being held in a man's arms, but upon opening her eyes, the night's events registered as reality. The Dane beside her was awake, she realized with a start, for he was staring down at her with something akin to a smile. A tender expression from a face so hard. She sat up immediately.

" 'Tis a fine day which sails us home," the Dane greeted her.

She did not reply; indeed it was not *her* home to which the day was taking them. The Dane stood, and Ambyre adjusted the silk headrail which had come askew during sleep.

"Your customs do not apply on open sea. Why not discard it?"

Ambyre did not stop trying to set right the hair covering.

" 'Tis improper for a woman to leave her head uncovered—whether in Wessex or anywhere else."

"Not in my province," he countered. "There only the married women are expected to wear some sort of covering, and even that does not cover completely. Unmarried women do not hide their hair at all. 'Twould be a shame to cover such loveliness . . . at least while a man can still dream of sharing its beauty."

Ambyre glanced up at him, for those were unlikely words coming from a warrior. But he turned away and she could not see his face.

He affixed another fur across the corner where she sat, hanging it from two spears stuck through oarholes, blocking her view from the rest of the men. Before leaving her in relative privacy he told her, "I will return in a short while with a meal for us. The covered bucket holds water for you to wash in. Lift the lever in the center and hold it upside down for the water to flow out."

She thought it an uncommonly polite offer from a member of a race known to be so barbaric as to murder holy monks, but she was grateful nonetheless. He did indeed return not many minutes later with the promised meal, calling her name, or AElfwyn's, before pulling aside the fur partition. In a wooden bowl he carried salted meat, a flat, coarse bread, and a cheese which he called *skyr*. He also brought a cup of ale, which she drank eagerly, not even caring that they both shared the same utensils. The food tasted surprisingly good to her.

As they ate, Ambyre cast more than one glance in her companion's direction, though neither spoke. He was a handsome man, she thought, and had he been anything but a Dane she might even have wished his plan for marriage to bear fruit. Aside from the abduction itself, he had treated her with kindness and utmost respect.

But there was more than the fact of being a Dane which stood in the way of his unseemly proposal. He wished to marry AElfwyn of Mercia, not Ambyre of Athelney. She could not tell him she had deceived him into kidnapping the wrong person. Kind he may be, but what if he learned he was duped by this Saxon? She did not believe this kind facade, put on for the sake of a possible bride, would last long if he knew his plan had been foiled by her deception. The memory of AElfwyn's guard lying dead outside her door still weighed heavily on Ambyre's mind.

She hoped he would not broach the topic of that marriage, for she did not yet know how to make her refusal. She also hoped, if he allowed her to refuse, that he would simply send her back home and try to think of another plan for resisting the Norwegians.

Little did she know the depth of determination in this warrior, Rathulfr the Ruthless.

III
Yorkshire

On the coast of the very province toward which Ambyre's captors were headed, a celebration was in progress. To an outsider, it would have seemed an occasion of unmatched joy. Those at the trestle-tables caroused, drinking from vessels made of bulls' horns, swallowing great and continuous amounts of the fermented potion the horns contained, without thought to waking the next morning. Food abounded; there was bread of rye, meat of pig, lamb, goat, various fish—herring, cod and ling. There was also a variety of beverage, but only the beer and mead were consumed, leaving the milk untouched. And throughout the feast was their laughter; it was a celebration.

Not far from where they sat in this gay, garrulous company, stood a tent. It was a small shelter, with no one nearby. Inside, however, a woman worked, an old woman, wrinkled and gray, who carried a humped back and used her hands slowly but meticulously. She was alone, though she dressed a man who lay on a cot. He was dead.

This woman, so accustomed to attending the dead, was not unaffected by the youth of the one before her. It was not sadness she felt; she had known death too well for too long to be burdened with the sadness of it. Regret would be most accurate, for the man had not died in battle. It was winter and all battles ceased from late autumn until spring. Nay, he had not died valiantly, for if he had, those celebrating outside the tent would be even more boisterous than now; and she herself would not feel this regret. Instead, this young son of Olaf, named Dyrk, had died a straw death, upon his bed, and though none cared to speak of it, he had died without his weapons. It was said that Dyrk was strangled by the *maran* from the spirit world, and that was most shameful, because the *maran* of the night were women.

Dyrk would have been a great warrior, they all said. This was to be his first season in battle, and as one of the chieftain's sons, though not the eldest nor the heir, he was nonetheless well trained and had possessed the bearing of a fierce and noble warrior. He would be missed, but the only tragedy lay in the manner of his death.

Mourning among these people was short-lived. When they learned of his death ten days ago, they had been saddened by the circumstances. So young and healthy, and found without his weapons. Surely it was the *maran* who had claimed his life. There could be no other cause. But now, they went about the burial as if he had already been a warrior. It was commanded by the chieftain, and because those present were not averse to celebrating, they agreed to send off the body of this beloved but unfortunate young man.

Hauled ashore, not far from where the grave tent stood, was a ship. It was large, one of the chieftain's favorites. But it was not too fine to give to his son, for Olaf, the grieving father, had loved his son dearly and hoped this craft, in all its greatness, would allow Dyrk to go to the afterworld in some amount of comfort. Surely it was known there, in the afterworld, how his son had died.

Around the ship was a massive pile of wood, and on board, inside a tent, was a wooden bench, covered with brightly painted silks and cushions. It was fit for the burial of a leader.

Soon, the celebrants gathered near the ship. Among them stood a woman, finely dressed and ornamented, surrounded by those who had attended her since the death of her master. She hardly looked like the slave she was.

The body was brought from the tent, dressed in finery. Because of the coldness of winter, there was no odor from the dead flesh. The only alteration was in skin color, blackened from the fairness it had held in life. Dyrk had been

NORTHWARD THE HEART

provided with food, drink, weapons—all placed near his body after he was laid upon the soft cushions of his bier.

When this was done, several warriors came forward with animals to be slaughtered, cut in pieces and placed on the ship with the corpse. The cries of a dog, two horses, two cows, a cock and a hen were heard before the attention was focused on the slave girl. She had been given much to drink throughout the days past, and now, as was her duty, she cheerfully gave herself to the owners of the different tents nearby. They took the offering of her body for her master's sake.

Later, she was led back to the death ship. What jewelry she wore was given to the old woman who had earlier attended the dead man. She was given another cup of the fermented drink, and she sang words of farewell before emptying it. This was repeated once again, as she was given another cupful.

After this she was brought to her dead master, inside the tent and out of sight of those who watched. Other warriors followed inside, along with the old woman, and the slave girl was given to each of those warriors in the presence of the old woman. The warriors then left the ship, all but two, who stayed aboard with the old woman and the slave. Those who left joined other warriors on the beach, holding their shields high, beating on them with wooden sticks to deaden any sounds which might have emitted from the ship behind them.

Maureen Kurr

The slave girl lay beside her master, the old woman placed a small cord around her neck, which the two warriors were instructed to hold at each end. The crone pulled out a shiny, broad dagger. She held it up and directed the warriors to pull on the cord. At the same moment she plunged the dagger deep into the girl's heart.

The slave lay dead beside her master. The noise made by the warriors outside had not even been necessary. There had been no cries of fear to camouflage for the sake of other slave girls who might one day be in her place.

The warriors came out with the old woman, indicating their duty was done. Olaf, the chieftain, now came forward, who, despite the cold, was unclothed. He was the first to ignite the wood beneath the ship. Others brought burning branches and wood and added to the fire until all that remained was ash.

One man, standing apart, watched the pyre with an ill-concealed smile upon his face. This smile was not noticed, but had it been, who would have thought it strange? He was merely saying farewell to his brother. Only he, another of Olaf's beloved sons, knew the smile was one of triumph.

IV

Ambyre sailed northward with her captors for two days, never far from the east coast of England. When they headed for shore, she felt her pulse quicken, knowing she would soon be expected to give her answer to the proposed marriage.

No such trepidation existed on the part of the Danes. Near home after a successful venture, they were spirited and eager for the feast which surely would greet them once their victory was known. Humorous banter and wild tales of bravery brought quick laughter. Boasting became rampant; warriors vied with one another. Raff, as his comrades called their leader, was challenged to a race. Ambyre watched curiously. Surely there was no room aboard this crowded vessel to hold a test of speed.

She quickly learned the race was not to be inside the hull. When Raff jumped on one side rail and another warrior opposite him, she guessed at a swimming race in the wintry waters. Though the men did jump downward, she saw their heads still well above water as they ran from bow to stern. She popped up for a better view and saw they took their footing on the precarious position of the jutting oars, moving with each step as the ship continued toward land. She marveled at their dexterity, until she heard a splash of water from the challenger's side. Only Raff sprang back over the rail, his race won.

Cheers greeted him while laughter met the loser, who, shivering, was helped aboard and handed a fur to warm him.

Not much later, the ship pulled toward shore. Their voyage apparently over, Raff carried Ambyre over the short distance of shallow water to the beach. Then the vessel was tilted to one side which let both horses and oarsmen hastily disembark. Afterward, the crew rolled the empty ship up onto the sand, using large tree trunks placed underneath its wide, low hull. They worked so methodically that this took only minutes.

"My home is not far from here," the Dane told his captive. "Once there you can rest properly."

Ambyre did not reply, for in truth she felt no fatigue. But she was not sorry to leave the Danish vessel. Undeniably seaworthy and buoyant as it was, it nonetheless tossed her too close to the waves, and she found herself glad to be back on dry land.

Once again, Ambyre and her captor shared the powerful, saddled stallion. Raff, the sound of which she thought suited him, seemed as comfortable upon the horse as he had in the longship, and she did not wonder that these men allowed him to be their leader. Strong and able, his prowess seemed superior, even to Ambyre who had known him so briefly.

They headed toward the province ruled by Olaf Trondsson, east of York among the Yorkshire Wolds. To the south, the old Kingdom of Lindsey was not more than a day away by warrior's pace, and to the north lay the Moors. The North Sea, with its blustery winds and angry waters, could be seen to the east.

But now they turned inland, the Sea to their backs, and soon Ambyre could no longer smell the salt and fish upon the breeze. They passed farms that looked to her as peaceful and familiar as those between Athelney and Winchester. But she quickly reminded herself that this was not the Danes' homeland; it was merely a portion of her own island, conquered by them.

The town, too, was not unlike one in Wessex. Many of the peasants' houses, built of timber, turf, or stone, were small, resembling those she'd seen for years. The largest home, into which now they led her, was the only unfamiliar structure. Large and long, its walls were curved, not straight and square. It resembled an upturned longship, and she could not help but marvel at the architecture.

"This is my father's home, and will one day be

mine," Ralf told her as he took her through the entryway. She noticed the pride in his voice.

Darkness contrasted with the sunlight outside, but once her eyes adjusted, Ambyre realized the large room was really quite well-lit. A hearth burned in the center, its smoke escaping through an opening above. There were even windows, not open and drafty as they were at the Wessex palace. Instead, these were smaller and covered with a stretched transparent membrane, letting light pass through, though the view outside was not clear. While most of the room was long and narrow, as might have been expected from its outward shape, smaller chambers were partitioned toward the opposite end and closed from sight. Along each curved outer wall was a low, wide bench, which Ambyre imagined could be slept on. Above, at various intervals, hung extra furs she assumed were used as blankets.

At once, people thronged around them—servants, slaves, even children, greeting their returned masters quite happily. Several women appeared whom Ambyre guessed to be wives or family by the jewelry they wore. She was soon introduced, and her surmise proved correct.

Raff presented his mother first, a tall, sturdy woman. Ella was thin, even guant, compared to the women of similar age Ambyre was accustomed to seeing, but she appeared healthy and strong. Her blue eyes twinkled youthfully, and her skin, though very pale, was relatively free of wrinkles, except for those around her eyes.

Beside her was a younger version of herself, obviously Raff's sister, at the prime of her beauty. Her large, blue eyes were quite fetching. Blonde hair, completely uncovered, flowed thick and straight, bound at the nape of her neck. The likeness she shared with her mother included a smile that greeted Raff eagerly.

Other women present were not yet introduced, wives of warriors who had stayed in Olaf's home until their husbands returned. Now they went to their men and soon disappeared, though with mention of a celebration feast, Ambyre was sure she would see them again.

Raff asked his sister, Sigrid, to take the monk's cloak from Ambyre. It had been her only wrap and proven surprisingly warm. Then Sigrid led her to one of the smaller rooms, closed off at the back of the building. The hearth here was dwarfed by the huge one in the outer room, but it warmed the area well. A large, ornate bed stood in one corner, and opposite an alcove was cut off from view by the matting of an unfinished tapestry hanging from the ceiling. Next to it, sewing material overflowed from a leather-covered chest.

Sigrid smiled as she closed the wooden door behind them.

"My brother says Saxons value privacy more than they do cleanliness," she said. "Is this true?"

Ambyre lifted a brow, wondering how to react to such a statement. "I can only tell you of myself. I value both equally."

"Then you are to have this room to yourself," Sigrid told her.

"Do you not have your own room, Sigrid?" Ambyre asked with some surprise. Was not Raff's family of Danish nobility?

"We do not need whole rooms to sleep in, milady. I have a bower closet off the Mead Hall. This is the sewing room, which we converted especially for you, knowing your customs are different from ours."

"How long... have I been an expected guest?" she asked hesitantly.

Sigrid smiled easily, unabashed by her brother's tactics. "We've awaited your arrival for many days now, ever since my brother learned you were at your uncle's palace and left for Wessex. He chose an appropriate time before... inviting you to come here." She could not help but grin at her own choice of words. Obviously, Sigrid knew the exact manner in which Raff had planned to bring AElfwyn to his home. "As you can see," Sigrid continued, nodding toward the unfinished tapestry, "our weaving is not complete. But you shall have your privacy, Lady AElfwyn."

Seeing the smile remain on the Danish girl's face, Ambyre realized how lovely she was. The largeness of her eyes was enhanced by dark, thin lines of paint surrounding the very rims of her lids. Her skin, fair and flawless, had a glowing healthy tone, and her body, beneath loose-fitting gown and pinafore, was tall and shapely.

Sigrid excused herself. Alone, Ambyre had time to become accustomed to her surroundings. Too wary to give in to sleep, she glanced around the room. It would take more than privacy to make her feel comfortable, she thought. Even the familiar sewing articles visible in the corner added to her unease. Many of the tools were undoubtedly Saxon, and she supposed they'd found their way here as spoils of war.

Sigrid returned later with a bundle of clothing and jewelry. A servant followed, carrying water and an open box of pins and combs.

"This is Kirsten," Sigrid announced. "She will be your maid." The girl bowed her head submissively, and Sigrid continued. "We've brought fresh clothes for you to wear at the festivities. Perhaps you will be more comfortable."

Even as Ambyre thought of the custom these Danish women had of letting their heads go uncovered, she dismissed her own reluctance. Surely it was a small price to pay to avoid unpleasantness with her captors.

For the first time, the coppery hues of Ambyre's hair were given freedom from the headrail, and the Northern girls marveled at its texture. Kirsten washed it, combing it dry with an ornate comb of antler and silver inlay.

Finally, bound with a silver clasp as Sigrid's was, it was allowed to flow down her back. With their own light, fine hair, these girls were not used to seeing the dark fullness so natural in Ambyre's. The few Saxons they'd seen in neighboring villages always hid their hair under headrails.

Next to Ambyre's skin, instead of her own linen gunna, came a white, pleated garment, tied with a ribbon around its circular neckline. The pleats went clear to the floor, even down the sleeves. Over this they added a double-sided pinafore, bright reddish brown and made of the finest wool Ambyre had ever touched. It attached front to back over her shoulders by a pair of curved, oval brooches. These were ornate in themselves, with animal designs of gold and silver over a bronze base. Between the brooches, from shoulder to shoulder, hung a string of beads, intricately painted glass interspersed with gold.

The only difference now between Ambyre and these girls was the color of her eyes and hair. For a moment she imagined herself back in Wessex, and the surprise, even hatred, she would engender by allowing herself to be seen dressed like the enemy. Why then did she not want to fight them, to reveal this hatred she should feel? These people were Edward's enemies; many lives had been lost because of them. But she looked at Sigrid, smiling and laughing with her maid, adding rings for her wrist, arms and fingers. Could this be the enemy? Ambyre would merely bide her time. While no one knew she was going to refuse Raff's proposal, she would be safe.

In the large hall, people already had gathered. A long, flat board had been set upon trestles to make a table, with chairs and benches alongside. The smell of roasting meat welcomed her.

Raff stood with many other warriors. They carried weapons still, though helmets and shields were laid aside. Upon sight of Ambyre in the dress of his people, Raff's eyes lingered over her, she thought, with pleasure.

And he was not the only one staring at the prospective new addition of his family. His three brothers lingered nearby, all looking upon her with varying degrees of admiration and envy. But only one of them too deeply coveted his eldest brother's newest acquisition.

Raff stepped toward her, taking one of her hands. "I would like you to greet Olaf, my father, milady. He is anxious to know you."

The way was cleared, and behind the warriors a man sat near the hearth on a stone bench. He was old and fair, still in the habit of wearing a sword at his side. The portion of skin showing above his beard was finely lined, but his body looked to be as strong and hard as that of any young warrior. The combination of age and strength made him look to Ambyre like a King. His bearing was kingly. He sat erect as if upon a throne, and at his side was his wife. Ella gave Ambyre a smile, her blue eyes adding a twinkle.

"I have known of you for at least twenty-five

years, AElfwyn," Olaf said, with one brow lifted as he gazed at her with keen blue eyes. "Yet you do not look such an age."

She bowed her head as if in thanks for what should have been a compliment, had she been the true AElfwyn. "I am thirty, milord."

The old man lifted a brow and murmurs could be heard from those nearby, but Ella spoke above the whispers.

"You must tell us this secret of your youthful appearance, AElfwyn," she said in a kindly manner. "Never have I seen one at such an age look so young."

"Perhaps the southern dampness does well for the skin, milady. I have spent much time there." But even though Ambyre answered confidently, she felt uneasy with such a subject.

A young man stepped forward, boldly touching Ambyre's backside. As she flinched, Raff commanded the man away.

"He assures himself you are not a wood spirit, milady," Raff explained. "Such women are said to roam the forests, enticing men with their beauty and softness. It is only when a man nears one that he realizes they have no backsides, and are apparitions. Yet the woodwoman may cast a spell upon him, seducing him and making him her captive."

"I assure you, I am no such apparition," Ambyre said to the man firmly.

" 'Twas more a compliment to your beauty than indiscretion," Raff said, easing her embarrassment.

Ella spoke up in a surprisingly harsh tone. "We will not speak of such beliefs, my son."

Raff turned again to Ambyre, explaining his mother's anger. "My mother has accepted your Christian God, though many of our people have not. She wishes us to follow her in such beliefs, but some are slow in leaving the ways we have had for centuries."

Ambyre wanted to ask him if he, too, had accepted the Christian faith, for it would have made him even less an enemy than he already seemed, but Olaf commanded the feast to begin. Servants suddenly mingled among the warriors, filling horn drinking vessels, laying out wooden dishes, antler spoons and iron knives along the table.

Olaf and Ella shared a large chair at the center of the table, nearest the warmth of the huge hearth. Opposite them sat Raff, who requested Ambyre to sit beside him in the place of honor. Next came Raff's brothers and Sigrid, and beyond them warriors. At the ends of the table sat servants and slaves. Ambyre was quite surprised that slaves were allowed to eat with their masters, but she was quickly learning of the kindness with which they were treated.

They drank mead, a sour tasting fermented potion, very dark in color. Raff told her it was made from honey. Though she had never tasted it before, many at Edward's court were accustomed to such a spirited drink. She could not, however, after sampling it, fathom why.

The meal was lavish, with several varieties of

meat. Goat and elk, even reindeer, and fish as well, all roasted or boiled. Vegetables steamed with butter, were served alongside milk and cheese, bread and apples. There was kale broth and porridge, flat bread and nuts. What was consumed most, though, was the mead, despite various jokes of waking with "a stiff head."

Talk and laughter dominated the meal, not unlike suppers at the court of King Edward. Ambyre remained quiet as she watched the strangers around her. Raff, too, was quiet, speaking mainly to Ambyre, and she found herself pleased by his courtesy. She almost wished she was the real AElfwyn, and that his plan could work. Not, she hastily assured herself, because she wished to be joined to a Dane, but because they seemed to enjoy peace as much as the Saxons. Perhaps this Dane's plan could have succeeded.

After the meal, a man not much older than Ambyre herself sat near Olaf and Ella, a harp in his lap. He sang a long and detailed saga of heroes and monsters, battles and death, but through it all was the sense of victory achieved by the hero. Olaf listened very closely, as did Ella. But others continued garrulous discussions full of jovial laughter, oblivious to the poet's song.

Boasting seemed the favorite sport, sparking challenges between the men to prove their claims. Wrestling bouts demonstrated physical strength, races proved who was the fastest, drinking contests proved who had the most stamina. Ambyre thought they must all be very drunk, but none of them appeared very much affected by the mead, as she would have been had she consumed only half as much as they.

Raff did not drink as much as the rest. His brothers were like all the men, boisterous and rambunctious, and she imagined Raff would be little different when not concerned with a prospective political alliance.

Ambyre steered conversation away from the matter. She was uncertain how to proceed, whether to confess her deception or merely refuse without explanation. Certainly she didn't owe them one, but she did not believe Raff would settle for a simple "no" when he believed, and rightly so, that his offer was quite noble.

She looked across the table at Ella and Olaf, wondering if she could seek their protection. Ella was Christian; surely she would try to intercede on another Christian's behalf. Olaf seemed a fair man, not brutal—though it may have been age that mellowed him. He showed a certain sadness as he listened to the poet sing his tale of valor, but Ambyre hoped the sadness did not spring from having lived too long to still summon valor of his own. She prayed he would demand her peaceful return to Wessex, despite what it would mean to his son's plan.

"You're very thoughtful," Raff observed, "but I doubt the poet caused this with his tale of battle."

She smiled.

"Have you dwelt on my proposal?" Raff asked. His voice was soft but not eager.

Ambyre breathed deeply, knowing to delay would only prove more awkward. She could not prepare herself for the outcome; she did not know this man except as a rather benevolent captor. He could kill her in an instant, the same way he or his men had killed AElfwyn's guard, or he could accept her decision and send her home. There seemed no other alternatives.

She did not raise her eyes to his. Men and women all around caroused and laughed, enjoying the mead as well as each other. Olaf listened to the poet. Speaking in low tones, Ambyre was confident no one else could hear, even if interested. She put aside any fear his reaction might cause. Her father had told her there was no shame in death at the hand of an enemy.

"I cannot marry you, Raff."

Her voice was quiet, but she knew he heard her, for though he remained still, she heard him expel a deep breath.

"I won't ask if you have considered the benefits; I explained them to you and I don't believe you are ignorant," he said. "I don't understand your refusal, I admit, since the alliance could save the lives of as many Mercians as Danes. Your mother seemed a less selfish woman, in that she cooperated so thoroughly with her brother, King Edward."

His words, still spoken in low, even kindly tones, were harsh to Ambyre's ears. How dare he accuse her of something so personal as selfishness; he could not possibly know what sort of person she was.

"The reasons are many for my answer. Selfishness has naught to do with it."

"I ask your pardon, then, milady," he said, and Ambyre wondered if she had only imagined the sarcasm, "for what appears obvious to me must not be so. I will speak once again of your mother. In January of last year, the leaders of my people made an agreement with her. We gave your mother allegiance, and she promised support against the Norse. If she had lived, that agreement would stand to this day. I am not surprised you know nothing of it; if you had, perhaps it would not have died along with your mother. You might have fulfilled it yourself, and left behind something from your brief reign. But Edward was always there, was he not, even before he stole you away from your throne?"

"Why do you not offer the same agreement to Edward? He now rules there. 'Twould be a more peaceful way."

His smirk told her allegiance to Edward would not come so easily. Instead, he said softly, as if wishing to coax her, "If your mother were alive, I can only believe she would agree to my plan."

"Well, *I* do not believe so. She was distressed when all of you *Danes* first infiltrated England. Do you think she cared for *your* people just because she found use for you against *other*

Northmen she did not want in her homeland?"

He laughed instead of taking offense. "Nay, milady. We both found use for the other. Would it not be better to unite and be rid of another who seeks control, then afterward see who shall be the final victor?"

"You mean this is to be just a temporary alliance?"

"Of course."

"And the alliance offered to my mother," she said suspiciously. "Was that, too, to be temporary?"

His smile showed respect for her perception, but his words were solemn. " 'Twas an oath, milady. If she had lived, if she had upheld her part and helped to expel Ragnold and his Norwegians, then our allegiance would have been binding. But this agreement between us, milady, because of its delicacy, should not inhibit us both for the remainder of our lives. Do you agree? We should use this agreement with more power than the one between my people and your mother. We shall use it, and then discard it. Divorce is not difficult among us; it must only be agreed upon by the two involved."

"Marriage is a sacrament, is it not?" she asked, appalled at his proposition. She had always been taught it was for life. "I will go back to my homeland a woman without a future, having been married to an enemy of my uncle's people. Do you believe my mother would have sacrificed her only child to a barbarian?"

Again, her words did not insult him, though she wanted them to. He smiled. "If your mother had had the opportunity you have at this moment, to live among us as one of us, then she would have seen we are not the savages your bitter race calls us. We are a strong people, milady, and our needs have surpassed what our homeland could provide. We came to your country to settle, and now we live among you. We've accepted your ways, for the most part. Some of us have married your people, even adopted your religion. In many areas you would find it difficult to tell a settled Dane from one of your natives."

"Only after years of bloodshed! What of the monasteries you pillaged? Perhaps not you yourself, but those of your father's time. To murder defenseless monks—"

"Defenseless but very rich, milady," he said. "Those attacks were sporadic, and not the will of the chieftains. We could not control those few, perhaps many by your count, who sought riches in the misfortune of others. And they were Norwegians who struck those first blows, still spoken of by your people. Yet you blame the Danes."

"You hate the Norwegians, and so you blame them for all unpleasantness," Ambyre accused.

"Nay, milady. Look around you. These men are not all Danes; some are Geats, some Lapps, some even Norwegian. Admittedly, most are of my homeland, but we have nothing against the Norwegian who does not wish to usurp York from us. It's been under our control for many years now."

"Why don't you call upon the Northumbrians for alliance? They were eager enough to help you against Edward." She spoke her last words with ill-concealed bitterness.

His smile was as bitter as her tone. "You know as well as I, milady, that the Northumbrians are in worse straits than we Danes. Still, almost ten years after Tettenhall, they have not recovered their strength."

Ambyre regretted the thrust of her words. Everyone remembered Tettenhall; it had been a great victory for Edward, but she could see its wounds remained raw to those who suffered the loss. In desperation, she spoke again.

"What of the Scots? Can they be of no assistance to you?"

"Aye, as they have been already," he said, adding in a convincing, low whisper, "but they are not enough. The Norse have already defeated them once, just months ago."

She could not look at him, for she found herself believing his words, believing his plan was indeed the last alternative. But she spoke with a quietly determined voice.

"My decision remains the same, despite all you say. There can be no alliance with Mercia based upon a marriage between us."

"As you wish," he said in a low, vaguely angry

voice. He reached for his horn drinking vessel, drained it with one swallow and requested more from a nearby servant.

Ambyre, knowing only that her presence seemed no longer welcome, was grateful she had not been forced to reveal the truth. Shameful enough for him that his plan failed simply by her will not to wed, but certainly for his men to know she had fooled him would be intolerable.

Ambyre stood, her tension attracting more than one glance. Olaf and Ella looked on, frowning. Others stared in interest, seeing their guest leave the hall even before the feast had reached its peak.

The noise abated somewhat at her departure, and had it not been for that, she doubted she would have heard the voices calling her from the entryway. But they were urgent and familiar, and in astonishment she turned to them.

"Fauntley!" came her incredulous gasp. Her eyes were wide in disbelief. Cuthbert stood next to him, and she ran toward them, arms outstretched.

By then the quiet had turned to silence; all heads turned to the foreign threesome. Tears filled Ambyre's eyes. She hugged her brother to her. Tears of gladness, relief, confusion. Had Edward sent a fleet after her—but why allow Fauntley along? He was an unlikely soldier to be leading any rescue.

Raff arrived at her side before Ambyre had the opportunity to question them. He demanded the reason these Saxons had been brought.

"They claim to be the maiden's family," a warrior announced. He lowered his voice, though Ambyre could still hear. "Husband and son."

Raff was visibly astonished. He looked first at Ambyre, who tried to hide her own surprise, then his eyes passed to Cuthbert, and finally to Fauntley, at whom he frowned in evident disdain.

"I understand now the reason for your refusal, milady," Raff said softly. "It was not known that you were already wed."

Fauntley listened in confusion, wondering what refusal he referred to. He was eager to be alone with Ambyre, inform her of his plans, but she was already speaking.

" 'Tis not known anywhere, my lord," she said.

Fauntley intercepted quickly, afraid she would confess the truth without realizing the deception was his own doing, and with good cause.

" 'Twas a secret marriage, years ago. Our son, Cuthbert, was born shortly after."

Ambyre looked at Fauntley, hiding her bewilderment, fearful for his life as well as her brother's should the truth be revealed.

"You will take them to the room you have been given, AElfwyn," Raff said. "Await my word."

Grateful and eager to be alone with them, Ambyre led the way. Once inside the private room, questions spewed from each of them, until Cuthbert quieted them both with a pleading tone.

"They didn't hurt you, did they, Ambyre?"

Ambyre smiled down at her brother, and hugged him to her once again even though she knew he disdained such conduct as being only for children. But at this moment, he did not regard the embrace regretfully.

"Nay, dear Cuddy. They have been most courteous."

"Danes—courteous," Fauntley grumbled, unbelieving, and Ambyre glanced at him in surprise. This tone was unusual.

"They brought me here thinking me to be AElfwyn, to arrange a political marriage. The chieftain's son, Raff—the one you just met—is whom AElfwyn was to marry. Of course I refused, because once my identity is known such a marriage would be useless. But I did not expect to be followed by my tutor, claiming to be my husband."

"I did it for your safety, Ambyre," he said, flushing. "They will not . . . despoil you if they believe you to be married."

Ambyre did not feel the embarrassment Fauntley so obviously did. "As I said, they have been only courteous, even kind and friendly."

"How could we know? We feared many horrible things, milady."

Ambyre shrugged. "It makes no difference now. At least they have a reason for my refusal. Perhaps they will just send us home. In the meantime, we must continue with the lies that have been told. You must call me AElfwyn, not Ambyre."

"And you must regard me as your husband, milady," Fauntley said softly. He wanted to smile, but he was afraid she would be displeased, so he merely gazed at her sheepishly.

And Ambyre sighed, wondering how she could regard Fauntley with a convincing display of love. Affection would have to suit, she decided.

There would be no such difficulty concerning Cuthbert. Love for a brother or love for a son, she thought, made little difference, and she was grateful for the resemblance they shared which strengthened their tale. There could be no denying this youngster was indeed of the same blood.

They waited several hours for word to come. Noise from the festivities never resumed, and Ambyre assumed they had abruptly ended, with no more to celebrate. While waiting, the three traded tales of what had taken place since Ambyre's abduction. But she omitted how she slept aboard ship, as well as how she felt watching Raff race across the oars. In fact, she said nothing of the race, for Cuthbert always warmed to stories of strength, and she did not want him admiring these Danes in any way.

It was not Raff but Kirsten who finally came to the room. She brought food for Fauntley and Cuthbert, remaining silent through the questions they asked.

"You will stay here tonight," was all Kirsten said, and they could pry no other words from her. She refused even to look at them.

After the girl left, Ambyre realized she was not eager to spend the night with Fauntley. When they finished their meal, she spoke firmly.

"Cuthbert and I will share the bed," she announced. "Fauntley, you must sleep by the hearth. You may have the pillow and one of the furs."

He did not argue, glad to be staying in the same room. It was necessary in order to avoid questioning by the Danes, and he considered that his good fortune.

As for Ambyre, though the bed was soft and she was glad to have two familiar faces nearby, she could not help but wonder at her thoughts. What she truly missed was not her own scented mattress in Wessex. Strangely enough, it was that animal-smelling fur bag she had shared last night.

V

Morning came before they had gotten much sleep. Water was brought for them to wash with, a courtesy that plainly amazed Fauntley, though he had no kind words for those who provided it. Once refreshed, they were summoned to the hall. Raff was there, among servants and slaves.

"A message has been dispatched to your King telling him your whereabouts and that you remain unharmed."

"Then we are to be retrieved by Edward's soldiers?" Fauntley asked.

Raff looked at him before speaking, but it was to Ambyre that he directed the answer.

"I cannot allow this plan to be completely destroyed. There are too many lives involved, lives you may be able to save once spring has come and battles resume. When we spoke on board ship, I told you it was not my desire to set you upon the throne of Mercia, which would surely rekindle the wrath of your King. However, since no alliance can now be reached between the two kingdoms otherwise, I have informed Edward that is precisely what I intend doing."

Ambyre tried not to betray her anxiety at Raff's words. "How can you risk war with Edward when you intend fighting the Norwegians?" She dreaded this plan much more than the last.

"I don't believe it will come to that," he said. "I've merely invited Edward to think of all the possibilities. I could set you back upon your throne; there remains enough loyalty to you and the memory of your beloved mother, the Lady of the Mercians. With your command to fight the Norwegians alongside the Danes, Edward could do nothing. But he does not want to lose the kingdom of Mercia he waited so long to add to his domain. He wishes to rule all of this isle, does he not? Then let him fulfill my wishes; fight with me to be rid of the Norwegians, or lose Mercia to you so that the Mercians will fight with me. 'Tis a simple matter, one he should agree with."

"A Saxon would never fight alongside a Dane," said a firm, bold young voice. Horrified, Ambyre tried to hush Cuthbert, but Raff was already directing his attention to the boy, and she felt her first hint of fear. Yet the Dane did not frown; he looked at this Saxon stripling closely, perhaps seeing the resemblance he bore to Ambyre, and finally he smiled.

"You are not the shy young child I presumed," was all he said, and though it had not been intended as a compliment, all present sensed it to be one. Cuthbert would have smiled had it not been for the hatred he must show this enemy.

"Until we hear from your King, you will stay here, as our guests."

Fauntley grumbled, while Ambyre found herself amused at the choice of words. Cuthbert was unsure what he thought; he did know, however, that he was glad not to go back to Wessex and his lessons.

Thinking they had been dismissed, they stopped abruptly when Raff spoke again. "If I do not hear from your King by midmonth, I will assume he does not agree with my plan. You shall be held until one month before spring; at that time I shall take you into Mercia, to appeal to the loyalists who would see you back on your throne."

"And if Edward should attempt to rescue us?" Fauntley inquired. "Will you then risk the lives you claim you are trying to save?"

"Edward will be allowed to search for you if he so wishes, peacefully or otherwise. 'Tis his decision. He will not find you until I desire it."

With that, Raff walked out of the hall, and so the three were left to their own company. Fauntley, seizing the moment, looked outside the door to see if they could slip away unnoticed. But what he saw discouraged him.

Women were busy at the riverside, craftsmen

occupied with iron work, smithying, and other trades. Warriors burnished weapons, polished helmets, or practiced with bow and arrow. It was a bustling, contented scene, but Fauntley knew how quickly they would be detected if they made a run for the forest. Those very warriors now laughing and gaming with each other would, in an instant, become as fierce as their reputation warranted. He returned to Ambyre, disheartened.

"Perhaps if we told them who we are, they would send us home," Ambyre suggested, seeing Fauntley's dejection.

He spoke quickly, with a glance to see that no one heard. "Nay! We could not risk our lives. What reason would they have to go to the trouble of returning us if we were of no value to them? 'Twould only be an admission of their own failure. Nay, milady, we remain as we are, until we are brought to Mercia. Once there it will be easier to escape. We'll have all of Mercia there to help us."

"But that isn't for over a month," Ambyre reminded him, though her concern was not that they must remain here among the Danes. She was worried what Edward might do, what AElfwyn might implore him to do. No lives must be lost over her.

"Don't you see, Ambyre? This is our chance to escape unharmed and defeat our country's enemy!" Fauntley laughed, proud and pleased. "Only we know you are not the real AElfwyn. Won't our pompous captors be thunderstruck when they parade you before the Mercian loyalists and learn they've been set up as fools!" He laughed again. "I cannot wait!"

"But what if Edward should send men to rescue us?" Ambyre asked. "Would you wish to see any one of them die because of us?"

"Edward is the only one who can make such a decision, the only one who can take such a risk. You are very close to his heart, milady; more so than AElfwyn. And these self-exalted heathens have betrayed all rules of sovereignty. Edward may wish to teach them obedience, and I could not blame him for that decision. I would support it."

"But to have lives endangered over three people who mean nothing to the future of our kingdom—"

" 'Tis not the issue, maiden! The issue is pride, and the King's honor. 'Tis Edward's decision, wholly his own, and we can afford no guilt when none of this our own doing."

Ambyre looked away; Fauntley, as always, was quick in his assessment. His words made sense, but her heart did not so easily agree. He stepped closer, venturing to put a hand on her shoulder in his exuberance over their assured victory. "We need fear them no longer, milady. They'll not harm us while they believe us to be of value. And when they find out we are not, it will be too late for them. We shall be revealed as the victors. *We* shall laugh when this is over, and that alone can make our days among them tolerable."

Further conversation became impossible as Kirsten approached. She looked more than usually pale and her pace was quick.

"There is someone who wishes to speak with you, milady. Will you follow me?"

When Ambyre stepped forward, so did Fauntley, but Kirsten stopped him with a gentle touch to his chest. He was surprised by her boldness. "You must stay here, milord. My master wishes to speak to the Lady AElfwyn alone."

"I'll not allow—"

" 'Tis all right, Fauntley," Ambyre cut in. "As you said, they'll not harm us while they have need of us. And they'll do no harm to me."

Fauntley continued to frown, but he stayed behind with Cuthbert, as he was told.

"Is it Raff who wishes to see me alone?" Ambyre asked, unable to hide her own hopefulness.

"Nay, milady. 'Tis Torquil, Raff's brother."

Ambyre remembered the tall, younger brother. His eyes were not unlike Raff's, but his features were measurably softer, and he smiled quite often. She thought him to be the friendliest of the three brothers.

"Torquil is your master?" Ambyre asked with interest. "But I thought you were Sigrid's maid."

"My duties for Sigrid are during the day. My duties to Torquil are at night."

Ambyre flushed. "You are his ... concubine?"

Kirsten smiled. "I have no such status, milady. I am a slave, owned by Torquil. He merely allows me to use my time to help Sigrid, and now you, if I can. But I would die for Torquil."

Ambyre thought those words to be a profession of love.

Kirsten led Ambyre outside. They passed several small huts before coming to the last, well away from the others. Inside, she found it windowless and dark, in spite of the small fire burning in the center hearth. She heard rather than saw Torquil's presence. He came nearer, yet she could not make him out until he was quite close. Taking her arm, he seated her beside the warmth of the fire, which Kirsten stoked before leaving.

"I welcome your presence, my lady."

He smiled as he took a seat by the revived firelight. Though his tone was assured, his youth was apparent. Torquil's face, smooth and fair, had only a faint showing of hair, too soft to be called beard. He was not handsome in the rugged cast of his brothers Raff and Piers; rather, he was almost pretty, though his manner bespoke nothing effeminate. His mouth was thin-lipped; cheekbones stretched a fine layer of fair skin over them. His nose, narrow and somewhat aquiline, was unremarkable. What was striking were his eyes, of a blue as deep and clear as a mountain tarn. Above them were brows of great delicacy. Thin and arched, they would have been perfectly shaped had they belonged to a woman.

NORTHWARD THE HEART

"Has my brother explained why he brought you here?" he asked at last. He moved closer to her on the bench, and although his words were impersonal, Ambyre had to resist the desire to move away.

She nodded in response.

"Mayhap this is not loathsome to you, then," he said, watching her closely. "Mayhap you welcome this new plan to regain your throne."

"King Edward has taken it from me once; he will do so again, if need be."

Torquil seemed intrigued by her reply. "Do you respect your King, then?"

"Of course!"

Her assured and speedy answer sent an unabashed smile to Torquil's face, and Ambyre could not help but wonder at such odd behavior.

"You wish to return home, do you not?" he asked.

Ambyre nodded.

"And I wish..." he began, but hastily amended his statement. "Let us just say that I wish to avoid further war between my people and yours—war my ambitious older brother is all too eager to ignite. Raff is a soldier, so anxious to fight he cannot see that the enemies are only in his imagination. He wishes for an ally against the Norwegian, does he not? Either Mercia, by giving you back your throne, or Edward himself if he will bend to Raff's threats. Yet we need not fight the Norwegian at all! They are staying to the west and the north—

they've already taken the disputed land of the Cumberland Coast—but who should care? They'll not be foolish enough to attempt taking York. Yet that is what my brother fears. He believes the stories that this Norwegian called Ragnold lays claim to York through his kinship to the first settler there, Ragnar. Ragnar is long dead, milady, but both the house of York and the house of Dublin, to which Ragnold now belongs, spring from that very Ragnar. Would cousin fight cousin? Nay, milady. My brother is mistaken. But in the spring Raff would have us fight against these two imagined enemies, one of which has defeated us already. Your King will merely beat us again."

Ambyre was surprised at such an admission from a Dane. Young as he was, no more than seventeen, he had been trained for battle, and yet spoke this way. These were not the words of a warrior. They *were* the words of a sensible man. It was true, Edward had beaten the Danes. Why threaten battle with him again?

"Have you spoken to Raff about your thoughts?"

"Of course," he said. "But he will not listen. He is beginning to believe me a coward, and in truth, at times I do not blame him." He sighed. "I see before me a land of peace, milady. A land of fruitful farms and happy farmers. In many areas this is an established way of life. Yet Raff would have us pick up our weapons again and fight one imagined enemy while stirring up yet another old one. I cannot agree with his intentions. And he risks you, a woman of noble birth, to help him instigate these wars. It is hardly worthy of a warrior."

"But he doesn't believe the Norwegians are an imagined enemy. He sees them as a real threat to both the Danes and the Saxons, real enough that Edward will agree to his plan and fight alongside him."

Torquil smiled. "I see he has spoken of this to you."

"Aye, he wanted me to understand the reason for my part in his plans."

"And my brother can be quite persuasive at times." He went on slowly. "Milady, if you could, would you prefer to return to your home, and let my people work out this war on our own? Certainly now that we have your King's attention, we might spare you needless danger."

Ambyre almost laughed. The answer to Torquil's question was obvious.

"I know a way to return you home while avoiding the risk of war that my brother so easily takes. But though this strategy may seem suitable enough for us, Raff will be against it."

Ambyre looked at him with interest. "How could it be done? You have spoken to him already, and know his mind."

"You must understand before I tell you my intentions, that my plan is only to save lives—so many Danish and Saxon lives that would be lost because of your throne. In order to save many, however, it is sometimes impossible to spare some . . . We could not spare my brother."

"Kill Raff?" Ambyre blurted, so surprised she was unsure she had understood his words. "He is your brother!"

"Aye, and greatly loved," Torquil assured her. "But 'tis the only way for your release. I've tried to persuade him through talk, but he is determined. I believe he enjoys battle above all things, though I cannot blame a warrior for that. My father's word has been given that should something happen to Raff, then you, his responsibility, would be returned to your people."

"But to kill him. . ." she said, uncertain.

"Why do you hesitate?" he asked, as if impatient. "He is your kidnapper, your enemy."

"He has not harmed me."

Ambyre was not sure if she saw a smirk on Torquil's face, for when he spoke again it was softly. "You Saxons fear death too much. Aye, Raff will die, but he will be just one in the place of many. And he is better prepared for death than any Saxon. Do you think he wishes to grow old like Olaf, our father? Do you think he wishes to become feeble, useless, unable to fight? Nay, milady. He would willingly give his life for a hero's death, now at his prime. And this death, to save so many, would truly be heroic."

"I doubt he would see it as such," Ambyre ventured. "He believes his plan to be noble. Yet yours is not."

"Which would you have, milady? Noble war or ignoble peace?"

She did not answer. Her father, she knew, would have said war, if anything was to be gained by it. But was there? Torquil seemed to believe Raff was imagining the strength of the Norwegians. She breathed deeply.

"What would you have me do?"

Torquil now spoke eagerly, with excitement, convinced that he had persuaded her to his way of thinking. "You are a valiant woman, AElfwyn, but I would not have you commit an act your religion counts as sin. I merely need you to take Raff to our holy ground. It is not a building, as you Christians have churches. We worship and sacrifice to our gods on consecrated ground, marked off by rope and rocks. There, because it is holy, no weapons are allowed. Simply ask Raff to take you to this place in order to view if for yourself, to tell your holy men of it when you return. Make sure no one accompanies you, not your husband nor your son. Bring Raff alone to the holy ground. I will be waiting for him. Tomorrow, milady. Tomorrow after midday."

"Tomorrow!" she repeated in sudden dismay. It was too soon. She wanted to think.

"The sooner it is done, the sooner you will be free. We cannot wait, lest Edward act faster than we anticipate. He is bound to punish my people for this violation of you. And Raff has said if he does not hear from your King by midmonth he will take you away, to hide you from Edward's forces. I must get to him quickly."

Ambyre nodded, though not at all sure she

could go along with such a plan. True, Raff was her enemy, and all Torquil said seemed to make sense. Then why did she hesitate?

She was allowed to leave. Kirsten waited outside the door to escort her to the longhouse. Both were silent all the way back.

Ambyre said nothing when she returned to the room and her "family." Fauntley pressed her with questions, but she kept to her own thoughts. Could she do what Torquil wanted? She knew what Fauntley would advise if she told him; there would be no hesitation in his voice as he voted for Raff's death. So Ambyre remained silent.

Two meals a day were served to the household, and Ambyre, Fauntley and Cuthbert were allowed the seats of honorable guests nearest Olaf. But Raff and those nearby did not speak to them. Tonight's dinner had a different atmosphere from that of the evening before, reflecting the failure of a plan they all had pinned their hopes on—all but one. Torquil continued to smile in Ambyre's direction, but she did not look his way. She had not yet made up her mind.

The meal ended and many of the warriors went off to their pallets. Making Ambyre promise to join them shortly, Fauntley allowed her to stay in the hall after he and Cuthbert retired. Servants and slaves finished their duties, and all was quiet. She sat on the stone bench near the hearth, staring into the flames and wondering if Torquil could be right about Raff. Would he prefer an early, heroic death to an old, peaceful one?

Opportunely, he came in from outside, saw her by the hearth, and sat beside her on the stone.

"Has your husband allowed you to be alone among my pagan race?" he asked, and she noticed a quickly passing smile.

"He is unnecessarily mindful of me here. He fears for my safety."

"Then you should tell him, madam, that he has naught to fear—for you, for himself, or for his son. We have taken an oath; we may be pagans to you—barbaric, savage, uncivilized—but we will not break an oath."

"I do not fear you," she told him steadily.

His gaze seemed to say he knew, but he did not reply. Yet, logically, as a defenseless prisoner, she *should* have been afraid: in the power of a man hated by her father, her King, her God. They were different in every way—he a Dane, she Saxon; he a pagan, enemy of her faith, a savage warrior; she schooled in the gentler ways which had been respected since King Alfred's time, ways of education and grace.

Yet there was an affinity between Raff and Ambyre, intangible, mysterious. He could stand before her in full armor with the reputation of his blood-stained race, and still she would not quake. She sensed his strength, and knew instinctively it was the same her own father possessed.

But now, somehow, she was the one with power of life and death over *him*. Her decision should have been made already, but was Raff's death the only answer?

"You have put yourself in a very dangerous position, my lord. Was there no other way to gain an ally than to steal the Wessex King's niece?"

He regarded her silently, as if choosing his words. When he spoke, he looked into the fire. Ambyre gazed at his profile.

"There is a saying, milady. A wolf in his lair never gets meat, nor a sleeping man victory. Could my people sleep while the Norwegian tries to take land we have fought for? We have suffered enough loss in recent years."

"Because Edward has taken back much of what your people tried to claim?"

He nodded, looking at her closely, as if wondering if she could understand.

"But now there can be no more; we must pull back what forces we have and sap our strength to keep what we have. We attempt to do so peacefully, through an alliance. If your King can look past his pride, past the manner in which I gained his attention, then we will fight the Norwegian together. Perhaps even that can be avoided, for Ragnold would not be so bold if he knew our forces were allied. He takes advantage of the mistrust between your people and mine, invading and hoping we are too preoccupied with each other to pay any attention to him."

"But you have added to that. You have threatened Edward's honor by making him bend to your wishes."

"To rule wisely, a true king must listen to his subjects' wishes."

"Even so arrogant a subject as yourself?"

He smiled at her words. "A king must learn to deal with the arrogant as well as the meek."

"I pray he deals with you peacefully. Now that I have seen both kingdoms in peace—yours and my own—I have learned there is not so great a difference between us."

"Yet we rise easily enough to war against each other, as the past has proven."

"True enough, though as a Christian I abhor such bloodshed."

"All things must die, even oneself. What remains is a man's reputation. Will the name of a warrior who died upon his bed be sung through the ages? What is left of him once his spirit has left his body? Would a fighter wish for any other death than in battle?"

"You talk as if you do not want peace."

"As a warrior, I cannot shy from battle. There is but one way for me to reach Valhalla—or Heaven, as you Christians call it. I must die in battle, and then be carried from earth's battlefield to the battlefield of Odin, where I may fight again and again, but never die."

"Then it is your religion that drives you to fight?"

"Perhaps—for some. But I will tell you a secret. I am uncertain that Valhalla even exists, so I'll not count on it. But if afterlife is questionable, glory is not. That, at least, I can leave behind, since where I go may be an abyss of nothingness."

"Then you do not wish to grow old, to make sons, to live peacefully?" Her tone was low, somewhat sad. He seemed to be making the decision for her.

"An old man is no better than a corpse upon a pyre."

"Do you believe that of your father?"

Raff spoke easily, as if his words were a fact no one, not even Olaf, would dispute. "He believes it of himself."

She now had the knowledge she needed, yet thoughts within her conflicted. The more she knew of Raff, the more real he became. He was no longer unknown, faceless, some symbol of evil. Here sat a man she was quickly coming to know.

Yet she was a captive, a prisoner. Her life was endangered each moment, and her brother's, and Fauntley's. What would they say if they knew she had a chance to free them? What would they say if they knew she hesitated? Their lives weighed heavily upon her mind; Fauntley, with his new found belligerence, and Cuthbert, young, impetuously brave, naive about how seriously he could be dealt with for an insult. If she did not act and something were to happen to them, it would be her fault.

And what of all the men who might come to rescue them? Could she balk at saving their lives to spare one half-civilized Dane?

So it was against Raff that the decision must

be made. He himself said he did not fear death, in fact, expected to die young. Torquil, she now saw, had good reason to show surprise this morning when he told her his plan and she had not eagerly and immediately agreed. It was no less than her duty, to freedom, Cuthbert, Fauntley, and her people. She should not have hesitated. She would act with honor.

Ambyre stood. Only one more question to ask. She must know if Torquil had spoken the truth.

"If a battle must be fought, either over my throne or over a rescue attempt made by Edward, what should happen to me if you were to die in such a battle? Would I then be under the oath of your father?"

Raff stood also, hands resting on the weapons at his side. " 'Tis my oath, which I took to enact this plan; you are my responsibility, not my father's. Upon my death, that oath is broken, my plan a failure. You would be released to your people."

"You have given me information which inspires me to wish you dead," she replied. "If you were to die, I would be set free."

"That is true."

"But why have you told me this?"

Raff smiled down at her. "You have said you do not fear me," he replied. "Can I do less?"

She looked away. Perhaps if he had some inkling of his brother's intentions, he might fear *him*. But no. Fear was not to be found in Raff.

She left his side. There were no doubts now. She did not respond to his quiet good-night. After all, she was going to help murder him.

VI

The small wattle and daub hut belonging to the woman called Angel of Death was rarely visited after dark. Villagers who still worshiped Odin came during the day, when the sun shone to frighten away the spirits.

Only one visitor came at night, later than most would venture outdoors. This man was accustomed to the dark. He liked the way it frightened people. For him it was a cover, a sure friend to give him aid.

The woman beside the hearth barely acknowledged Torquil's entrance. She had not expected him, but he was one who came often enough to wear away any surprise.

" 'T'will be a fine day on the morrow," Torquil pleasantly announced as he sat beside her.

"Have you taken to reading the oracles that you may predict such things?" she questioned affectionately.

To Torquil, the wrinkled face, sparse hair and

half-toothless grin did not seem so ill to look upon. She was an old woman, the very oldest he knew, and it was her age that Torquil felt drawn to. He thought this woman had the secret of life and would live forever.

He leaned toward her and laid his head upon her lap. One of her hands, thin and frail, came to stroke his hair, a loving gesture his mother had never made, and Torquil peacefully closed his eyes.

"Tell me why you anticipate tomorrow," the woman asked. She continued to caress him, her movements slow with age.

He smiled, his eyes still closed, and the woman recognized that look of confident assurance. He had a secret. Ever since he was but four years old, when she first took such a liking to him, Torquil had been unable to hide his thoughts from her.

"I merely said tomorrow would be a fine day," he said. "Do I not have the right to predict fair weather?"

"Aye, of the weather you can say anything. But 'tis not to that you refer."

He opened his eyes, focusing on hers. Such familiar eyes, he thought. Eyes that held more love for him than any other person. Never once had his mother looked upon him this way. Nor had his father.

But Torquil shut these thoughts from his mind. Why dwell on how little love Olaf had for him when his scheme was so near to succeeding? Soon he would be loved best of all.

"You will know tomorrow," he told her.

The old woman did not speak again. She stroked Torquil's hair and forehead until he fell asleep. But sleep would not come so easily to her.

If she had been able to have a child of her own, she'd have wanted that child to be like Torquil. She gave him love of a depth his true mother did not begin to understand, with four sons to divide her attention. And Torquil needed what she gave, having to share it with no one.

That was why now she frowned. She worried when he kept secrets from her, secrets that most often endangered his own welfare. But she knew better than to demand the truth. She would find out... tomorrow, as he said. She knew there was naught to do but wait.

VII

The day dawned cold and windy, and to Fauntley it seemed unusual that Ambyre should desire to walk alone with her captor. Wearing a warm cloak with fur hat to match, she seemed mysteriusly secretive, but looked so beautiful that Fauntley gave in to her as always. He watched the couple trudge against the wind as they left town and people behind. Still, he would have followed had he not been prevented by two strapping guards.

The cold air refreshed Ambyre. The longhouse, while much warmer than the bower she had occupied at Wessex, was stuffy. They had had to close the smoke-hole because of sleet during the night, causing smoke from the hearth to grow quite thick.

Yet this was no mere outing. Murder was the intent, and she was nervous, unwilling.

They soon reached a meadow marked off as holy ground. Raff did what Ambyre had been told. With his cloak clasped on one shoulder, leaving an arm free to reach his weapons, Raff took off his sword, his dagger, and laid down his spear. He had used the shaft as a walking stick on some of the steeper pathways of the wolds and greenswards, aiding Ambyre in their ascent. But now the weapons all lay on the ground, and it was the first time she had ever seen him separated from them.

The meadow was empty but for three wooden statues, tall, intricately carved, made from the trunks of large oaks. Raff stood before one which was only a head with a single eye and a snarling expression.

"This is Odin," he told her, "the father god. When war comes, we sacrifice to him for aid. Then, if any warrior dies in battle, he goes to Valhalla."

Ambyre said nothing, barely listening. She had expected Torquil to be waiting here, yet he was nowhere in sight. She was unsure how long she could keep calm.

Beside Odin sat another idol, holding a large hammer. "This is Thor, the Protector. If famine or plague threaten, we sacrifice to him. But," Raff added with a sneer aimed disrespectfully at the statue, "such sacrifices only seem to make famine worse."

Ambyre realized Raff respected little about his religion. Last night he told her he doubted Valhalla's existence, but this cynicism was sweeping. He laughed about various animal remains before the idols, claiming scavengers had no doubt enjoyed them rather than gods.

They came to the last statue, where Raff smiled for the first time. "Frey is the god of fertility," he told her, "for both men and harvest. Sacrifices to him are supposed to give peace and pleasure to mortals... but I must admit to having enjoyed pleasure without a sacrifice to Frey."

Ambyre glanced up at him, hearing the softness in his voice. She might have paid closer attention had not her thoughts been on Torquil. What had Raff said? Frey... the god of pleasure? She would have blushed ordinarily, but her tension left little room for embarrassment.

Aware of her distraction, Raff grew curious. Why did she want to see this holy ground, especially without husband or son? Did she not love her husband? Even so, no woman of noble birth would seek adultery in such a manner.

Ambyre began to wonder if Torquil had had second thoughts about killing his brother. Perhaps he would not come. Eager to believe this, a sigh of relief escaped her. Instead of murder, this was merely to be a moment alone with a man—the enemy, but still a man. And she had never known anyone of such forcefulness, even smiling as he was at the moment.

She smiled in return, then realized how improper he must believe her to be. She suddenly flushed.

"I would like to understand you, AElfwyn," Raff said. "You don't love your husband, it takes no one wise to see that. You did not come here to be alone with me, yet I cannot think of another reason. You are not interested in pagan gods."

"I *am*..." she said lamely, in little more than a whisper. The words rang false.

Gently, Raff lifted her face toward him with one hand, and his touch was so soft she barely felt it.

"Why, AElfwyn?" he asked.

She had no answer, and could not have replied even if she had not seen Torquil. Face hidden behind his helmet, he was so suddenly there that Ambyre cried out. She saw him lift his heavy sword, as if to follow through with a blow that surely would have beheaded Raff had not her cry warned him. Raff turned in an instant. The sword, held in both hands of the attacker, sliced the air with a whisper, missing its agile target. Raff fought unarmed, unprotected—Torquil with both advantages. The sword swung again, grazing Raff, with the clatter of metal hitting mail chain. It tore his cloak. At last, when Torquil again brought down the heavy blade, Raff lunged forward and struck a blow with hands entwined. It came down upon Torquil's wrists, releasing the sword which fell heavily to the ground. Raff then turned his attacker around, grabbing the dagger from its sheath at Torquil's hip, and in an instant plunged it into his chest. Blood spattered down the tunic onto Raff's hands. He let the dead body fall to the ground. If there was a Valhalla, this was how to find it.

Ambyre turned from the sight, never having seen death before. She pressed a hand to her quivering stomach, closed her eyes, and wished she could blot the sight from her mind.

But when Raff reached for his attacker's helmet, she forced herself to look again, to see Raff's face when he unmasked his own brother.

Ambyre was thunderstruck. It was not Torquil under the helmet. It was someone she did not know. Though she hid her confusion, Raff did not hide his.

When he stood beside her he reached out, but in her turmoil and guilt, she shied away from him. He could not realize how much more there was to her aversion than the blood staining his hands.

Upon returning to the longhouse with Ambyre, Raff went to his father and told him what had happened. Olaf summoned several men and warriors who went with him and his bloodstained son back to the holy ground, where the corpse still lay. There they would hold an assembly, calling a *Thing*, to include the victim's family and a committee of lawmen. In this case, Sigrid explained there survived only a brother, another warrior.

"What will happen to Raff?" Ambyre asked, fearing condemnation.

"I cannot say," Sigrid answered. "Was it

Raff's knife which killed the man on holy ground?"

"Nay. He took the knife from the attacker's hip. Raff had no weapons."

Sigrid was visibly relieved. "Then Raff need only show them what took place; the man he killed was unholy, to have brought weapons to that place."

Seeing Ambyre's continued concern, Sigrid went on. "If Raff had killed a man without reason, he would indeed have to be punished. A price paid in silver to the victim's brother, or banishment from the land, or being pronounced an outlaw no longer under the protection of our society. If the victim's brother wanted to kill Raff, he would have the right. My brother would be forced to abandon his home and belongings, to flee the territory. Those are our punishments for murder. But if he acted to save his own life and perhaps yours, the man who attacked him was the wrongdoer. It was he who defiled our holy ground. Have no doubt, Lady AElfwyn, Raff will not suffer."

"I wasn't really worried..." Ambyre said, suddenly embarrassed that Raff's sister should think her so concerned about him. "Just curious about your customs."

But Sigrid smiled knowingly.

The men soon returned, having pronounced the victim unholy, with Raff given no punishment. Fauntley scoffed—only to Ambyre of course—how savage these pagans were to treat a man's death so casually. At the evening meal there was as much boisterous laughter as ever, with no reference made to what had taken place earlier. Not even the victim's brother seemed affected by the event.

Ambyre looked about for Torquil, who did not appear. Was he afraid of being linked to the attack? Was he sulking that his plan failed? Would he try again if he truly believed killing Raff was best for his people? Was she herself in danger, knowing who instigated the attack? What would Olaf do if he learned the truth? Her head swam with the heat and the shock of what had happened. She had to think of something else, or faint.

Ambyre thought of Raff. His hand upon her face felt as gentle as the touch of a babe. Yet the next moment those same hands killed. No, don't think of that. He had to defend himself. What was he really? Gentle and brutal? Everything in between? He was again so tender with her afterwards, reaching out, covered with blood. There was no hesitation to kill, no interest in questioning motive. A warrior, one of his own people. How much easier would it be for him to kill a Saxon?

No words were exchanged between them that evening. Ambyre's guilt forced her to wonder if Raff were beginning to guess the truth. But no, she was safe. If the dead warrior had known of her collusion in the matter, he couldn't speak now. The secret was hers and Torquil's.

Torquil himself stayed away for several days, which no one seemed to think unusual. As one day followed another, the episode receded and her anxiety passed. She grew accustomed to living among the Danes. She saw Cuthbert less and less, for Kirsten had introduced him to Raff's youngest brother, Alf, who was just two years older. Ambyre was not sure she approved of their friendship, but there was little she could do. And Cuthbert could not be expected to stay alone.

Fauntley, however, was eager to turn this friendship to their own gain. If Cuthbert could steal a dagger or an axe, something easily hidden, this camaraderie with Alf could prove worthwhile. The lad promised to do his best, though secretly he had no wish to alienate his new friend. He was learning the ways of warriors as an equal, the type of life his father had meant for him. Secretly, he never wanted to return to Wessex.

Ambyre spent her days treated as an invited guest of some importance, Kirsten continuing to wait on her. One day she learned with surprise that the slave was over five months pregnant. Though she never complained, at times Kirsten's hand went to her back as if it pained her, or to her stomach with a smile. With the loose fitting pinafore strapped at the shoulders over a shift, it was impossible to see any physical sign. But when asked, Kirsten eagerly admitted the truth.

Though the girl herself appeared content with her predicament, Ambyre could hardly believe

Kirsten was truly happy to be carrying a child out of wedlock.

"Why does Torquil not marry you, if you are giving him a child?" she asked.

Kirsten lifted a brow in surprise. "I am a slave, milady. Neither Torquil nor his family would condone such a marriage. He is the son of a chieftain. I am fortunate to be treated as kindly as I am; I have heard how cruelly some slaves are treated in other lands—"

"But you carry his child! Surely his Christian mother would wish her first grandchild to be lawful."

"Oh, it will be," Kirsten said. "If he is healthy, then Torquil will accept him and he will be lawful."

"And if it is a girl?"

Kirsten hesitated. "If she is healthy ... she may be recognized." She did not admit all the possibilities, possibilities which would have shocked Ambyre much more than the fact of simply raising an illegitimate daughter.

No Saxon upbringing would condone such immorality. And to think she had been appalled that unmarried women did not cover their hair! Nay, it was far worse than that, and perhaps Fauntley was correct in his total condemnation of them.

Supplies and foodstuffs were collected early one morning. Ambyre learned that two ships would take her and her "family" to a place with the unwelcoming name of Iceland. The North-people gathered every provision necessary to set up a very lavish camp on any foreign shore. Tents and beds were dismantled for easy handling, and a variety of kitchen necessities, from soapstone dishes to iron cauldrons and chains, were all stowed aboard ship.

Two slaves struggled to carry a wooden tub. Ambyre was delighted the Danes would think to bring such an item. How clean they were! They bathed more frequently than Saxons; they even washed their hair every day, that long, fair hair she found so striking. Fauntley, however, considered them conceited to pay so much attention to their bodies.

Raff had not spoken to Ambyre since that day at the holy ground. He spent much of the time with his brother Piers, who was closest to his own age. Piers would be joining them on the voyage, heading the second longship. He, Ambyre had noted, was a quiet sort, watching all that went on around him, rarely saying much, and feared because of this by many of the men. Not that he was a great warrior, for he was not; it was that they did not understand him. They were accustomed to boldness, with no inner thoughts kept hidden. But Piers was called the Fox, because it was never certain what he was thinking. Yet he had to be trusted among them, for she was told he would be the next lawspeaker, a position almost as powerful as chieftain.

Two warriors who introduced themselves as Wulfstan and Erling announced to Ambyre they would take her and her family to the seashore where the laden vessels waited. Once there, Wulfstan spoke to her apart.

"You are to come with me, Lady AElfwyn. Erling will see your husband and your son to their ship."

"Surely there's been some mistake," Fauntley protested, led firmly away from her toward the second longship. "My family should travel together."

"It has already been decided otherwise," Wulfstan replied, and turned away.

There was nothing any of them could do. Ambyre, who had been last aboard, waved to Cuthbert and Fauntley, who waved unhappily in return.

Almost immediately, the warriors rowed the ship out to sea. Now, with some unexplainable satisfaction, Ambyre realized the ship she was on was commanded by Raff.

When evening came and the open sea was calm, Raff allowed the men to sleep in shifts. They erected a tent from the mast and, because of the cold, the warriors doubled up in their fur bags. And as she watched the men in twos, Ambyre wondered if she would again spend the night with Raff. Such a thought would once have surprised her. But what was once so familiar was now far away and so, it seemed, was part of Ambyre herself. A short time ago she could not have imagined herself so cordial to an enemy, yet here she sat, hoping for the company of the very leader of this Danish pack.

Because of the cold, she quickly told herself. The cold.

It was very late and she was tired. Nonetheless, she remained sitting until he approached with the familiar bag. He still did not speak, but as he laid it on top of a fur for further insulation against the cold, she did not protest as she once had. Silently, they both slipped beneath the covering, after which Raff added more furs. He lay close and slept with his arms about her in the same manner as before.

The voyage was long and uncomfortable, made worse by Raff's cool attitude. Even at night, enfolding her in his arms, he did not speak, and she could feel the tension in him before drifting off to sleep.

The warrior Wulfstan spoke to Ambyre after two days of exchanging smiles. Despite the glances Raff directed their way, Wulfstan was friendly and she welcomed his company. He was not young, she was certain; he told stories of battles she knew took place twenty years apart. Yet he was robust, virile, and still quite handsome, with hair so fair she could hardly tell how much of it was white. His face was toughened like leather, lined and worn as the well-used jerkin he constantly wore. When he smiled, many wrinkles showed along his eyes and mouth, and he laughed so often they never disappeared. He spent what time he could with her, teaching her to play draughts and other board games, with pegged pieces that would not move regardless how rough the seas became.

And they did indeed turn rough. It grew so exceedingly cold, that as water sprayed upon the deck it turned to ice, causing the ship to become top-heavy. Men kept busy chipping it away, singing sagas and other songs to keep their minds off the frigid temperature.

Ambyre had never been so miserable. A small tent gave her some privacy and cut the wind, but did little to warm her or improve her disposition. Her only comfort was Wulfstan, with whom she became great friends in spite of Raff's often wrathful gaze.

Because of Raff's aloofness, Ambyre found it easier to remind herself he was the enemy. She no longer regretted having played a part in his attempted murder. If that had succeeded, perhaps she would now be at the warm hearth of King Edward's palace, not shivering on these icy waters. If there was another opportunity, she would not hesitate to do whatever she could to gain her freedom.

That moment came quite unexpectedly. As always, Raff was never without his weapons. He did not sleep with them beneath the furs, but they were within reach. The thought rose suddenly, and she was surprised it had not occurred to her earlier. He had said she would be returned to her people should his life be taken. Would that still be true if she herself took it? That had to be tried. She was becoming desperate. It was either freedom, or death.

The hour was late. Only a few men could still be heard moving about outside the small tent she shared with Raff. He lay asleep beside her, legs intimately entwined with hers, as if he were her lover. His hands about her waist were relaxed. The jeweled handle of his dagger was dull in the darkness. She must reach past him, press herself closer against him. If she moved carefully he would not wake.

She waited several moments before her attempt. Her heart pounded so, she thought the noise might wake him. She breathed deeply, trying to relax, to gain control. This time there would be no hesitation, no regret. He really was a savage after all. It would be like killing an animal.

The dagger was further away than it seemed. She had to press tighter and tighter against him, moving slightly upward to reach the weapon's handle. A stretch, and one finger touched it. She had now moved so close and so high that his face nestled at her breast. She could tell by his breathing that he slept, though it felt for a moment as if a kiss had suckled one nipple through her shift. But this was the time to prove her own valor, to make use of what her father had taught her. She took the dagger into the palm of her hand. Another moment to relax, to grasp the dagger with both hands before plunging it through his back into his heart.

She held it tightly, ready to strike. Her fingers felt quite numb. She looked down his back, eyeing the spot where she would strike. Lifting the dagger above him, she could still feel his rhythmic, warm breath on her chest. In a moment it would cease; in a moment he would be dead.

The dagger came down, swiftly at first. But she could not prevent herself from closing her eyes, knowing as she did how displeased her father would have been at such cowardice. She *was* a coward! She, the warrior maiden taught to kill the enemy, weak at the last, most crucial moment. She deflected the blow, wanting to cry out her failure, but allowing only a low whimper instead. She did not want to wake him.

VIII

Ambyre gazed at Iceland's coast, searching for some sign of grass or trees. Only the harsh outline of tall, unyielding rock stood firm against the onslaught of the relentless ocean. Barren, cold, forsaken.

She pulled her furs closer in a futile attempt to resist the gusting wind. Compared to this, the North Sea had been relatively clam. But when those around her began to shout and curse, she knew this was no ordinary occurrence.

"Go back to your tent, my lady," ordered Raff from behind her. When she turned to face him it was already too late. He was on the other side of the deck, issuing orders, giving her no further notice. The first icy rain drops pelted down just as she reached the shelter.

From inside, she could hear their urgent voices.

"Thor protect us!"
"Curse this wretched storm!"

NORTHWARD THE HEART

"Don't waste your strength praying and cursing!" It was Raff. "Get to work bailing us out!"

The ship tossed from side to side. In panic, Ambyre peeked out the flap to view the growing intensity of the storm. Water gushed into the vessel faster than it could be bailed. Some men, to save their few belongings, tied sea chests to the deck. But soon every hand was needed for bailing, and when a bucket was tossed at her feet, she too set about to help in a task she believed hopeless. They would all drown in these dark, icy waters.

Spray soaked her despite the fur she was wrapped in from head to foot. Soon the bail felt frozen to her hands; her feet were numb from the water in which she stood. But the frantic activity of scooping bucketful after bucketful warmed her somehow, overcoming the fiery pain.

Ambyre could not be sure how long the storm lasted. The furious night wore on, testing her physical strength for the first time since those lessons with her father. When dizziness assailed her and her knees threatened to give way, she kept on, fearing they would all die if even one pair of hands was idle.

Once Raff came to her side, forcing her back to the tent, but she fought him away with the help of a huge wave that suddenly swept them both off their feet. He had no choice but to continue bailing frantically.

Morning brought respite. The sun rose slowly

in this northern latitude, giving little warmth. The wind died down, leaving the water, which had last night been so threatening, suddenly calm. It now carried them toward their journey's end. Once the danger had passed, Ambyre fell panting onto one of the sea chests. The men did likewise; all were exhausted. The deck was strewn with discarded pails, rolling gently with the ship.

Raff was there; she did not know how long he had been staring down at her. It was an effort to look up at him. She didn't want to move. Cold was creeping through her again now that the danger which had quickened her blood was past.

Gently, he picked her up. She wanted to laugh deliriously when he grunted from the effort, but she hadn't the strength. Both were wet to the skin; his body offered none of the warmth it usually did. He brought her into the tent, and as he set her upon the furs that even there were soaked, he rested on his knees beside her. Stored inside a nearby chest were relatively dry clothes and furs; he reached over to get some of each.

"Take off your clothes," Raff whispered. There was not enough warmth in her to blush. She could neither argue nor obey. She hesitated not to wait for privacy, but to gather strength.

Numbness in her fingers made a chore of removing gloves and boots. Without a word, Raff pulled them from her. The hat came away as easily, but when he reached for the brooch upon her cloak, both seemed suddenly aware of something other than the cold. Their eyes met. A new emotion replaced fatigue. He did not hesitate long. Unhinging the clasp, he removed her cloak, then went for the brooch on her pinafore beneath.

"Raff, I..." she began, covering his hands with one of her own, "I can... do it myself."

His eyes held hers once again, and she saw the coolness return at her words. He left her then, but she was too tired to think. She fell asleep.

Ambyre did not feel the steady sway of the waves cease beneath her as the longship was hauled ashore. She was barely aware that Raff carried her to the beach; her vision was clouded and she could do nothing but shiver. Would she ever be warm again?

That was her last rational thought before the fever gripped her. When he lay her upon a fur-lined bed inside a tent on shore, she reached out to hold him as he stood to discard his weapons. In her delirium she clung to him, seeking his warmth. And he stayed as close as she needed, supplementing the furs with the heat of his body.

Only Wulfstan was allowed inside the tent with food and water. Later, when Piers' longship arrived and both Fauntley and Cuthbert came ashore, they were prevented from disturbing her until the next day.

Wulfstan stayed with Raff and Ambyre that night. He brought in his sleeping bag and lay on the ground near the bed, while his captain never stirred from her side beneath the furs. Neither of the men slept much, listening to her soft, incoherent mumbling. She spoke her name several times, not the one they knew her by, but her own. The Danes made nothing of it.

Morning came and she remained hot with fever.

"Shall we see if she'll take some broth?" Wulfstan asked Raff. He frowned at the sight of Ambyre's pallor, wanting to do more than merely sit idle while the fever continued unchecked.

Raff nodded, stroking her hair. There was no mistaking his concern.

When Wulfstan left to get the broth, several warriors asked after the Saxon's welfare. They had witnessed her efforts during the storm. Such strength for a woman! Above all things, these men respected courage and strength. This maiden showed both.

Seeing Fauntley head decisively toward Ambyre's tent, Wulfstan rushed forward, spilling some of the broth but reaching him just as he was about to open the flap.

"Milady is still asleep," Wulfstan said, putting himself between the tent and Fauntley.

The answer was curt. "She has been asleep for more than twelve hours. I wish to see her."

"When she awakens, I will tell her."

"Look here, I demand to know why *you* have been going in and out of this tent as freely as if you were her husband. And where is that savage Rathulfr? I demand to know what is happening.

NORTHWARD THE HEART

How is my wife?"

"Go back to your tent, *kjerringa*."

The name angered Fauntley. He knew in this sense it meant "old woman," which he had been called far too many times by this band of barbarians. Though blind with fury, he quickly assessed the unequal match; the Dane was twice his size and carried full weaponry. He turned away, looking over his shoulder as he did so, seeing the Dane go into the tent. Then, before anyone else could stop him, before Wulfstan could emerge he ran back and burst through the flap. What he saw inside paralyzed him. Ambyre, small and pale in the center of a large bed, was in the arms of the Dane he had come to hate most.

Fauntley's senses were overwhelmed; his rage was born of pure jealousy. He did not realize she was asleep, or that Raff caressed only her face, to check for fever. He saw only his beloved girl in bed with a savage, another standing by to take Raff's place. Mad with fury, lunging forward, he screamed an oath he had never before used, bounced off the surprised Wulfstan, and reached for Raff with two hands he hardly recognized as his own, full of unexpected power.

With all of that, Fauntley, of course, was no match for Raff, who stood in an instant, and with one back-handed blow sprawled this intruder on the floor. Raff ordered Wulfstan to take the *kjerringa* away.

Ambyre first came to herself late that day.

Raff had felt the fever leave her body, but he stayed at her side as she slept. When finally her eyes opened, she recognized Raff beside her and Wulfstan hovering nearby. She looked exhausted.

"Welcome back, milady," Raff whispered to her.

"We're glad you've awakened at last, milady," Wulfstan greeted.

She smiled, though her eyes were slits. "Do not pretend concern for me, you pagans." Her tone was weak, but not unfriendly. "You feared losing your prized captive, nothing more."

Raff smiled, Wulfstan guffawed, both relieved, happy the sickness had left and her mind was once again her own. Wulfstan observed his captain, seeing deeper emotion reflected in him. This maiden was politically vital, no doubt. But there was more than mere politics under Raff's happiness at her recovery.

Ambyre gasped at Fauntley's bruised face, purple and swollen from eye to jaw. He attempted a smile which was decidedly crooked.

"What happened?"

" 'Twas a misunderstanding. I'm glad to see you are recovered. They told me you became ill during the storm. Cuddy has been terribly worried . . . as have I."

She sat, fully dressed, upon her bed inside the tent, and smiled. "I would like to see him whenever it's permitted. They haven't increased their

NORTHWARD THE HEART

guard on you?"

He shook his head. "The opposite is true. I suppose we could hardly return home without their help, or at least their ship. I'm ignored much of the time, and find it infinitely better than being watched like a suspected leper. They plan to move us in here with you."

" 'Twill be good to have your company again," she told him sincerely, and his smile broadened before he winced under the pain. "What sort of misunderstanding could have merited that?" Her tone was angry. Fauntley was gentle, a holy and learned man; no warrior, God knows. These Danes did not need to prove their strength on him.

" 'Twas nothing," he said awkwardly. "I'm sure it looks much worse than it is. Please try to ignore it."

"How can I ignore it when it covers your face? Have you attended it at all?"

"My knowledge of medicine, limited as it is, is worthless in this strange land of foreign and frozen plants. Pay no attention, Ambyre. I myself can ignore it better if you can."

She said no more, deciding to speak to Raff about it. Surely he would reprimand whoever did this. She would tell him of Fauntley's staunch belief in the Christian God, of his unwillingness to fight even when attacked, his religion requiring him to turn the other cheek. She would make Raff understand that Fauntley was bred to be gentle, and should be treated gently.

Raff had not been back to the tent since Ambyre's fever had broken. She had spent the night alone. She refused to admit missing his warmth beside her though the tent kept out the wind and a number of furs covered her well. The large, transportable bed kept her off the frozen sand. Admittedly, they had made her as comfortable as they could. So there was no real need for Raff's warmth. She convinced herself she welcomed the privacy.

Because of the storm, they'd landed west of their objective. Ambyre knew little of Raff's plan, but piecing together bits of conversation Fauntley overheard, it became clear they had been heading for a farm near a river, run by a local chieftain. They were to set sail the next morning.

Those not occupied with repairing storm damage to the hulls rested before the final voyage. Ambyre stayed in the tent, teaching Cuthbert the game of draughts Wulfstan had given her. Fauntley sat quietly nearby. At suppertime, feeling sufficiently revived to eat a solid meal, she stepped outside to test the weather.

The wind had died considerably, though the Icelandic gusts were never absent for long. Taking advantage of the relative calm, the Danes, as always, enjoyed their meal. Mead was passed about freely, warming their bodies and heightening their spirits. Ambyre allowed Cuthbert a cupful, which put him into a premature but comfortable sleep.

NORTHWARD THE HEART

Fauntley drank none despite the cold, then soon woke Cuthbert, helping him to their tent. Ambyre pretended still to be eating, an excuse to be left behind.

She reached for Cuthbert's goblet, downing what liquor remained. Its fire shot to her veins. Wulfstan gave her more. Soon she felt pleasantly drowsy and warm.

Raff sat across the fire from her. She watched him. He had finished eating, and now laughed and drank with his fellows. Noticing her gaze upon him, he rose and came to her.

"You appear well-recovered," he said as he sat.

"I am," she admitted; her smile thanked him. She had hoped for a moment between them. After all, the matter of Fauntley's jaw... "I know that you are making my... captivity as comfortable as you're able. I would ask only one thing of you: that you try to do the same for... my husband."

Raff averted his gaze and drank deeply. "That one is treated no differently."

Bravery bolstered by the mead, she demanded, "What of the bruise upon his face?"

"That, my lady, was his own fault."

"How so, my lord?"

"Did he not tell you?"

She shook her head.

"Then 'tis because he admits his own folly and is ashamed. I put that color in his face."

"*You!*"

"With good reason, and will do so again if he

raises a hand to me. Your husband is a fool, lady. He instigated an attack against me which he never could have won."

"I thought your people respected bravery!" she exclaimed.

"Bravery, aye, foolhardiness, nay. He has not the first notion of how to fight, yet attacks someone twice his size and strength."

"Is not the fact that he is a prisoner—desperate—reason enough?"

Raff was amused. " 'Twas not his wish to escape. That might have warranted respect. Nay, AElfwyn, it was blind jealousy."

"Jealousy!" she repeated, and asked without thinking, "Who has he to be jealous of?" Didn't she know the answer?

"In truth, madam, any man," he replied. "In his addled mind, myself. He rushed into the tent whilst you were still with fever. I lay beside you, if you can remember. The dolt conluded I was despoiling you."

Color rose from her neck to her cheeks. She averted her gaze. When she looked at him again her eyes sparkled angrily. "If my husband fought to save my honor, then 'twas an act of bravery."

" 'Twould have taken but a moment to clarify what was happening. He would have seen you were out of your mind with fever, that no man here would have wronged you in such a state. But because of his rashness, he received a blow to the face. I say again: 'twas his own fault."

"Was it necessary to strike him? Surely there

can be no honor in wounding someone so ill-equipped to fight."

"*He* attacked *me*."

"If you had been truly noble, you yourself would have pointed out my illness. Instead your instincts were those of a barbarian."

"I doubt your husband would have listened to words; he was in a rage that only force could speak to. He looked quite . . . *barbaric*."

Ambyre ignored the retort. "He would have listened," she insisted. "He may be physically weak but his mind is strong. He has intelligence which is highly respected in Wessex—even by King Edward."

"Such knowledge has been of little use to him among my people."

"Aye, proving only more firmly your own barbarism."

Scorn from a woman was not easy for Raff to accept, as his expression now betrayed. Had she gone too far? But after a moment the hardness of his face turned to laughter.

"What sort of man allows a woman to defend him?" He gave her another grin and took a huge gulp of mead. "It grows late, my lady."

"Does that mean I am dismissed?" she challenged.

"You may do as you please," he snapped curtly.

"Then I would be pleased to return to Wessex." His stern glance made her smile with satisfaction.

"We will board the ship early tomorrow."

Obviously, he wanted her to be the one to leave.

When she remained seated, he regarded her curiously. Why was she content to remain? She returned his gaze evenly.

His tone was quiet. "Why, milady, do you always appear so composed? Even now, after the mead has tinted your cheeks and brought forth your smile. 'Tis as if you hold some secret, some inner knowledge that conquers any fear you have of being held prisoner. And that is what you are, AElfwyn. A prisoner at my will. Yet you are unafraid. Your very manner proves it. I wonder, why?"

She lifted her chin, slightly but perceptibly. "I cannot say, my lord. Only that my upbringing has not produced a simpering female. My father could not have been proud of such an offspring."

"Your father?" he seemed puzzled. "I'm surprised you still speak of him; dead almost nine years. 'Twas your mother, AEthelflaed, who set such a fine example."

"Aye," she agreed, glad her mistake was so slight. The mead had slowed her wit, dispelled her caution. "Aye, 'tis because of her, then."

He leaned closer, but still Ambyre did not move. She could not guess his intentions, but she forced herself to remain still. He had been nearer to her than this. Was she afraid now?

"Do you still control yourself, AElfwyn?" he asked, so near she smelled his breath. It was sweet from the honey.

"I have no fear of you . . . unless you wish to

strike me. Only a fool would not fear that."

"I will not harm you; I have taken an oath."

"Then I am not afraid."

Slowly, Raff stroked her face. He looked at her with softness, appreciating the view. Still, she did not move.

"I would like to know what secrets you hold, lady," he whispered.

She looked away. "I have none, my lord."

"I hope . . . you do not."

"For if I do? . . ."

He gazed at her fixedly before answering. His hand dropped from her face as he became mindful of others nearby. Though he did not move away, distance came into his eyes.

"I serve my people. As Olaf's son, I can do no less. They alone concern me. You, your King, your King's soldiers and subjects, all mean nothing. Can you understand what I am saying?"

She nodded slowly. Indeed, she understood—understood that only one thing could disrupt his plan—her own identity. Not till now had she realized the full danger of being revealed as Ambyre of Athelney.

They were at sea again, hauling eastward, Fauntley and Cuthbert with Piers, Ambyre sailing with Raff. It was dark and cold, with a steady wind as chilling as it was welcome, for that meant a swift journey.

The men had become more friendly to her. They played board games, told her stories, taught her the words to their favorite ballads. One even created a saga about her, singing of her courage and strength during the storm. She was honored by their respect.

Only Raff remained aloof. Cheerful around his men, playing games as any of them did, he did not come near her until night. Then, when they lay together for warmth, he never spoke. It was mere necessity, little different from sleeping with one of his men.

On the second day at sea, the air took on a painful chill. But these Danes went on without complaint.

Wulfstan laughed about the weather; he had learned to withstand the cold long ago. And what else was there to do? He shared his evening meal of cheese and dried meat with Ambyre, in a mood of good cheer that somehow added to her obvious discomfort. But when he made an offhand reference to her nights with Raff, Ambyre blushed a deep red, deriving at least some warmth from her embarrassment.

"You should not be shy to speak of such things, milady," he said. Though in her tent, she knew they could be overheard. " 'Tis a very practical way of keeping warm—though I wager any man aboard would wish to be in Raff's place on a night such as this."

"Wulfstan!"

" 'Tis true, milady, which is why 'tis Raff who lies beside you. He could not trust one of us—especially not your husband. How would it be, milady, if we poor men outside could hear your bliss and only turn to the brawny lad next to us? 'Twould be torture and Raff is right to save us from it. 'Tis only himself who sleeps so close to Paradise, but unable to—"

"That will be enough," said Raff from the tent flap.

Wulfstan stood, pretending contrition, but grinned as he left. Raff, wordlessly took the sleeping bag, laid it out, and waited for Ambyre to slip between the folds. He then joined her.

Perhaps it was what Wulfstan had said that made her so suddenly aware of Raff. Certainly she had forgotten the cold by now; he was familiarly warm. However, for each time she had thought it improper to share such a sleeping arrangement, she had never once wondered what effect, if any, her proximity had upon him. He believed her to be married. To despoil a married woman meant death under the Dane's penal code. Did that suffice to keep his mind clear of any desire? Or perhaps, and Ambyre thought this more likely, he just did not desire her. He had always been kind, even friendly at first, but never once had he betrayed any interest in her—had, in fact, told her she did not come before his countrymen. And certainly, since she had complicated his plans for alliance, he had reason to remain cool.

Such contemplation kept her awake, and by Raff's touch, she knew he lay awake as well. When he slept, his hands on her waist would loosen, but now they held her firmly.

She could not tell how long they lay there,

tense, unable to relax. She wondered why he was sleepless, but did not ask. She was not sure she wanted to know. Anyway, it was impossible to converse. She did not forget that the tent provided no privacy when it came to sound.

What she did forget were the differences between them—their roles of captor and captive, the impending war between their people, surrender or battle. He alone filled her mind, with nothing about politics. Perhaps attraction had been there all along; neither would have admitted it. But their tension proved it now.

She shifted once. Raff's eye caught hers. He attempted to smile. She glanced away, wishing foolishly for morning.

Perhaps dozed; the tension seemed to subside after a while. She stopped shifting, forced herself to relax. Though her body soon obliged, her mind did not. She was too aware of him, of herself. Soon her heartbeat slowed, her limbs became less stiff. He no longer seemed hard to the touch. For a moment she believed him asleep. But when one of his hands moved from her waist, slowly, with direction, she knew he was as awake as she was. It came to her face, rested against her cheek, fingers reaching into her hair, palm almost to her neck. He barely touched her at first, until she turned to face him. Then he increased the pressure.

His mouth came down on hers easily, without hesitation. And once contact was made, Ambyre forgot all else. His lips felt smooth against her own, firm yet gentle, testing her willingness.

She knew he could not doubt that willingness. Though she quivered ever so slightly, she did not pull away. Never before had she been kissed in such a way; never had she even imagined the pleasure it could bring. She seemed to lose all conscious thought, as if her body became fused into his and everything—even her breathing—depended on his movement and not her own.

Then, slowly, the pressure of his mouth upon hers deepened. She welcomed it, reveling in this need to get closer. His hand slipped to her back, pressing her against his broad, hard chest. His legs, already entwined with hers, hugged closer. One went between hers, stirring a desire she had never known.

With a long sigh, his lips softened against hers. He brought his other hand from underneath her and buried it in the thickness of her hair, smoothing it between his fingers.

"I'm glad you no longer wear that head covering," he whispered, so softly she barely heard.

But she did not reply, too afraid to speak. If she had allowed her lips to utter what she felt, she would have begged for another kiss—and more, though she knew not what. So she kept silent, not only because of unwitting eavesdroppers just outside the tent, but because she could not bear the thought of begging him for anything. Surely he already thought her shameless.

But how could she stop him when his lips

lowered to hers once more? How could she resist him when every fiber of her being had so newly discovered what a kiss was? As his mouth descended, she felt her own arms pull him close as his did her. She felt his hardness along her entire length—from the muscled breadth of his shoulders beneath her fingertips to his hard chest against her soft one, to his thighs and calves and feet, all solid as stone, all so welcome to her touch that she trembled with new-found desire.

She would have spoken then, in a haze of longing so thick that rashly she wanted to confess she'd never in her life been kissed that way. But he put a finger to her lips, motioning toward those on the other side of the flap.

Then he shifted position to let her head rest against his shoulder. Still wrapped in his arms, she knew beyond doubt that never again could she feign indifference to Raff Olafsson. Hadn't he awakened something within her that went as deep as her soul?

IX

Sailing inland up the river, Ambyre saw more of Iceland's black, forbiddingly angular landscape. She wondered what sort of life this land could possibly support, but Wulfstan assured her the farm they headed for was both independent and habitable for man and beast. Cattle provided hide and leather, while a nesting ground brought even higher profit, eiderdown being the largest export of the land. But she only hoped, since the farm was reported populous, that it would prove warm and comfortable as well.

Piers' longship fell behind, ice having redamaged the repairs given it after the storm. He signalled Raff on, shouting a message that he would stop to patch the hull and finish the final trek the next day. There was no reason for Raff to be delayed as well.

Despite the ice floating in the river, the remaining longship sailed almost to the border of the farm. There it was rolled ashore into a large shed, where Ambyre noticed others already stored.

Once again on land, they were greeted with Iceland's ferocious wind. Blowing snow stung Ambyre's cheeks and eyes. She pulled her furs up over her mouth and nose until she could barely see or breathe. Even though it was early afternoon, twilight already darkened the day. Why would anyone choose to live in this sunless, windswept place?

Light from the farmhouse could be seen in the distance, but the snow was too deep for them to walk. From the ship they took sticks of wood long enough to use as poles, a pair for each person. Weaved, oval accessories were attached underneath their shoes. Ambyre did as they told her; these people knew every way imaginable to meet nature's demands. The wideness of the leather weaving dispersed her weight, enabling her to walk on top of the snow without sinking.

Raff trudged beside her as they left the river's edge and headed toward the farm. He had spoken little during the final part of their journey, but his manner had warmed from aloof to a friendly distance for the benefit of his men. He still came to her only at night, though he was quick to smile in her direction. She began to wonder what had inspired him to kiss her. Had it been an impulse? A desire of the moment? Something easily forgotten?

Not so for her. Every waking hour contained at least one brief recollection of what she'd felt in his arms. And her dreams were full of Raff and his kiss. How could she forget? Never, she thought, would this memory fade, no matter how much time passed.

Yet other thoughts plagued her as well. Often she'd been torn between the wish to tell him she was not married and the fear of exposure. Raff believed himself to be kissing a woman who should not have been kissed. And she'd let him—no, more than that. She'd wanted him to kiss her, it could not be denied.

What was impossible was to tell him the truth. A kiss did not mean any mercy would be shown if he found she'd made a fool of him. He had been tricked into kidnapping the wrong person, which negated his plan. Could some small carnal desire mitigate the punishment he would carry out?

No, she must allow him to believe he had kissed a woman willing to betray her marriage vows; not yet an adulteress, but thinking of it, meriting punishment by her own kingdom's code of morals. She must be ready to give up his respect rather than the secret which guarded her life.

Now, as he walked beside her, she alone seemed to be tense. He was assured, confident, even eager to be alone with her. Since the kisses they'd shared, he had seemed more relaxed in her company, as if doubts had been resolved. In any case, matters were getting out of her control and would surely come to a head soon. When that happened, she must force herself to be firm. Her life, and Fauntley's and Cuthbert's, depended on it.

The farmstead consisted of several buildings, separate quarters for slaves, a hay barn for grain and other such food stuffs, a smithy and several sheds. The main house was really three buildings in one, with a privy nearby. It was seeing the smoke that made Ambyre rejoice, eager as she was for the warmth of a home hearth.

Raff directed her inside. The room was large and long, spacious enough to hold all of their thirty men with ample margin to spare. He took her to the hearthside, warm and welcoming. The men soon discarded their heavy cloaks, though she retained hers, not yet trusting to part from it until assured of her own warmth. After a while Raff took it, saying the mistress of the farmstead was eager to meet her.

Ambyre first saw her hostess standing among the men. Dressed in a green, smooth pinafore with an underdress of ivory, she was pouring wine for them, greeting many familiarly. When Raff approached, she instructed a young girl beside her to continue serving while she welcomed him with a firm embrace and a resounding kiss.

"Raff! How good to see you! Bjorn has itched to go a-viking with you, but now you have come before he could set sail! I'm so glad."

"Where is that brawny blood-brother of mine?" he called out, still in the woman's arms.

"Here! Watching the hands you've laid upon my wife!" a voice boomed from behind, and they both turned to it. " 'Tis a sad place you've chosen to winter, my friend! You should be in the Turkish warmth rather than the Iceland ice!"

"The Turks do not welcome me as you do, brother!" In a moment, the two men embraced.

"Welcome! Welcome! Of course you are welcome—and for as long as you wish. We have food aplenty, and 'tis the time of year for feast and celebration."

With a hand on Raff's arm, Bjorn would have led him to the wine, had Raff not detained him, indicating Ambyre. She stepped closer at his bidding.

"We bring with us a special guest. For safekeeping."

A guffaw thundered from Bjorn, but Ambyre was more amused than startled. He reached for her without warning, hugged her close and kissed her cheek loudly. He was a large man, very strong, as she felt from his tight embrace. Several years Raff's elder, gray sprinkling his dark beard, it was nevertheless the hair atop Bjorn's head that Ambyre noticed first. He was crowned with the brightest red shock she had ever beheld.

"Safekeeping from all those brothers of yours, no doubt," Bjorn joked. "And well worthy! She's a treasure, my boy. A beauty!"

"A beauty not mine, nor my brothers'. We

NORTHWARD THE HEART

have brought her here to hide."

"Stole her away, did you?" Bjorn asked with a grin.

"Precisely, my friend, but for reasons which are more complex than obvious. I will explain it all to you in detail later. First we wish to impose upon your bathhouse and share the feast you promised."

"Of course! Of course! Explanations later, as you wish. But you needn't tell all. I can see reason enough for wanting to steal this one away."

"Bjorn, do not take too much for granted," chided his wife, who stepped closer to Ambyre. "I am Gytha, mother to this one's children. You shall come with me, away from all these loud men. Raff, she and I will use the bathhouse first. You and your men will wait!"

Raff grinned, obeying Gytha, who took Ambyre away, leaving the men to finish their wine and refill their cups.

Gytha was probably close to the real AElfwyn's age of thirty, with an eager, dimpled smile and gray-blue eyes. Her hair was light blonde, very long, plaited at the back in the usual style to keep it out of the way.

The bathhouse lay at a quick sprint from the back of the farmhouse. There, Gytha spoke easily as she began to undress, undoing her braided hair, combing her fingers through its length. "Have you ever taken the mist bath before?"

Ambyre shook her head, shy about showing her body in front of anyone.

"You will like it," Gytha promised, letting her pinafore fall in a heap. "In winter, we bathe more often. 'Tis the best way to be truly warm. It will relax you after your cold voyage."

Ambyre, playing with the silver clip in her hair as if she had difficulty with it, merely smiled in response, a timid, half smile. Never before had she bathed *with* someone. Only servants with obediently averted gazes had ever been present. This was far different.

"What is it, dear?" Gytha asked, now fully unclothed and prepared to go through a wooden door to the bath. "Can I help?" She was completely unselfconscious.

Ambyre did not look directly at her. " 'Tis my hair; I cannot seem to loosen it."

Gytha had the clip free in a moment. "There," she said with a smile. "Now hurry; I shall start the bath."

Ambyre caught a glimpse of her body as she went through the door. Tall and trim, built sturdily, looking healthy with creamy white skin. Still Ambyre stood, fussing with the brooches upon her chest, holding the pinafore to her. She peeked behind the door, wondering what sort of bath she was headed for. To her surprise, with equal amounts of delight and relief, she saw thick, hot steam, so dense she could barely make out her own arm in front of her.

"Come in!" Gytha called. "I know you are there; I feel the draft. 'Tis wonderfully warm once inside. Come in!"

Reassured, Ambyre thrust off her shift and entered the steaming room. When the door closed behind her, she was surrounded by the hot vapors, caressing and warming every part of her body, clinging to and moistening her skin.

"There is a seat along the side, my dear. Can you find it?"

Ambyre walked hesitantly, arms outstretched. "Aye. I've found it."

" 'Tis comforting, is it not?"

Ambyre sighed, leaning back with a smile. " 'Tis the warmest I've felt in over a month. Nay, in all the winters of my life."

"I will make more steam."

Ambyre heard the swish of water scald against something hot before a new outpouring of steam spewed forth. At first it was almost overpowering, but in a moment it settled and she felt each pore of her body cleansed from within.

"What is your name, dear? I did not hear Raff say."

Ambyre's eyes, shut in such warm comfort, opened. She had almost said her real name.

"A— . . . AElfwyn. I am niece to the King of Wessex in England."

"Niece to King Edward!" Gytha's voice revealed her amazement.

"You know of him?"

"Aye; we all know of him. 'Tis a strong leader you have in your uncle, AElfwyn. My own husband has fought against his men."

"In England?" Ambyre asked, surprised.

"Bjorn likes to go traveling and adventuring between seasons. 'Tis how he met Raff. But tell me, then, how come you to know Raff? Surely your uncle did not allow him to court you?"

Ambyre laughed at the very thought. "Nay, milady. Raff and my uncle have never met, eye to eye. Only politically, and that because of land they both want. Raff is holding me for ransom from my uncle."

Gytha made no quick response, but soon Ambyre heard an amused, light laugh. " 'Tis so like Raff to choose such a manner of gaining Edward's attention. He can be quite romantic."

"Romance has had little to do with it."

"Oh?" Gytha sounded genuinely surprised.

"I am married, milady."

"Oh. . ." said Gytha, somewhat deflated.

"My husband and my son are being held as well. They follow us in a separate ship, with Raff's brother Piers."

Gytha spoke again, her voice apologetic. "I am more of a romantic than Raff, I must confess. You are young, and very beautiful, and for a moment, when he presented you, my romantic mind leapt to a romantic conclusion. He is also young, and very attractive, is he not? But 'twas my imagination, I see now."

"Aye . . . it must have been," Ambyre replied, wondering if it had indeed been that alone.

NORTHWARD THE HEART

After their bath, Gytha provided Ambyre with a complete set of new clothes, stored in the anteroom. A linen shift was stark white, as white as she had ever seen. Gytha told her this was achieved through soaking it in boiled cow's urine. After being rinsed and delicately scented with dried flowers, it was then pleated with hot flat chunks of cullet. Over this came a pinafore, dyed crimson red with madden dyes. Neither had she ever seen so deep a red. This pinafore, unlike others given her by Sigrid, was puckered at the waist, more becoming to the female form. Gytha wore the same style.

Like the women in Yorkshire, Gytha used cosmetics freely. Without the thin, dark lines drawn along the lids, her eyes were small. Now they seemed to sparkle and grow larger. Ambyre's eyes, already large, were enhanced by the color placed around them. They appeared even darker by contrast with those of Gytha, who told her they were quite alluring.

When the two returned to the Hall, Raff's men began to leave for their own baths, a few at a time, while he waited with Bjorn until all others were through.

Ambyre could smell the makings of the promised feast—beef and pork, fish, porridges and bread. Much wine and mead had already been consumed, judging from the empty calfskin containers lying underneath the table. She offered to assist Gytha who left to oversee the preparations, but was pleasantly commanded to be seated.

She found a place near Raff, who was listening to Bjorn's deep, resonant voice laugh over times past. She heard adventures retold that had taken the two friends from the northern fjords of their homeland to the southern deserts of the Islamic Caliphates.

When most of Raff's men had returned from the bath, Bjorn stood to accompany the remaining few, expecting Raff to follow. But he hesitated, telling Bjorn he would join him in a moment. Raff let Bjorn leave before facing Ambyre.

He moved closer to her, seated as they were on the same bench near the hearth. He took her hand, squeezed it, then let it go. He looked at her as he spoke. She could do little else but stare back, unaware and foolishly uncaring if his men watched from afar.

"We will talk, now that our every word cannot be heard. I have spoken to Bjorn; you will be staying in a separate house, a comfortable home that is warm and private. Your husband will not arrive until tomorrow. I will come to you tonight."

Her heart beat wildly within her. She protested before any thought, any emotion could make her hesitate. "Raff, I cannot—"

He laid a finger to her mouth, withdrew it quickly. "We will speak later of what can and cannot be done. Have no fear, milady. Whatever happens, whether 'tis nothing or . . . Know that you will be safe."

He was gone before she could say another

word, before he could see the sudden dismay upon her face. Confusion ... emotions erupting and attacking, causing physical pandemonium within. She could not think clearly; her cheeks burned. She wanted to run, to sort things out, but Gytha was coming. Suddenly the smells of the feast seemed nauseating.

She got through the celebration, though later remembered little of it. She was aware only of Raff, who seemed to pointedly ignore her. She ate so little—was Gytha offended?—that Wulfstan inquired after her health. Then she painstakingly tried to force food into a stomach that was churning with emotion.

Feasts were never short for these people; they caroused between courses to make the meal last well into the night. As for Ambyre, she could only hope it would last until tomorrow night, when Fauntley returned and gave her an excuse to avoid this new danger. Raff would not approach her with her "husband" present.

Though the robust laughter was at its height, Gytha suggested taking her to her new home, for she looked quite fatigued. Wanting to stay for no other reason than to be safe from what she couldn't control, Ambyre had no obvious argument against Gytha's logic.

Outside, Gytha led her toward what appeared to be a hill covered with snow, small, graceful wisps of smoke escaping from its peak. But as they walked around the side, Ambyre saw that the snow had been shoveled away from a door. Gytha took her inside.

A fire burned in the hearth to give the small, one-room home warmth. Circular, wood-lined walls built into an earthen hill provided extra insulation from the air outside. To one side was a large bed; near the hearth, a bench. A washing table stood near an open chest, revealing furs and extra clothing. Scented rushes strewn on the floor made a clean, earthy smell. There were no windows, but the hearth was bright. Ambyre thought it an inviting place, warm and clean, and especially private.

"You should be comfortable in here, my dear," said Gytha. "I will come for you in the morning."

Gytha retreated toward the door as Ambyre thanked her, but hesitated before leaving. "If you should hear anything during the night, 'tis only Gorm, the dog. She is prone to follow unfamiliar scents, and if she picked yours up, she may chase it to your door. Do not worry; my gentle Gorm could harm no one, especially now when heavy with young. Sleep well, dear. Prop a bench against the door if you wish."

After Gytha had left, Ambyre's eyes sought the bench. She was tempted to follow the advice, though not solely to keep Gorm from entering.

Time passed slowly, with her mind alert for any noise from outside. Twice she went to the door, imagining she heard Raff's voice, but no one was there. At last she went to the bed and felt its softness. She added another fur, then sat down, finding it warm and comfortable. She imagined sharing it with Raff, remembering his hard body next to hers aboard ship. But a noise made her spring from her guilty reverie. She ran to the door, opened it, finding to her amazement a gray, swollen dog, obviously near her term. The tail wagged furiously. Ambyre could not help but laugh and kneel to pet her. The dog muzzled against her ear, leaving half her face soaked with saliva.

"I wager the bitch gets a warmer welcome than I," said a voice from the dark. "At least, she stood before your door merely a moment before having it opened and being welcomed. Expecting her, perhaps?"

She stood. Raff came into the light. "Gytha did warn me of her..."

"And it was only her you expected to find," he finished. "May I intrude, or are you disappointed to see me?"

"No..." she said, then added hesitantly, "Yes..."

"Yes?" he repeated, apparently surprised.

"I—I cannot know why you have come."

He smiled, though he seemed more confident than amused. "I have grown accustomed to having you beside me at night. Shall that suffice as reason enough?"

"And when Fauntley arrives?"

He shrugged, stepping over the dog to enter the small room, closing out both the dog and the cold.

" 'Tis not necessary to remind me of your husband, my lady. We both know he exists."

"Then why are you here?" she asked.

He faced her, standing only a short distance away. He spoke softly. "I am here because both of us want me to be."

"Perhaps not both," she told him, though she did not look up at him as she spoke.

He placed a hand on each of her shoulders. "I know better than to believe your shyness. I remember well what was in that kiss."

"It . . . 'tis unexpected. . ."

He laughed outright, holding her against him. "Unexpected! Hardly! Both of us were lying there that night, taut as bows, ready. AElfwyn, you cannot deny it."

He kissed her then, just as lingeringly, just as demandingly as he had that night. And she let him for no other reason than sheer desire, pressing herself against him as urgently as he pressed to her. And she realized, as thrilling as those first kisses had been, this one was more thrilling. Unrestrained by either a sleeping bag or alert warriors within earshot, she felt the freedom it gave. No inhibitions marred it. His mouth, warm against her own, was more eager, more gentle. His arms around her were no tighter than hers around him, but when his tongue darted against her lips, an emotional door opened deep within her. She reveled in the unfamiliar sensation, surprised at the smooth softness of his tongue. Never before had she felt such arousal. The pleasure spread uncontrollably. She felt caution slipping away.

But somehow, at the last moment, she managed to pull herself away. The choice was to indulge her senses or save her life.

"No!" she said, staggering back. "How can you? How can you think... How can you demand from me something which deserves death as its penalty?"

He frowned, but did not touch her again. "True, milady, 'tis not something I would care to have anyone know about, not your husband nor my own men. But I don't demand this response from you. I don't force you to enjoy my kiss. What is between us has nothing to do with you being my prisoner. I demand you stay here, and I'll not bring you back to your kingdom, but I don't demand anything further. What I came here for tonight is something both of us want."

"Fornication?" she challenged in an unsteady voice, then quickly corrected herself. "Adultery?"

"I have now kissed you twice, and feel your body saying something contrary to the protests from your mouth. Do you deny the desire I know you have?"

"How can I admit it when it will lead only to sin?" she asked. Her voice was calmer, as much of the truth as possible under it. "How can I lie with you when in little more than two months you will resume being my enemy? Would you have me only in lust, to be cast aside and dishonored once you war with my people?"

"What are you asking for?" He was puzzled. "Love?"

" 'Twould make little difference in the future."

"And now, this moment?"

She did not want to answer. When she spoke it was reluctantly. "We cannot be in love; we know too little of one another."

He looked at her closely. "I wonder..." Then abruptly: "I wonder, milady, if you truly know what love is. Did you ever love your husband?"

"We have a son," she declared, as if that were proof.

"And you love him now, to this day?"

"Yes, yes of course."

He laughed shortly. "I do not believe you."

"You seem such an authority on love," she countered, glad to focus on him. "Yet you remain unmarried. Why is that?"

"I have never loved a woman," he admitted, "so I am not such an expert. But I want you, knowing you are married, knowing you can never be mine. Perhaps I shouldn't say that the moment I saw you I hoped my plan of marriage could succeed. Nor should I admit you have come before my thoughts of my people's future. You are an unusual woman, AElfwyn. Intelligent when most are trivial, brave with the enemy, strong against a stormy sea. And beautiful as well. I cannot convince myself you are happily married; I can't stop remembering the night we first kissed. I can't ignore the desires I feel when I look upon your face, nor the pleasure your company brings. I want you, aye, but 'tis not as simple as lust."

She was silent. He understood her refusal—understood but did not accept it. Only one persuasion remained to him. He stepped closer. Her words denied what she wanted; he knew her body could not.

He moved slowly. She saw the longing in his eyes. His kiss was stubbornly demanding, forcing her to reveal her own, equal passion. It was in the inviting softness of her lips, in the willingness of her arms encircling him, in the way she strained herself against him. They needed no more discussion; the truth could not be denied.

This time when his tongue thrilled her, she obeyed the surprising desire to open her mouth to him. His exploration of her own tongue and teeth were pleasures she had never imagined. She trembled. Who would have thought a kiss could be so intimate?

Carefully, without lifting his mouth from hers, he guided her backwards. She was aware only of his kiss, not that he moved her toward the bed. His hands loosened from around her only to unburden him of his weapons. The sword and dagger fell silently to a fur on the floor. One hand resumed its hold around her waist, the other went to the smoothness of her neck, caressing it as he continued to kiss her. She became aware of that hand, more aware now than of his kiss. It seemed to tease her, wanting to move, but lingering nonetheless, either from uncertainty or from experience, either shy or wanting to build what passion its hesitation would create. She wanted that hand to move, to caress her in places that felt so alive, so dominant that they consumed all thought or hope for anything but satisfaction. It did move, ever so slowly, so deliberately, so knowledgeably. That hand went beneath her pinafore at its opening on the side, so that only the soft linen shift lay between it and her skin. It moved to unfasten the brooch and then the ribbon on her shift. Soon his fingers were directly against her skin, caressing her, teasing her. She felt the peak of her breast stiffen to his touch.

The second brooch came away as easily. Raff gently slid the pinafore and undershift from her shoulders. He stepped back ever so slightly, watching as the garments fell to the floor. Ambyre stood naked, looking at him without shame. His eyes were alight with appreciation.

In a moment they were lying down. Raff's kisses never ceased, though now his lips traveled to the areas his fingers had already explored. Ambyre no longer felt any fear. Desire left no room.

Her arms clung to him until he placed one of her hands under his tunic, the other following automatically. Beneath the soft, curled hair, his skin felt taut against his muscles. Her fingers encountered several scars, some small, others large, which spoke of his bravery and strength. It would be so easy to love this man, she thought to herself.

His close-fitted breeks were bound at the waist by a smooth cord. Ambyre had not noticed, at first, that he had unfastened that cord. Till then, only pleasure had been able to penetrate her desire-ridden mind. But when she felt him against her she realized they were both naked. There was no longer any protection between him and her virginity. The words repeated in her mind...protection...virginity. Suddenly her blood pumped faster from something other than passion; suddenly her mind realized what her body had made it forget. She was a virgin; surely he would know, surely he would learn of it if allowed entrance. She must stop him. She *must...*

Her protests were taken at first only as moans of desire. Her tongue was slow to obey, but when her eyes opened, her voice became more urgent. She was fully alert now, alert to the danger. How could she have allowed this to go so far? How could she so easily betray herself? Betray those depending on her? Her body had driven duty and fear from her mind. But they returned in time, and their rebirth caused a stirring which even Raff, lost in his own desire, recognized as more panic than passion. His eyes sought hers, seeing them wide and fearful. He stopped his caresses, though he did not move.

"Do not be afraid," he whispered. "I swear to you Fauntley will never learn what is taking place. I give you my oath."

"No...no I cannot. I cannot finish what should not have begun. Please...please, Raff, release me."

"AElfwyn—" he began, pleading, but when he heard his own tone it seemed alien to him, and he did not go on. He would not plead, not with her, not with anyone.

He rolled away, pulling down his tunic and closing his breeks. Then he did not move, but merely watched as she clutched at a fur to cover herself. He breathed once, deeply.

"I—I'm sorry," she whispered, tears filling the eyes she averted from him.

"Sorry," he laughed, scoffing at the word.

He stood. Now she felt his disdain and could not bear it.

"So much for your confession of 'more than lust!'" she accused. "So much for any feeling beyond that within your loins! You look upon me now with disgust, with your frustration the price of my morality. But do not leave without knowing I too suffer. I wanted it to happen—yes, I did. Just as much as you. But I wounded your pride by being able to resist at the last moment. So leave! And do not be fooled into thinking I believed any of your words of respect."

He gazed down at her during this outburst, first confused, then angry. Didn't she *want* him to go? It wasn't *he* who stopped. Was she mad? But he listened, hearing her earnestness, saw tears glistening in her eyes. Understanding was beyond him. Was what they had already done somehow less than actual culmination? Did not this incomplete act count for some portion of adultery? Why had she stopped him after they had gone so far?

"Look at me, AElfwyn," he quietly demanded,

and had to repeat himself before she obeyed. "I am standing here, not touching you; I have done as you asked. I could have forced you; the god Frey himself knows I could have entered you and neither of us would have borne a mark to show what took place. But here I stand. What cause have you to say my words were untrue? How this ended was as *you* wanted, and I respected your wish. Tell me, is not that evidence of something higher than lust? Might that not be love?"

His words only increased her agitation; tears turned to sobs and she could not stop herself. She turned away from him, but he sat again and pulled her to him for comfort. He held her close, aware of her nakedness, but now reining in his desire. She sobbed against his shoulder, coming under control at last, clinging to the fur covering and not to him.

"I cannot ... I cannot lie with you," she choked. "Our personal feelings don't matter; what cannot be done is what must be remembered, and this *cannot* be done."

"All right," he soothed, and bent closer to kiss her forehead. "All right."

Before leaving, he paused long enough to say, "But remember all I've said, AElfwyn."

Piers' longship arrived the following afternoon, when Raff was conspicuously absent. He appeared at the evening meal, but acknowledged neither Ambyre nor her family. Afterward, he and Bjorn dressed for the snow and went out. Neither of them appeared again for the remainder of the evening.

Many female slaves inhabited the farm and it seemed each of the men found at least one to their liking. Fauntley found this custom of having a body slave detestable. He was glad to have separate sleeping quarters, especially for Cuthbert's sake.

The boy spent time with Wulfstan, while Ambyre worked with a spindle and distaff given to her by Gytha. Fauntley stationed himself nearby, as always finding his greatest pleasure in simply watching her.

He had been instrumental in keeping them separate by day as well. Scandalized when simultaneously a fight broke out at one end of the main Hall, while at the other a warrior mauled a slave who seemed to be enjoying it, he demanded privacy. Gytha, accustomed to these ways, was surprised at such a request from a man; but after all, he was a foreigner. So she brought them to the private room where she slept with Bjorn. Her children were there, a boy no older than seven or eight and a girl with the same red hair as her father. The daughter was about Cuthbert's age and looked at him with shy interest, but he felt it best just to ignore her.

Because the room built into the hill was so small, Ambyre and her two charges spent only their sleeping hours there. With little sun by which to gauge the time, she soon found herself following the schedule of her body. When she became tired, she knew it grew late, and when she woke hours later, she knew it to be morning. It was easy to sleep longer, with no sun to brighten the day and only cold outside of the furs. She and Cuthbert occupied the bed, while Fauntley slept on the rushes near the hearth, warmed by it and extra furs.

Days went slowly for the three hostages. It seemed everyone else had ways to stay occupied and entertained. Gytha had unending tasks presiding over the household; Bjorn, reunited with his best friend, spent the days with Raff, in between duties of overseeing his many slaves with their winter duties and repair tasks. Even Raff's warriors, visitors as they were, were not idle. They either practiced the many sports which improved their battle skills, or amused themselves with slaves. Even Cuthbert became initiated in the ways of the warriors, despite Fauntley's concern, for he followed Wulfstan about whenever Raff was with Bjorn.

Ambyre was supplied with a lap loom to create ornamental hair bands or borders for her dresses. To decorate the objects she made, she was given fine silk and threads of silver and gold, thick enough to be used without a needle, stiff enough to pierce the material. The ornaments, though of her own design, were of imported material and quite costly, so she did not keep them for herself but made gifts of them to a surprised and pleased Gytha.

After three days she became aware of a growing languor. She missed the time spent outdoors at Wessex. Here she could not be so bold as to follow these warriors about as Cuthbert did. She envied him. Riding horses and practicing with a sword were permissible for the daughter of Dunstan, but not the daughter of the Lady of the Mercians. So she remained with her stitchery.

Fauntley, too, became restless without a tablet to write on or a pupil to teach. Ambyre saw an opportunity for him to end his boredom when Gytha complained of the speed at which her storeroom was emptying. Ambyre suggested he inventory what remained and log what was used, so that Gytha would always know what was plentiful and what should be rationed. The process intrigued Gytha, who could not write. She watched Fauntley list the supplies on a length of bark peeled back from a felled tree. He wrote with a knife dipped in ink he created from animal oil and ash. When he had finished, Gytha urged him to teach her such wonders. He'd found a student.

When Bjorn learned that not only his wife but his children were learning to make strange symbols which spoke only to those who understood, he was at first very angry. To Bjorn it was magic, and those who knew magic were not to be trusted. But Gytha told him it was merely a system which would unburden her of worry about winter supplies. Seeing it then as a household craft, Bjorn forbade only his son's participation. If it were part of woman's work, then certainly a future warrior should avoid it.

Gorm had her litter of pups, which indirectly

broadened Cuthbert's social life. It was how Gytha's red-headed daughter, whose name was Helga, broke through his indifference to her. When she brought him a pup, he melted. From then on he cut down on his time with the warriors to spend regular hours with Helga and the eight mewling pups.

Ambyre grew to anticipate frequent visits to the bathhouse. She went alone or with Gytha, while Fauntley accompanied Cuthbert. Gytha wondered aloud why they did not go as a family but never received a suitable reply from any of them.

One afternoon when Ambyre inquired if the bathhouse were unoccupied, Gytha replied she would check. Gone only a moment, she returned smiling warmly to say the bathhouse was free.

"Would you care to join me today?" Ambyre asked, but Gytha was already shaking her head.

"Nay, not till later. Better that you go now."

Ambyre left, not noticing the smile lingering on Gytha's face. She went to the bathhouse eagerly, by now well-accustomed to pouring the correct amount of water over the heated rocks in order to create the comforting steam. She undressed quickly, but to her surprise the room was already filled with the hot vapors. She assumed it had just been vacated.

She sat down on the side bench, breathing deeply and feeling her body relax. This was her favorite comfort, and she planned to suggest King Edward have one installed at the palace in Wessex.

The steam began to subside, and, about to stand and replenish it, she suddenly heard the hiss of water against the rocks.

She was not alone.

"Who is there?" she demanded, sitting alert, attempting to cover herself. She could still see no one.

"AElfwyn?" said a surprised, familiar voice. She saw Raff's outline come near, and fought to control sudden panic.

"Yes!—But no, stay where you are!"

She heard him laugh, though he obeyed her request.

"Still shy when I have memorized the vision of your body? You need not be ashamed, my lady. You are lovely."

She stood, inching nearer the door, hoping he would stay clear.

"I—I must leave," she said urgently. "Should someone find us—"

" 'Tis the custom to check with Gytha before entering. She keeps track of who is here. She'll not allow anyone else in with me."

"She allowed me!" Ambyre declared, which made him laugh even louder.

"I must remember to thank her." At his last word he was suddenly in full view, her arms ineffectually trying to hide what they could not, and he took her hands. When she looked away, he put a finger under her chin and turned her toward him for a kiss. He pulled her up, pressed her close, their bodies damp, smooth against each other. She fought her desire to let him kiss her again.

"You must let me go," she whispered. She felt the hairs on his chest tickle her breasts, and tried to break away. How could she refuse if she felt him like this? She remembered too well what magic his body could create in hers. "Gytha will wonder why I did not immediately leave, once she realizes her mistake."

" 'Twas no mistake."

"Then she *knows* we are here together?"

"Milady, she intended for us to find each other."

Ambyre could only gasp, trying once again to escape his touch. "Doesn't she know the penalty for adultery? Doesn't she care for your life—or mine? Would she have us killed because it amused her to see what might happen?"

"Hush, milady." He stroked her damp hair. "Gytha would not betray us. Whatever her reason for this, it cannot only be amusement. Do not worry; she is an honorable woman."

"Honorable, to have set up such a situation! Intentionally! 'Tis shameful."

He laughed agin. "I feel no shame. To be honest, I rather enjoy it."

"Raff, let me go!"

He did so, and she was unsure which affected her more, his body upon her or his eyes, for he looked at her without embarrassment, boldly taking in the sight of her. She attempted to flee, but he caught a hand and pulled her back to him.

"Wait!" His voice was more serious. He brought his mouth to hers for another kiss. She did not struggle. His body pressed again to hers, hard strong, demanding as his lips, his tongue teasing hers. "Stay here with me, AElfwyn," he insisted.

"Raff..." his name poured out sadly, reluctantly. " 'Tis impossible."

"I know your husband has not satisfied your needs," he challenged, separating himself from her, suddenly angry. "He has been with you at night while I lie alone, yet your kisses betray your unquenched thirst. Admit it to me, AElfwyn, Fauntley cannot satisfy you."

"No!" Only a whisper came out when she wanted to be firm.

"Which is it? No, he does not, or no, you will not admit it?" he persisted. "Tell me, AElfwyn, and I will let you go."

With bent head, eyes downcast away from his body, she told as much truth as she could. "Nay, he does not satisfy me. He has never done so."

He seized on the word. "Never!.. Then why did you stop me the other night? I would have shown you how it is, AElfwyn. I'd not have given up until you knew—and you would want to stay with me now, to know it again. Stay, AElfwyn. Let me show you."

She emitted a cry. With a sudden wrench her body slipped from his. Then she was gone to the outer room, hurrying into her clothes so fast she did not take time to fasten her pinafore or tie back her hair. She stumbled toward her little home and rushed inside, not even noticing the cold.

Fauntley was there, and he stood in amazement at her disheveled, half-clothed appearance.

"Ambyre, you must be frozen from being outside like that! Damp hair turning to ice... carrying your pinafore and cloak. What is it? Has someone threatened you?"

"Aye," she said, but stopped herself quickly, as much for her own protection as his. "Nay... no one. 'Twas nothing. I was startled, no more. Please, you must excuse me to finish dressing."

He suddenly flushed, seeing how the damp linen shift clung to the generous swell of her breasts, providing little concealment. He immediately turned away.

"What startled you?" he persisted suspiciously from over his shoulder.

" 'Twas nothing," she said again, more firmly. "An animal."

"Ambyre, if someone has threatened you—"

"Nay."

"I am supposed to be your husband," he continued, not letting her interrupt further. "You must tell me the truth, Ambyre. If someone needs to be reckoned with then I shall play my role."

"Fauntley, your words are ridiculous." She spoke with exasperation. "Any one of these Danes would kill you in an instant if you challenged him."

He seemed crushed. Still not facing her, he found a seat on the bench and held his head in his hands, elbows propped on his knees.

" 'Tis expected of a husband to protect his wife," he murmured at last.

Ambyre was distracted with the clasp in her hair, not noticing the dejection upon his face or in his voice. "You aren't playing the role of husband completely, Fauntley. There is no need to endanger your own safety."

"I suppose I haven't been much good to you," he sighed.

Ambyre stopped fussing with the clip, aware now of his depression.

"Fauntley!" she chided, coming to sit beside him. "You've saved my life! By coming after me—you've served our kingdom! Without you, my identity surely would have been learned."

"I've done nothing more than follow you into captivity, unable to free any of us."

She put an arm about his thin shoulders. "We'll be free soon," she encouraged. "Don't forget, Fauntley, 'twas you who knew what to aim for: when we return to England and go into Mercia, our enemies will be revealed as the fools they are, and be forced to free us."

He turned to her. "I want you to tell me the truth. If someone does threaten you, I want to know. I want to protect you, just as a real husband would."

"There is no need—"

"Ambyre," he interrupted, "I want to play the role of your husband . . . because I want to *be* your husband. I love you."

She stared unmoving, her arm still comfortably about him. "Fauntley," she gasped, slowly withdrawing from him, "you've never even hinted this to me before."

It spilled out of him now. "I've always loved you. I love your mind, your curiosity, your strength. And . . . and I love the rest of you, too. You are a lovely woman." He was dizzy with relief.

"I never realized . . . I've always believed your life dedicated to God and to teaching."

"Can't it be dedicated to God, to teaching, and to you?"

She smiled without looking at him. "In that order?"

He shifted uncomfortably. "God must always be first," he said. "But teaching . . . that is third. You come second."

"Fauntley . . ."

He did not like the tone of her voice, nor the fact that she stood, moving farther away. "Say nothing yet, not while we're both held prisoner here and nothing can be done. I should not have spoken while we're forced to live in such close quarters. Please forgive me; I showed no foresight."

She turned back to him, smiling again. "I see no reason to ask my forgiveness. 'Tis I who should ask yours, and show you my gratitude as well. You have already protected me well. You need do no more."

She kissed his cheek. He silently reckoned that all the tribulation suffered at the hands of these Danes was suddenly worth this moment with Ambyre.

X

Fauntley had never known such extremities of emotion. He, a prisoner in a forsaken, ice-covered land, had at last revealed a part of himself which he had long kept hidden.

He was no hero, like in the sagas. Not broad of shoulder nor strong of back. But Ambyre credited him with saving her life, a deed which was by most standards heroic. He had done nothing, he thought, to deserve her praise, but he reveled in it nonetheless. It was enough that it was she who praised him.

This became the foundation of a new measure of self-confidence for Fauntley. Sullenness gone, he no longer scowled when a warrior teased him or called him *kjerringa*. He was no longer tormented by the obvious differences between himself and these virile men. He knew his own shortcomings but his strength lay elsewhere, and it concerned him only that Ambyre saw that. He never before had self-respect. Now

NORTHWARD THE HEART

that he knew she respected him, he felt the measure of his own worth.

Only one person could penetrate Fauntley's new self-confidence, and that was Rathulfr Olafsson. Since their arrival in Iceland, he noticed the warrior regarding him with a bit more interest. Before, he had simply been ignored, but recently he had been surprised to catch the man boldly staring at him. What's more, he didn't flinch under the steady, rude gaze. He held the stare of those blue eyes regarding him curiously, eyes with barely-concealed anger behind them.

Fauntley did not wonder what he had done to deserve this new attention; he had long since concluded this race of pagans possessed very little intelligence. So he let the man stare; it was a barbarian's pastime. He would win in the end, and Ambyre knew it.

With this new contentment, he was even unperturbed when the savage requested to see him. A slave brought him to the center hearth where Raff sat with Bjorn at a trestle-table. They were playing draughts by lamplight; neither looked up for several moments, though they surely heard him come in.

"We have something to ask of you," Raff said at last. He did not take his eyes from the amber gaming pieces before him. "My friend Bjorn knows a neighboring chieftain, Thorvold by name, who wishes someone to decipher various symbols inscribed upon utensils and weapons he has come to possess."

He had spoken so slowly, with such lack of interest, that Fauntley questioned him before Raff could continue in this manner. "You wish me to read these symbols?"

Raff looked up as if seeing an intruder rather than the invited party he was. "Yes," he said. "This chieftain's territory is a day's journey from here. Bjorn will accompany you with several of our men."

Fauntley, knowing the decision had already been made, merely accepted. "Is my family to travel with me?"

Raff's eyes, and with them his attention, had turned back to the draughts. He looked up again in annoyance.

"I would think you'd rather they stay here than travel in the cold."

"Of course," was Fauntley's reply, barely heard as Raff moved a game piece and sat back on the chair, causing Bjorn suddenly to thunder. He'd been beaten once again.

Fauntley was given snow shoes, and for long passages of ice he was provided with a pair of boots made of animal skins, with the dewclaws left attached for extra traction over the glassy surfaces.

Early in the dark morning, Ambyre came to see him off. Cuthbert was still sleeping.

The embrace they bestowed upon each other, bundled in furs, was barely felt through to the body. When she caught a glimpse of Raff coming to say his good-byes to the departing Bjorn, Ambyre quickly pushed aside the fur over her face and kissed Fauntley full on the mouth. Perhaps that would show Raff where her duty lay.

To Fauntley, the kiss was more than just part of a role; he had not instigated it. She had kissed him as a wife should have done—but which was certainly not necessary under the circumstances. Instead, it held hope. Unable to think of anything else, he then told himself it held more than just hope. It held promise, security, an eagerness to return home where all would be different because of these weeks spent as captives together. The memory of it warmed him throughout the day.

Ambyre gave no thought to what lay ahead. She was alert only to the present. The days past had been full of Raff, though they had barely spoken. She realized her foolishness, but despite scolding herself, her remorse, her trepidation about these feelings, she no longer ignored them. She warned herself that thoughts of Raff could lead only to pain; nothing could ever come of their relationship.

But still the emotions remained. She remembered their brief time together, his kiss, his words, his profession of love, and she found herself repeating those very words, silently, in her mind. At night, when she lay upon the bed they had shared, she closed her eyes and remembered him there with her, their eagerness, her hands upon him, even the many scars upon his body.

But those very scars warned her of who he was: a chieftain, or soon to be one, who could hardly marry a Saxon maiden who betrayed him. If his bride were to be a Saxon, then she must be of political value, and Ambyre could not provide that. Instead, her very identity might well thrust him into another war. And those scars would increase in number, fighting against her people, until one day he would receive a wound that would not heal, would not have time to scar. Someday he might achieve his warrior's death.

The thought unnerved her; she could not tolerate such visions for long, especially that she might be responsible for his death. If he had kidnapped the right person, couldn't his plan have succeeded? Couldn't peace between Edward and these Danes be gained by a true political marriage? AElfwyn would have been afraid—Ambyre still remembered her terror— but that would have passed. How could she say that AElfwyn herself would not have fallen in love with this Dane, as she had?

The admission came as no surprise; she'd had an inkling of emotion for him from the moment he lay next to her that very first night away from Wessex. She had found him to be more man than barbarian; illiterate, it was true, but not without sensitivity and intelligence, certainly strong and brave beyond measure.

When she learned yesterday that Fauntley was to leave with Bjorn, unwelcome hope came to her. Had it been Raff's idea to volunteer her "husband's" services? She hastily dispelled such a thought. Certainly he could not have arranged the need of the other chieftain. And if it were a ruse, wouldn't Cuthbert, too, have to be taken along in order to free her from her family? Her brother now remained her protector.

Raff's intentions became apparent when Cuthbert ran to her that very afternoon. His cheeks were flushed with excitement, his eyes sparkled in a way their father's often had, and his voice was high-pitched and fervent.

"Wulfstan has invited me to hunt falcons!" he exclaimed. "He told me how they capture them with nets and bring them back to train. They have to be young, so first we have to find a nest, take the young from—but 'tis a kind sport, Ambyre. The falcons are fed better in captivity than they are in the wild. And they're treated kindly, Wulfstan said so. Can I go, Ambyre? You won't make me stay behind, will you?"

"What sport can be kind if a living thing now free must give up that freedom? You should know best of all, Cuddy; you know what it is to lose your freedom."

His smile disappeared but his eyes remained alight. "I tell you truthfully, Ambyre, I have never been so happy as I have been among these people. Father would have approved, I know he would. Except that they're Danes, they're exactly the way Father would have wanted us to be."

She frowned, though his words reflected thoughts she herself already had. She tried to dissuade him, but in his enthusiasm he barely noticed her unwillingness to have him leave. He soon ran from the room, looking for Wulfstan to ask what provisions he would need. They were gone within the hour.

At the evening meal almost half the men were absent, so the festive qualities of other nights were lacking. Raff ate silently, while Ambyre found she had little appetite. She delved into conversation with Gytha, hoping to pass the evening hours ignoring the conflicts within her.

She did not deny the guilty hope that Raff had set this up, in anticipation of spending time alone with her. It was that hope which frightened her so, for certainly she did not wish to suffer the humiliation of putting him off again, the frustration of which must come if she were to keep her secret safe.

Despite Ambyre's wishes to the contrary, Gytha excused herself, and she was left to do so too. With the evening meal particularly short, her mistrust of the older woman grew. Since the episode in the bathhouse, she had had the distinct impression that Gytha was pushing her at Raff, regardless of her supposed married state. So when Gytha retired, taking her children and excusing most of the slaves, Ambyre left as well, without word to Raff, who watched her go.

Sleep, as expected, eluded her. She stoked the fire, brightening the little room, then sat beside it rather than face the bed alone. She tried thinking of other things, of what Edward might be doing at that moment, of what AElfwyn must think and how she must worry; she even attempted to think about her freedom, of returning to Wessex and to the life she had before. She could hardly imagine it, yet that was the life she had been reared and prepared for.

These thoughts were sporadic. The recurring theme was the truth before her. Fauntley had been sent away with Bjorn, for at least three days. Cuthbert would be gone with Wulfstan for the same amount of time, leaving her as alone as on that first night in Iceland, before the second ship had arrived. This must have been Raff's doing.

She heard a sound at the door and, unlike that other night, she had no hope that it would be the dog; she knew who it was. She hesitated before moving, hoping he would go away if she did not answer, wondering if she possessed enough sense to let that happen. She stood, her decision made without rational thought, for if she'd been wise, she would not have opened the door.

He smiled upon seeing her, a smile as friendly and platonic as any he'd given her in full view of his men. She could not be so glib. He stepped past her into the warmth of the room. She noticed he seemed particularly warmly-dressed, with not one fur but two, his helmet atop his head and fur accessories warming his hands and feet.

"You're not tired, are you, milady?" he asked brightly.

She shook her head with some hesitation and confusion.

"Good, good," he said, looking toward the

chest at the foot of the bed. "Tell me, did your husband leave behind any clothes Gytha had made for him? She'd been very generous, don't you think, regarding payment for these lessons he's giving her?"

"Well . . . yes, but why do you want to know about Fauntley's clothes?"

"You're about his size—height, weight, and so forth. Do you think you could fit into his breeches?"

Her eyebrows raised in obvious surprise. "Why?"

He laughed. "Women's clothes are exceedingly silly for outdoor sport."

"What?"

"Don't frown until you've seen what I have in mind. Are you willing?"

Now her brows knitted. "I believe you've been possessed by your trickster-god Loki."

"Perhaps . . . but 'tis contagious. You'll feel it any moment now."

She could not help but giggle at his enthusiasm. He laughed with her, going to the trunk, pulling out apparel.

"Answer one question before I go with you," she stipulated. "Why have you decided to do this at night? Couldn't it wait until morning?"

"Does it make a difference? There is almost no sun."

"Yes, but at night . . . it seems so secretive."

"And so it is," he answered, holding up the masculine clothing. "Once you don these breeches you will be committing a crime—a social crime so horrendous many a divorce has been had over such an act. 'Tis unseemly for men and women to wear the clothes of the other sex, and therefore a punishable wrong-doing. We must tread in utmost secrecy, milady, lest your crime be found out."

The ludicrousness of his words made her laugh, and she donned the clothes eagerly as he politely turned his back. Adding a fur cloak and accessories, from a distance she looked much like Fauntley with her long, slim legs and narrow shoulders.

They slipped silently from the farmstead. Raff paused only to bring a smooth wooden sled from one of the outbuildings. He invited her to be seated, took the rope and pulled her along. Gorm heard them departing. With a yip she followed. However, when they could barely see the lights from the farmstead, her maternal instincts outweighted her love of adventure and made her turn back.

They stopped at a hill virtually clear of trees, as most of the land was. All that grew were a few willows and naked birch. This tall hill led to a series of slopes and hills beyond. Raff boarded the sled behind her, and with one shove they flew down at speeds Ambyre had never before experienced, not even on King Edward's finest stallion. Despite the cold, she felt exhilarated. She laughed aloud, leaning against him, letting him hold her close.

Traveling at such speed, she wondered how they would ever get back to the warmth of the farm, but such worries did not last long. This was a country he knew well; she knew he would not let them come to harm.

As if in answer, the sled slowed by itself. Raff stood again and resumed pulling. He seemed to have a destination in mind, so she did not question him.

Ambyre had been told that beneath the deep snow lay fields covered with gray-black lava which had once flowed red-hot from erupting mountain tops. These mountains spewed fire, the land becoming a battleground of flames and ice. Always, in the end, ice reclaimed the land. It was said these gaping holes from which the fire came were entryways to Hell, and from how it was all described, she could well believe it.

With an occasional glance at the stars, Raff found his way to the haven he sought. Ambyre did not see it until he began brushing snow away from its very door. With a grin he disappeared inside. Then the candle he lit showed her the way.

It was little more than a cave—indeed, had been a cave, once. Now it was paneled and floored, a door added to hold out the elements against which mankind always fought in this land. The room was set back in the cave, entered though a passageway so narrow and low they had to walk singly, he even having to stoop.

It was just as cold inside, but they were protected from wind by the earth itself, so it seemed warmer. Soon Raff had a fire going, the smoke escaping through a winding passageway deep within the earth.

With her surroundings better lit by the fire, Ambyre looked around. The place was sparsely furnished, only a heavy wood table with one low bench alongside. No bed, just a pile of furs in one corner. But she could tell it had not been vacant for long. Near the hearth was a stack of fuel. The table was laden with food: a barrel of cheese, a basket of dried meat, nuts, and flat bread covered with cloth to keep it fresh. On the floor fresh rushes left a clean, ash-like scent. She had never smelled it before; the rushes in her home were scented with dried flowers, which, though sweet, did not smell nearly as clean.

"What is this place?" she asked.

He continued to play with the fire, answering casually. "A haven for outlaws. 'Tis the Desert of Evil Deeds we are in; barren, desolate, but safe from any intrusion. Outlaws have often fled to this country, and if they survive here on their own, they are likely to become heroes with such proven strength. There are many such caves as this; from the doorways a man can watch the horizon for any who may come in search. But those foolish enough to pursue an outlaw must be well-directed or exceedingly lucky. 'Tis not easy find a place such as this. Not many come in search; 'tis more often than not a very foolish errand."

"How did you come to know this place for outlaws?"

"Bjorn once had a warrior in his service who was accused of killing a man and concealing the crime. 'Twas many years ago, and the man is long since dead. When he grew ill and mindless from age and aloneness, he found his way back to Bjorn. Before he died, he was able to show this place to Bjorn, proud of all that he had done with it. A bard sings of him sometimes at Bjorn's table, even to this day."

There were other questions upon Ambyre's mind which weighed more heavily than the history of this place. She wondered at the supplies and fresh food; she wondered how they would get back. Was it really only a short journey in the opposite direction, over the hills they had crossed? But she could not bring herself to ask. Not yet.

"How often do you come to Iceland?" she asked. "You seem so familiar with it."

"I've come once or twice a year since meeting Bjorn. There is not much habitable territory, just the coastline, so there isn't much to learn of it."

Conversation dwindled after that. Ambyre sat near the fire. Raff discarded his own cloak, then reached for hers. Suddenly self-conscious about her clothing, she handed him the furs with hesitation.

"Is wearing clothes of the opposite sex really grounds for divorce?"

He laughed, affirming the truth. "And many a husband has been cuckolded that way. But you needn't worry about yours. He is far away and I doubt would let you go for any reason, certainly not one as silly as that."

At his mention of Fauntley, she lowered her eyes, embarrassed. "But perhaps he would not feel that way if he knew I was here... with you." Her voice was not much louder than a whisper.

"Are you sorry I brought you here?" he asked gently. "It's all quite innocent, you know. A ride on the sled... a little meal in a warm shelter..."

"Where *did* this food come from?" she asked.

"I had someone bring it here earlier."

"Then... you were planning..."

He smiled. "Of course. I sent Fauntley to look at some sword hilts Thorvold has had in his possession for nearly twenty years. He mentioned to me some years back that he would like to know what the symbols meant, but I think he has been content enough without such knowledge. As for Cuthbert... I thought you knew what I was up to when you let him hunt with Wulfstan. Upon that, I had the food and fuel brought here, thinking you would approve."

She did not look at him. "How can I say I approve when we should not allow ourselves to be alone together?"

"We've done nothing wrong; I brought you here only to enjoy yourself, nothing more. There is an inlet not far from here. We can go fishing. And there are bone skates to give us a little exercise."

"But when did you plan doing all this? Surely by morning we should be back—"

"We have three days, milady," he told her quite seriously.

"Three days!" she repeated. "But certainly those who remain at the farm will conclude—"

"Nothing," he finished. "I have given instructions for Gytha to say you've become ill and I've gone hunting. We'll not be missed, milady. Gytha alone will tend your supposed illness, so no one will wonder why you do not leave the confines of your shelter. Have no worry; she can be trusted."

Still, Ambyre could not help but blush. Surely the woman believed the worst of her.

" 'Tis late," he said, going to the furs in the corner. "Tomorrow we will catch fish and you will learn to skate like a Dane. So you must sleep well in order to be a good pupil."

At her hesitation, he stood aside from the sleeping area. "I'll not touch you, milady," he promised.

It took Ambyre an exceedingly long time to fall asleep that night.

She woke early the next morning, but not before Raff. He had already brought in water for them to wash with and was gathering articles they would need for fishing. When she sat up, he smiled, saying nothing as he continued packing.

In multiple layers of fur, she followed him outside. There was a river not far away where he cut a hole in the ice and invited her to sit beside him. A stinging chill in the air made her uncomfortable at first as they sat in companionable silence on the ice. But soon she forgot her chill in the excitement of catching her first fish.

Despite the cold, they spent more time outside than in the cave, and she was relieved. Either way they were alone, but outside the privacy seemed less pronounced. She could relax with him. He seemed to have noticed that, for they were back out on the ice before the fish had settled within their stomachs.

Of the two sports he taught her, she greatly preferred skating. That took up much of the afternoon as they braved the cold rather than return to the shelter. She soon learned to balance upon the deer-bones attached to her shoes, assisted by wooden poles to propel herself forward. He urged her to greater speeds, and before long she was sliding along beside him, oblivious to everything but the fun they shared.

"You have the energy of a young warrior, AElfwyn," he marveled. "I've never seen a woman of your age with such abilities and strength. Do you know you're even older than I am?"

"You make me sound quite ancient," she replied, trying to sound unconcerned. But secretly this banter distrubed her. "I'll show you how 'old' I am. I challenge you to a race!"

In the lead already, Ambyre sped forward as she tossed the words over her shoulder. He soon pulled up and skated at her side for a few moments. Then he caught her eye and grinned, proceeding to pass her easily.

She reached his side again only when he slowed to a halt. With friendly anger, she shoved him hard and laughed as his feet slid out from under him. But as he went down so did she, losing her own balance in reaction.

"Never challenge a warrior, lady," he warned her, a little short of breath from the fall. "We cannot bear to lose."

"Nor can I, which is why you warm the ice with your backside this moment."

Laughing, he reached for her in one nimble movement and pressed her close. "You have the pride of a Dane, my girl," he whispered. Then he kissed her.

All that Ambyre had suppressed surfaced with that kiss: desire and fear, frustration and need. When he looked at her he sensed the confusion.

"You are as fearless as the falcon among the birds, in all things but love. Why do you quiver like a captured sparrow? 'Twas only a kiss."

She sat up. "Perhaps because I *am* a captured sparrow."

He laughed at such an admission, sitting up as well. "You are no such thing. You are a guest, invited and highly respected by all my people. If 'twere up to me, I would have you remain among us for the rest of your life."

"And Fauntley as well?" she asked with amusement.

"Well . . . I suppose I could conjure up many assignments for him."

She smiled, allowing him to help her to her feet. They skated back to the snow line arm in arm, holding the poles at one side to thrust them forward in unison.

The small shelter seemed awkwardly quiet. Evening was always when the warriors were most boisterous. But they seemed as far away as Wessex.

The fire danced within the confines of the hearth, sending shadows to and fro, giving welcome warmth to the two beside it. Ambyre's eye caught the light reflected from Raff's discarded helmet. It looked skeletal and forbidding. Next to it lay the sword, for once not upon his hip. She smiled, remembering how he referred to it by name. Of Frankish make, ornate but strong, he called it *Kappi*, meaning "great champion." All the warriors had named their swords, from which they were never separated.

" 'Tis beautiful," she said, admiring the carved animals on the silver handle.

His eyes went to it as well, resting upon it as if it were a pet, there to serve and to please. For him it did both.

"My father presented that sword to me when I was sent from his side. He told me it would be there to protect me, since he could not."

"Where did you go that he was not able to follow?" she asked with interest.

He looked from the sword to her, seeming to ponder the question. "Do you want to know the past of a warrior? The past of an enemy? We should look to the future, toward the alliance between our people, rather than dwell on the past which holds only war."

"You aren't my enemy," she whispered boldly.

He smiled slowly. "True enough, my lady. We are as alone as two lovers, and the politics of our people seem unimportant."

"I wish to know about you, Raff. I wish to learn of your life, of your past, of everything which brought you to this day. I wish to know you as though I had grown with you, by your side. Will you tell me?"

He laughed at her earnestness. "We are known for our sagas, AElfwyn. Can you bear to hear all I may speak of?"

"I shall welcome each word as a bee does nectar."

"But we have only two days left to us," he teased. "How can I sum up my whole life in two meager days?"

"By beginning this moment," she said with mock severity.

"Why do I feel I can tell you all of it, each part—the battles and the blood—when I couldn't tell another? Why do I know you won't shudder nor be repelled, but will listen and understand?"

He needed no reply but her smile of encouragement. Indeed, they knew each other already.

"My father wasn't home much when I was young," he began, "but each time my mother welcomed him back meant I'd have another brother or sister soon. When he set sail for some new adventure, he always left behind his seed in my mother's womb. I shudder to think how many brothers and sisters I would have if there had been raids for my father to go on.

"He spent must of his time pillaging the Frankish coastline, but when that began to settle he moved on to England, to aid the Danes already there fighting against your uncle. He sent for us soon after, but I still saw little of him—except of course when he came home to father Torquil and Alf. So I trained to be a warrior, and with each visit my father would tell me how I'd grown. Then we would spend some few precious hours alone, while he watched to see what sort of warrior I was learning to be. Afterward we'd sit and he would tell me about his battles. Those are the lessons I remember best. Others taught me to use a sword, but my father taught me honor.

"I was sixteen when I went into my first battle. Your uncle's army of Mercians and West Saxons had us outnumbered, and before long we had to accept peace on his terms."

"Was that so bad?" she asked, remembering Edward's fairness. He had let the Danes keep much of their land, even their own customs. Was that so hard for them to accept?

But Raff's eyes hardened at the question, which was answer enough. "We took your uncle's peace, but only through the winter. The following year we invaded Mercia while Edward was in Kent waiting for the fleet to arrive from Wessex. We believed most of his men were aboard, so we were bold enough to go as far as Bristol-upon-Avon. We were at our finest, even with so few, because advance is what our people know best. We felt again all that strength Edward had continuously sapped away.

"But it was short-lived." His voice was low. "We thought Edward's army to be on shipboard, but we were mistaken. They came against us in force, making us pay yet again for our raids. 'Twas August, hot and humid. They overtook us near Tettenhall. Even with the Northumbrians at our side we couldn't win. Win! We hadn't a chance. Annihilation is the word. Countless dead or left to the war-hawks and wolves. I myself was left to die, but managed to crawl among the bracken and birch scrub till I gained the strength to search for my father."

Ambyre remembered the stories of Tettenhall. The glory belonged to Edward that day.

"It was after Tettenhall that Olaf sent me away."

"Because he feared for your life?" she asked.

Raff shook his head. "It saddened him that I knew only defeat. He had always spoken of the victory, the glory of war, and instead of being able to show that to me, he had brought me into battle after battle which proved Edward's strength and our own weakness. He said this could not be tolerated for his son, the next chieftain of his settlement in Yorkshire. So he sent me to where he had learned the glory of a warrior: he sent me to the coast of the Frankish Empire, where King Charles of France was being harried by Rollo and his men. How it saddened my father to make me leave! Each of us was needed in those days, each warrior a hand well used.

"So for five years I fought with Rollo in Northern France. Bjorn was there for the action as well. I learned the triumph that my father was so anxious for me to know." He laughed as if seeing once again some amusing sight. "I saw Rollo confirmed as lord over Normandy. What a day that was!

"King Charles stood with Duke Robert on one side of the Eptis, Rollo and the rest of us on the other. When the agreement was made, Rollo and a few of us crossed the river to show our loyalty to Charles. Once there, some of the Franks suggested Rollo thank King Charles for his generosity by kissing his foot. Ha! Rollo would hardly bend a knee to another man. So he reached down, picked the King's foot up to his mouth, sending Charles promptly onto his backside.

"The Franks, of course, did not welcome this action, but the rest of us could only laugh. Did they really think it was a gift, when Rollo had conquered that land? Charles had offered it because his people could no longer withstand our raids. The land was no gift; it was protection from complete defeat. They should have been grateful to us."

Ambyre could not help but imagine the scene with amusement. How typical of a Dane to uphold his pride at the risk of future warfare. His voice settled to a quiet, almost respectful tone as he told her more tales of battle. She envisioned it all, from defeat to victory, remembering her father. He would have understood Raff. For enemies, the two were remarkably alike. Cuthbert was right.

"So you've spent more years away from England than in it," she observed. "Yet you treat Edward as the greatest enemy of your life."

Raff spoke slowly, letting his gaze travel once again to *Kappi*. "Do you remember that I said my sword was given to me by my father?"

She nodded.

" 'Twas after the Battle of Tettenhall, with defeat in his eye which I hope never to see again, not in my father nor in any warrior. This is my talisman, my greatest reminder of that battle which has lain more heavily upon my memory than any other I've known. 'Twas Edward's victory, my people's defeat."

He said his last words quietly, but she could not mistake the glimmer of hatred in those dark blue eyes. Never before had she seen it so vividly. Bitterness, aye, even hostility for the king of his enemies, but never before had she been aware of this hatred. How could it be that the King she loved was hated by the man she was in love with?

"Doesn't it wear on your honor," she asked, "to ally yourself with someone you so thoroughly detest?"

He stood, going to the sword, handling it with a gentle touch.

"This alliance is more necessary to my people than my personal honor," he said, more to himself than to her. It was as if he needed to remind himself of the fact, particularly when holding the embodiment of terrible memories that caused his hatred.

So these proud Danes were left to take the scraps, land which the Saxon did not want, high up the wolds of East Anglia, where water was a constant problem. But even this was better than what they had come from, the barren lands of Scandinavia. In Anglia they had cultivated and produced. It was now his duty as a warrior and leader to see that that land was not taken away.

They had no place else to go.

It was an uneasy peace between their people. Even here within this very room, peace seemed threatened by a new silence. Ambyre did not look at Raff, but she felt his eyes upon her.

"Perhaps what lies outside this refuge is not so distant after al," he said bleakly. "We are alike in many ways; we share a healthy respect for strength, for pride, and we both will remain loyal to our dying breath. 'Tis a shame our loyalties lie in opposite corners."

She wanted to deny it but could not. What lay in her heart was obvious to them both.

When she spoke it was to say, "I should not have come."

He moved closer to her on the bench, so close that their legs touched and his mouth was very near her ear. "Nay, my lady, you should not. But not because of our divided loyalties. You should not have come because you are not mine to have. I should not have asked you to come."

Slowly, she found herself responding to his smile. "I want to have nothing between us in this place but understanding. I don't want Edward, or your heritage, to come between us. I don't want to be your enemy."

"You're not," he said. "You're anything but an enemy."

His face was just inches away, and with one slight movement he met her mouth with his.

NORTHWARD THE HEART

But he did not wait for her to resist. Instead, before she knew it, before she wanted it, he had stopped himself. He gave her a quick hug, more friendly than passionate, and began talking animatedly.

"Now I will make you laugh, because we have been foolish by looking to the past when it is over. I will tell you the story of Bjorn's young brother, who tried to trick his friends into believing he was Odin incarnate. 'Twas a bad omen, so they said, to tamper with the gods . . ."

Soon Raff was telling her stories not only of his family and friends, but also sagas of old, of brave warriors, of daring, courageous feats they performed. Eventually, warm and drowsy, they were lying down upon the furs, his arms comfortably around her. Before long in the middle of one of his stories, they both fell asleep.

Ambyre woke some hours later. The fire in the hearth had died down and the small cavernous home had grown cold. Raff lay next to her, his arm thrust casually across her middle. Asleep he looked like a young boy, except for the moustache above his lip.

She had longed to know him, and he told her his stories. Now she felt all barriers between them gone. Yet what did he know of her? He professed to know her spirit, which he claimed so proudly was like a Dane's. Perhaps, in part, that was true, but what would he think of her when he knew the truth?

Gently, she touched his face, stroking the sharp line from cheekbone to jaw. He did not stir. She looked upon him for a long while that night, wanting to tell him everything. But she remained silent and eventually fell into a troubled sleep.

XI

When Ambyre woke the next morning, she was alone. She smiled as she remembered the night before and wished Raff had not left their bed of furs so early. She had relished the feel of him beside her through the night. More than once, she had felt an almost ovewhelming urge to wake him with a kiss, a caress, to show him how deep her love for him went. But that would have destroyed something more. Last night had possessed a magic of its own, one not of the powerful physical love she knew she could feel for this man, but love of a different sort. One of mind and soul and spirit. While joining their bodies might have completed that union, she couldn't help feeling what they had shared had been special enough for its own sake. And for now, that was enough. It had to be.

Rising, she spied a bucket Raff had filled with water, and used it to refresh herself. Before she finished, he returned.

"Good morning!" she greeted him cheerfully. "I wondered where you. . ." Ambyre let her words drift off, seeing him turn away. She waited silently for an explanation. He was far too somber after the closeness they had shared the night before.

"Will you walk with me?" he asked.

Outside, the familiar dark had an odd aura to it. A mist had rolled in from the sea, thick and uninviting. She wondered why he wanted to go out into it.

"My people are afraid of this; they call it *wendol*, the black mist. They believe it brings fiends and monsters who eat the flesh of humans. No one knows where they come from; they're black and hairy, gruesome to touch and smell. What do you say of such a story?"

She breathed deeply. " 'Tis a frightful tale, but a tale and nothing more."

"Then you do not believe the mist to be an evil omen, a covering for such fiends?"

"The mist is like rain, natural and harmless. Fauntley could explain it better than I."

He paused, a frown creasing his brow. "Your husband has much . . . knowledge."

She smiled, knowing what such an admission cost him. "Aye," she replied.

"And what do you think of me? Do you think I am savage, uncivilized to believe the mists belong to monsters?"

Her smile faded at the tone of his voice. They stopped, facing each other. "I do not think you believe in such tales. Else why would you be out here?"

"I could be a fool."

She shook her head. "Nay, if anything, you would be brave to truly believe in those fiends and venture among them. But you have brought me with you, therefore I don't believe you're either a fool or fooled by ancient superstitions."

"I shall tell you the truth, milady; I have never welcomed the mist. I've heard the stories since childhood, yet I never asked myself if I believed or disbelieved. On the sea, I think of the mist only as a hindrance, a danger to our journey because 'tis easy to sail off course. But even on land I do not like the mist. There is no reason. This morning when I woke to see it, I turned back to you and knew you would be unafraid of such things. I thought of your husband, puny as he is, and knew he, too, would be unafraid. It reminded me of the differences between us, AElfwyn, when last night I thought we had become so close. I remembered your telling me Fauntley has another sort of strength, not of body but of mind, and I scoffed at you for respecting him for it. Mayhap such strength is not useless—though in my land 'tis not necessary. You have defended your husband, and I have been blind to what qualities you see in him. I wish to know which is more worthy in your eyes."

Ambyre was silent for what seemed a long

moment. His words surprised her, but they were not unwelcome.

"With all the knowledge Fauntley possesses, you yourself have no less. It isn't the learning itself which deserves respect; your lives have taught you differently. 'Tis the *ability* to learn that is worthy, which you both have equally."

His relief was slow but came at last. "Your compliment is one I shall always remember, milady," he told her. Briefly, he kissed her cheek, adding with a frown, "But may we get out of this mist nonetheless?"

Laughing, they ran back to the shelter, arriving out of breath and still giggling like a couple of children. Inside, they quickly shut the door against the mist as well as its fables.

With inclement weather, Ambyre knew the day would be spent indoors. She no longer felt awkward in this reclusive privacy. He kept his distance, dispelling any worries she had.

The wind soon picked up, and she grew hopeful that it would disperse the dank mist. But the gale itself grew to such intensity, she knew its force would keep them within. Conversation slowed; they listened to the wind. It did indeed sound threatening, yet Ambyre knew they were safe with the earthen walls as their cover.

Raff stood to stoke the fire. As he did, she watched him appreciatively. He added fuel, then sat, his massive back to her, dagger as always hanging from one hip, sword from the other. Though without his mail shirt, he wore the leather tunic which usually accompanied it. Black trousers were gathered from ankle to knee by bright red cross-garterings. His hair had grown since their first meeting and now reached just beyond his neck, tied out of the way with a silk band.

Ambyre, still in Fauntley's clothes, stood and looked down at herself before joining him at the hearthside. She should have suspected that he would not desire her, dressed as she was.

"Is it still storming?" she asked.

He nodded.

"Will we be able to get back tomorrow?"

He did not answer immediately, giving her a gradual smile instead. "Thinking of returning already?"

"Nay," she said hastily. "I've never been as happy as during these past days. I'm grateful to you for bringing me here."

" 'Twould have been no fun without you."

They were quiet again after that, both staring at the fire, caught by the fascination of its ever-changing dimensions. She was still thinking about their return to the farmstead. Fauntley would be arriving soon, as well as Cuthbert. Neither would suspect how friendly she had become with this man beside her. Neither would know of these days, these very few, quickly-disappearing days, which she had truthfully proclaimed her happiest. They would be yet another secret for her to possess, one she would dwell upon often.

"I'm almost sorry we ever have to go back,"

she heard herself say, quite without thought.

"Almost?"

She smiled at the word. " 'Twould be you, my lord, who would be greatly missed. No doubt you soon would be itching to return, to rule your men and lead them into their next battle."

" 'Twould be a hard choice to make, milady, if such were possible. But you have your people and I allegiance to my own. Neither of us could choose to stay without some regret."

"You did not mention Fauntley in my obligations to return," she observed. "Only my people."

" 'Tis only a better comparison to my own responsibilities."

If she had spoken again, she might have pointed out that his next battle could very well be against her own countrymen. Where would her loyalties be then? So she said nothing, unwilling to admit her fear of that possibility.

"I shall miss you, AElfwyn," he told her, still staring at the fire. She heard the sincerity in his voice, warmed to it, wanting to savor his words. "Not only later when you return to Mercia or Wessex," he continued, "but tomorrow, when we go back to being captor and captive. 'Twill be a hard role to play henceforth."

She nodded, wondering how she would ever be able to look upon him again and hide her love. She should have learned by now how to keep the truth out of her eyes.

There was one truth Raff had found in her,

one truth which, when discovered, he would not let her deny: her desire for him. The danger of it seemed easily forgotten when she was near him. Questions were denied answers; passion negated fear. Beside him here, knowing their time together would too swiftly end, it was nearly impossible for her not to acknowledge that aspect of their affinity. It seemed only to heighten as they got to know one another.

She lusted after a pagan as no Christian woman should. She longed right now to touch him, kiss him. Would she ever have the chance again? Whatever the consequences of her desire, she was ready to face them.

Once Raff discovered her virginity, her deception would be revealed. Indeed, she would have given him her maidenhead the night he had first kissed her if she had not feared for others' lives. Now that she believed in his love, could it be he would love her still as Ambyre of Athelney? Not at all a princess? She would want *him*, be he the next chieftain or the lowliest of slaves. Perhaps love would sustain them through her lies.

Raff's gaze left the fire that warmed their cavernous shelter. Now she saw a different flame in his eyes, one that burned within his body. Was she surprised to see that reflection of the blaze within herself? She was glad. He had sensed the growing passion that merely sitting beside him created in her.

His mouth met hers with vivid evidence of the

flame they shared. Their separate sparks were united with the kiss, and sprang up as one fire, flowing through their bodies. She knew then with certainty that there was no turning back now. No fearful retreat this time. Perhaps what he had seen in her eyes was the decision to use this little time for a union both had known all along was inevitable.

Her arms went about him as his went about her. They pressed together, barely breathing, consumed by the fire, yet feeling vitally alive.

He paused only once, giving her a last opportunity for words of caution or retreat. Hearing none, he stood, lifted her in his arms, carried her to the furs in the corner. He lay her down gently, standing back only long enough to discard his weapons before leaning toward her again. She raised a hand, not in caution but entreaty, pulled up the heavy leather tunic he wore. He smiled, lifted the garment over his head. She admired the muscles which moved in unison under his taut skin, the fair, curled hair meagerly covering the strength beneath. Her hands touched eagerly, relishing the feel of him.

He was just as eager. His fingers, long and slim, deftly untied the belt at her waist. The masculine clothes hiding her femininity were discarded easily, breeches following quickly after woolen tunic. Ambyre again felt the thrill of having him look so appreciatively upon her body. Warm flesh touched hers, created more warmth in its very contact.

Her awareness heightened. No more questions. She became filled with the sensations of her body. Her skin, sensitized by passion, felt as it never had before. Desire made his touch intoxicating, sharpening every reaction. Each pore seemed to register pleasure, every area his fingers caressed awakened to the spreading titillation. A river of molten lava flamed through her veins, flooding her senses wherever he touched her.

His hands left her body just long enough to remove his breeches, the last garment between them. Instinctively, she turned modestly away.

"I love you, AElfwyn," Raff said softly. "Do not be afraid."

He smiled down at her between more kisses, but Ambyre knew her inexperience had shown. She was shy, unaccustomed to the unclothed body of an aroused man—a man aroused by *her*. And she wondered if her lack of skill marred his pleasure, for she was too uncertain to touch him boldly as a woman of experience might.

" 'Tis not fear," she told him, "not fear . . . as you think."

"What then, if your husband will never learn of this?"

She did not answer, but when his hand paused on the curve of her hip, she looked at him again, waiting for him to speak.

"Then why, if you do not fear me?" he whispered.

She looked away.

"AElfwyn..." he said the name gently, and turned her face toward his. "You have nothing to fear from me. I have not hurt you; I would never hurt you. Has it been painful for you before, with him?"

She kept her eyes averted.

"Has he hurt you?" he persisted, and his tone did not hide his anger.

"No ... no, not him," she answered. She did not want to face these questions. She wanted only to feel the pleasure of Raff's touch.

"Someone else?"

"No ... no one."

He kissed her then, and desire blotted out everything save the sensations he created in her. "I'll not hurt you, either. You need have no fear of me."

She heard his words, believed him, for she expected only more of the pleasure he had already given. She never wanted it to end.

"Your body is as youthful as your face," he told her. "You're lovely, AElfwyn. There is no reason for you to be shy." He smiled at her reddened cheeks. "I shall have fun coaxing you out of that shyness, my love, if only you let me."

"I've seen the women of your village ... the way they approach men. I—do not share their boldness."

"We Danes are not like you. And I've never made love to a Saxon woman before, so you'll have to teach me how."

"I like the way you love me," she said, her eyes clear of shyness now.

His caress was gentle, as he promised, and patient, as he sensed she wanted him to be. He discovered the pleasures in her as she discovered them in herself. They learned she had a spot at the hollow of her throat that sent shivers along her body when kissed. His tongue brought exhilaration to it, then to each nipple, then down farther, to her tiny navel.

Her body could deny him nothing, not even when his kiss traveled lower, to the spot she never imagined would be caressed. But it was there that the feeling intensified, making all else pale in comparison. She could only close her eyes, trembling from fingertip to eyelid, limbs tense, as pleasure emanated from the center of her being—pleasure so fierce it almost frightened her. But it was Raff giving her this fulfillment. She accepted all her body could take, consumed with desire she had neither power nor wish to control. It enveloped her, making her no longer a creature of flesh and bone but of pleasure—a being of white heat, of throbbing passion. Until at last it began to subside, returning her slowly to balance, bringing her again to an awareness which had been obliterated by sensation.

Soft and swollen, sodden with the balm of desire, the center of her felt him shift within. Their bodies seemed designed for this. He looked down at her, kissed her, and she wondered what more there could be. Surely she had experienced the ultimate delight. But what of him?

His body felt hard, from his firm chest against her own to the muscles in his thighs with the swollen member in between. He pressed closer; she had enough knowledge of nature to realize this was to be the culmination of their intimacy. Would he now experience what she had done only moments ago? She was aware of nothing but him, seeing him, feeling him, being filled with him, wanting to give what he needed.

He was so gentle she did not expect any pain. When he moved against her, his expression betrayed a new curiosity. She wondered if now he knew the truth.

With his thrust, her sighs of pleasure became an unexpected cry of pain. He had promised not to hurt her, but could not have kept that promise. No man could. Sudden tears moistened her eyes; she felt him pull away.

"AElfwyn?"

But Ambyre clung to him, unwilling to allow those questions he must surely ask. She was a virgin and he knew. Yet she had one wish; moments ago he had given her delight beyond imagination. She would not let him stop until he experienced the same.

Briefly, she wondered if this pain must exist in order to create his pleasure, but soon it diminished and the same wondrous voluptuousness she'd felt before began again. Whatever questions he might have had were forgotten as the rhythm between them quickened. Her arms entwined tightly about him as if to bring him with her to that plane of desire, to have him become through her an entity of passion, to lose all reason, all thought, to be aware only of her and these wonders they exchanged.

She felt him cling to her as well, heard him call her name as he knew it, vibrating with his body when the point of abandon was reached. The climax engulfed them.

Release lingered, carrying them gently back to the recognition of sensations other than delight. She lay still, not wanting to open her eyes, to postpone the return to reality.

But he gave her no choice; she looked at him unwillingly.

"AElfwyn..." His voice resounded in her head, the very name an attack on her judgment. She lay beneath him, wanting to look away but unable. "A virgin..."

Slowly he moved away, glancing back at her as though he had been betrayed.

"Why did you lie?"

The question was expected but not the desolation in his tone. She reached to touch his face. He caught her hand and held it in mid-air, waiting for her answer.

" 'Twas because of being kidnapped; Fauntley said your laws would protect me from defilement if I were married."

He laughed harshly. "And not if you were a virgin? I confessed *love* to you, maiden! How could you think I would hurt you? You do believe me barbaric, don't you?"

"Nay," she denied. "Nay, but I did not know what to believe before I came to know you. A prisoner has little power. I sought the protection of lies."

"Who is he?" Raff demanded suddenly.

She knew to whom he referred. "Fauntley is our tutor."

"And Cuthbert? He resembles you enough to be your son."

"He is my brother."

Raff lifted a skeptical brow. "Then the Mercian throne would be his, not yours."

"He is illegitimate, unrecognized, unknown to the Mercians."

She might have gone on, told the complete truth of her identity, anything to help restore his trust, but he was standing, pulling on his breeks. When he turned to her there was no trust, no compassion nor understanding, only anger in those eyes.

"So you have lied to me all along, letting me make a fool of myself as the secret lover."

"Raff—no! Would I have given myself to you—my virginity—if I were laughing at you?"

"Only Odin himself knows why you gave away this secret. What did you hope to accomplish? To thwart my plan and get revenge for kidnapping you? Is it only me you hate for that act, or the whole Danish race? Are you like your uncle, forever wishing to expel the foreigner?" He laughed bitterly. "I shall no longer worry that my people are less civilized than yours. Lies are not tolerated among us. We are honest, without deceit. 'Tis you and your race who have proven unworthy."

Tears flowed unchecked down her cheeks. She stood, carelessly flinging a cloak over her shoulders to cover her nakedness.

"And you have proven unworthy of what I told you earlier!" she accused in an unsteady voice. "I honored your intelligence, yet you seem to have lost it. Don't you see what has happened? I *gave* myself to you—I love you! I love you more than my own life, to have jeopardized it so."

"There would have been no jeopardy if you had been honest."

"How could I know that? My life has been in danger since the night you stole me from Wessex! I am a prisoner—I owed you nothing, certainly not the truth, for what you did. I have no rights, no way to protect myself or my brother. My only defense was to lie."

"Which you continued to do even after you knew you could trust me."

Her shoulders could only slump under the accusation. "I was afraid."

"Then 'tis you who lacks intelligence. You were afraid yet you gave yourself away—your duplicity as well as your maidenhood."

She said nothing. The silence was unbearable. When he spoke again his voice was low, controlled, yet filled with anger.

NORTHWARD THE HEART

"There was no mention of marriage until Fauntley was brought to Yorkshire after you. He is the one with the professed knowledge of our laws, so this ruse was his idea, was it not?"

"Yes, but only for my sake. You cannot harm him for that!"

He scoffed. "The *kjerringa* is unworthy of a moment's consideration, even for punishment. You were aware of my plan for a political marriage, yet before he came you had already refused me. I believed him to be the reason why, but since he is not, you must have had another motive. Why did you refuse?"

Ambyre's tears ceased out of new fear. She should have known he could not put her before his people.

"My . . . my allegiance is to Edward. I'll not marry except at his command."

Angrily he grabbed one of her hands, holding it against him. "You shall have that command, lady. My original plan can now succeed. You can no longer spoil it. Consider what has taken place here a pre-nuptial consummation of our vows, AElfwyn. We now know how deeply our loyalties lie, do we not? Yours to your King is equal to mine toward my people. Perhaps yours is greater. You were willing to give me your virginity but not your hand in marriage. Is it only because your precious King Edward may see fit to use you as a pawn elsewhere? To marry for some other potential gain to his kingdom? Is your allegiance to him so complete, so all-encompassing?"

"And what of yours?" she retaliated. "Isn't your loyalty greater than any so-called love you professed for me? Wouldn't you have willingly left me once I had done my part in your plan to defeat the Norwegians? Once you had used me for the security of your people? Love had little to do with your intent, this political marriage you hoped for."

"True, lady, love has nothing to do with it. Marriages are business contracts, partnerships. Few have any love in them; they're meant to produce heirs. So should you desire any offspring, you had better hope my seed takes root in your womb this day, for 'twas the only chance this marriage will have to get heirs. My plan will succeed. Edward will give his consent. He is not about to pass up an opportunity for peace. Once the Norwegians are defeated with the help of your Saxon soldiers, then you can go back to your prized King to be used in whatever manner it pleases him to do. I'll no longer care."

He had put on his cloak during that bitter speech. At the last word he stomped outside, slamming the door. Moments later, he returned to douse the flames in the hearth. Ambyre was dressing. When she finished, he thrust her cloak at her and strode again from the room. He brought the sled to the door, commanding her to be seated.

"I can walk," she said icily.

"Sit down." His tone was threatening. She obeyed.

The storm had not dissipated. Snow blew so

wildly they both were blinded by its density. Yet Raff would not delay. He pulled the sled along as she sat huddled in her furs, face hidden among the folds. Only once did she peer out, seeing little to ease her fears. How could he know in what direction they were headed? This world of whiteness had no landmarks to point the way.

As the cold went through her cloaks, Ambyre's body ached from it. She shivered beneath the furs, prey to the wind. How long would he go on, oblivious to the raw weather which tormented her so? Yet after a while, as he continued, immune to the blizzard, she too seemed to forget the pain. Her jaw, sore from trembling, loosened and ceased its convulsive movement. She no longer tried to see outside the furs; she remained still, curled up, drowsy. She imagined the warmth of a hearth so vividly, its presence seemed the reason her shivering ended. She dreamed that what she lay on was a soft bed of furs, not a rough-hewn sled.

It was a cruel awakening to be thrust roughly onto the ice. In dazed astonishment, she fumbled to free her hands and face from the cloak. What could have happened?

Raff stood formidably over her, his foot upon the upturned sled that caused her rude landing. She wanted to scream what she was thinking, words most unaccustomed to Christian lips, but found herself too cold to speak. Her bones felt brittle, as if they would snap as easily as icicles if moved too fast.

"You will walk beside me," he commanded, and turned away without helping her up.

She watched him turn his back to her without a glance, wondering if she could perform the simple task he demanded. Yet why should she? She wanted only to sleep...

Ambyre was only half-aware of being dumped back onto the sled. By the time it later pulled to a halt, she was completely asleep.

Pain awakened her. Limbs which had felt frozen quite through now seemed ablaze, throbbing unbearably. Or was she on fire? She saw the flames ... they seemed much too close, and she could not move away. Something held her prone, her back upon a hard surface, legs and arms pinned at her sides. Vigorous rubbing accompanied the pain. Though she tried to pull away she knew she would not succeed. Soon sleep returned; discomfort no longer registered.

When she woke again, her suffering was a memory except for the stiffness. Beside her lay Raff, holding her, sharing the fur coverings. They were in another cave, a crude uninhabited shelter unlike the one they had occupied. It was dark, for the fire was low, yet she could see how small it was. They were tucked in one corner, away from the open mouth, protected from the wind and biting snow.

She had believed him to be sleeping, but his eyes were open, the anger in them riveting her gaze. Was there no reprieve to be found there? No hint of understanding?

If he detected her silent imploring, he hid it from her. He stood, going to the entrance to assess the weather, returning to the fire to extinguish what flames remained. She quickly realized they were to be on their way, yet not a word came from his mouth.

It angered her that he could treat her so harshly, especially after endangering her life with petulant, foolish insistence on returning to the farm before the storm had passed. Who could blame *her* for being angry? Yet she was treated as though the storm had been her fault.

"Why didn't you just leave me to die out there?" she demanded, so suddenly irate that even Raff seemed surprised.

But he did not reply.

"You want to punish me for this great injury I have inflicted on your pride?" she persisted. "Then kill me now! Your people are tolerant enough of murder—as long as you claim to have done it for a good cause. Who would blame you? With your whole race made up of arrogant, prideful, ignorant barbarians just like you—"

He stepped closer, his face so ominous that she ended her tirade abruptly. He did not lift a hand against her, but when he spoke the words were more painful than any blow could have been.

"I saved you because you are the niece of King Edward, milady. Yet I swear by Odin's eye that I'd have left you had you been anyone else."

Though it was still early when they reached the farmstead, in the darkness no one saw them.

Raff did not seem as concerned over secrecy as he had been at the outset of their journey a few days before. He took the sled to the storeroom, letting her walk alone to her quarters.

XII

Ambyre's heart was heavy. Never before had she known this desolation. And loneliness, such bitter loneliness. As if something vital to her existence had suddenly been denied. Indeed, it had. She had found complete happiness with Raff, only to have it taken away.

What a fool she'd been! Had she really hoped, even for a moment, that he would overlook her dishonesty? He, who had more pride than anyone she'd ever known? Had she been so stupid as to think he could love her that much?

But that's how she loved him! Without bounds. So totally, nothing could stand in its way. At least she did at the moment she gave herself to him. No power in heaven or on earth could have stopped her then.

And now? Pain riddled her body like a fatal disease, permeating her so thoroughly she could find no refuge from it. Could she still love him knowing he was the cause?

Worse. Only half of her deceit had been revealed—and how close to death he'd let her come even so! She had no doubt that if he had discovered her true, worthless identity, she would at this moment be lying frozen in the icy wasteland of the Desert of Evil Deeds. The man she loved would have left her there to die.

So fear had its part in her desolation. Fear and the shattering knowledge of how deep his scorn for her went. How could she live with that? How could she face him? And how would she ever find peace again? She could never forget the sincerity of his oath that he would have let her die.

At times, when she reached the deepest pit of despair, she felt tempted to reveal the rest. Let him kill me, she thought numbly. What does it matter now?

But always that part of her which fought back, that stubborn resiliency found its way to her senses. Contained in that part of her was the strength to go on—not only strength but anger. Anger that could save her from this utter despair.

She still had one weapon left: her identity, the very deception which had saved her life. Perhaps it could save her again.

Let Raff try to fulfill his plan. Let him contact Edward with his intention of marrying AElfwyn of Mercia. Who but he would suffer the consequence? She would merely bide her time, wait until they returned to England. Perhaps

Edward would even agree to such a plan, as Raff seemed to believe. It would mean some sort of peace between them, such an alliance. And if Edward agreed, they would be off to Wessex where Ambyre's identity could be revealed. There she would be safe ... Raff would marry AElfwyn.

She ignored the pang in her heart at the thought of him marrying another. Let him, she thought bitterly. Certainly she didn't want him now, not after what he'd done to her. How sweet her vengeance, seeing him learn the whole truth. Duped by her yet again! That should bring some comfort. Shouldn't it?

But would he, with that pride of his, accept an alliance out of such deceit? Wouldn't he mistrust all Saxons forever and not hesitate to draw his sword, even if it meant his own death as well as his people's defeat?

She did not sleep that night; she did not even lie down. She sat by the fire, stoking the embers absently, wishing her mind could freeze as her body had done the day before. Yet thought would not stop, making her fearful of what lay ahead.

In the morning Ambyre went to the Hall, finding many warriors still absent. Only Gytha sat at the trestle-table. The meal had been served and cleared away, leaving her uncommonly idle.

So odd was it to see the head of this large

household with no task before her that Ambyre approached with concern. But a sharp utterance cut off the smile she'd intended.

"He is not here, lady."

"You refer to...?"

Gytha's face was hard, eyes cold as she looked across the table. Those dimples, so obvious when she smiled were now just as obvious when she frowned, but not so pleasant to look upon. "He has left orders to have the ship ready to sail."

"Back to Yorkshire?" she asked, already knowing the answer.

Gytha nodded.

Ambyre remained where she was, not sitting, not retreating. She spoke calmly.

"He told you, didn't he?"

Gytha dropped her eyes momentarily. "Nay, but I can well guess at the truth. Why do you not give yourself to him? Do you believe yourself superior to him, the greatest of our warriors?"

Ambyre laughed uncontrollably, not caring who heard. When several slaves peered out from a storeroom, Gytha hushed her.

"I believe you are quite mad, you know," Gytha said harshly.

"*I*, mad?" Ambyre repeated, sobering somewhat. She teased her hostess maliciously. "*You* would have had me commit a sin punishable by death. If only you knew the truth!"

"Who would have been executed for it? Who

was there to press the matter? Your puny husband? Ha! He has no power here."

"Why is it, milady, that you concern yourself so with the satisfaction of Raff's loins? Since your husband is away and you condone such behavior, why do you not give *yourself* to him?"

Gytha stood. With one quick movement she reached across to plant a stinging slap upon Ambyre's face. Then, ashamed, she turned away from anger-filled, triumphant eyes.

"I demand to know what has taken place!"

Fauntley's words fell on Ambyre without effect. He sighed, breathing so deeply that she heard him clearly from across their little room, her back to him. When he spoke again his voice softened, closer now.

"I returned only minutes ago, and was told immediately to remove my belongings from here into the main hall. No explanation, neither from these illiterate pagans nor from you. And you, I can see, are decidedly overwrought, yet you'll not let me help you. You've spoken not a word since I arrived. Won't you even look at me, Ambyre?"

Slowly, she peered over her shoulder. Her eyes were large and mournful, their pain so evident he wanted to rush to her side, hold her, soothe her, convince her that the cause would soon be removed. But he possessed no such boldness. All he could do was return her gaze, unable to speak.

"He knows," was all she said.

Fauntley came another step closer. "Who does? Raff?"

She nodded.

"He knows your identity?"

She shook her head, looking away.

"What does he know, Ambyre?"

"That you are not my husband, Cuddy is not my son."

He frowned. "But how... certainly you didn't tell him?"

"I did not tell him," she said. "Not intentionally, that is."

"Then how did he learn of this? Did Cuddy misstep in some way?"

She shook her head once again, still not looking at him. " 'Twas my fault. 'Twas my sin."

"Sin," he repeated with an amused laugh. "You are too harsh on yourself for a simple mistake. Do not worry so over this. They don't know your true identity?"

"Nay."

"Then there is no great worry. 'Tis that which holds our lives, nothing else."

"We're to sail to Yorkshire within the week. From there Raff will send word to Edward of his plan to ally himself with the Mercians by marriage to AElfwyn."

Fauntley laughed. "Let him! If Edward agrees, 'twill not be you who marries the brute. But I heartily doubt that Edward will have any part of this Dane's plan."

" 'Twould mean peace."

"Aye, and so 'tis apealing — for all but AElfwyn. She was born to be a political tool, aware all her life that marriage would be a matter of state. Many marriages—nay, most—are set up this way. Why should it worry you?"

"When he learns he has been duped yet again he will surely renege on any peaceful settlement."

"This man has no heart, no love to give a woman. If he does not learn of your identity until we return to Wessex, then we shall be safe. Once there, he won't care who he is marrying; he will care only that his plan has succeeded, allying him with Edward and the Mercians. There will be no war when the Norwegians hear of it. They would not be foolish enough to take on the whole of united England."

Fauntley's approach to the future made it seem simple and clear. Certainly Raff no longer wished to marry *her*. Perhaps the true AElfwyn *would* be welcomed by him. Indeed, had she not already learned thoroughly enough that nothing mattered to this Dane but the good of his people?

Still, her depression did not lift.

Fauntley gathered his clothes, folding them inside an extra cloak to carry to the Hall. He did not look forward to living among those barbarians; he left Ambyre's side with the greatest regret.

"I shall continue to spend my days with you, to assure myself of your welfare."

NORTHWARD THE HEART

She did not look at him, afraid he could read the guilt on her face.

"Do not fret," he reassured her. "No harm has been done. 'Twas a simple slip of the tongue ... was it not?"

She nodded before considering it was another lie she told.

"It could have happened to me too, Ambyre. Do not worry any longer."

"No ... I won't."

She watched him walk toward the door. How could she ever tell him the truth?

XIII

When Cuthbert returned from falcon hunting with Wulfstan, Fauntley warned him of the changes. He was allowed to remain with his sister, though in only two days they were to sail for Yorkshire.

Ambyre had not spoken to Raff since they had returned from the Desert of Evil Deeds. She did not even see him until the day before they set sail. Her eyes lingered but he turned coldly away. She could not feel anger, though she wished to. She had given him her virginity. And what then? He believed she used it merely as a weapon, to shame him. For a warrior, that was harder to bear than death. His shame was to have been tricked by a woman, an enemy.

The ship was provisioned and good-byes were said, though she had no part in them. Who was there to take leave of? Gytha? Not after their little exchange the other day.

Fauntley sailed again with Piers, but Cuthbert was allowed to travel with Ambyre. It appeared obvious to her that Raff no longer wanted physical contact, not even to share warmth at night. Cuthbert was glad, mostly, to be with Wulfstan. He trailed him like a puppy, and the patient warrior made him feel welcome. Ambyre was grateful to Wulfstan for not letting the boy's spirits flag, now or during their weeks of captivity.

The other warriors were baffled. Raff had announced that his original plan of alliance through marriage would succeed after all, and they had shouted their approval. But as his coolness became apparent they could not hide their confusion. They trod carefully around him and were more distant, though not indifferent, to her. Would they too feel betrayed if they learned of her dishonesty? Would they shun her as quickly and easily as Raff had done?

Still, she had won a permanent portion of each man's heart that night in the storm. Since then, many were more than a little in love with her themselves. Cuthbert, too, was well-liked, yet not beyond Raff's new coolness.

Ambyre knew her time among them was close to its end, and she greeted the thought with ambivalence. Though pained to endure Raff's disdain, what would she feel not to be with him at all? In time he might come to understand. Wounded pride would give way to memories of love. He would finally realize there had been no malice.

Yet, when? How? No time. No means. They would go to Wessex. Raff would marry AElfwyn. Forgiveness or lack of it would be irrelevant. There was to be nothing between them. Ambyre was just used goods.

The fourteen-day journey to Yorkshire was by far the hardest of all. In the midst of winter, with unyielding winds and relentless outpouring from the sky, there was little comfort to be found throughout the dark, dismal days. And where was she to seek it? Cuthbert provided the warmth Raff now denied her at night, and while the result was the same, the effect was different. She could remember his presence, while now he was cold as the season, and as formidable. Those eyes were bleak as blue ice, frigid as a fjord in winter.

Before leaving Iceland, Wulfstan had constructed a sturdy square box which he filled with sand. Neither Ambyre nor Cuthbert knew what purpose it would serve, but once at sea they found out, to their great delight. Insulated by the sand, a small fire could be built in the center. It not only provided warmth, but could be used to cook meals as succulent as any on dry land in a home hearth. And Wulfstan loved cooking.

That little stove was Ambyre's only respite from the chill. She missed the steam baths, longing to feel their warmth against her skin. Seated at Wulfstan's carefully-tended fire, she imagined herself in that small room, heat engulfing each part of her, releasing perspiration

NORTHWARD THE HEART

as though she were sweltering under the midsummer sun. In that way she managed to bear the rest of the voyage.

Returning to the Danish settlement in Yorkshire was like returning home, even for Ambyre. Olaf and Ella greeted her familiarly, and later Sigrid came to welcome her as well. When she inquired after Kirsten, she was told the slave had been confined to bed; though not yet near the end of her pregnancy, the signs did not bode well.

When Raff told Olaf his plan of marriage could succeed after all, the old chieftain was not content to have the details left unexplained. He frowned when he learned they had been lied to. The warrior's blood in his veins began to pulse with thoughts of retribution. But it was curiosity that soon outweighed wrath.

"Surely she did not admit the truth," Olaf said. "This girl is no weakling's spawn; how did you come to this knowledge?"

"It makes little difference now," Raff evaded. "I came only to inform you, to confess my loss of honor in having been fooled."

"You have lost no honor, my son. 'Twas a mere delay because of the enemy's fortitude, but you persisted and now 'tis you who have succeeded."

"Then I shall send word to Edward immediately."

About to go, his father detained him with a brief, quiet question which had the impact of a well-aimed arrow.

"Was she a virgin?"

He faced Olaf again. When he said nothing, the old man stood and placed a hand on his son's shoulder.

" 'Twas a bitter way to learn of the maiden's falsehood," he whispered. "Have you come to care for her?"

"No longer," Raff exploded savagely.

Olaf patted the shoulder under his hand.

"She has proven a worthy enemy, a quality to be proud of. It makes your own victory finer. To conquer a falcon is greater than to conquer a sparrow."

Raff scowled. He had spoken the same maxim to the "falcon" herself. "She will be conquered only when the alliance is made, when the Norwegians are expelled. Till then there is no victory and she cannot be trusted."

"Never trust the enemy, my son, not even, as you have learned, one who shares your bed."

Ambyre visited Kirsten frequently, their friendship easily renewed. Though a slave, this girl carried the child of one of the chieftain's sons. Sigrid had therefore excused Kirsten from her duties when the pregnancy began to prove difficult.

Sigrid visited as well, and on one occasion she brought with her so unlikely a companion that Ambyre could not help but stare in bewilderment. It was an old woman, hideously ugly, with a sharp, protruding nose, a small snarl of a mouth covering a half-toothless grin, and stark white hair. Garbed completely in black, she stood no taller than four feet, with her hunched back and crooked legs. Still, she moved agilely, and her long, skeletal hands appeared strong and quick. This old crone, Ambyre was told, worked magic among those Danes who had not accepted the Christian God. She was called the Angel of Death.

"Have you brought them?" Kirsten asked anxiously from her bed.

The woman smiled an ugly smile.

"Please," Kirsten pleaded. "Please proceed now."

From her sack, the Angel of Death produced bones of various shapes and sizes. Ambyre could not tell what kind of remains they were, but from the looks of this woman she would not have been surprised if some were human.

The witch cast the bones haphazardly before her, stooping to read the oracle their positions revealed. Then she silently retrieved them, replaced them in her bag without a word, and left the room.

Expectantly, Ambyre looked from Sigrid to Kirsten, who averted her glance in sudden tears. Sigrid offered a comforting hand, but the act was hardly noticed.

"What is it?" Ambyre asked. "What did it mean?"

"The child shall not live," Sigrid answered quietly. Kirsten's tears turned to sobs as the augury was uttered.

Ambyre stepped forward, angry at the old

crone as well as these two for being so superstitious. She sat beside Kirsten and put a hand on each shoulder, gently but firmly. "You cannot believe such foolishness. She uses tools of the devil and everyone knows how the devil lies. You must not let her upset you, or you yourself will make her prophecy come true."

Kirsten looked at her, confused. Sigrid knelt beside the bed, eager to join in the encouragement even if she was not convinced. "AElfwyn speaks the truth, Kirsten. Being overwrought near the time of birth will only bring harm. You want this baby to be strong and healthy, accepted by Torquil, do you not?"

Kirsten nodded, still crying.

"Then 'tis up to you more than the old crone's oracles. *She* is not the one carrying."

"But the omens..."

"Are the work of the devil," Ambyre finished. The smile upon her face and Sigrid's could not be ignored by poor dejected Kirsten. Though she herself could not smile, her crying ceased, and before long the two had made her forget the Angel of Death.

"It should only be a matter of days before we set sail for Wessex," Fauntley said, sitting next to Ambyre at the hearth. They were alone, though various slaves went about their duties at the far end of the long, narrow room. He put a hand over hers, his boldness surprising even himself when he let it linger there. "I haven't been as strong as you throughout this."

Patting his hand, she smiled and stood, not wanting to prolong the contact.

Fauntley stood too, bringing up courage from some unsuspected well, not backing away as he usually did. "Please don't, Ambyre. When I touch you or look at you you always run away as though you cannot stand the sight of me. What have I done? Are we no longer friends?"

She smiled again, turning to him. "Of course, Fauntley. How could we not be? Here among the Danes we have only each other—the three of us."

He grinned. "And things will be different when we return home, won't they? This experience has brought us closer than ever before."

"Aye, it has. I know you better now than when you were just my tutor. And I suppose you know me better, too."

"Yes... but... not as well as I would like. That is, I would like to... I mean, Ambyre you know how I feel. I meant it when I told you I loved you. I wish to know you better than just a friend."

Ambyre bristled at his words. How little he really knew her. How weak she had proven herself to be! He was so trusting she felt ashamed, but attempted to laugh. "How can we speak of this now? What can I say in these surroundings? What good would it do either of us?"

He abruptly leaned forward to give her a kiss. Brief as it was, it had been carefully aimed and executed, so when Raff entered at that moment he could not mistake Fauntley's intentions. Quickening his step, a scowl on his face, he stepped between them immediately, as though protecting some prized morsel from being devoured by another predator.

"Your masquerade is at an end," he said harshly, grabbing Fauntley by the collar. " 'Tis now my woman you violate. If I see you touching her that way again, I shall punish you as you deserve."

Fauntley remained unperturbed by the threat. How he longed for this pompous beast to be revealed as the fool he was! The vision of that made him smile, which Raff dismissed as idiocy and let him go with a sigh of disgust, stomping out without another word.

This behavior had been unusual. Lately, even at boisterous mealtimes when they shared the same drinking vessel, he acted cold and distant, looking through her as if she were invisible.

But Torquil was not so indiffernt. He had welcomed her back as though they were old and dear friends. Uneasy at his effusiveness, she thought it best to keep some distance between them.

On the third day after her return there came a great commotion outside the longhouse. Several warriors carried Torquil inside, his tunic torn in several places, blood pouring from gashes on his skin. Awake and alert, insisting he could walk, he was gently settled near the hearth, two slaves ministering to him immediately. Olaf and Raff came in, assessed his wounds and waited for him to speak.

" 'Twas Johannes," Torquil hissed. His eyes were full of hatred.

"What provocation?" Olaf asked.

"He took offense at the game we played."

Raff's lips tightened. "The game of words should be played only within our family, Torquil."

"He started it!" Torquil exclaimed, adding levely, "and I finished it. Johannes is dead."

Olaf frowned, turning to Raff. "Go to your mother and request the silver. We shall have to amend what Torquil has done before this goes any further."

"*I* have done!" Torquil repeated incredulously. He brushed away the slaves administering sea-water and cow's-urine cures. "Look at me! Johannes attacked *me* and I killed him for it! Any warrior would have done the same."

"You still live. We shall have to pay for Johannes' life, as is the custom."

"And I say nay! I want revenge upon that family! I'll not allow blood money paid for one who sought to kill me first."

Olaf sighed at his son's determination, knowing what was best for the good of his province. "We will hold an assembly."

"They'll not be part of it," Torquil said confidently. "And they'll not accept blood money. 'Tis no secret that chieftain Freyvold prized his son above all things. He'll be satisfied only with my death—your son for Freyvold's son.

"He would not be so foolish as to feud over this, not when we have silver to pay."

Torquil smirked. "Let us await word from them before you send your silver. Do not forget, Johannes was the heir. They'll be satisfied with nothing less than your son."

The crowd began to disperse, spreading the tale throughout the village. Raff went with Olaf, both obviously worried, while Ella came to tend her son's wounds. Torquil seemed very self-satisfied.

Word from the neighboring chieftain came in the form of death. The villagers spent a boisterous evening without thought of impending danger. Tired after the feasting ended, no one heard the stealthy intruders. Not until two slaves were found dead the next morning did they know of the secret invasion.

A new maid had been assigned to Ambyre since Kirsten's incapacitation, and it was she who told her of this vengeance. The girl's brother had been killed along with another slave not yet sixteen years old.

Ambyre sought Sigrid for answers to the questions this raised and found her at the loom in the storeroom, conspicuously unhappy.

"Will the bloodshed end with this?" Ambyre asked, anxious, not wanting to appear so. But she had come to care for these people. "Two lives for the price of one?"

NORTHWARD THE HEART

Sigrid set aside the weaving sword, looking at her with a sad smile. "Lives of slaves mean very little compared to a chieftain's son. They'll not stop until they have taken a member of my father's family."

"Torquil?"

Sigrid shrugged noncommittally.

"But 'twas he who killed Johannes. Why should they seek anyone else?"

"Vengeance will be had only if the next chieftain, as Johannes was to be, dies."

"Raff?"

Sigrid nodded.

Ambyre could not hide her dismay. A gentle hand was laid on her arm.

"You should look forward to his death, milady. Were he to die, you would be free."

Ambyre said nothing, did nothing.

"Would his death pain you so?" Sigrid asked softly, causing Ambyre to blurt out what she had kept within.

"Yes!" she cried. "I do not wish to be free at that price."

Sigrid held Ambyre to her, encouraging tears with tenderness. "Does my brother know you care for him?" Silence revealed the truth.

"You must tell him, AElfwyn." Ambyre could have laughed at the irony in that statement. "You must tell him you love him."

" 'Twould make little difference. You have seen the way he acts. He disdains me."

Sigrid frowned. "He has not taken well that your loyalty is similar to his. How alike you are!

You must tell him your love is real. His doubt of that is tearing him apart. Then he will be able to concentrate on ending this blood feud."

Ambyre regarded her closely. "You understand, don't you? You can see why I have lied."

"If Raff would let his spirit see yours for only a moment, he would know that Odin himself would have done the same had fate put him in your position."

"I have insulted his pride. He will never forget."

Sigrid did not offer empty hope. "Nay, milady. He will not. But he will come to understand. If you love him, your loyalty to *him* will convince him of it. Prove to him it outweighs your loyalty to Edward. But first prove it to yourself."

Uncertain, confused, Ambyre stood to leave. "And Freyvold?"

"Will seek to kill him."

She left with a heavy heart.

Guards were posted that night to prevent further attacks, but there were no other signs of anything unusual. The evening meal seemed especially garrulous, Raff drinking and laughing as much as any of his men. Ambyre wondered at his lack of caution. Fauntley thought him a fool.

The next day a group of Freyvold's warriors attacked a small band of men outside the village. Angry, Olaf swore he would not let this go on. Two of his warriors had been killed and

Freyvold had lost three. It would only get worse, wasting lives so desperately needed to stem the Norwegian advance into Yorkshire. The threat of Ragnold never left Olaf's mind.

He sent a messenger to Freyvold with a proposal: he would pay silver for the life of Johnannes, dismiss any charges because of the warriors and servants he himself had lost, calling it even in view of the loss of Freyvold's three warriors. Thinking this fair, he was enraged when his messenger was found dead at the border of his territory.

Ambyre spent her days anxiously waiting for word from Edward. Raff could then leave this village where his neighbors sought to kill him, for safety in Wessex or Mercia.

Cuthbert added to her ill temper. It had long been his custom to follow after Wulfstan and other warriors, but with this new threat, she wanted to keep him close. He told her haughtily that he could take care of himself, refusing to stay inside.

It was mid-afternoon, two days after they'd found the slain messenger, when Ambyre lost all track of Cuthbert. Usually he could be found near the longhouse with Alf and Wulfstan. But when she went to check, he was not there. Instant panic assailed her and she went to Wulfstan immediately.

He smiled at her concern. "He was here just moments ago, milady. He could not have gone far. No reason to fear for his safety. He'll no doubt be back before long."

She took little comfort in his reassurance, scanning the area for some sign of Cuthbert's dark hair among so many blonds. Not seeing him, she went into the longhouse and questioned several servants. He had not been seen since early morning.

Fear gripped her, redoubled by everyone's attitude. No one seemed concerned. She left the longhouse quickly and walked the length of the village asking after him, calling his name. But he didn't answer and people didn't care.

Tense, she tried to think of all the places he could have gone. Only one possibility was left—the forest—where Olaf's warriors had been attacked. Had he been foolish enough to venture there?

Dread filled her. She knew the answer. He always tried to show these Danes he was as fearless as they. Fearless, she thought, and foolish, if he had indeed gone into the forest. There was no choice but to search for him there. To go back to the longhouse and wait idly would be intolerable. Nor could she ask anyone for help. Who? Raff? Ha! Fauntley? She had enough to worry about as it was.

The forest was dense, its ground covered with needles, rocks and moss, all grass having long since been suffocated, overrun with huge trees and their seedlings. The sun shone in rays through the tall branches; the air smelled moist and earthy. Where the forest was thickest it seemed a world of its own, shadowy, dimly-lit, alive with birds and small animals, heard yet barely seen even by the quickest eye.

She hadn't meant to leave the outskirts of the village, intending to stay within sight of the houses, within earshot of the voices. But concern for Cuthbert sent her deeper into the wood, where tree trunks looked black in the sunless density. She called his name to hear only the flapping of birds' wings in response.

She walked and walked, losing sense of time. Between periods of calling his name, she offered up silent prayers which brought her no comfort. She wanted to be angry with her foolhardy young brother but couldn't. Find him first, then tell him what hell he put her through...

At last, with a pebble in her shoe, she stopped. Leaning against the wide base of a tall pine, she shook out the stone. Finally allowing herself a moments rest. Then, as she looked around, her heart froze.

Where was she? Where was the village? When had she lost track of it? From which direction had she come? The forest was the same everywhere, thick, dense, dark.

Replacing her shoe, standing tall and rigid, she looked around again. Nothing to fear, she told herself. How far could I have come? Not very. How long could I have been walking? The sun is still high in the sky, isn't it? If only I could *see* the sky. But the branches are too full, the trees too close together. There isn't even a decent shadow to reckon the sun's height, just the same dim light everywhere. Well, at least it's not gone completely ... yet.

She resumed walking, her pace considerably slower. Had she passed this way before? Did that tree look familiar? That rock? That bird's nest?

Ambyre didn't know. So intent had her mind been upon finding Cuthbert she had noticed little in passing. Now it all looked the same. Had she passed that fallen tree? Ever? More than once? Only going in circles? She was completely disoriented.

Even if she found Cuthbert now, she couldn't bring him to safety. Heart pounding heavily in her breast, she felt fatigue more acutely than ever.

At last, praying that with a bit more rest she might be able to recognize her surroundings, she sat down against a large smooth rock. Leaning against it, eyes closed, she fought tears of frustration, willing herself not to cry.

With deep breaths, she calmed herself. The way back would soon be found, Cuthbert would be safe, blissfully unaware of all she'd gone through because of him. Why did you think I was in danger? I can defend myself, he would scold ... He had such an impudent way about him now, half his own, half learned from these Danes he'd come to love. Aye, he'd be a fine warrior one day, in a few years...

With these thoughts she allowed her exhaustion to give way to sleep, deep, sound, motionless.

When she awoke, conditions in the forest had changed. Before, there had been at least some sunlight, vague, hazy, coming from nowhere in particular. Now everything was black as midnight.

And there were noises, night sounds. The hoot of an owl, the chirp of a cricket, the call of a frog echoed all around. But was that what woke her? There was something else.

Then it sounded again and she was on her feet in an instant. Howling, neither human nor the wind, made its way through the trees. How many times had she heard wolves? When she was a child the unearthly sound had made her run crying to her father. One of his men overheard and the next day teased her unmercifully. Such big teeth wolves have, he'd said. So large they could tear a man to bits in moments—and a little girl in the wink of an eye.

What foolishness! Hadn't her father said wolves have no need for human flesh? Still, when the woeful cry rose again, her back tingled.

She could not spend the rest of the night here. She *would* not. More desperate than ever, she tried to shake the twinge from her spine, square her shoulders and keep to a brisk pace. But walking was difficult in the blackness.

Fear plagued her, nudging at her senses, threatening. But she did not give in, forcing herself to believe she was *not* afraid.

Suddenly, from the corner of her eye she saw

a flash. There in the distance was a light passing through the forest, sporadically eclipsed behind tree trunks. She stopped. The light kept moving.

Her first impulse, to cry out to her savior, died on her lips even as she formed the words. Something kept her silent.

Fear hit her now like a physical blow. She fell back, away from the light, even though whoever carried it could hardly see her from where they were. She stepped behind a tree, her mind racing with possibilities.

It was imperative to identify the torchbearers. Could she force her quaking limbs to get her close enough? She must! Perhaps, by the grace of the Almighty, it was Raff or one of his warriors. She would be saved.

In any case, she must remain undetected. These midnight walkers, if they were Freyvold's men, were up to no good. Perhaps, if they planned a deadly attack on Raff's village, they could lead her where she wanted to go.

Carefully, she stole from behind one tree to another, always quick, always quiet. The light grew larger, brighter, as she drew near. Then she saw the shadows of four or five men in the torchlight. She heard the clatter of their weaponry as they walked at a steady pace. She could see no faces, recognize no silhouettes. They kept abysmally quiet.

If this was a search party looking for her, would they not call out her name? And why have four or five men together? Far wiser to split into smaller groups, to cover more area.

Her heart pounded heavily. These men could only be Freyvold's. She implored God: let them not have done their evil deed already! Perhaps, if she continued to follow them, she would be able to warn the village.

Her prayer was heard. As she followed stealthily, none of the warriors looked behind. A fallen branch tripped her. She hit the ground with a thud, terrified, closed her eyes and shielded her face from what she knew would be the head of an axe or the tip of an arrow if she dared look up. But the warriors did not hear, did not even look her way, so intent were they on their grim business.

Before long, the torch was extinguished, plunging the forest again into total darkness. Moments later, through the thinning trees, lights of the village sparkled in view.

Ambyre heard the hiss of steel as blades were drawn, the whisper of arrows poised to shoot. She knew there wasn't a moment to spare; the men were ready to attack. Guards Olaf had posted outside the longhouse were an easy target.

What could she do? How could she warn them without falling victim herself? Her terror provided the answer; she did what she'd wanted to do since the first howl of that wolf had quickened her pulse.

She screamed. It was an unearthly, shrill sound, so loud the entire village must have heard. How good it felt! She'd held back so long, and now she let out every shred of terror she'd felt that night. Freyvold's men turned in astonished confusion toward the sound. At the same time, the longhouse guards looked toward the forest, glimpsing the lamplight reflected off the blades of the attackers. They raised their shields, poised for battle.

None ensued. The intruders, now discovered, knew they were outnumbered. Surprise had been their strongest weapon. Without that their objective could not be achieved. Still looking toward the scream, weapons drawn, not one warrior moved.

Ambyre stared at them, eyes wide, a night breeze billowing her hair and skirts. She felt nothing; the scream had left her exhausted, or perhaps, she thought, witless. At first it seemed they had not seen her, despite the glow from the village lamps, for they did nothing. Then one warrior turned, not drawing his sword against her but dropping it and fleeing as fast as a rabbit before a wildcat.

"A wood spirit!" he cried. "Run before she has you!"

The rest of Freyvold's men were gone before the words stopped echoing around them, two dropping their weapons in fright. Within moments, the blackness of the forest enveloped them.

Olaf's guards came quickly to Ambyre, Wulfstan among them, plainly amazed to see her.

"Lady AElfwyn!"

Awash with relief, senses returning, she fell

against Wulfstan's sturdy form. She was back; she was safe. And she'd saved the lives of Olaf's guards.

She told her tale in bits and pieces, how she'd been lost, come across the torchlight and thought the men were a search party for her. How she'd assessed their plan to attack, then followed to warn the village. As she spoke, they were joined by more of the village who came to see what caused the commotion. Even Olaf and Ella came from their bed. But Raff was nowhere to be seen.

Olaf listened to her story passively, his face revealing nothing of what he felt. Even when several warriors suggested a feast in AElfwyn's honor, he gave no clue as to whether or not he approved of the idea.

"We will discuss it again on the morrow," he said with his usual stoicism. "It is late."

With that, he was gone, and Ambyre might have felt deflated had she not been so utterly exhausted. It *was* late, and the only thing that had kept her awake since reaching safety was the hope of seeing Raff. Where was he? And what would he say when he learned of her exploit? Would he be pleased? Would it soften him, for her to have saved a few of his men? Wouldn't he at least smile at her again?

Then Fauntley and Cuthbert came to her side. They'd stood on the fringes of the crowd surrounding her and had heard the whole story.

"You're a hero!" Cuthbert gleefully

announced. "Just like in the sagas. A hero who saved the people!"

Ambyre tousled his hair affectionately. "I stopped one small band of men with a scream I couldn't keep in. Certainly I didn't save the whole village. But thank you."

Fauntley did not share Cuthbert's enthusiasm. He stared at her a long while, but when she started to walk past him into the longhouse, he held her arm.

"Why did you do it? Why save *them*?"

She faced him, silent, offering no explanation.

"All right," he said. "But they *are* pagans. Enemies of God. And you're too good. You shouldn't have endangered your life for the sake of a few Danes. Even God wouldn't expect that."

How could she tell him? She hadn't done it for God. She had done it for Raff.

"I couldn't stand by and watch them slaughtered," was all she said.

"Then you truly are a hero, as in the sagas," Fauntley whispered, the admiration in his voice all too apparent.

Bristling, she turned away. A hero? Hardly. She'd been afraid all the while. And once she'd followed them back she'd done what any coward would have done; she'd screamed. It had been the grace of God that made those warriors think she was a wood spirit.

Now she turned scowling to Cuthbert who still glowed with excitement and pride.

"Where are *you* this afternoon? Did you know I was searching for you? That is why I was in the forest to begin with."

"Aye, we knew," he answered. "Why did you do such a silly thing?"

"Silly!"

"I was shooting arrows with Alf behind the longhouse. You didn't look there. When we realized you'd gone off after me—because you weren't there for the evening meal—Raff was almost as angry as I was. Why do you worry about me, Ambyre? I'm a warrior—"

She cut him off. "Where is Raff?"

Fauntley spoke. "He was quite angry. He's out looking for you now. Cuddy and I were waiting up for word of you."

"Raff . . . in the forest?"

Both nodded.

Her exhaustion fled. What had she done? Saved the guards, sent Freyvold's men back into the forest, only to have them find Raff instead? Conspicuous, vulnerable, the very target they wanted?

"I think it's time we all went to bed," Fauntley said.

She barely heard him. Sleep? With Raff out there?

They helped her into the longhouse where Fauntley headed for his pallet, surprised when she stopped at the center hearth.

"Aren't you going to bed?" he asked.

"I'm waiting for Raff."

He was mystified, but by the set of her jaw,

the steadiness in her eye and the certainty in her voice, he knew she would not be dissuaded.

"You must be tired."

"I suppose. I'll just sit by the hearth. Goodnight, Fauntley."

His good-night was barely audible. He went silently to his pallet at the rear of the long-house.

"Why do you want to wait up for Raff?" Cuthbert asked. "He's angry. See him tomorrow."

Would he be alive tomorrow? Could he possibly defend himself against at least five vengeful warriors, most still fully armed?

"I'd prefer to confront him tonight," she told Cuthbert. "Please go to bed. No reason for you to hear an unpleasant argument."

Would that were the worst possibility!

Raff again heard the cry of the wolf and unwitting chill passed through him. How could he forget that long-ago vision of hungry animals forced toward man because of one harsh season after another? Then, when countless villagers fell victim to a dreaded, fatal illness, their bodies too numerous to bury or burn properly, the wolves had quickly developed a taste for human flesh. Those shallow graves offered easy prey to a hungry pack.

He shook off the horribly vivid image of AElfwyn, whose body he'd come to know so well it invaded his waking and sleeping moments, torn to shreds by the angry white teeth. He would find her. He must.

He called her name again, ignoring the dryness in his throat. His eyes scanned darkness lit only by the torch in his hand. In the distance, through the trees, he saw another torch, and another, other warriors he'd ordered to search. He heard them call her name. But never any answer.

Why had the fool gone into the forest alone? How far had she gotten? Had she walked halfway back to Wessex?

He scowled. Perhaps that was her idea; perhaps she wasn't lost at all, but running from him. If she were desperate enough, leaving behind her little brother and that simpering scholar would be a small price to pay. They were of no use to him. Only she, having political importance to Mercia and Wessex, could do him any good.

That was why he must find her. His worry was only for the alliance. Yet the sweat on his brow, the twist of his heart increased painfully with visions of what danger she could be in.

His grip on the torch tightened. When he found her she would be alive, safe, well. And then he would happily wring her neck for putting him through this.

He wasn't sure what warned him first. Was it the light that caught his eye, one from behind which shouldn't have been there? Or the dousing of that light? Or the rattle of weaponry? He turned in an instant, with barely enough time to raise *Kappi* in defense, before he was assailed, a man on each side of him with raised swords and battle cries on their lips.

The commotion brought the rest of his men to

Raff's side. Torches were dropped, igniting dried needles on the forest floor. The scene was bathed in heat and flickering light, casting sinister shadows of battle.

Then another shadow joined the ghostly crew, a warrior with no weapon. He saw his comrades outnumbered by those reinforcing Raff.

"All Valhalla is on his side!" the warrior cried. "The wood spirit warned us—I told you it was a sign! We cannot win."

Raff's sword, poised for a fatal thrust, found no target. Freyvold's men fled behind the wall of flames around them and disappeared into the night.

Raff and the rest stood motionless, their weapons still raised for combat, staring after a vanished enemy. Gone—truly, amazingly, gone. Never before had any of them seen such flight from battle.

"Freyvold's men must all be cowards," said one. Raff and the others laughed. It was the only explanation.

Then, suddenly aware of the spreading fire, took up their torches, stamped and smothered the flames, and resumed their search, eyes sharper than ever. A wood spirit, one of them had said. A wood spirit meant certain death if gazed upon too long.

Waiting alone, surrounded only by snoring men and slaves, was far more difficult than she anticipated. Each moment dragged by interminably. How much longer would it be? He had to come in soon, if only to see if she'd found her own way back.

She watched the fire; she paced; she sat on Olaf's bench. At any moment now, Raff would walk through that door. And oh, how she'd welcome him—glad even for an argument. She paced again, fears heightening, aggravation growing. Wasn't anyone else worried? Didn't Olaf realize his son was out there among Freyvold's warriors? Wasn't Ella concerned? How could they sleep so soundly when Raff was in danger? These people accepted fate too easily!

Too angry to listen to any more snoring, she left the longhouse at a determined pace. Wulfstan and the others were still on guard.

"I'll escort you," Wulfstan offered. It dawned on her with some annoyance that he must think she needed to use the privy.

"That won't be necessary," she retorted coldly, driving his smile away. It was too difficult to regret having snapped at him. *He* wasn't worried either. "You haven't seen anyone yet, have you?"

"No, milady." His tone stayed respectful. "To worry over him does him dishonor."

"Dishonor! What a foolish race you are!"

"Do you seek to disgrace my people with your insults?" A joyously familiar voice sounded from behind her.

She wheeled about, eyes filling with inadvertent tears at the sight of him, angry as he was. But she fought them down and resisted the overwhelming desire to fling herself into his arms. That scorn—so much a part of him since their fateful night on the Desert of Evil Deeds—was still present. Scorn too deep to ignore.

Fatigue made her reckless, giddy. She loved him, worried over his welfare, and he was angry, bitter, savage. Rashly, to hurt, she said, "you and your people disgrace *yourselves*."

Suddenly, so suddenly it seemed a surprise to Raff himself, he grabbed her arms in a viselike grip that made her flinch. On his face was a fury so livid she couldn't hide her fear.

His grip tightened. How he wanted to hurt her! Why not? She'd brought him nothing but agony, an aching emptiness born the moment he no longer had her. Tonight he'd been tortured with gruesome apparitions, from her being devoured by wolves, to her falling and breaking her neck. Now here she stood, forever taunting him and his people. What made her so superior? He should break that lovely neck himself!

It struck him that she wasn't struggling; she seemed resigned. He wanted to put terror in her eyes—those eyes, so dark, so large he could lose himself in them. And that skin just below his savage touch, so soft, smooth . . . that mouth, the very one that taunted him, so inviting. He had the urge to crush her to him, an urge that infuriated him further.

He thrust her away. He knew if he held her a moment longer he would be lost. He would drag her to bed and nothing else would matter.

But what mattered had nothing to do with the

tightening in his loins, the bitter ache in his body from denying her to himself. Now he took out his rage on Wulfstan.

"You and the others are as much to blame for wasting my time running after her. She is a prisoner who shouldn't be allowed to wander freely about. She could have escaped. Thor help you, Wulfstan, if you let this happen again."

"I wasn't trying to escape!" Ambyre was defiant.

Raff turned back to her. "Your brother was safe all along. You should have come to me."

At that, hysteria rose and she laughed. "To you? What do you care how I feel?"

Wulfstan backed away, leaving the two discreetly alone.

"I am responsible for whatever concerns you."

"Then you were to blame for my being lost. Not Wulfstan, not Cuthbert, not even myself. You."

He could have thrashed her, knowing she was right. "Then perhaps I should keep you under lock and key, opening the door only to serve you meals. Otherwise I cannot guard your every movement."

"You've not been much of a guard," she retorted, "avoiding me like a disease."

"And you've no doubt missed my company." His tone dripped with sarcasm.

Without another word, she turned and disappeared inside the longhouse, going at last to an exhausted death-like sleep. Raff pulled *Kappi* from its sheath, held it high with both hands, and drove it into the hard earth.

The following morning the whole village hummed with stories of how the Lady AElfwyn had saved them from attack. Exaggerated tales reached her of how she'd shot an arrow at a hundred of Freyvold's men who took flight in fear, thinking she was a Valkyrie.

Everyone smiled at her that day, or spoke to her with unabashed admiration. Even Olaf seemed grateful. Her being thought a wood nymph was a good omen. It meant Freyvold might believe the spirit world had chosen to side against him. It would be up to him to make the next move.

Olaf agreed to the feast his warriors had called for. During a roistering dinner, the poet sang a newly-composed saga of the Lady AElfwyn and her bravery. Everyone listened, nodding along, even the fiercest warriors paying respect to her with their attention. Torquil, Ambyre noted, was absent, no doubt sore from his wounds.

There were more tales too from those who had been attacked by Freyvold's men, of how their enemy ran from a wood spirit. Ambyre was triumphant. *She* had been that spirit which, it seems, had saved Raff's life.

He sat beside her in his usual place, sharing her goblet, laughing with Piers. When the saga dedicated to her had been sung, he was as deferentially silent as the rest. But never once did his eyes meet hers, never once did he speak to her. The smile she'd hoped for never materalized. Bitter, she called herself a fool. Let him hate her, then. If only somehow, she could learn to hate him in return.

In the middle of the feast, the rowdy gaiety was unexpectedly hushed. A fat, squalling boy was dragged in by a couple of guards. Word quickly spread he had been sent by Freyvold.

"A likely messenger," said Wulfstan, who sat on Ambyre's other side. "A charcoal-chewer of less value than a lap dog."

"Charcoal-chewer?" she repeated.

"Look at him, milady. With that fat carcass, what more must he do than sit by the hearthside, eating all day?"

Some began to mutter that they ought to send the boy back to Freyvold in bloody pieces. But Olaf signalled for silence.

"Just as well to hear what he has to say," Wulfstan whispered. "What harm would killing this piglet do to Freyvold? That's why he was chosen."

"But surely they *won't* kill him!" she whispered back. "He's a child."

"A child on his way to becoming a worthless man, if he shows no talent other than overeating."

They quieted then, and the boy spoke tremulously.

"Freyvold wishes to resolve this bitter feud." His voice was high, nasal. "He wants no more loss of life when our people are so few already in this land. He will take no payment for the life of his son; he says no amount of silver can compensate. He wishes you to give your heir to him."

Ambyre glanced from the boy to Raff, now standing near his father, not surprised by the message.

Olaf scoffed. "So he may kill him with my blessing?" He raised one hand as if to give his permission to a nearby warrior to have done with this messenger and return him lifeless in any manner he saw fit. At that, the boy spoke again, urgently.

"Nay, milord! He wishes your son to fight our finest warrior. Should your son win the duel, Freyvold will accept the terms of your settlement. Should our warrior win, then you will be given the same amount of silver you offered to Freyvold for his own son."

Olaf looked at Raff, who, imperceptibly, nodded.

" 'Tis agreed."

The boy was allowed to leave unharmed, but for being ruthlessly teased, tripped and spat upon by several who were bitter because of losing friends. Once outside, he scurried frantically away, moving his plump little hams faster than he ever did before.

"There is nothing to fear," Wulfstan said, seeing the frown already appearing upon Ambyre's brow. "Raff can best any of Freyvold's men."

Nonetheless, sleep eluded her that night. Would this fear for his life never leave her? But the answer was grim: he was a warrior.

The duel was set for the following day. In the morning several of Raff's men, along with Olaf's retainers, went to the designated spot, a meadow between the provinces of the two chieftains. There they lay a hide upon the ground, stretching it smooth, affixing it firmly with four laurel poles.

Everyone but the lowliest slaves would be there, it seemed, excepting only those who could not leave their duties. Kirsten was not allowed from her bed, so she, too, would be left at the village.

Sigrid offered to walk with Ambyre, among the last to leave. Fauntley, in his disdain for what he called barbarian violence, refused to go. Cuthbert had already left with Wulfstan.

Ambyre caught a glimpse of Raff before leaving. With polished sword and helmet he looked more than fierce. Surely he could win against anyone. She wanted to speak to him, give him some word of encouragement. But she did not know what to say. She longed to rush to his side, ignoring disdain, immune to rejection. This was to be a duel to the death, and though she believed him a great warrior, she saw the possibility that he would be killed. What if he died believing she looked upon him only as her enemy?

Sigrid watched her closely as they walked. "Go to him, milady. Your face reveals what is in your heart; surely my brother will see your love through the pain he feels. Go to him." She watched Ambyre run back as a smile softened her face.

No one was in the longhouse, not even the slaves who were to stay behind. She ran out again, following a different path through the trees. God, had she missed him?

Then she saw movement in the foliage and hurried toward it calling his name. In a moment he appeared, coming to meet her with concern.

"What has happened?" he asked sternly. "Why are you alone again in the forest?" His blue eyes shone through the metal surrounding them, and seemed brighter.

"I—I must speak to you, to tell you—"

His sidelong grin was evident through the helmet. "Come to make sure you'll be sent home after I'm dead?"

"Stop!" she cried. "I have to tell you—I never lied about loving you. The rest was because I was afraid, knowing I mattered little compared to your people."

He laughed, a harsh, cruel laugh that overflowed with contempt. "Afraid, milady? When you so thoroughly believe I am off to my death this moment? Could a man incapable of winning this duel inspire any fear?"

Her tears brimmed. "I don't mean that! I don't believe you'll die."

"Then why make amends as though you'll never again have the chance? That's like sending for a Christian priest to perform the last rites. I commend you, lady. You've thoroughly convinced me of the honor you bear me. Pray that I don't disappoint you by surviving."

He turned not allowing another word. At some distance, a young warrior stood beside Olaf. When Raff joined them he commanded the young man to make sure their captive did not take advantage of the circumstances to escape. She would remain hostage, at least until the end of the duel.

The Angel of Death chanted the rules of the ancient rite. Each man was allowed one sword and three shields; if all shields were broken the fight would go on without protection. The battle must be fought upon the stretched hide between the laurel poles; at least one foot of each warrior must remain upon the hide at all times, assuring close proximity to each other. The battle would, of course, be to the death.

Amybre did not want to watch, but she, like everyone, could not take her eyes from the muscular bodies ready to hack at each other. Raff, strong and lithe, was nonetheless outweighed by his opponent. They were of equal height, but Freyvold's prized warrior had massive arms almost twice the size of Raff's. His legs, too, were like trunks of young trees straining against the threads of his breeks. And his shoulders looked strong enough to bear Valhalla, as if he were the son of Odin himself.

Once they were both on the stretched hide, neither hesitated. Freyvold's man struck first, using his sword as if it were an extension of his arm. Ambyre quickly realized the value of their shields, constantly thwarting forceful swings of the heavy swords. They deflected blows with the shield's flat surface rather than with the rim. At first she'd thought that to strike the rim, forged with iron, would break the opponent's sword. But when Raff parried in this manner, it wasn't the other sword that broke, it was his own shield instead. All gasped as the first of Raff's three defenses splintered.

Despite the cold, the duelists wore nothing above but padded leather jerkins. Ambyre could soon see sweat stains coming through from their chests. She feared for Raff, for the other's strokes were mightier, and with such a heavy sword it was strength, not speed, which counted. Raff struck a blow while fending off another, and once again did not lift his shield to accept the swing upon the softer flatness. His second one broke. A hush fell over the onlookers. Only one left now to protect him.

Ambyre was beside herself. Surely this one could not outlast the other's three. She wanted to turn away but was fascinated, watching as intently as everyone else.

With careful footing the men circled each other, mindful to remain on the hide, dodging blows when the shields were not needed. Raff was agile, but those who had known him in battle saw that he held back, slowing himself intentionally.

His opponent did not lose a shield and thankfully, Raff's own third one seemed better designed to avoid the final, fatal loss. Ambyre thought she was about to be sick when he took a slash to his sword arm. Dark, thick blood was added to stains of sweat.

Their swords sliced through the air with deadly strength behind every swing. At last, Ambyre saw a change in Raff. At first it was imperceptible, and she wondered if her hopes made her imagine it. But no, those around her began to murmur and whisper; they saw it, too. As his opponent began to tire, his own pace seemed to quicken, strengthen. The blows he dealt came swifter, harder, as the other's strength dwindled. Yet, though Raff quickly became more aggressive, Freyvold's champion never dropped his defense.

Then, a sickening crack. The opposing sword had come again onto Raff's shield, his last defense gone. But with some expert, mysterious move, he was able to twist his shield somehow. Wedged into it, the enemy's sword was pulled from his grasp and fell with a thud to the ground.

This was the end. Freyvold's man had kept his shields but lost his sword. A final slice would finish him, one last blow to his neck or chest, for he was tired and no shield was enough against a sustained onslaught. But Raff brought his sword down slowly, without force behind it, pointed to the ground. Then he thrust downward, leaving it to stand upright beside the other, fallen one. He looked up at the man's face, placid, resigned, expecting death.

Everyone was absolutely quiet. Raff looked over the crowd, dumbfounded by his action. Their surprise angered him. Only in Ambyre was astonishment missing. In her face he saw relief, and she alone among them did not disgust him. She alone was glad of the lack of bloodshed. He knew that if ever she had reason to call them barbarians, this was the time.

They waited. They had been promised blood. Would they feel cheated, he wondered, out of their sport?

But as his gaze continued to pass over comrades and neighbors, his anger faded. They were part of him, bound by blood, tradition, ancestry, now like children as they stood there waiting.

"I'll not kill this countryman," he announced to their amazement. "I have won this duel and won the right to speech; you will hear me out, both my father's people as well as Freyvold's."

He continued slowly, eyeing each of them.

"Our warriors are known for their strength and valor, but we will only weaken our race as long as we continue with these feuds. We've lost many a battle to Edward and his armies. Why? Why when we have warriors like this man before me? Strong enough to defeat any of the Wessex breed, Edward himself would attest to that. Then why have we failed? Why has Edward been able to bring us to submission?

NORTHWARD THE HEART

The evidence is here before you; we have lacked *unity*.

"That is the basis of Edward's success: unity, planning, strategic aggressiveness. We can boast of our skills at raiding, but how many of us are left after years of warfare against Edward's united armies? They have one leader, a strength which comes not from stubborn individualism, but from unity and purpose."

"And who will lead us?" came a scoffing voice from among Freyvold's men. "You?"

"I claim no such honor," Raff declared. "I speak here only to enlighten, because as surely as I stand here, Ragnold will be coming to take our land from us. Would you rather succumb to his tyranny than unite now and be rid of him forever? Would you lose York to him, and see our trade go with it? We can keep it only if we unite. What strength we have left can only be drawn from unity."

"The Norwegians have always been there," said another of Freyvold's men. "Yet York is still ours."

"False hope. Ragnold has already defeated the Scots. We are next on his list."

"You dishonor the title of warrior with your talk of defeat," said Freyvold himself, with a firm voice not to be ignored.

Raff looked at him squarely. "I have never known you to recoil from what is true, Freyvold. You now have no heir to leave your people. Do you also wish to deny them a future free of Norse tyranny by not facing facts?"

Olaf stepped forward, seeing that mediation was necessary. "None here can deny the reality of Ragnold. True, his people have been a threat for many years. Yet lately we Danes have been too occupied with the Saxons to pay much attention to them. Their number grows while our number lessens. No one here can deny that if we joined forces it could only strengthen us against the Norse."

"Then I ask again," came the disrespectful voice, "Who will lead?"

" 'Tis more important," Raff resumed, "that for now we agree to work together and not against each other. Feuds like the one ended here today must be avoided."

Freyvold, to Raff's surprise and relief, said, " 'Tis only the talk of defeat I object to. You have made sound sense. I call for an assembly where we can discuss the issue of joint leadership. We will look toward renewed strength and end this fear of defeat."

Cheers came from both camps. Raff shouted as well, in approval of their approval. There would be an assembly. It was a beginning. They were not the children he had feared them to be.

XIV

Kirsten had had a difficult night. The next morning she was left with dark circles around her eyes and a drawn, fatigued pallor.

Ambyre offered to bring a cup of warm milk, but Kirsten shook her head.

" 'Tis, I, milady, who should wait upon you. I am only a slave."

"And what am I? A captive as well. We are the same."

"Nay, milady! You are to be the next chieftain's wife; keeper of the keys of this great household."

Ambyre frowned with a shrug. "That, my dear friend, is something I would rather not discuss. Now how can I make you more comfortable?"

"Only the babe can do that, milady. He has shifted so low, I fear he's near birth, yet my term should not end for two months yet."

Ambyre's eyes went to the swollen belly

beneath the blanket. She spoke regretfully. "I am of little help in such matters; I know nothing about pregnancy."

"You shall," Kirsten said, but looked away in such discomfort that Ambyre wondered if she truly wished such an experience for anyone else.

Leaving the hut in which Kirsten lay, Ambyre met Torquil just outside the door. He greeted her with a smile, his wounds healed into several new scars.

" 'Tis a cold winter day for you to be out," he observed.

She smiled wryly. "You've never been to Iceland, have you, Torquil? There this would seem most comfortable."

She thought he would continue past her into the hut to see to his coming child, but instead he walked along with her, chatting amiably. When they reached the longhouse he stopped her before she went in.

" 'Tis the third day of the assembly, and still they cannot decide on a leader to fight this imagined enemy," he said. "Most have decided for Raff, even many of Freyvold's men, but there are too many rivals."

"I see you continue to believe Ragnold an imagined enemy," she countered.

"Aye, and I am not alone. Some are in favor of Raff's plans, though, in case Ragnold proves strong and Edward does not join us."

He had obviously left the assembly before the others; this seemed ususual, and she could not help but wonder why. So when he continued to keep her from going inside, she was curious about what he wanted.

"Will you walk with me a bit?" he asked. "Since the air is not too uncomfortable for you."

She saw no harm in a little stroll with Torquil, so unlike his brothers, so mercurial. He began to tell her of the games he played as a child on that spot—or that. He was, she thought, still a child, his changeability a facet of his youth. Though he claimed to be a warrior, she could hardly imagine him wielding a heavy sword and carrying an iron-edged shield. He seemed too... delicate. Now he was pointing out a mound in the earth, a hideaway which he had used with his friends as an outlaw's den. It was cavelike, small, damp, and dark, perfectly suited to a young boy's imagination.

They walked on and before long were well away from the longhouse and its surrounding huts. The trees grew dense in this area, blocking out the sun, which made her realize how far they had come.

"We should be returning." She stopped.

He came back to her, a frown evident on his face. "Are you cold?" he asked solicitously.

"We have walked too far, and 'tis a raw day. The way back will seem longer."

He stepped closer. "But you are accustomed to the cold, after Iceland."

"I'd have taken an extra cloak if I'd known we were going to hike."

"I've no wish to hike," he said, taking another step closer. "I only wish to be alone with you."

She almost laughed, surprised at Torquil's declaration. He may have seen it before she turned away. For a moment his eyes flashed with anger.

"You wish to be alone with the woman who is to be your brother's wife?" she asked over her shoulder.

"But you are not yet wed." He stepped in front of her, stroking her arm through the cloak. "I can think only of what I want this moment; I want you."

She smiled, as patiently and maternally as she could. After all, AElfwyn of Mercia was a woman of thirty. Torquil could be barely seventeen. "Not only am I to be your brother's wife, but I am nearly twice your age. What do you want with an old woman like me?"

"Old!" he exclaimed in disbelief. "Desirable but not old. All the women envy you; I've heard them talk. They wonder how you can look so young. Tell me, Lady AElfwyn, does the rest of your body look as young as the little you show?"

Ambyre began to head back toward the village. "You have said quite enough, Torquil. I'll not tell your brother what has transpired if you promise never to speak to me in such a manner again."

Roughly, he grabbed her arm and wheeled her about. "*What* has transpired?" he demanded to know. "A few words? An admission that I desire you? That should come as no surprise; most of Raff's men are in love with you. It makes me wonder what went on during your long sea voyages. Perhaps they know you as well as I would like to."

Before she could stop herself, she slapped him. He was no longer the carefree, jovial youth. He was suddenly lustful, lecherous, when only moments before he'd been merry. Pulling her to him, his kiss was brutal, insulting. As he pressed his mouth to hers, she bared her teeth and bit him as hard as she could for as long as he continued. He freed himself with a shove, putting a hand to his wounded lip, seeing the blood.

The look in his eye was venomous. He raised a hand and struck her firmly across the face, causing her to fall back with its impact. He would have gone on hitting her had she not reached up for the dagger at his side, grabbing it and holding it in front of her with a look of sincere menace.

He smiled through his pain. "Many of our women offer a fight for this sport. So you think I won't master you? A Saxon?"

"Come closer and see," she invited warily.

He did so, not expecting the agility of this new foe. She was on her feet in an instant, keeping a short distance away, still poising the dagger to strike. He had no doubt she would use it, but did not intend to give her the chance. She was a mere woman, not even a Dane. Saxon women were weak and soft.

His mistake was to underestimate her. Light-footed and swift, she proved much stronger than he expected. When he lunged at her she dodged him easily, until at last she made him trip over his own stumbling feet and watched him fall face down on the ice-covered ground.

"I'll not kill you because you are Raff's brother," she said, kneeling over him with the dagger against his back. "But I'll not be treated in this manner again, or I shall tell every warrior in the village how I bested you today. Won't they think that amusing? So do not provoke me again, Torquil. Do you understand?"

The nod came awkwardly because of his prostrate position. She lifted the dagger away from him, taking it safely with her as she walked haughtily away. No fool, she listened carefully for his footsteps in case he decided to follow.

By the time she reached the longhouse, the assembly was over and people were milling about. Her absence had been noted, and as she entered in a disheveled state, more than one curious glance was cast her way. Unknown to her, Torquil's blow had raised an ugly welt along her jaw.

She would have gone on through the hall, ignoring the stares, had not Raff stopped her when she passed his chair. He did not reach out to her, but his voice, though quiet, was enough to halt her progress. She faced him, standing not far away, and he neared her with eyes that never left the bruise on her cheek.

"What has happened?" he asked evenly.

She looked away, trying to leave, but he caught her shoulders in his hands.

"Who did this to you?"

Instead of speaking, she held up Torquil's dagger. He took it, turning it in his palms, recognizing it.

"Did he . . . violate you?"

She smiled bitterly. "Nay, milord. Your bride remains intact . . . but for what you yourself have already taken," she added with a whisper.

Her words went soft but clear. For a moment he wondered if she were sorry to tell the truth. Wouldn't she like to see his reaction if another man had taken her?

A swift order brought a servant scurrying to attend her bruise. Raff went out. Much later, when Torquil appeared, she saw that he had several fresh welts of his own, aside from the swollen lip she had given him.

"Word has come!" Cuthbert ran in shouting. "I just saw the messenger arrive! Edward has agreed to the wedding!"

Fauntley smiled. At last! At last they'd be going home. His gaze fell on Ambyre. Soon, he thought happily. Soon she would be his. Oh, he knew she felt some attraction to Olafsson, but put the barbarian in King Edward's civilized court and he'd be revealed as a total fool. She would see that. And he could hardly wait.

"Did they say when we would be sailing?" Ambyre spoke without emotion, much to

NORTHWARD THE HEART

Fauntley's surprise. Wasn't she glad?

Cuthbert now began to realize how much he'd be leaving behind that he loved. His joy at breaking the news turned to gloom. "I imagine it'll be soon. I didn't ask."

"What is the matter with both of you?" demanded Fauntley. "We're going *home*."

Ambyre smiled at him. "Of course, and we're glad. Aren't we, Cuddy?"

The boy gave an uninspired nod.

"Such happiness overwhelmes me," Fauntley said.

Sigrid had come to the door and listened for a few moments. Now she spoke warmly to Cuthbert.

"Captivity among my people has suited you well. You will make a fine warrior one day, whether you serve your king or someone else. You've been a good pupil with Alf and Wulfstan." Then she turned to Ambyre. "And Lady AElfwyn . . . you've many reasons for uncertainty. You will soon be marrying my brother. Marriage often brings happiness and sadness at the same time, even for those who love each other."

All of them knew the truth but Sigrid.

Just then a maid approached. She bid the Lady AElfwyn to the hall where Olaf awaited.

She found him seated, Raff standing stoically at his side, not looking at her, barely listening as his father spoke.

"Your king has sent us word that he agrees to this alliance for peace. He has, in order to show his support of this union, invited my son to accompany you to Wessex, where the ceremony will take place. From there you will travel into Mercia before returning here to live among us. King Edward believes, as we do, that support must be rallied inside of Mercia itself to make strong this new bond between our lands. You are willing, milady, to follow the commands of your king?"

With a surreptitious glance at Raff, she answered proudly and truthfully. "I am."

"Very well. Banns are being announced at your Christian church immediately; the ceremony shall take place as soon as possible. I will reconvene our assembly tomorrow to tell them of this. My son will see you back to Wessex within the week so that you may plan your wedding and see your uncle again. He eagerly awaits your return."

"Did he . . . say that in his message?" Ambyre asked curiously.

"He did," Olaf answered. Ambyre knew then that Edward had some strategy to insure her safe return.

She was dismissed, without a word from the prospective groom. Nor did she acknowledge him. She had tried to tell him the truth before the duel. He would not listen to her then. It was too late now.

The pains began late at night, urgent, premature pains coursing through Kirsten's body. She wanted to cry out but clung to her pillow instead, knuckles white, her delicate face twisting in anguish.

Ambyre was summoned in the morning. Sigrid was there with several other women, whom Ambyre knew were capable enough without any assistance from her. She had never before witnessed childbirth; she wasn't sure she wanted to see her young friend suffer. But the women ushered her to the bedside where her hand was thrust into Kirsten's, thankfully and urgently accepted.

Soon that grasping hand numbed as the throes of childbirth proceeded. Ambyre was not even sure Kirsten knew it was she who held it. The girl was delirious with pain. She could only offer words of comfort, do little else than distract her from the pain between spasms. When Kirsten at last cried out, Ambyre encouraged her, urging her to give full vent to it, to shake the very walls with her screams.

Exhaustion soon touched everyone. As the final stages began, the women placed their hands upon Kirsten's belly to help push the baby downward. Kirsten could not do it without them. An ominous silence followed the birth, but once the child's mouth was cleaned of mucous, he let out a wail which almost matched his mother's in volume. Kirsten did not hear it; she lay back, spent, unaware.

By the time the babe was bathed and swaddled, the hour was late. But instead of being laid at his mother's warm breast, he was taken to the longhouse. Curiosity overcoming her fatigue, Ambyre followed the woman who carried him, leaving Kirsten to be watched over by a servant.

There was a small group gathered in the longhouse. Torquil was there, Olaf, Ella, and in the corner stood the old crone, the Angel of Death. Ambyre wanted to smirk at her; Kirsten's baby was alive and healthy; her oracle had proven wrong.

Raff was there, too, standing apart. He had not spoken to Torquil for two days, since beating him for Ambyre's bruise.

The child had ceased crying as the blanket was opened and he was laid on the floor, uncovered in the chill. He just lay there, and even to Ambyre's untrained eye seemed listless. His tiny hands would move, but slowly, with such effort that his weakness was evident. She despised this custom, thinking the child should rather be in its mother's warm arms than made to suffer such cold perusal by men of the clan.

Though she did not see it immediately it was there nonetheless, as tiny as the newborn was. A deformity. Not instantly noticed, but as their squirming stopped, the crooked, ill-shaped legs became apparent. The infant lay bent and weak, a small helpless being stared at by all present.

Ambyre watched Torquil look down at him, impassive at the slow, labored movements. But when he saw the legs, he reacted with disgust. He wanted no weakling for his offspring. He turned his back. No one uttered a word. They let the child lie there.

Ambyre was about to step forward when Sigrid firmly grasped her arm, forcing her to be still. She watched as the old crone, garbed in black, moved closer, stooped over the child and picked it up without the blanket.

"Where is she taking him?" Ambyre whispered fearfully.

Sigrid's voice was low and sad. "He has not been accepted by his father. The child will be taken outside."

"And then?"

Sigrid merely looked at her.

"And then?" A tinge of hysteria was in her tone. When Sigrid remained silent, Ambyre grew frantic. "He will be exposed...in this cold...to die?"

Sigrid's eyes closed in confirmation.

"No!" the cry wrenched from deep within, loud, desperate, as though Ambre herself had carried that child and just labored through its birth. Kirsten had suffered too much for Torquil to turn his back so easily, so quickly, and doom a young life. Is this what these people call tradition? No one stood forward, no one protested. The Angel of Death moved freely to carry out her duty. Ambyre's cry did not affect her. There was nothing any foreigner could do.

But Ambyre would not allow it. She freed herself from Sigrid's touch and ran toward the old woman holding the naked child. All those around, shocked into stillness, merely watched as she tore it from the woman's arms and fled from the room.

She did not know where to go until she spied the wood where Torquil had taken her. Relief overcoming panic, she remembered the games he told her of. She sought the outlaw's den, thinking only of the child in her arms. By the time anyone in the longhouse had moved to follow, she was out of sight.

The shelter was hardly a room, more like an animal's den, dark, cramped, dank. She clung to the baby, holding it inside her cloak against her own warm skin. He did not cry.

She knew nothing of babies, indeed, she had very rarely seen one, so excluded were they from her life at Athelney and Winchester. She had no food to offer it, no way to build a fire to keep them both warm; she had only her cloak and this muddy, dreary cell, too small even to stand in. There was no door, just the small opening through which she had come, through which she could see if anyone approached. She heard nothing, saw no one.

She looked down at the tiny child in her arms. Had she done it any good? It could not survive here, alone with her. Both would freeze before long, or starve. Ambyre was hungry already. She had been with Kirsten and had not eaten since the day before.

Ice on the ground outside the opening left no tracks for the others to follow. She reached a hand toward it and broke off a chunk. Tearing a piece of her shift, she wrapped the ice in its fold, holding it in her free hand until it melted. She put it to the little mouth, which sucked eagerly although the liquid was still quite cold. Then she watched the child against her bosom as it fell into a peaceful sleep. She felt its little chest breathe deeply against her own and knew this baby was stronger than they'd thought.

Morning came and they were still alone, undetected. Light filtered through the opening. Ambyre longed to stretch, but could not. When the baby cried out, a soft, gurgling noise, she held him closer, muffling his gentle protests in the folds of her cloak. He remained warm. After a while she gave him more water. Then he slept again.

Of the two of them, the child seemed better adapted to the conditions. Ambyre's cloak, damp where she sat on it, was slimy with muck. So was the bottom of her pinafore and shift, not to mention her shoes. Her hands were dirty but dry, and the only clean place left on her was where the baby rested against her chest.

Neither of them would be able to survive this way. Before long, she would have to go back. But to what? Had any good at all been accomplished? Would she return only to have the child given back to the Angel of Death? The thought was intolerable but there was no choice. She could not remain here. The baby needed his mother's milk or even with Ambyre's protection he would die.

She waited until dark, hoping no one would detect her before she was able to take him to Kirsten. Her cloak was heavy with earth and dampness, but she no longer noticed. Her mud-covered shoes slipped on the ice. She balanced herself quickly, mindful of the child.

Kirsten's hut was the farthest from the cave. It was quiet and ominously dark. She peered around the open door. No hearth was lit. Empty. Where had they taken her?

"AElfwyn," the familiar voice sounded through the darkness, and she found herself relieved to hear it. "Come here."

She obeyed.

Raff fumbled with a strike-a-light against a flint, lighting the hearth, sending warmth into Ambyre's numb limbs. The child squirmed under her cloak. Raff looked at her, a filthy sight, defiant, firmly holding the child.

"There is nothing you can do," he told her bleakly. "He will die."

She lifted her chin, her determination unwavering.

He stepped closer. " 'Tis the right of the father to decide the fate of his child. Torquil has made that decision."

"He cannot allow this!"

"The babe is weak," Raff stated.

"And so you condemn him for leaving the womb too early? Perhaps that is all it is! He'll get stronger, Raff—he'll grow and straighten and . . . and be strong. Already he is better, only after being given water."

"Weaklings do not survive, AElfwyn. 'Tis better if he dies now than to suffer through life."

"You condone this abhorrent practice!" she

exclaimed. "Never before have I believed you truly barbaric; now I see. Fauntley was right! Ignorant savage who cares nothing for life! I shall be *glad* not to marry you!"

He stepped forward, taking her shoulders roughly in his hands, shaking her despite the cries of the child.

"You shall marry me, whether or not you care to. You shall be my wife for as long as I need you, and when I discard you, you can return to your own supposedly civilized race. Call us what you like, but while you are my wife, you shall be one of us."

"Never!" she retorted with hatred. "I shall never lower myself to your standards, never condone the murder of any child. The admiration I once had for your strength has turned to loathing. I see now why your people are strong. You murder the weak so that none exist. I'll respect no strength gotten by such means!"

His fingers tightened so that she felt his grip even through her turbulent emotion. Seeing her aversion and disgust, he pulled her to him regardless of the child between them. His mouth came down on hers harshly. He wanted to conquer that look of hatred. She struggled but was no match for him. The child's cry was muffled against them. Raff persisted; his mouth bruised her, his tongue invaded her, his arms pressed her to him. Then, in one unexpected movement, he snatched the child, taking it from the hut. In horror, she dogged his determined steps, tears staining her dirty face, following him to the longhouse.

The warriors were not yet asleep. When Raff entered with the child, they sat up, watching. She was at his heels. He went to her own room, which, to her surprise, was not vacant. The hearth was lit, and Kirsten lay in Ambyre's bed. Raff deposited the child next to its mother. Straightening to his full height, he looked at Ambyre impersonally, coldly.

"Consider yourself the victor, milady," he shot at her. "You have brought us 'civilization'—the breeding of weaklings."

He strode from the room, not looking back, leaving Kirsten in tears of gratitude and Ambyre triumphantly disheveled.

XV

The assembly of the nearby chieftains and warriors came to an end. Raff was chosen to lead the Danes into battle, since through him the alliance had been achieved. Should Ragnold attempt to take York, he would find a resistance he might not be anticipating. Some of the Danes were reluctant to fight alongside Edward's men, but others were eager to join this new source of strength. Most felt confident they could show their Saxon allies a few points about being a warrior.

So with this business at an end, preparations to sail were made once more. Only one ship was to go; Piers would stay behind while his brother went to Wessex to unite, through matrimony, the two races which inhabited the land. It would be a short journey compared to the others, so little was needed in the way of supplies.

Fauntley was jubilant. His happiness was

contagious even to Ambyre, whose emotions were in constant conflict.

The last meal before they were to sail was a feast, a wedding celebration to send off the bride and groom with blessings and hopes for a peaceful future.

The warriors seemed especially rowdy that night; there were countless challenges and great quantities of mead were guzzled. Torquil, somewhat subdued since the decision concerning his son had been reversed by Raff, now approached Ambyre with his old smile. He held out his horn goblet, offering her a drink to peace between them.

After the briefest hesitation, she agreed, finding his laughter preferable to Raff's scowl. She forgave him for his assault on her; she forgave even his abandonment of the child. Since it had been allowed to live it had grown strong on mother's milk. And though its legs turned sharply inward, who could say how that would affect its growth? But for the present it seemed healthy enough, and Torquil had even gone to visit. True, it had not been made legitimate, but Ambyre felt the gift of life to have been enough.

Raff said little to either of them, though gradually he lost his scowl as the aura of the evening intensified. It was a festival and he could not resist the merriment of his people. With the others, he bantered and boasted and sang sagas. He was challenged many times to contests with weaponry or bouts of wrestling.

He lost only once, in a contest which Ambyre thought merely amusing until told it was a battle skill that came in handy from time to time. One warrior, Orm by name, boasted he could jump the height of one tall horse while fully burdened with his weapons. Raff challenged him, saying with a laugh that Orm would have to possess the strength of that very horse in order to lift the bulbous belly he was forced to support.

The contest began; they donned the heavy accessories. Raff, as challenger, proceeded first. His legs proved strong, as if mighty springs were coiled inside. He jumped as high as his own height, but Orm still contended *he* could jump higher, as high off the ground as the tip of an ear of the tallest stalltion.

All gathered round as he made himself ready. He breathed deeply just once and stooped momentarily to prepare for his upward thrust. Then he jumped. A gasp sounded. Then cheers, for Orm had proven his boast to be true. Laughing, Raff accepted defeat and the two toasted each other with generous draughts of mead.

The evening was one to remember, a time out of time, capturing the hospitality of these people and the easy friendship they shared. Even Fauntley was laughing, for Sigrid had taken a liking to him and used her ready sense of humor to make him forget the past weeks of degradation.

He was going home the next day, and that was

enough to lighten his spirits. Once there, he could speak to Ambyre again of his love and petition Edward for her hand in marriage. It would not be easy, he realized, to request that of a man who held her as close to his heart as one of his own daughters. Even knowing he had the king's respect, Fauntley was still somewhat frightened of him. Perhaps it was only because he *was* king, for otherwise Edward was kind and generous. But Ambyre was so precious to him it gave Fauntley pause.

His eyes went to her across the table, seeing her laugh at something Torquil had said. She was so beautiful; even that frightened him. Who was he to dream of having such a wife? He often thought of what it would be like; he could refuse her nothing, of course. Still, Ambyre would never ask too much. He had little money, but life would be comfortable as long as the king continued to commission him as tutor. And with Edward's passion for knowledge, there was little possibility he would care to lose Fauntley's services. So Ambyre's life in Wessex should be little different from before, and he hoped that would help his cause. She could be sure what the future would hold. He knew women wanted security, and felt he could provide it.

He continued to gaze at her, unable to help himself. The pinafore she wore was tied at the waist, giving evidence of the shapeliness of her body. Each time such thoughts arose, he told himself to dispel influences of the devil. But just now it was exceedingly difficult. He longed to have her for many reasons, not the least of which was a carnal desire for every inch of her body. At times these thoughts were overwhelming.

"Be careful when you stare at a woman promised to another," Sigrid whispered.

He turned to her with a smile of chagrin, glad she was mistaken, that it was not really Ambyre promised to Raff. "True, milady. I shall keep my expression more guarded."

"It doesn't seem to matter though. My brother has noticed your stares and does nothing."

"Perhaps because he is assured of the alliance." Fauntley was glad that it would be another AElfwyn who married the barbaric Dane.

Outside, where the brawling clamor of the feast could barely be heard, two dark figures spoke in somber tones.

A circle of turf had been cut from the earth and hung suspended above them from an ornate spear. Where the turf had been cleared stood two boys drawing a dagger across the palms of their hands, their blood spewing free. They mixed this blood together, each other's with the earth, then fell to their knees as they swore an oath: from this day they were brothers. Brothers now reborn under the circular womb

NORTHWARD THE HEART

of Mother Earth, their blood one blood, to avenge or protect, until the last breath was drawn. A final, firm, solemn handclasp was the seal.

When Alf and Cuthbert returned inside, the evidence of their private ceremony was not overlooked. Their hands, crusted with dried blood and earth, were proof enough of the bond. Warriors laughed and cheered.

Olaf became aware of the covenant and called the boys to him with a grim expression. The room quieted as he spoke softly so that only those nearby could hear. Ambyre listened with curious concern.

"This oath is not a game for boys to play," he said.

Alf stepped forward, raising his chin, trying to grow to manhood before his father's eyes.

"I am almost fourteen, my lord," he announced. " 'Tis old enough to bear responsibility.

"This responsibility is not yours alone. You've made this Saxon your brother, a part of your family. A part of my family. Did you not consider my approval?"

"Raff did not when he took Bjorn as blood brother," Alf said defensively.

"It was not possible when they took their oath. They were across the channel, in Northman's Land. You had only to come to me, here within this room."

Cuthbert spoke boldly. "Would you have allowed it, milord?"

Olaf looked at him for a long moment before answering. "I have watched you among my household for only a short time, yet I have seen your eagerness and bravery and I commend you. But you are a Saxon nonetheless. You lived among us under the lies of your sister and tutor, allowing us to believe you were their son. Can Alf accept one who has been deceitful, even to himself?"

Alf spoke again. "He was not deceitful, my liege. He was true from the beginning, and under my oath I told no one of his secret."

Ambyre's eyes widened. Her identity had been threatened long before she knew it.

Olaf frowned. "You knew this, yet felt no obligation to your family to reveal it?"

"I had two obligations. One to my family, one to my friend. I did not think this minor truth to be worth breaking my friendship."

"And who is to say what is a minor truth? Your brother has planned many months for this alliance."

"And will have it, with the Mercians at least, whether or not this marriage comes to pass. I feel no remorse, my lord."

Olaf leaned back, recognizing the truth of his son's words. "Then I can expect no more. Your oath to this Saxon is recognized."

Joyous shouts were heard, and before Cuthbert completely understood, Alf clasped his arms and smiled with victory. He was welcomed with warm approval, and the festival went on with renewed buoyancy. Ambyre had

NORTHWARD THE HEART

no chance to confront him, to question him about how much of their secret he had revealed to Alf, for he was soon being challenged as Danish warriors had been. His acceptance was quick and immediate.

"It seems I have been too harsh on your Saxon race," said Raff quietly to Ambyre. "At least one of you possesses the knowledge of love."

She shuddered, and he took it for revulsion. "Are you offended that a barbarian has accused you of lacking the civilized ability to love?" he asked.

"You, my lord, are a fool."

He guffawed at her statement, throwing back his head, revealing a goodly amount of even teeth. "You would not be offended if I did not speak the truth. You call me fool; you attack rather than try to convince me my words are untrue."

"What would you have me do?" she asked angrily. "I have already tried speaking to you, but you will not listen. My attack, as you call it, is justified. You are, I truly believe, a fool."

Had those words come from any other mouth, slave or free, warrior or woman, Raff would have put a quick end to the life of the one who uttered them. Insults were not easily taken. But Ambyre sat, eyes defiant, chin held high, and he knew he could do nothing. Because she was the woman he loved—or once loved, he quickly amended his thought.

"In what way?" he asked. She glanced at him

quizzically. His voice sounded far too sincere. "In what way am I a fool?" he persisted.

"You are a fool for overlooking the obvious. I allowed you to find out about me because of the very love you say I do not have."

"You used your virginity as a tool, a way of avenging yourself," he told her. "You lured me to you, using your beauty, your laughter, to make a fool of me so I would act in just the way I did—as your secret lover. You seduced me."

Ambyre's mouth fell open and she spoke louder than she had intended. "*I* seduced *you*?" Immediately she lowered her voice, seeing Fauntley glance their way curiously. It was her turn to laugh as he had done.

"Who was it that came to my room in Iceland so late at night?" she insisted. "And who was it that sent you from that room before anything had happened?"

He remembered that first unsuccessful attempt. "You were merely building your web around a poor fly to insure your final victory."

"Who made it possible for what finally took place? *You* took me to that secluded cave! *You* seduced me!"

He waved off her protests. "I have had time to consider why you have done what you have done," he said. "You are proud, AElfwyn, and more dedicated to your King than to any living being. Your loyalty to Edward even outweighs that for your own kingdom. You *wanted* to see Mercia ruled by him, didn't you?" His tone was incredulous. "And because of me, Edward's reign there was threatened. So you attempted to destroy my plans, in order to keep your precious king's new domain safe. But you are to be commended nonetheless, Lady AElfwyn. You have proven the strength of your loyalty by extending it even to such personal property as your virginity. You will make a fine Dane, with your pride and dedication. 'Tis a shame your allegiance lies elsewhere."

Before she could answer, he was called away by a warrior, bow and arrow in hand. Though it had been dark for sometime, they went toward the door to proceed with a contest by lamplight.

Amybre was now out of tune with the festivities around her, depressed by Raff's attitude. The jovial villagers around her suddenly sounded loud and disorderly, creating a clamor in her head and making it ache. The feast had gone on for many hours. She realized with surprise how very tired she was. Raff had left his cup behind. She reached for one last swallow before excusing herself. Perhaps the heavy mead would put her to sleep before she could dwell on his words.

The vessel at her lips was suddenly scooped from her by a pair of firm hands. In confusion, she did not at first hear the nearby laughter. As another one was thrust into her hand, she looked up to see Torquil's merry face.

"You were to share mine this whole night through, milady. Had you forgotten, or did you wish to offend me?"

She gave him only a half smile, too tired for more effort. "I wish to offend no one."

She put his cup to her mouth, drinking thirstily, full swallows she had never allowed herself before. She felt the liquor warm her immediately. Sooner than she reached her bedchamber she felt the dizziness reach her head.

XVI

Ambyre opened one eye at a time, her lids heavy, reluctant. On seeing Cuthbert's concerned face hovering over her, she rubbed her puffy eyes and propped herself up on one elbow.

"It can't be time to sail already?" she inquired groggily.

"Nay, Ambyre," he whispered. " 'Tis not yet morning."

She laid her head back on the pillow. "I do not wish to rejoin the feast. I wish to sleep."

"The feast has ended . . . 'tis about Raff, Ambyre."

Her eyes opened again, focusing on her brother as if to discern the meaning of his words. "What has happened?" Her tone was alarmed.

"He's become ill . . . they say he may die."

She was on her feet before Cuthbert had finished the last word. "Where is he?"

He watched her don her pinafore and shoes as he answered. " 'Tis why I came to you. They've put him a tent, far from any hut or shed and will not allow anyone near. They've left him there to recover on his own . . . or die. They say it must be done with his own strength."

The words were hardly out as she stalked from the room. Such a custom was ridiculous, she thought to herself. Surely they would let her help him; they assumed she was to be his wife. Would they keep his wife from him?

A few warriors were still in the hall, those still awake reluctant to settle down for the night. Olaf sat by the hearth.

"I demand to see Raff," she stated imperiously, oblivious to the stares at her tone of voice.

Olaf said nothing. His eyes were circled with fatigue, his mouth drawn in a frown fixed upon his creased face. He motioned toward Wulfstan who came toward her and began leading her away.

Struggling, she spoke louder. "You must let me help him—or see that someone does. You cannot just let him die—your own son—your heir! How can you be so savage?"

"Hush, milady," Wulfstan whispered. "Say no more to our chieftain. He'll not allow you to break another of our customs."

"But this is wrong! What has happened to Raff? Do you let all your people die without help?"

She was brought to her chamber where Cuthbert opened the door, as Wulfstan explained, "Raff does not suffer from a wound, milady. If that were the case, he would have the finest care. He has become ill; an inner, unknown sickness has invaded his body to test his strength. It may take him to Valhalla or it may let him remain here to achieve a valiant death, but he must fight it on his own."

"I demand to see him!"

"You cannot. No one can, not even Olaf, until Raff walks from the tent by himself . . . or we smell the stench of death within. He shall remain there alone."

"Nay!" she cried, and attempted to run for the door, but Wulfstan caught her, holding her firmly as he spoke.

"You will not be allowed to interfere with another tradition, my lady. The most you can do is pray to the gods."

She sank in defeat onto the edge of the bed, holding her forehead in her hands. "What sort of illness is it?" Frustration gave way to hopelessness.

" 'Twas sudden when it took him," he told her quietly. "Many of those at the feast had already fallen asleep; there were only a few of us left when it happened: Piers, Torquil—"

"And Alf and I," Cuthbert quickly supplied.

"We were retelling stories for the benefit of the boys," Wulfstan went on. "One moment Raff was speaking, the next moment he was doubled over in pain, clutching his middle. 'Twas sudden, milady, as though he were struck with an arrow to the belly. But whatever it is strikes him from within. There is naught to do but wait."

Ambyre stood restlessly. "Not even go to his side? Comfort him? Wait on him? 'Tis now he needs me, Wulfstan, and I am held back by rules which can serve no purpose but to hasten his death."

She had not noticed the door being opened, nor the countenance of Fauntley as he heard her words and knew to whom she referred. He said nothing, and when her eyes fell on him with surprise, she was silent as well. She might have denied that she worried over a man supposed to be nothing more than her captor and enemy, but she did not. What purpose would it serve?

Fauntley stepped inside, ignoring Cuthbert and Wulfstan. He stood before Ambyre, eyes never leaving her face. "When I learned that Raff might die I came here to rejoice in our good fortune. But I see I am alone in my attitude."

She was annoyed by his words. What did he expect of her? To continue to deny what he must have guessed by now? No, she would not rejoice in this, nor would she cater to that forlorn look on his face.

"I'm sorry," he whispered, and she wondered about it. Was he sorry for Raff? For her? Himself? Indeed, he had reason only to be sorry for himself, for his dreams were being shattered.

He turned and left. She let him go. There was nothing she could do.

"I want to see where the tent is," she said after his departure. Wulfstan frowned. "Surely I can just look upon the tent?"

He led her outside. Dawn was near, but the village was still asleep after the night's feast. There was a hush, as if the earth and all its inhabitants held their breath out of respect for her concern.

The tent was well away from the last house of the village. There were no trees along the rolling wolds at this end of the province, so her view was unmarred. The shelter was small, with its flap closed. She could not imagine that it was very warm. Had they allowed him blankets? or a mat to protect his body from the frozen ground?

She could do nothing but look. Several of Olaf's retainers had been assigned to stay near the edge of the village, to discourage intruders. She had no doubts they were there for her benefit alone.

Wulfstan returned her to the longhouse. Once back in her room, she was left with Cuthbert and told to get some rest before the village awakened. As he withdrew, Wulfstan announced what she already suspected. "We will not sail...not until the outcome is known."

But when he was gone she could not sleep. There would be no rest until she knew that outcome.

"Tell me again how it happened," she asked of Cuthbert when they were alone.

He obliged, eager to be helpful. He recounted the event in detail, including even the story Raff had told before the seizure, which she recognized as one he had told her in the cave in Iceland. That seemed so long ago.

"And there was no warning?" she persisted, trying to find some cause. "He was not pale, nor drawn, nor tired?"

"We were all a little tired from the feast. We were the last awake."

"He looked no more tired than you yourself?"

"Nay," was his definite reply.

Ambyre stood decisively. She went to the door, stopped short, paced back and forth. "I must see him," she said. Though it was little more than a murmur, Cuthbert recognized her determination.

"You saw yourself that the tent is guarded," he warned.

"From the village side. If I could sneak out of the village and approach the tent from the other side..."

"But how? The sun is almost risen already."

"Then we'll not delay. Cuddy, give me your clothes."

"My clothes!" He was astonished.

"Aye, and this moment."

"But I've heard 'tis a crime to wear clothes of the opposite sex."

"And who is to punish me?" she demanded. "I'm not one of them. I'll neither abide by their laws nor their foolish customs. I *will* see him, and I can move easier if I'm not encumbered by the long folds of this shift. I'll need your cloak, too. 'Tis shorter than mine."

Cuthbert's clothes were not as comfortable as Fauntley's had been, but they were unobtrusive nonetheless. With her hair concealed under his fur hat, she resembled him at a quick glance.

Knowing there was safety in speed, she was out of the longhouse at a rapid but not urgent pace. She wished to attract no curious eye.

The sun, not yet visible but casting a pink announcement of its coming, was another cause of concern. Some of the villagers were just awakening, and she passed them by swiftly, ignoring any comments directed her way.

She went to the opposite end of the village from where the tent was, with its guards, and left from there. Hidden by the forest, she backtracked through the trees toward her destination.

The tent was at the top of a small, treeless hill. She went past it to the opposite base, creeping upward where the guards could not see her. At the summit, she peered in their direction. The tent flap faced them, within their view.

Their orders from Olaf had been to keep the Saxon maiden from entering the tent. It was only she, disrespectful of their customs, who offered any threat to tradition. So their eyes were directed more often toward the village, where they looked for any sign of her dark hair among the fairness of their own race. She didn't have to wait long before scurrying inside the tent, undetected by the watchful guards.

The smell of sickness filled the air. Raff lay on a cot draped in furs which he had kicked aside and left strewn about. He was unaware of her presence.

Though there was a chill and most of his covers were off, he wore no clothes. For a moment Ambyre merely looked at him, his hands upon his abdomen as though it still pained him.

When she stepped forward her foot caught one of the fallen blankets, causing it to pull away from his legs. His head tossed toward her.

"Who is there?"

Her anxiety heightened. The sun had risen, casting the tent in translucent brightness. Surely he could see her?

" 'Tis I, AElfwyn." She came closer.

He expelled his breath with disgust as his hands moved the blankets to cover himself.

"Was it not enough that you made me a fool?" he asked. "Do you wish to see me like this as well?"

"I wish to help you."

He sneered, and his next words came with undisguised sincerity. "Get out."

"Raff—"

"Get out!" His voice was surprisingly firm for one so pale.

Ambyre would have stayed, disobeying the command, had anyone but Raff ordered her to leave. Against his wrath, if even on his deathbed, she was helpless.

"I love you, Raff," she said, and then she was gone. She slipped from the tent under bright rays of sunlight filtering through early morning clouds. She went back the way she came, and, though less concerned about detection, she remained unnoticed.

Cuthbert was sleeping when she reached their room. She laid his clothes at the foot of the bed for his use, then redressed in her own and left in search of Wulfstan. She wanted to ask him again what had taken place, though she didn't imagine he would welcome her persistence. But there must be something, some reason for it, some warning or indication they had missed.

Wulfstan, however, was now asleep. As Ambyre returned to the room, she heard many who knew of Raff's sudden illness whisper in worried tones, pointing after her. 'Twas a shame, they said, that it had to happen during a wedding feast. Could it be an omen? She disregarded the curious glances cast in her direction.

Fauntley avoided her for the next few hours. As he thought about things, he saw what he had hidden from himself till now. How could he have been so blind? She actually cared for the savage! This was no silly, brief infatuation. No mere "interest" or respect because Raff, to his countrymen, was some sort of hero. This was love! She *must* love him if she cared more for his life then her own. Why had he never seen it before? Why had he fooled himself into thinking it was something so much less important?

But he knew the answer. He'd had such dreams. It was hard to admit jealousy, yet finally he could not deny it, not to himself. He should have known he was no competition for these virile warriors. It was true, even the youngest and weakest of them could best him. But he'd thought Ambyre could see beyond that difference! He thought she'd seen the strength in him, too.

To prove his strength, one not of brawn but of spirit, if only to himself, Fauntley stirred himself to action. If he could also prove that strength to Ambyre, he may not ever win her love, but he might at least earn her respect.

He found Piers in the stable tending to his horses. The two men had sailed for many days on the same small longship, and even though Fauntley did not entirely trust Piers, he did believe he could go to him for help.

When he mentioned his interest in Raff's condition, he was met with a curious look.

"Why should it concern you that my brother lies on his deathbed? I do not believe you would save his life for its own sake."

Fauntley's confidence ebbed a bit. Certainly Piers wouldn't understand his need to prove himself.

"I do it for my God," he said before he'd even considered the answer. That was at least partly true. "It is my Christian duty to help mankind."

"Even someone not of your faith?" Piers asked with an undisguised smirk.

"My God loves all mankind."

The smirk only grew. "Your god must wear himself weak, if he tries to answer the needs of all mankind."

"Perhaps He is powerful enough to succeed."

Piers was impressed with that, and it was Fauntley who now felt like smirking. Power, he thought, was another thing these barbarians understood. But he smiled politely, knowing he needed the young Dane's help.

Piers repeated what had taken place, describing Raff's actions during the evening as thoroughly as he could remember, up to and including the seizure that prostrated him. Fauntley listened carefully, finding little real evidence to work with.

"Did he eat anything the rest of you did not?" he asked when Piers had finished.

The response was thoughtful. "None of us had eaten for some time. The feast ended earlier, and only Torquil and I were still drinking. Raff hadn't had anything for quite a while."

"There are some poisons which delay their symptoms," Fauntley mused. "The body accepts them only to reject them much later."

"Poison!" Piers was thunderstruck. "I had not even considered it. But who could have done it?"

"I accuse no one. It could have been quite

innocent; a bad cut of meat, a soured vegetable. Has anyone else complained of illness?"

"Not to my knowledge. But perhaps we should keep this suspicion to ourselves for a while. 'Twould do no good to raise everyone's fears unnecessarily. Perhaps Raff is not seriously ill, and will be completely recovered on the morrow."

Fauntley nodded, though he wasn't quite willing to keep the idea to himself. Surely time was already against them if poison was indeed the cause. He left the stable, deciding to stroll through the village to see if anyone else complained of illness.

When Ambyre learned of his inquiries she went to him without delay, her mind too full to offer any more than a smile of gratitude.

"Then you will help him?" she asked in a soft, almost desperate voice. Fauntley could not refuse. "Do you think he has taken poison? Is that what his symptoms mean?"

"They might mean any number of strange diseases, milady. God only knows how many, and so few can be cured. But the severe pains in his stomach came on too quickly to be natural. Without warning or indication, it seems strange that his body would react in that way."

"Have any others fallen ill?" she asked, undeniably hopeful. Perhaps if some sort of unintentional food poisoning had been the cause, Olaf would no longer withhold treatment for his son. Surely once the sickness was understood, he would not let it ravage those who suffered.

But his answer crushed that hope. "No one else has been affected. If poison it is, then 'twas for Raff alone."

"Intentional . . . murder?" He nodded. "Who would do such a thing?" Then her eyes narrowed with suspicion. "Do you think Freyvold could have tried to take revenge for the death of his son despite everything?"

A shrug. " 'Tis possible."

She stood. "Then certainly they should treat this as a battle wound and not an inner illness testing him. They should let us help him now."

Before Fauntley could reply, she was off to find Olaf.

As usual, he sat by the hearthside, and again she forgot to address him in the manner expected. When she aired her suspicions and he remained aloof, she continued in her disrespectful tone. "Surely you'll do something now! You cannot just wait for this poison to take his life. Already it may be too late. You must—"

"Sit down, maid," he commanded with quiet assurance. She did so, restlessly. "You are not one of us," he went on. "You defy our customs. You are quick to mistrust even after an oath of peace. Should we send an envoy to Freyvold accusing him of this he would take great insult, and rightly so, if 'twas not his doing. Then all that Raff has put together would unravel. There would be no unity, no direction to work and fight side by side to expel our enemies. Raff himself would forbid the accusation of Freyvold."

"At the cost of his life?" she asked bitterly. "If they are to blame, will you continue this travesty of peace after the murder of your son?"

"We would have one assurance. There would be no more reason to resume our feud. Unity will be upheld."

"So you value the end of a feud more than your son's life."

"What I value is the beginning of harmony, of strength among our people. Raff would feel no differently."

"Can harmony be based upon revenge and murder?"

"If murder is the case. Only you suspect Freyvold. I do not."

"Who else could have done this? Who would want to?"

"Each of us has our enemies, Lady AElfwyn. Even you and your friend Fauntley have reason to wish my son dead."

"*We* are trying to help him—"

Olaf ignored her indignation. "I accuse no one. 'Twas not I who suspected poison to begin with. It may be Raff's own body revolting against him and no one is to blame."

"But you must find out!" she insisted. "You must send someone to Freyvold—"

"Nay." He spoke firmly, decisively. "If Raff was poisoned, the one responsible will step forward. Not one of us would commit a secret murder, not a Dane."

"So you will just let him die," she said quietly.

"There is no proof of intent to kill. 'Tis not for us to interfere with the proving of strength. Raff would not tolerate such an insult to his honor, whether he lives or dies."

"Your value of honor causes more death than battle," she told him with disgust.

"Without honor, a man has no reason to live."

More dejected than before, Ambyre seemed to have no luck petitioning Olaf. How could he be so obstinate when his son's life was at stake?

She left, found Fauntley and relayed all that was said. He took her back to her room where both sat in heavy-hearted silence.

"Fauntley!" He jumped as his name exploded from her. "Why have I been so dullwitted? Surely if Raff *knew* he had been poisoned he would *wish* for help. Which I can give him. I've broken their rules before and I shall do so again. Give me your clothes."

"Milady!"

"Tell me all you know about treating those who have been poisoned." She unhooked the bronze brooches at her shoulders. Fauntley watched, appalled.

"Little is known." he began, suddenly turning his back as she dropped her pinafore and stood in her linen shift. "Poisons are widely used for their effectiveness. Few have antidotes."

"But what can be done?"

"Milk can be given to dilute what has been

taken... induce vomiting... speed up elimination... food to absorb what residue may be left. But this must be done right away. The poison has worked within his body for hours now—they say the attack did not come until long after he had eaten. It must already be absorbed, else the symptoms would not be evident."

"Then we cannot delay. Are you going to give me *those* clothes or will you bring another set? And whatever else... milk, food, whatever I shall need to help him."

Fauntley did as she asked, deciding at that moment to accompany her regardless of her wishes. He would not have her sneaking around alone in men's clothing to help someone forbidden to receive it.

When Cuthbert entered and saw her again in masculine attire, he quickly recognized the plan.

"I want to help!" he insisted, but she shook her head. As it was, she didn't welcome his knowledge of her intentions. He kept no secrets from Alf.

"You can help by acting as guard. Let no one into this room, and tell anyone looking for us that Fauntley and I are here, not to be disturbed."

"They'll not take well to *that*, even if Raff is on his deathbed," the boy countered with wisdom beyond his years.

"Then 'tis your job to make it appear as innocent as it is," said Fauntley, and Cuthbert found the difficulty of such a task duty enough. He pressed for none further.

The longhouse was empty except for the slaves, so they had no trouble leaving. Outside, however, they attracted more than one curious glance, yet kept to a steady pace. No one actually interfered, for Ambyre's lithe body transformed well into that of a boy under the looseness of Fauntley's cloak.

They followed the route she had taken early that morning, now more than three hours past—three wasted hours. Fauntley carried what they would need, lithely dodging trees and shrubs, doubling back with her till they reached the hill behind the tent.

The guards at the edge of the village seemed occupied, backs to them, and Ambyre would have scurried forward had she not seen in time what held their attention. Olaf was between them, facing the shelter.

She crouched, frustrated, telling Fauntley what she saw.

"We'd best wait until he departs," he suggested. "At his age his eyesight should be weak, but I've seen no evidence of it before. 'Tis better not to risk being caught."

The wait seemed interminable. Each time she peered over the summit, Olaf was there, unwavering, staring at the tent flap as if willing it to open and bring froth his son.

When at last he turned back to the village, she seized the moment. The guards watched him go, their backs still to the tent. A quick motion to

Fauntley and they were inside, undetected.

Raff was motionless, pale as death. The urgency with which she went to him tugged at Fauntley's heart. Beckoned to follow her, he began his ministrations.

Raff woke at the touch, unsteady, eyes out of focus.

"Drink this," Ambyre gently commanded, holding a cup to his lips. She held his head with her other hand but he would not open his mouth except to inquire groggily what it was.

"Oil and water," she replied. "To help bring up the poison."

"Poison?"

" 'Tis the cause of your sickness."

He shrugged her hand away, letting his head fall back to the pillow. "Nothing left to bring out. Done nothing but puke till only dry fits."

"But there may be some residue—"

"Take your potions. Need no help."

She reached for the leather pouch of milk. "Drink this, at least. 'Tis just milk to coat your stomach—and dilute anything which may be left."

To her surprise, he sat up. "I tell you there is nothing left."

Without reply she stared, seeing his renewed strength, strength he had not shown earlier. He rubbed his eyes, then saw Fauntley for the first time.

"Now I am sure this is a plot to see me dead. Do you Saxons like to watch an enemy in pain?"

She helped him as he got unsteadily to his

feet. "Raff, you are well!" Her arms were about him. For the first few moments he did not resist, Fauntley watched, appalled at her contact with a naked man.

Raff's gaze began to focus on her. "I see you have returned to wearing men's clothes. You are determined to flout our customs."

She smiled uncertainly, too glad of his recovery to heed any scolding.

"Hand me my breeches, will you?" he asked of Fauntley, who obliged with great relief. Once dressed, Raff rubbed his eyes again as if to force them into service. He breathed deeply, coughed, then turned his back on them as he headed toward the opening.

"You will follow me to my father," he said over his shoulder. "You will tell him that you come here deceitfully, but that you only woke me. You must tell him that I accepted none of your potions. Do you understand?"

Ambyre spoke as she neared him. " 'Tis the truth."

The guards were plainly stupefied to see Raff emerge with the two Saxons at his side. Knowing that Olaf would be angry at their failure, they followed, ready to take whatever punishment he issued.

Olaf was not alone when they got to the longhouse. To Ambyre's angry surprise, Freyvold was seated with him. She could not put suspicion of him out of her mind.

When Olaf saw his son, he abruptly stopped speaking to Freyvold and stood, eyes wide with joy, hands rising to greet Raff, returned from the dead. No words were exchanged, just a firm, eager grasp of each other's arms. Words were not necessary.

Freyvold, too, stepped forward, then offered Raff his seat, which was accepted without hesitation.

"Tell him," Raff commanded, his voice breathless.

Fauntley then revealed how they had crept inside the tent with their remedies. But he finished in a firm tone that could not be doubted.

"They are all still untouched within our sacks. His recovery was unassisted."

Olaf now turned to Ambyre, his mouth grimly set.

"Go, change into your own clothes and return here."

She could not believe he thought her clothes more important than the current confrontation. Beside him was the man she suspected of having administered poison. How could he send her away with so petty a command? Raff was supposed to be her betrothed. Did that not give her a right to stay?

For a moment she didn't move. But, unwilling to be disobeyed before a fellow chieftain, Olaf cast her a glance that penetrated to her better judgment. She turned on her heel, determined to be quick to return.

Though gone for only minutes she found it long enough for Freyvold to have taken his leave. Raff looked as though the task of sitting alert was almost beyond his strength. And Fauntley stood like some underfed warrior, sacks of antidotes beside him instead of weapons.

Since Olaf had commanded Ambyre to return it was he who had, by custom, to speak first. But rashly she now demanded to know where Freyvold had gone.

"Be still," he warned her, striking fear into Fauntley that she obviously lacked. How could she dare disregard someone not unlike a King? Instead, she disobeyed yet again.

"Your son has been poisoned and the only enemy he has is the man you just let go! Did you at least question him on the matter?"

Surprisingly, Olaf responded kindly. "There is no need, lady. He came here because word had reached him of the suspicious nature of Raff's illness. He knew there would be those, like you, accusing him, and he came to put aside those rumors. He assured me there was no poisoning done by his hand, or by any from his province."

Her face was set in angry disbelief, until his next words brought on astonishment. "You were wrong when you said my son has only one enemy. He has many; some Saxon, some French from his years spent in Northman's Land across the Channel. There are even some among us who would hope to see another succeed me, who count Raff as a natural enemy. There is also you, milady."

Stunned to silence, she let him continue.

NORTHWARD THE HEART

"My son kidnapped you forcefully from your home. He thought, before knowing you, that an alliance between yourself and our people would be welcome. Not only would it strengthen both armies against the Norwegian Ragnold, but it would also restore some of the honor you lost at the hand of your uncle. You would be wed to a strong leader; your Mercian loyalists would be eager to look again to you for leadership.

"But now we see your allegiance is to Edward alone, that you have no desire to keep Mercia separate from Wessex. To this end, to insure your King's hold upon the whole of Mercia and all the reaches of this isle, even to my own doorstep, you have tried more than once to thwart this plan. Because of your loyalty to Edward, you do not wish for an alliance by marriage, for the very reasons we thought you would welcome it. You do not want the Mercians looking to you, thinking you are capable of ruling them at the side of a strong husband. You wish them to look to Edward alone. For that reason you thwarted the plan to set you back upon your throne. Now you wish to crush the idea of marriage to my son, fearing that, too, may jeopardize Edward's new leadership of Mercia. So you, lady, are the enemy nearest to Raff."

"You accuse *me* of poisoning him?" she whispered, aghast. Would no one believe she loved him?

"You have been disruptive many times during your short stay among us. First you led us to believe you were already wed, then when we planned instead to return your throne to you, you revealed your deceit in hope of gaining time. Time for Edward to plan against us.

"May I also remind you, lady, of a day not long after you first arrived here?" Olaf continued steadily. "You coerced my son into taking you to the holy ground where he would be weaponless. You wanted him there alone. You led him into ambush. It was fortunate the man died before he could name you as the one who bribed him. Of course, as I said, Raff has other enemies eager to do him harm. Without proof, there are only suspicions."

Raff, who seemed to be enjoying her discomfiture, now spoke with a wan smile. "And let us not forget one night on shipboard. I have told no one, milady, how you reached for my dagger to plunge it into my back. 'Twas only your cowardice which stopped you then. You prefer someone else to bloody his hands as most women do."

Ambyre, recovering her pride if not her defiance under this litany of condemnation raised her chin. "If you believe any of this, why do you allow me to live?"

Raff answered. "Because, as you see, I am still here. And for now you are worth more to us alive than if we indulged our vengeance with your death. I shall, of course, be more wary of you, since your methods seem to be proving more successful, but you will be allowed to live and fulfill the alliance."

Ambyre wanted to run away, finally

accepting the fact that he did not and would not believe the truth. For Olaf to doubt her was to be expected. He had reason to look everywhere for enemies of one of his clan. But for Raff to doubt her, she who loved him and had tried to tell him so, was too much to bear before them.

Fauntley, however, did not have the same emotional problems. "You are a witless fool!" he blurted at Raff. "You have her love, which by no means do you deserve, and you toss it away!"

Raff gave him a sidelong grin. "She has a most unusual way of expressing it, wouldn't you agree?"

"She had nothing to do with any attempts to murder you!" Fauntley rose like a warrior to Ambyre's defense.

"What of the night when she held the dagger in her own hands. Surely you cannot deny intent to kill?"

"But she didn't go through with it! Believe me, if she had wanted to kill you, if she had not suspected her love even then, she would have done it. A coward she is not."

Silence. Ambyre whispered gratefully to Fauntley, "You have proven my dearest friend, but 'tis no use. Let us go."

He followed her, as she bade him, to the privacy of her room. Once there, neither spoke. She sat dejected; he sat worried about her. He wanted to shake her, shake her free of that stubborn love so she could see the foolishness of it. But it would have been useless.

"They are so convinced 'twas I who tried to

kill him," she said at length. "It seems they are willing enough to believe 'twas poison, if 'twas I who gave it to him."

"Some of their evidence is indisputable," he replied. "The dagger... the lie about our marriage. Tell me, Ambyre, *did* you lure Raff to their holy ground as they said you did? I remember that day; you were acting so strangely, I knew something was astir. Yet you knew nothing of their customs about holy ground. Why did you not tell them that and defend yourself on one count at least?"

She breathed deeply. "Because I knew."

His eyebrows shot up. "You *knew*... then you *did*—"

She nodded miserably. " 'Twas not my idea, but I cannot deny my guilt. Torquil instigated it."

"Torquil! Why didn't you tell them?"

"What difference would it make except to get the boy in trouble? It was my doing."

"Torquil is certainly no boy; he is old enough to have his actions noted and accounted for. What reason did he give for wanting Raff dead?"

"He thought Raff was risking war with Edward—that it was for the good of the people. But he regretted it later. Once war with Edward was avoided, he was sorry about the whole thing."

"How can you believe any of these barbarians?" Fauntley exploded. "If he tried to kill Raff before..."

But Ambyre wasn't listening, unable to pull her mind from the accusations made against her. "Have they forgotten that I broke their law to try to *save* him? All that I have tried to do is *help*. Why don't they see that?"

She groaned. "Can I do nothing right when it comes to this man?"

Later, Fauntley found Piers being instructed by Ouse, an elderly man with thin, blond hair and a beard that had become sparse with age. His skin had few wrinkles, but his body displayed its age in labored movement. Ouse was one of the lawspeakers, a privileged position among Northmen, for at assemblies it was he who recited each of the laws of their land. In one of the storerooms he was now teaching Piers to commit these laws to memory, in order to carry on in the old man's place.

"I meant no intrusion," Fauntley apologized as Piers hesitated with his repetitions.

The young Dane's smile welcomed him. " 'Twas not because of you that I stopped. I simply forgot which law comes next. Truthfully, I welcome any intrusion to save me from this."

Fauntley stepped closer. Ouse laughed. "Perhaps this Saxon youth could teach you, Piers. I've heard tales from the men that he was trained for the mind rather than the body."

He did not add the scorn that had gone with the comments, nor the epithet *kjerringa*. Ouse, unlike his clan brothers, respected wisdom and education, even if they did not bring glory.

Fauntley welcomed his praise. "I have very little knowledge of your laws, though I have heard they are respected by whomever comes to know them. I would welcome an opportunity to learn."

The old man was gratified. "When Piers learns, he will teach you. I am too old for more than one pupil."

"At least if the pupil is as slow to learn as I," Piers laughed. His teacher stood, with a gradualness imposed by age-stiffened bones, giving him a smile that bespoke compassion. Ouse remembered how long it had taken for him to learn all these laws, learn them without error, for his people depended upon the law-speaker to hand them down through the generations.

"You are not slow," he said, "just filled with the impatience of youth. You will learn."

He headed toward the door, seeming to know the lesson had ended for the day, and left with one final admonition for Piers to recite everything again before going to sleep.

As the door closed, Fauntley spoke without the lightness his tone had held. "I came about these poisoning suspicions again."

Piers did not seem to welcome the topic, but asked nonetheless, "Has my father accused you of poisoning Raff?"

"Not I. AElfwyn."

"I should have warned you. Olaf will sooner suspect a Saxon than a fellow Dane, even if that Dane has motive. But you should realize that if *you* stop talking about poison the whole thing will be forgotten. Perhaps that would be best for all concerned."

"Even if I know it was Raff's own brother who poisoned him?"

"Do you accuse me?" Piers developed an angry twitch at the corner of his mouth.

"Torquil," said Fauntley with assurance, adding, "Perhaps my eagerness to clear suspicion from AElfwyn has pushed me to recklessness, but I truly believe him capable."

Instead of the rash of loyalty he would have expected between two Danish brothers, Piers invited him to go on. He related Torquil's plan involving Ambyre, instigated in the name of devotion to the people. He made it clear that if Torquil had once sought to kill Raff, he could have done so again.

"I have not known him to be so eager to avoid war," Piers replied slowly. "If indeed he told AElfwyn he wished to kill Raff in order to avoid war with Edward, 'twould have been most unlike him."

"There can be no doubt she speaks the truth."

Piers expelled a breath, his brows drawn into a frown. He turned from Fauntley, pacing the room once in slow, preoccupied steps.

"Torquil is my brother," he said, "and I should uphold him to the death, but in this I cannot. I will tell you of him, though I, son of the same father, cannot tell much. He has few friends; he is very secretive. Yet I remember well enough what sort of child he was, before he learned to hide what he felt. He was always envious, toward anyone or anything, especially within the family. He was furious when Alf was born, who was now the youngest and received more attention than he. Alf was not expected ... my mother was getting older ... he was a pleasant surprise and because of that, perhaps a bit spoiled."

"Seems a natural sibling jealousy," commented Fauntley.

"Aye, toward Alf I could understand. But Dyrk, just a year older than Torquil, suffered the same resentment. Even as they grew up to be the best of friends, at times Torquil's feeling was obvious. Dyrk was exceptional in everything. He would have made the finest warrior in our village; the strongest, the quickest, the most brave. He was smaller than Torquil, but that didn't matter. He outlasted him in any challenge, and so the rancor grew.

"And I? I am probably the worst of warriors, but have abilities Torquil doesn't. I am to be the next lawspeaker and will be considered very important to our village. It will depend upon *me* to hand down our laws which are sacred to us. Torquil covets the position this puts me in, one of respect and a certain amount of power. I shall be almost ... *almost* as powerful as Raff.

"Then, of course, there *is* Raff," Piers continued with a sigh. "In him Torquil has many things to begrudge. He is next in line to be Chieftain. But beyond that, Olaf and Raff are more than father and son; of all his children, Raff is closest to him. 'Tis more because of this that Torquil hates Raff. Even Sigrid, our sister, enjoys more love from Olaf than Torquil. I have seen this hatred in him, bitterness at not being the most loved. There were times when I suspected him of..."

His voice dwindled, as if he were reluctant to share surmises he was not proud of.

"I always thought he had found a friend in Dyrk; they were like twins. They trained together. For years they were as close as Cuthbert and Alf are today. And yet... when Dyrk died mysteriously in his sleep, I could not stop the thoughts from forming. Even with that closeness there were times when Torquil would look at him with hatred. When Olaf commended him for superior skill and said nothing to Torquil, I would see the hatred he was too young and inexperienced to hide.

"The night Dyrk died the two of them had been drinking heavily. They both got sick, since their youth had not yet given them a tolerance for the mead, and slept in the hut that Torquil still uses, which they built together. They were alone that night, and when I came to wake them in the morning, I found Dyrk dead. Torquil was sleeping at his side."

"Do you think?..."

"No one accused him, of course. 'Twould have been secret murder to kill and not admit it.

That is the most shameful of all crimes—much worse than to confess for whatever reason, even an accident. Instead, our people called it death by spirits. They could not accuse one of Olaf's sons, the very brother of the victim. So they said the maran spirits of the night took Dyrk to the their world. He died not only upon his bed, shameful in comparison to a battle death, but also without his weapons. 'Twas not a proud passage for him; during their drinking, Dyrk had become separated from his weapons. People said he must have done something wrong no one knew of; that spirits took his weapons away so he would not be remembered as a warrior."

"But you do not believe this?"

Piers smiled. "I have a confession for you, Fauntley. I may not believe in your Christian god, but neither do I believe in any maran of the night. Certainly none powerful enough to take a man's life. I'll not forget Torquil's face when I woke him; he seemed to know already. He asked me if I'd wakened Dyrk, and I saw the anxiety in his face."

"If you suspected him, why did you never speak to Olaf about it?"

"These are suspicions I have admitted to no one, save you. I am not proud of them; Torquil is my brother and I do not want to believe ill of him. But I cannot deny that I believe him capable of killing one of his brothers."

"Will you tell Olaf now if I go with you?"

Piers' face clouded. "I cannot. Not without

evidence. What father would be willing to believe this of one of his sons with no proof beyond mere conjecture?"

Fauntley could only admit the wisdom in Piers' words. "Then we must find evidence," he said. "Are you willing?"

The nod came, reluctantly, perhaps a bit sadly, but it came.

XVII

Kirsten led Torquil through the quiet longhouse toward Ambyre's room. Most of the warriors, after sporting with their favorite wenches, had fallen asleep. Torquil himself was tired, but curious. He'd had a full evening, with his choice of the new slave girls recently purchased at York. But as the Saxon had always intrigued him, he could not refuse her invitation. She was proud as any Dane and courageous enough to defy Olaf, whom Torquil himself had difficulty opposing. Even more intriguing was her beauty. She had never flashed him a smile to nurture any hope. Quite the opposite. Yet obviously she'd forgiven him for past grievances and now sought his company. As he went in, Kirsten discreetly left.

Ambyre's smile of greeting was not the sultry one he wished for. Friendly enough, but hardly an indication of what lay inside her heart. He waited for her to speak, his own smile not betraying the hopes he bore.

"Sit by me, Torquil," she invited. He did so after the briefest hesitation.

Their backs were to the room's single decoration, the unfinished tapestry left from the room's former use as a sewing closet. It hung like a heavy curtain, separating one small corner from the rest of the room. Torquil took no notice of it.

"Do you remember when I first came here, Torquil?" she asked. "You summoned me and explained what troubled your mind. You expressed your fears and loyalties, your ambition to see your people safe, even at the great cost of your brother. You explained why you would sacrifice his life for their benefit."

"Aye, milady; I had little choice, as I saw it then," he replied. "But now, Raff lives and we should be glad my misguided scheme never succeeded."

She turned to him, their faces close. "Are you?" she asked earnestly. "Are you glad he still lives?"

He shrugged off her sobriety, answering in a light, friendly tone. "Of course I am glad. He is my brother, born of the same blood."

She frowned. "I had hoped... but no, I cannot go on. I should not have disturbed you at so late an hour, Torquil. Please... forgive me. You must go."

She was about to stand when he grabbed her

wrist and forced her to stay, his face covered with confusion. "My lady, do not send me away without some word, some reason. Have I not been honest with you? Will you not be the same with me?"

She breathed deeply. " 'Tis hard, Torquil, in view of your new devotion to your brother."

"Do not be afraid. Whatever is said here will go no further. Did we not share the cup of friendship at the last feast? You have my trust, let me have the pleasure of yours."

She nodded slowly, almost imperceptibly, still allowing him to hold the wrist he had taken moments before. "Do not hold against me what wishes I shall reveal. Do I have your promise?"

"I shall always respect you, milady."

She gave him a grateful smile, at the same time gently pulling away to stand with her back to him. He could see it was hard for her. He was patient.

"I was hoping for an ally as well as a friend," she began. "I cannot do alone what I wish to, and am without hope now that you refuse to help me."

He stood behind her, laying his hands upon her shoulders. He was tall, and though Ambyre stood higher than most women, he rose above her. His lips fell gently on the back of her hair, sucking in breath as if to taste the very scent of her. Her aversion was mixed with relief that he was so eagerly taken in by her plan.

"Do not discount me yet, milady. What is it

you wish?"

"Your brother . . . this betrohal. I cannot go through with it."

He turned her to face him. "But why? You have given your word."

" 'Tis true," she said miserably. "But only under such pressures that it cannot be binding. What choice have I had in this? If I do not agree, Raff will force war against Edward by restoring my throne. He does not understand; I am not like my mother; I cannot rule. I was not bred for it—and haven't the desire my mother had. I have only loyalty to my king, with whom your brother risks war. For that I can never forgive him. I cannot marry him. I must marry only at the command of my sovereign, for his good, not at the threat of someone who forces his will, as Raff has done."

Torquil perused her so closely that she felt heat rising from her chest. He spoke before the blush darkened her face.

"I am surprised, milady, since you seemed so concerned about my brother during his recent illness. Why is it you tried to help him?"

She laughed, which sounded harsh even to her own ears. "Have you, a Dane, not reckoned the truth? I hoped he would die, but if there were any chance of recovery I wanted to make it shameful for him—so shameful he would wish he hadn't recovered. What man would wish to live if he owed his life to a woman's remedy? I meant only to steal the victory he now claims."

Torquil's laugh was filled with genuine surprise. "You are a formidable enemy, AElfwyn. You've learned to attack with the mind. To a Dane that is more fierce than the sword. My poor brother Raff hasn't a chance."

"I would have used those very words, having enlisted your help. But I am abandoned."

"I don't understand. I thought you wished for peace. By marrying Raff you will insure it."

"At too great a price to my king! How can he allow another to dictate to him? One who kidnapped me, who now threatens to marry me by force. Hardly the conduct of a man offering his allegiance. Through you, I hoped for an answer. You were not loath to do away with your brother when you had reason . . . I sought to give you reason again."

"You think war would be avoided if Raff were dead?"

" 'Twould be an end to his plan, would it not? Edward's honor would be upheld, with no reason to retaliate against your people."

"But Edward has agreed to the betrothal."

"For my safety!" she insisted, believing that much to be true. "Torquil, listen to these thoughts I've had—thoughts you've been part of. Should Raff die, Piers is in line to become the next chieftain after Olaf. But with your help I could convince my uncle to make his peace with you, for saving me from Raff's ruthless tactics. Then who would your people turn to? To Piers, who did nothing, or to you, their deliverer?"

Torquil raised his hand, causing her to

hesitate in surprise.

"True, I did seek to kill my brother once ... and I also have known hours of regret over it. 'Tis not I you should ask. By your own admission, Piers now has most to gain. Speak to Piers, milady," he finished quickly.

"But all that would change once I spoke to King Edward. Peace would have come because you helped me—your people would want *you* as chieftain then."

Torquil was shaking his head. "Nay, milady. I would not kill Raff to become the next chieftain—even though I have reason to want him dead."

"What reason?" she asked curiously.

He looked away for a moment as if deciding whether he could trust her. Then he spoke slowly. " 'Twas not only for peace that I arranged the ambush. That was just a small part of it. Truth is, I did it for my father's respect."

He suddenly laughed, full of bitterness. "But 'tis only Raff who has it," he continued, tense with emotion. "Raff is the one he loves. Does he ever look to me for counsel? For the future welfare of our people? Only to Raff. Aye, I would have seen him dead when I had that chance—I would have saved our people from war, and Olaf would have been proud of *me*, of his son Torquil, for the first time." He sighed heavily, his voice seeming to lose urgency. "Instead, Raff is alive and his plan will succeed without war. And Olaf will have more reason to be proud of him. As for me . . . if my father ever learned what I tried to do he would forsake me. I could never add that to the suspicions he already has. Then he would surely blame me for Dyrk's death."

"What has that to do with this?"

He seemed reluctant to answer. "My brother Dyrk died suddenly . . . under mysterious circumstances. 'Twas murder, everyone is sure, but they all resorted to our pagan beliefs by calling it a spirit-murder instead of accusing me, since I am a son of the chieftain. And my father too must think that I killed him. Who else could have done it? Even I myself sometimes . . . We had been drinking too much . . . I can't remember that night."

"Do *you* think you killed him?"

He returned to the bench, holding his forehead, running his fingers through his hair.

"I don't know," he whispered. "I loved him . . . he was my brother, my friend. I did love him . . . more than I envied him. But I did envy him, too. My father loved Dyrk more than any of us, it seemed. He would have been the greatest warrior of our clan."

Ambyre heard the pride in his voice. At that moment she could not believe him responsible. But Torquil himself did not seem so sure.

"Being envious doesn't mean you wished him dead," she told him gently.

He was grateful for her comfort. "I've tried to

convince myself of that, milady."

She did not speak for several moments, but sat beside him. As she did, she glanced at the tapestry concealing the alcove. Behind it hid Piers and Fauntley, waiting for her to lure the truth out of Torquil. And in her opinion she had done it. But did they think so? They wanted him to be guilty. Would they condemn him without a confession?

"I cannot ask you to help me, then," Ambyre said quietly. "Though I must admit, I thought I might have a partner in you. Do you know, Torquil? I thought *you* had put poison in Raff's cup. I remembered how you bade me drink only from yours. I thought you had known what was in his."

"Nay. Had I known, I'd not have let him drink. But if poison it was, it's gone now and we can be thankful." He stood, gazing down at her for a long while. She did not meet his eyes. "I came here tonight hoping for more than conversation, Lady AElfwyn," he whispered. "But perhaps we should both resign ourslves to your coming marriage. You will grow to love Raff. Most do."

"Do you?" she asked steadily.

He smiled slowly, then turned away and walked to the door. With one hand on the latch, he said as he left, "Aye, milady, I do."

* * *

Ambyre and Fauntley stayed away from the hall the following day. If their absence was noted, nothing was said. Through the day Raff regained much of his strength, and if poison had indeed been the cause, then it no longer mattered. He proved stronger than it.

The two Saxons stayed in her chamber, hungry but stubbornly refusing to share a festive evening meal with heathens who thought them capable of intent to kill.

They discussed it at length, going over each word Torquil said the night before until they both agreed that without a suspect, without proof that Raff had indeed been poisoned, perhaps Olaf was right to say his body had tested him.

She fervently prayed this conclusion was correct. For if poison truly had been administered, someone meant to murder. And because the attempt failed once didn't mean another wouldn't be made...

Fauntley had been sure of Torquil's guilt... but even he, on hearing the young man speak, came to the same conclusion: innocent, at least in this.

By the time he returned to his corner of the hall to sleep, most of the warriors were already abed. It was not long before the crease upon his brow smoothed into sleep, for he knew, with Raff so swiftly recovered, sailing to Wessex would soon be at hand. Home!

'Twas a fine, clear morning, Cuthbert had noted to Alf when he bade him walk in the forest. The sky shone a bright blue with no clouds to mar its endless color. Sounds of the forest came sharp—a doe running from bow-distance, a rabbit scampering in fright. Birds' wings sounded just overhead, yet were far in the distance. Alf and Cuthbert leaned against a tall oak to watch and hear.

Neither spoke for a long while. When they heard footsteps on the frost-covered greensward, Alf subtly nudged his friend. They watched unobserved as Piers came into view.

The newcomer did not see the boys watching, though his eyes skimmed the area to assure himself he was alone. Then he dropped a small leather sack, wrapped both palms round the leather-covered handle of his axe, and chipped away at the firm ground at his feet.

Curious, the boys silently watched, not betraying their presence. Piers dug a sizeable hole for such a small pouch, covered it carefully with earth and dead fronds to make sure it would be unnoticeable to the eye. Once satisfied, he turned back toward the village. They heard his footsteps until he descended one of the wolds in the distance.

Neither Cuthbert nor Alf needed to speak their intentions. Both went forward in the same moment, without question, intent on learning what Piers had so secretively rid himself of.

They unearthed the contents in much less time than it had taken Piers to bury it. Alf lifted the sack, opening the corded top and peering inside. But what he saw made him frown. Not gold, as he expected, hidden from plunderers and pirates. It was a dried substance that looked more like shriveled mushrooms than anything of value. Alf handed it to Cuthbert who was equally puzzled.

"Shall we just bury it again or try to find out what it is?"

Alf laughed. " 'Tis my brother who hid it—I should not betray his secret. But there can be no harm in finding out what it is. Perhaps 'tis of some value—some magic brew he bought at York."

"Whom do we ask? Surely not Piers."

"Your Fauntley might know. Or the old crone; she'll know if he doesn't."

They were off in a moment, leaving a hole gaping in the earth which Piers had so carefully covered with fronds.

The boys found Fauntley alone in the storeroom repairing his shoes with needle and strip leather.

"Can you tell me what this is?" Cuthbert asked, handing him the pouch. "We thought it must be of great value, since someone took the time to bury it. Do you know?"

Fauntley set aside his shoe and opened the sack, pouring a portion of the contents into his hand. Puzzled for a moment, since such an oddly-dried collection of plant life was hardly worthy to be called valuable, he sniffed it and studied it closely. As it separated, the mushroom shape of certain pieces was soon apparent, and he frowned. Slowly, he returned the contents to the sack, then looked up at the boys from where he sat.

"Where did you find this?" He pulled the cord to close the contents carefully within.

"Among the northern wolds, outside the village."

"You just happen upon it? Did you say it had been buried?"

"Do you know what it is?" Alf asked, ignoring the questions.

Fauntley stood. "You will come with me," he demanded, walking decisively toward the hall, boldly calling after Raff who headed toward the door.

He turned, annoyed at such a tone. His men were outside the longhouse, some to go with him to the ship, being readied to sail to Wessex the following day. Others awaited orders to load provisions. Raff did not like them hearing him summoned so curtly.

"Look at this," Fauntley told him, carefully pouring some of the dried mushrooms into his palm.

Raff, uninterested, looked at him expectantly.

" 'Tis the death-cup mushroom. A poison—the same sort you may have taken."

"Oh?" he said with one lifted brow, adding derisively, "Did the Lady AElfwyn give this to you?"

" 'Tis nothing to scoff at, Raff Olafsson. If you ingest but one small portion of this you are doomed."

"Ha! I have passed that danger, have I not? Now tell me where you got it."

"We gave it to him," Alf announced. "We found it."

Raff's eyes returned to Fauntley.

"And what makes you think this is what rendered me ill? These boys certainly did not seek to kill me with it."

"Nay, but whoever buried it may have. There is a powerful evil within this mushroom, with many different poisons in one. Some you have already survived . . . the others you will not."

"You are a mad little man." Fauntley barely heard him as Raff turned away without thought, just as Piers entered the longhouse in search of him.

"Why do you linger? The men are impatient."

"I am coming—the *kjerringa* was showing me a poison."

"Oh?"

Piers' eyes went to the sack in Fauntley's hands, to the loose substance he was carefully returning to safety.

"He brings the omen that I am to die," Raff said, laughing. "For a Christian, he certainly sounds like our own old crone."

"Given to telling oracles, are you?" Piers asked lightly, but Fauntley spoke to him in earnest.

"This is it, Piers, the evidence we needed to convince Raff he has been poisoned—and *not* by AElfwyn, since she knows nothing of this sack. 'Tis the death-cup, a poison that works in two intervals. It first attacks some hours after eating, then retreats for a second—fatal attack—some days later. 'Twas found outside the village . . . we must find out who buried this."

Alf and Cuthbert watched with thumping hearts as Piers gazed at the leather pouch and calmly denied knowledge of it.

"Try our Angel of Death," he suggested. "To her this would be some sort of treasure worthy to be buried for safekeeping."

"Don't you want to look into the matter yourself?" Fauntley asked Raff.

" 'Tis of no interest to me."

"This could be your death!" But Fauntley had spoken to his back. He was already gone, following behind Piers.

Alf and Cuthbert spent the day in anxiety. They did not reveal what they knew to Fauntley. There was little *he* could do. They must wait and speak to Raff himself. Alone.

Fauntley, however, went directly to Ambyre with the sack and its contents.

"But Raff is well!" she insisted. "He said the poison rid him of all that was within."

Fauntley shook his head. "Somehow the body expels all but the strongest poisons. 'Tis part of the drug's power."

"Then we must find out who buried it," she said, suddenly decisive, unemotional.

She took the sack from him, forgetting all the decisions she had made the night before. Torquil was the first they sought.

"Is this yours?" she demanded, having spotted him with his bow and arrow behind the longhouse. Not far away was a runner and at the end of the clearing, a target.

Torquil faced the harsh voice.

"What is it?" he asked in surprise, thinking the previous night had made them friends at last. He saw the sack in her hands.

Fauntley spoke. "If 'tis yours, you would know what it contains."

When he was about to reach for it, she hastily pulled away.

"Where did you find it?" Torquil asked.

"Then it *is* yours?" she persisted.

"I have one like it, aye. It holds the true burnishing cloth for my sword and dagger."

" 'Tis no burnishing cloth in this pouch."

"Then 'tis not mine." His voice was getting testy.

"You have never buried such a sack?" Fauntley asked, more in control than she.

"Nay—what for? I've no gold to fill up such a pouch."

"You're lying!" she cried, angry fears overcoming good sense. She stepped forward, dropped the sack, at the same time reaching for Torquil who evaded her agilely. Fauntley grabbed her by the shoulders and led her off, trying to calm her.

Torquil, watching them go, spied the pouch on the ground, forgotten in the tussle. Picking it up, he looked at the contents, frowned with the unlikely discovery. Neither gold nor his burnishing cloth. He wondered what the strange looking matter could be to have inspired such odd behavior in the Lady AElfwyn. Archery forgotten, he made his way to the Angel of Death to see if she could supply an answer.

Evening came. Cuthbert and Alf awaited Raff's arrival as anxiously as Ambyre. They remained steadfastly silent about the sack. Cuthbert had never hidden anything from her before. She therefore determined to wait for Raff with them, to learn what made them so uneasy.

Fauntley sat beside her for a while, but as he started to fall asleep at the hearthside, she insisted he go to his pallet. He did not share her anxiety.

Alf brought forth the game pieces for draughts but as soon as they were set up, there was an interruption.

Near midnight came the sound of horses' hooves, and Ambyre restlessly stood to greet the new arrivals. But Alf and Cuthbert suddenly immersed themselves in the board game, hastily whispering for her to sit nearby, as if they had all been at the game for some time, not on obvious watch. And she instinctively obeyed, for they seemed wary of someone coming with Raff.

He entered the longhouse first, his men trailing behind. They laughed and joked. Ambyre realized they must have eaten during their time away, for none roused the cooks and some looked to be tipsy from too much of their favorite drink. Most went off to their benches to sleep or to the affections of their favored slave-girl.

Raff approached the hearth alone, seeing the three figures surrounding the game. The boys glanced anxiously around for Piers.

"Sleepless night?" he greeted them, though he directed his eyes at her.

"Did everyone return with you?" Alf asked, his voice cracking once.

"Aye," Raff said slowly, now looking at him curiously.

"Where is . . . Piers?"

"With the horses. They need attention after a long ride. You know it's a task he enjoys."

Ambyre spoke up, though she kept her voice low. "Raff, this morning Fauntley showed you a small sack, did he not?"

"Ah," he said enlightened. "So this is not a welcoming party after all, but a warning party. Aye, milady. Fauntley showed me the poison."

"And do you understand it creates symptoms not unlike those you have suffered?"

"I assumed as much, though I no longer see reason for blaming anyone for my illness. Is it to divert my suspicion from you? Very well; I no longer suspect you. Now, will that suffice for you to give up this notion that I was poisoned? Even if I was, I am well and there is no danger."

"But there is!" she insisted, her voice a little

louder. "There are other poisons in the mushroom that work more slowly. 'Tis possible they are . . . fatal."

He laughed softly. "So you, too, are given to oracle-telling."

" 'Tis no oracle!"

"Listen to her," Alf pleaded, much to his brother's surprise. He had never been one to tell tales—not even at saga-time, when asked to spin a yarn. It was always thought the boy lacked imagination for he would stammer and blush, and little was ever understood. But now he spoke clearly, in earnest, his eyes never leaving Raff's. "The poison was freshly buried . . . this morning. And if it matches the signs of your illness . . . we are right to fear it has been used against you."

"Aye—if you knew who buried it, we would know if this person has cause against me." He turned to Ambyre. "If, perhaps, the Lady Ælfwyn buried the sack. . ."

" 'Twas not I!" she insisted. "I tell you, I do not wish you harm!"

Her anger seemed to please him which only angered her further. But before either could wonder why, Alf spoke again and drew their thoughts away.

" 'Twas Piers . . . he buried it. 'Tis his poison."

Raff was silent.

Ambyre watched him, her eyes wide with surprise. He showed no emotion: not belief or disbelief. Piers? She thought. The very brother he favored with so much of his time? She herself could hardly believe it was true, but she saw he considered the possibility.

At last their eyes met. Still, the blue gaze revealed little—except that he'd made his decision. He looked grim. When he turned on his heel she knew where he was going. The boys would have followed, but she held them back. This was something the brothers must settle alone.

Her heart went with him as he walked through the longhouse doorway. Please God, watch over him. Let this awful revelation keep him from harm!

Piers was brushing a tall roan as Raff entered the stables. He did not hear him come in, whistling and humming as he worked. Raff watched his narrow back, thoughts full of questions. Confusion, not anger. He would learn the truth.

"Why don't you leave that to one of the others?" Raff asked. Piers turned in surprise as he finished with the horse.

"I should," he answered easily, "since I am the chieftain's son. But I am not to be the next chieftain, so what does it matter? Besides, all have their best duties; I, unfortunately, do not do well those tasks warriors so love. This is what I choose instead."

"Still, hardly work for a chieftain's son," Raff prodded.

"A chieftain should be recognized by his ability to rule, not by such activities as this.

You've never begrudged me this before. Why now?"

"I've never had much time to dwell on it. Now, though, since my seizure I've begun thinking about the future of our people, should something happen to prevent me from becoming chieftain."

Piers laughed. " 'Tis unlikely."

"Is it?" He approached his brother. "Is it truly likely that I may live to sit in my father's chair?"

Piers ceased his work, concern on his face.

"Such a strange tone from one as healthy as you."

"Perhaps I am not so healthy," Raff said.

"Oh? Do you feel illness coming on again?"

"Should I?"

Piers laughed, for the first time uneasy. He turned back to the horse, brush in hand. "Why do you ask me? Only you would know the answer to that."

"Look at me," Raff demanded, his hand going to Piers' arm, pulling him around. The horse whinnied at the sudden tension in the air. "You have lied to me, Piers. A secret, cowardly action in a man. Why did you not confront me, challenge me, as a warrior should? As a *man* should? Can such a coward wish to be chieftain?"

Piers tried to pull away but was held tight. "You are mad. The illness has affected your mind."

"And what has affected yours?" Raff asked, his tone quiet. "I *loved* you, Piers. You are my brother, my friend. Why have you lied to me?"

"What lie have I told?" He brazened it out in the face of Raff's conviction that he was guilty.

"The poison," Raff said, letting go of Piers' arm. "You buried it and denied it was yours. *Why?*"

Piers' shoulders slumped as he heard the words. He turned away, leaning against the horse, no longer holding back the truth.

"Who told you?" Piers asked at last.

"You were seen."

"No doubt by Alf and his Saxon foster brother who brought it to you this morning."

Silence confirmed the truth. "Have you done this to me?" he asked bleakly.

Piers stood straight and looked squarely at Raff. "Aye," he said. "I'll be a coward no more."

"Do you hate me so?"

At that Piers stepped even closer. He put a hand on each of Raff's shoulders and gazed at him seriously before speaking. " 'Tis not hate. You would make a great chieftain Raff, but did you ever *want* to be? It is yours, simply because you are the eldest, yet you are better suited to do the fighting than to stay at home and govern."

"A chieftain leads his men to battle," Raff said.

"Does Olaf? Nay—'tis more a king than chieftain that our people have come to respect. I would be that king."

Raff stepped away from his brother's touch. He was a stranger. Did he truly believe this was the way to be hailed as chieftain? Through treachery and deceit, rather than bold honesty? Even for one brother to challenge another to the death would have been respected by their people. 'Twas not unheard of, even common when the inheritance was so greatly coveted. Yet both knew why no challenge had been made. Such a duel would have been no contest, so Piers had tipped the scale in his favor by resorting to secret murder.

"Did you think you wouldn't be found out?" Raff asked. "Did you believe you would be accepted so easily?"

"There would have been no suspicion of me." Piers laughed. " 'Tis Torquil who would have been suspected. He killed Dyrk, didn't he?"

" 'Twas *you* who found Dyrk that morning," Raff said suddenly.

Piers laughed again, and with that laughter Raff felt his love for his brother quickly turn to hate. A secret murderer deserved only that.

"You will face me for a duel on the morrow," Raff said angrily. "Midday. I care not that 'tis unfairly matched. You challenge for the office of chieftain. You must fight for it."

" 'Tis too late," Piers said, his laughter dying slow. "You have lost already. The death-cup has seen to that."

"Perhaps so, but I may take you along with

me. In Valhalla we may see Dyrk, and then he too will have his turn at you."

With that, Raff walked away, never realizing that for Piers, honor had died already. He would have no reason to duel for his body to die with it.

Piers fled the village before morning, his hidden dream gone, ambition crushed in defeat.

Ambyre waited, but Raff never returned to the longhouse that night. Near dawn she went outside hoping to find him. Surely he must now believe he had been poisoned.

The village was dark and quiet. Most were still sleeping. Therefore, when she spied movement near the old crone's hut, she thought he might be there.

The Angel of Death, a black cloak covering her misshapen form, stood as straight as she was able, for she was embracing a man and bestowing a kiss upon his cheek. Ambyre walked closer.

" 'Tis early in the morning to be leave-taking," she said, seeing Torquil with a bundle under his arm.

He stood back, face hard, silent.

"I must apologize for my behavior, Torquil," she told him.

Still, he said nothing. The old crone glared at her, sending shivers up her spine.

"Where are you going?" she asked, trying to avoid the old woman's eyes.

"You should be glad to be rid of me," Torquil said at last. "Haven't you twice accused me of trying to murder my brother?"

"I have apologized for that. Have you not heard? Nay, you would not, if you have not seen Raff. 'Twas Piers who poisoned him. He confronted Piers last night and I have not seen either since."

"Piers?" Torquil repeated, his face a mixture of hope and dread.

"Aye. Alf saw him bury the poison, yet he denied it."

"So my brother did not think lawspeaker was enough."

But the Angel of Death was speaking more urgently.

"Piers gave Raff a portion of the death-cup mushroom?"

Ambyre nodded, not hiding her disgust at the old woman's eagerness.

" 'Tis fatal most often," the old crone went on, her hand going to Torquil's. "You must stay, foster-son. If he is to die ... and Piers punished for his death ... then *you*, Torquil, will be chieftain."

Aprehension and fear joined the astonishment already on his face. He took a step backward, shaking his head as if to deny the truth. "Nay! Not I!"

" 'Tis true," the crone insisted.

"Raff is *not* dead," Ambyre reminded them both, anger tinting her cheeks. And Torquil clung to the words.

"Nay, milady," he said, nearing her and taking one of her hands. "He is not, and we must not let him be. He will be the next chieftain, not I."

"Do not be afraid—" the crone said, but he silenced her.

"My father will not lose another of his sons." He led Ambyre back to the longhouse. The old crone watched from behind, the ill-tidings of Raff and Piers not causing her any grief.

XVIII

Like fire on tinder, the news spread through the village. Many warriors were angry that Piers had disappeared in the night, taking with him most of his belongings. Some demanded they go after the outlaw to bring him back for punishment. But Olaf would not have it. When anger subsided, only fear remained that the heir might soon die.

If Fauntley had been a wagering man, he would have bet the poison strong enough to kill even so virile a man as Rathulfr Olafsson. He had not known many to survive its evil poison. But Fauntley kept these thoughts to himself. Ambyre was troubled enough.

She spent much of the day with Torquil near the hearth in the center of the hall. Raff, upon the mind of every villager, was absent. A young boy had seen him near the seaside at midday, but when Olaf sent a messenger to him he was nowhere to be found.

Ambyre wanted only to convince him of her love. He knew she was blameless at last. Perhaps he would begin to believe other things as well. But the thought was cold comfort. In the end she was dishonest, she who was known as "AElfwyn."

It was evening before she saw him. There was no feast that night, just a sober, quiet meal. With no appetite, she came to the table looking for him. When he slipped in later, the eyes of those remaining went to him. Some were curious, others pitied him. She hoped he would not see it.

Mostly, slaves were left in the hall. When one detained him, Ambyre thought perhaps she offered him mead or hot food from the hearth. He smiled, looking appreciative, but shook his head. When another stopped him, then another, she was amazed that so many would offer him supper. But the next moment her cheeks reddened as it dawned on her what they were offering. She had seen the boldness of these women, free and slave alike. They were as eager to approach a man as men were to approach them, and she could well imagine they wished his last days to be spent with whatever pleasure they could give him. Her only comfort was that his answer continued to be a shake of his head.

Torquil, when he noticed her embarrassment, whispered in her ear.

" 'Tis nothing improper, milady," he assured her. "They wish to be his chosen one, if he is buried in the Northern tradition."

"His chosen one?"

"To accompany him to the afterworld."

As realization came, she was horror-stricken. She had heard that many Northmen burned rather than buried their dead; she had not known that a living sacrifice was burned as well.

Torquil put a hand over hers. " 'Tis his decision, though I know he does not hold to many of the old religious traditions."

Raff reached them as Torquil finished speaking. He stood, eyes upon her, waiting to be acknowledged. His day had been spent in reflective solitude, many of his thoughts on this woman before him. Throughout the day he wondered at himself; would his last thought and breath be spent upon a Saxon?

But as Torquil and Ambyre sat before him, still holding hands, Raff could not help but feel jealous. Torquil, sensing it, uneasily withdrew his hand.

"My brother will no doubt be accepted as our father's heir," Raff said. "Has he also inherited my betrothal?"

She could not tell if his words were in earnest or jest. Her eyes were riveted on his.

"Nay, milord." Torquil became increasingly uncomfortable.

" 'Tis an idea to dwell upon," Raff mused, sitting, leaning back to relax in perfect peace and tranquility. "Why should this plan fail simply because of my death? 'Twas not I you betrothed, but my title. Now he holds it. I should think Edward would be as willing to accept Torquil as he was me."

"Must you say it so crudely?" she inquired softly, not trusting herself to speak up.

"You accuse me of being crude when 'tis my death I speak of? How would you have me behave? With fear, grief, hatred for what's been done to me?" He laughed. "This knowledge gives me certain liberties, milady. Liberties to offend, insult, speak without reservation, since it matters little if anyone seeks retribution."

She replied tartly. "You have said to me before, my lord, what a man leaves behind is his reputation. Do not leave behind careless words to destroy what has gone before."

Her words, spoken honestly, did the trick. He straightened in his seat with a sobered smile. "You have always proven yourself wise, AElfwyn."

Her smile was bitter. "Have I?"

"When one sees what is in your heart, it has been wisdom guiding you."

At those words, her heart raced. Did he at last see what was in her heart?

Torquil was about to leave, hearing the words exchanged between them, but Raff detained him with words that Ambyre did not welcome.

"Stay, Torquil. 'Tis late, and I'm sure AElfwyn is overtired."

She was being dismissed! So the men could talk. Just a moment before she had hoped he had seen . . . yet now her presence was no longer desired. Pain made her go, not pride.

She went to her room, finding it too quiet, too lonely. She would spend the rest of her life with only memories of him; all she wanted was a little more time to create as many as possible. But he had sent her away.

Setting aside the two brooches holding her pinafore in place, she let the garment fall carelessly away. She freed her hair from its clasp, and combed it smooth with an ivory comb. She faced the bed. Near it lay a bow and arrow left by Cuthbert. He had been given many weapons since his acceptance here, this among the finest, which he kept inside the longhouse for safekeeping against the weather. Ambyre gently fingered its taut bow and slim, feathered arrows. A tool of battle to provide the kind of death Raff would have preferred.

She lay down, not caring that the hearthfire had dwindled to glowing embers. She would be cold before morning but it did not seem to matter.

Cuthbert no longer shared her room. Since becoming blood brother to Alf, he slept where he did, among the warriors. At times she'd thought of protesting, remembering some of the activities common to the men and their favorite slaves, but she knew he'd pay no attention. He seemed more Dane than Saxon. In any case, whatever happened in the hall could no longer be a surprise. So she gave him his way.

None of the usual noise could be heard from the hall; the night was quiet. Still, she lay awake, unable to disconnect from her troubled, restless mind. Raff would die; she could think of nothing else, lying uncovered, heedless of the dying fire and deepening cold.

The door opened slowly. She watched without fear. It opened wider. A tall figure entered.

"AElfwyn," Raff said the name gently.

Precarious happiness filled Ambyre's heart. Many words came to mind, confessions, explanations, questions, and always the overwhelming need to convince him of her love.

But neither spoke. Too much had already been said, leading to misunderstandings, anger, intention to hurt. She lifted her arms to him. There would be no misunderstanding between their bodies.

Both were tender, careful even in language not to offend. They sought the other's pleasure, not their own, giving the sweetness of love its own way. Whatever passed between them tonight had no room for other memories; this was their time, past, present, future. Nothing else existed.

The scant barrier of their clothes seemed to disappear without effort. He untied the ribbon atop her gown, which obeyed his gentle fingers and floated to the floor. His tunic and breeks quickly followed.

In the dim light from the embers, she could see his body in all its masculine splendor. How many times had she imagined him thus, lying beside her, his eyes devouring her the way hers devoured him? And now it was reality. Nothing, she thought, nothing could spoil this night.

She pressed her body erotically close to his, reveling in the feel of his hair-roughened hardness. She longed for his caress, for his kiss, and more.

Ambyre was not the innocent maid she had been that first night he took her. So much time had gone by, so often had she thought of this, longed for him, that she grew bold without knowing it. Her kisses were as fervent as his, her fingers as explorative. Her mouth strayed to his body, the body she had memorized so thoroughly. Her tongue was as eager to please as his, traveling with erotic patience. His hair tickled her lips. She smiled at the sensation. Her heart thumped wildly as she felt a shudder of pleasure course through him.

He did not wonder at this transformation in her. He claimed her body with equal abandon, finding his pleasure in creating hers. Never before had he received so much from seeing the reaction to his touch. It was as if she'd been created for him, as if only he could make her moan, writhe, find fulfillment in him. She filled his loins with ecstasy and with trembling control he prolonged the building fervor within.

He took his time, his tongue and his touch delighting in the perfection of her body.

She did not give him pause as his mouth explored the body she so lovingly offered. His tongue caressed her with intimate knowledge of what she enjoyed most. She quivered below his lips, her wonderment only that such passion was possible, so perfectly enhancing the love they shared.

His caress found the center of her fire, and with a gentle probing motion he sent the flames throughout her veins, so intense she lost all sense of reality—except for him. She was fully aware who gave her this pleasure. She cried his name. Her palms spread upon his shoulders pulling him closer, wanting him more. She wanted him inside of her, to feel his fullness become part of her body, to envelop him and let them both seek that plateau of transcendency.

She invited him to her womanhood as eagerly as his manhood desired. United, they took each other to that realm beyond, that plane where nothing existed but their senses. She felt her body engulfed in a fervor so great she could only repeat his name breathlessly. He filled her as never before. She arched against him to accept each thrust. That plateau stretched far, supporting and consuming their bodies until neither could hold back from the edge. Then, out into space. They sank into the furs, still pressed together, still one, in equal exhaustion.

The hours of the night were spent this way, speaking in every manner but through speech. If she had ever doubted he loved her, Ambyre of Athelney, she did not doubt it now. He knew her as AElfwyn, but it was not her name he loved, nor her past, nor her political importance. His body loved hers, fully, completely, undeniably.

And she, Ambyre, loved him despite the fear that she would lose his love, knowing there was little hope for tomorrow. If he was to die within the week, let it be with this knowledge, this truth. Nothing was truer than her love, and she would not destroy it by exposing a secret that no longer mattered. Not when his future might last only another day.

This secret confession of love made them bold. Perhaps they would have been more cautious had their lovemaking not been so joyous; but they lay in each other's arms, the love too real to be in jeopardy. So now they trusted themselves to words.

"We Danes are not given to much thought, at least not like your friend Fauntley. We're people of action, not reflection. But with knowledge of my own death, as often as I've faced it in battle, I've never let it spill over into my actions. Now I'm able to, perhaps forced to; I would not be here otherwise. 'Tis a sad truth but one I cannot deny. Yesterday I had the privilege of many tomorrows; I had the hope of our marriage, as strained as it might have been. A lifetime in which to exchange forgiveness. But those tomorrows have been taken away, and for this moment, because I am here, I'm grateful."

"Then you truly believe the worst of me?" she asked with a heavily pounding heart. "That I . . . seduced you to wound your pride, to save Edward from losing Mercia?"

He breathed deeply. She prepared herself for the accusations to come. He spoke softly.

"Your loyalty is to your king, and loyalty, if not love, is something I know. When I kidnapped you, you were forced to make a choice. When I threatened to end Edward's rule in Mercia, you could not tolerate it—not even if I gave it to you. So you made the choice that Edward should lose you, his pawn, rather than Mercia. You thought it better to wed me than to regain your throne at his loss. I cannot lay blame to this decision, yet I know it had naught to do with love—"

"Raff, you are wrong! Do you think I don't love you?"

He looked at her as she stared down at him from her position propped on one elbow. On her face, even in the darkness, he could see the earnestness. Slowly, softly, he caressed that face which had captivated him.

"I am not so much a fool that I cannot see the truth of your love," he told her, and had he stopped there Ambyre would have known happiness. But he went on. "I have accepted that I must share that love with your King, as you must share my love with my people."

She wanted to deny it, to shout that he had undivided claim upon her, to demand the same in return. But a small part of her kept silent. Perhaps those were demands she could not make; neither upon him nor herself.

"I wish to convince you of my love," she said slowly, her words forming even before the thought had settled upon her mind. If she could not give him all of her love, or even the honesty of her identity, then she would give him all else she had. "Tonight, Torquil told me that you must choose someone to join you in the afterworld. I do not believe in the afterworld of Valhalla and Odin, but I do know that life here in this world will be unbearable without you. Choose me, Raff. I want to be beside you on the funeral pyre."

Held in his arms, she did not see the frown tug at his mouth. His words were gentle.

"I shall choose no one to accompany me. I shall be buried in the Christian manner, in honor of my Christian mother, and you."

Ambyre could not hide her tears, hearing him speak of his burial. Those tears became unashamed sobs, too strong to hold back. He held her close, stroking her hair, wanting to comfort her but finding no way. He too was bitter. Life would have been worthwhile with this woman at his side.

They had slept, but restlessly, though now at dawn neither felt tired. Time had seemed too precious to spend in slumber.

He didn't want to leave, but it would be impossible for them to be seen emerging from her room together. She said she did not care, but he was more cautious, not merely for his own sake.

He left after a kiss, one that tempted him to stay, but he eased away from her, gone before either of them had another moment's hesitation.

She dressed, hurrying after him despite the

fact he'd told her to take her time. Only minutes after he'd left she followed. Only slaves were up and about at this time of morning. Some made preparations for breakfast, others rekindled the dying hearths. But most stood in various stages of dress, washing themselves or fetching fresh water for the warriors to use when they awoke.

Heavily cloaked even though the air had taken on an unseasonable warmth, she caught up with him. The two walked among the villagers, too engrossed in one another to greet them. They smiled at each other, laughed, spoke eagerly, then slowly; they were quiet for a time, paused to kiss or hold one another. They drew as much pleasure from this as from the night before, reaffirming a bond born of affinity, a friendship that had little to do with sex.

They did not return to the longhouse until dinnertime. Everyone's spirits seemed brighter because of Raff's apparent happiness, and he in turn enjoyed their revived joviality.

Fauntley watched them from nearby. He had seen Raff go into her room the night before and had lain awake on his pallet, waiting. He thought Ambyre would send him away, but the door did not open again. His heart was heavy, but he did not condemn her for being unchaste. He had no place in her life, therefore could neither blame nor forgive.

But he wanted to forget the images going through his mind. He didn't want her to guess that he knew about the night before, that he thought this union to be the Devil's work. A gentle Christian with a barbaric heathen was certainly no work of God. It can only lead to a bitter end, he thought to himself, dreading the day when she would learn this for herself.

As she approached him smiling, he pushed away such unhappy thoughts. "Fauntley, I have news. Tomorrow Raff will go to York to be baptized."

He lifted a brow, his surprise milder than she'd expected.

"Of everyone I thought *you* would be most pleased."

"And so I am," he replied, a belated smile appearing. But Ambyre saw his reluctance.

"Will you accompany us? 'Tis not a long journey, just a few hours, and we will be staying overnight at a Christian chieftain's home. Raff is going to ask Ella and Sigrid about coming along. Will you come, too?"

His eyes warned her of his answer. "I am pleased that he has consented to be baptized . . . whatever the reason, I believe only good can come of it, not only for Raff himself, but for his people by the example he sets."

"But Fauntley..." Her dejection almost changed his mind.

"I cannot go, Ambyre. Please, do not ask me again."

He turned from her, but her words halted him.

"You know, don't you?" It was a whisper so faint only he could hear. "About last night, and how Raff learned I could not have been wed to you, or be a mother."

"I know nothing," he insisted, the truth too hard to speak. "What I *believe* is that he is going through the holy ceremony of baptism to please you, not for himself or God. I have seen many Danes baptized for the wrong reasons—to marry, for rights to live peacefully in Christian areas, even to buy and sell in Christian towns."

"He has not lived according to pagan beliefs. He's never gone to their holy ground to pray, nor offered sacrifices nor performed pagan rituals. He doesn't lie with slavegirls, as all the others do. And he wants a Christian burial. What greater sign can he give his people to accept Christianity?"

"Only good can come of that."

"We have committed one sin," Ambyre said gravely, "which you are aware of though you deny it. He does not admit it to be a sin, and is unaware of Christian law. But *I* am not. I am aware of what I've done. I bear the guilt."

He leaned closer, taking her hands, speaking her name so wretchedly, so miserably she could not go on. "Forgive me, Ambyre. I too have sinned. I have been jealous, covetous, and cannot cast a stone against either of you. I have thought of him with hatred and bitterness. Those were my sins. How can I judge yours? 'Tis God's place, not mine. I am sorry."

The embrace which followed was mutual and instantaneous, heartfelt for them both. But he became aware of Raff's eyes upon them and separated from her. Yet honesty had been exchanged. He would not go with them tomorrow, but a deeper understanding of themselves and one another had at last been achieved.

XIX

They traveled slowly over the wolds and through the forests, for the sake of Ella and Sigrid. Several warriors were sent ahead to herald their coming.

Raff stayed beside Ambyre, at first as solicitous of her as of his mother and sister who rode only rarely. Yet when she trotted her steed alongside his as if she had been born on the back of such an animal, his grin showed pride and surprise. Teasing, he said he did not know Saxon women were allowed to ride.

At that, she challenged him to a race. There were no hindrances before them, only the subtly rolling wolds and greenswards. Before his answer came, she nudged her animal forward.

Sigrid and Ella laughed at his slow start. So unexpected was the challenge that she was several lengths ahead before he urged his horse onward. His mount seemed as surprised as Raff himself and reared, almost sending him to the ground.

Ambyre had been given a gentle mare, while he rode a powerful stallion. Once he gained control it was not long before he reached her. But they could see it was not her horsemanship that had lost the race.

He drew his mount close beside hers, leaning toward her for a victory kiss. They were far ahead of the others but the kiss did not go unnoticed. Instead of returning to the rest of the party, they stayed ahead, finding more animated conversation between themselves.

"See how closely your mother watches," Ambyre said with a backward glance. "Perhaps she knows."

"She knows," he said with such certainty that Ambyre raised her brows. "She knows you have given me more happiness than I have ever known."

Ambyre smiled, glad to hear him speak so.

"Will you meet me tonight?" he asked, his tone more serious. She looked at him, her face a mixture of trepidation and desire. "We will be staying in the home of Gunnar, one of the great chieftains of York. His home is large—larger than my father's. Underneath Gunnar's hall is a storeroom, quiet and private. Will you go there with me?"

"Raff . . . on the eve of your baptism?" Her tone did not hold the horror a Christian woman's should at an invitation to sin before a sacrament, yet he noted the reluctance.

"This should not be done until I have been in the church as long as you have?"

Reddened cheeks were all he received as answer.

"You count this as sin, then?" he asked with concern.

"According to the Church."

"And the circumstances... the limited time we have... this makes no difference?"

"I have lain with you for the past two nights, my lord," Ambyre said, her eyes downcast. "I cannot truthfully say that I regret any moment of it. Had there been time for us to wed, we should perhaps have waited. But time is a thing we do *not* have."

A smile played about the corners of his mouth. "You would have wed me, willingly, even though by doing so I would have shamed your uncle?"

"He has agreed," she said warily. Edward *had* agreed to his marriage with AElfwyn.

"So he has said."

"You do not believe him?" She caught a note of suspicion in his voice.

"I believe he is willing to make peace to eliminate risk of revolt from my people. But our marriage... I have been wary of his intention to see it through. My tactics, if they succeed, would place him in a rather embarrassing position, wouldn't you agree? He would be seen as bending to the demands of a weaker army."

Not realizing he had these suspicions, she became uneasy. Lies, secrets... when discovered were sure to destroy his love.

"What is it, AElfwyn?"

She attempted a smile. "You speak of failure, my lord. I know how it must grieve you. It saddens me as well."

He did not respond for several moments. Then it was hesitantly, as he carefully chose his words. " 'Tis a plan that should not be abandoned. Though I mentioned this before, 'twas with malice. Now I speak in earnest. Torquil..."

"Nay!" she said, before he could go on. Her eyes pleaded, her hand reached for his, which he accepted as eagerly as she gave it. "I'll not marry your brother—I'll marry no one if I cannot marry you! I'll go to the convent, by my oath I will!"

Torn between selfish relief and the loyalty which was too deep in him to ignore, Raff spoke again. "We both know what it is to love our people. Could you so easily turn from your Mercians if you had an opportunity to save them from war?"

That it was sensible did not enter her mind; that it was possible was not even considered, for the real AElfwyn *could* marry Torquil, with Ambyre's full blessing. But what stayed in her mind was his willingness, thinking her AElfwyn, that she marry another after his death.

Tears sparkled in her eyes, though her tone remained steady. "Is that loyalty so great in you that you can imagine me with your brother—as his wife?"

"By the eye of Odin, AElfwyn!" he cursed, his grip on her hand tightened and his mouth set in a scowl. "I wish for no other man to look at you ... touch you ... receive your smiles. I have love for my brother, but I could hate him if I knew he took your love from me."

The kiss that followed, though eager, was impeded by the horses beneath them. As Raff's threatened to rear yet again, they found themselves laughing.

York was a bustling town of such international composition that Ambyre was amazed it was part of the same isle on which she was born.

Surrounded by a tall stone wall built by Roman master masons, it was more than a merchant town. But merchants thrived here, of every background, every speciality. Slaves and animals were sold among silks and spices, pottery, furs, leather goods, weapons. People crowded the narrow walkways, haggling and bartering. For her it was a sight she would long remember.

She heard every language imaginable. A few she recognized, most she did not. And people dressed in such outlandish style! From veiled women—and she could not guess how they saw through such coverings—to men with wide puffed pants drawn in just below the knee, enlivened with colors she'd never seen. Some wore turbans, others were bare headed. People of all skin shades carried on their business, gradations of brown, black, yellow, olive. And such crowds! Never had she seen so many people in one place. It made her cling closer to Raff. How would she find him if they were separated?

A variety of food was sold in the merchant sheds. Tantalizing odors of roasting meat, sweet wines, and honeyed confections made her mouth water. Everywhere she looked, people were eating or drinking. It was like an outdoor feast shared by people from all over the world.

Gunnar welcomed his guests in the traditional Danish manner. He offered more than hospitality; his objective was to exceed any other host in the comfort he offered those who visited. Dinner was a feast more lavish than even Edward's bountiful table supplied. There were bards, dancers, tumblers, musicians, singers. Gunnar's wife served wine to the guests, offering words of welcome.

Raff's warriors did Gunnar's efforts justice. No one would go to bed that night without a smile, even those who had quarreled. A feast without quarrels was rare—and indeed, most felt that was part of the fun. This feast lacked for nothing.

Wine being superior to the mead most were accustomed to, there were warriors who had drunk themselves to sleep even before the women were shown to the bower. Raff, Ambyre noted as she left, seemed to enjoy the wine as all the others did. But for a slight heightening of his coloring, he did not seem any the worse for having consumed so much.

Still, she wondered if the sweet-tasting but potent drink would keep him from their tryst. She would be glad if he did not come; 'twould mean he kept from sin on the eve of his baptism. For that she would thank the Holy Spirit who watched over them, even in this strange guise. But she could not keep the heaviness from her heart at the thought of spending this night alone. How many did they have left?

The women's guest bower was separated from the hall by a curved, dimly-lit passage. Two slave girls showed Ambyre, Ella and Sigrid the way.

The room was large, a huge bed taking up most of one wall. It sat on a dais covered with numerous layers of furs. Opposite that was a table upon which sat two large bowls of water and several linens. Nearby was a pair of massive carved wooden chairs padded with soft embroidered cushions in a myriad of colors and stitched patterns. On the walls, all but the far one which had a tall, square, unshuttered window, hung ornate tapestries depicting various Christian stories.

After each of them freshened with the water and linens and the slaves were dismissed, Ella held a candle to the tapestries and studied each one.

"This is the thief on the cross at the Lord's

side," Ella observed as she stood before the largest. " 'Thou shalt not steal,' " she quoted. "Isn't that one of the Holy Commandments?"

Ambyre stepped closer to her, for the older woman looked to her for the answer. She gazed at the tapestry as well.

"Aye, that is one of the Commandments."

"And this man broke that law. Yet our Lord, as forgiving as He is, said He would see him in heaven that very day."

Ambyre felt Ella's eyes on her and wondered at her somber mood. She'd been so cheerful throughout the day, her pride and happiness obvious over Raff's decision to be baptized. But that was gone now.

"This means," Ella continued, "that our God is a forgiving God."

" 'Tis why He died on the cross."

"That is comforting," she sighed. "We hear too much of hell and punishment." She let her eyes rest on Sigrid for a moment, already abed and close to sleep. "My children are my life, Lady AElfwyn. My Sigrid, and her brothers ... Raff. I am glad my son has chosen to be baptized. It may only be to please those he loves, yet don't you believe God will see some good in it?"

Ambyre took one of Ella's hands in hers. "Aye, milady," she answered, and never had she been more sincere.

Ella held Ambyre's hand and her voice intensified. "Raff has not committed any great sins against God. And he loves a Christian woman. 'Tis easy to see he loves you, lady. If only there were time! Time for you to wed, time for him to come round to the Christian ways. So you must help him in these last days. You must speak to him of God, and keep him from sin . . . at least until we know. . ."

Unwittingly, Ambyre stiffened. Keep him from sin, Ella begged. But how could she? How could she, when all she wanted to do was be with him for whatever time they had left? Surely God would understand and forgive them both.

But seeing his mother tormented over the state of Raff's soul, she sought to comfort her. "As you say, milady, our God is a forgiving one."

They embraced and she felt a sob shudder through Ella's body. But when they separated, her eyes were dry. Even now, Ambyre thought, pride was not forgotten.

Ambyre snuffed all the candles as Ella climbed into the large bed beside Sigrid. A moment later, she followed.

She lay in silence, contemplating Ella's words. She should heed her, she thought, for she spoke out of love for Raff. But Ambyre knew she could not. Nothing, she thought, could keep her from him tonight.

Surprisingly, it was Sigrid lying beside her who broke the silence a while later.

"My mother worries over many things," Sigrid whispered. They heard her even breathing and knew she was asleep.

"Because she loves him," Ambyre said.

"And so do you. So do I. But 'tis you who will make his last days happiest."

Suddenly angry because all three of them, herself included, had come to the same awful conclusion, she said sharply, "Raff will not die!" The words, full of conviction, were out of her mouth before she could soften them. But Ella did not stir.

"We all pray he will live," Sigrid gently replied. "But we cannot deny the possibility. Your friend Fauntley seems convinced of this poison's power. It is hard to doubt him."

"Aye," Ambyre sadly agreed, "that is true."

"I did not bring this up to stir your fears, Lady AElfwyn. I meant only to tell you this: I, too, follow the Christian ways. Yet I know Raff, and I can see the love you share. Perhaps I am wrong to say this . . . perhaps I am being selfish on my brother's behalf. But you must love each other to the fullest, milady. Use each moment left to you to last you the rest of your life and . . . and to bring what happiness you can to him now. Go to him, AElfwyn. Go to him tonight. Do not waste time here in this woman's bed!"

Had the room been lit Sigrid could have seen the blush stain Ambyre's cheeks. But she might have guessed her embarrassment by the hesitation before she spoke.

"Raff and I are to meet tonight," she whispered at last.

Suddenly Sigrid giggled, gently but with pure

and obvious amusement. "I should have known!"

Later, as the appointed time grew near, Ambyre could still hear the merriment from the Great Hall. Her anticipation heightened, but so did her concern. If the feast lasted further into the night, could he sneak away while the others still caroused? If only they were all abed by now... Would she remain undetected all the way to a storeroom that she was uncertain she could find?

She sat up, easing herself ever so gently from the warm covers. Both women were asleep; when she moved away from Sigrid who was in the middle, she felt the girl's arm fall gently of its own will to the spot she had vacated. Her departure would not be noted.

The moon was high. It shone through the open window. None too early.

She was glad of the tapers that lit the way. Raff had given her directions, but had there been total darkness she doubted she would have kept her wits.

As she bypassed the Great Hall through a side passageway, sounds of revelry seemed ever louder. There was little fear her footsteps would be heard.

The storeroom door was heavy but moved silently under her efforts, as if its hinges had been oiled for just this secret use. But inside it was black as pitch. She hesitated to close herself in. She had seen the stairs plainly enough. It was what lay at their bottom that gave her pause.

Behind her came the footfall of someone approaching, and in the greater fear of discovery she closed herself behind the door, shrouded instantly in total darkness.

For a moment she stood with her ear to the frame, hoping to hear the night walker pass by. But no steps could be heard, and when she moved to peer out, the door opened by itself. With a gasp she stepped backward, almost losing her balance on the stairs behind her. She would surely have fallen had not Raff reached out to grab her.

His heart quickened, matching the beat of hers. He pulled her to him and laughed away the shock.

"You were not expecting me, milady?" he teased, pulling a thick, short tapered candle from his belt. He separated himself from her to light it from another in the passageway outside the door.

Taking her hand, he guided her down. He said things to make her laugh, dispelling any lingering qualms, so that by the time they were at the foot of the stairs, she felt secure. It could have been the most luxurious of rooms they were entering instead of a cold, dark storeroom.

Handing her the candle, he found blankets enough to make a soft bed for them upon the floor. Clean, orderly and dust free, during the winter the storeroom was used often in daylight hours.

He affixed the candle between the tops of two crates, smoothing the blankets before them. Then he turned, putting a hand on each of her arms, looking at her closely.

"Do you fear discovery in this place?" he asked, seeing that something was amiss with her.

"Many are still awake above stairs. None will come here... looking for more wine... or you...?"

He laughed gently, holding her closer. "I saw to the supply of wine before I left. They'll be needing no more. As for me, milady, my men know better than to seek me out."

His words comforted her, and when they kissed, she was less tense under his touch. It was as it had been the past two nights, and even before that, whenever he touched her. She could think of nothing else, and the release seemed sweet. She scorned consequences, relishing these moments with him. They shared momentary oneness, enabling them to forget the uncertainties of the future.

The feast upstairs could be heard from where they lay, but as they feasted on each other, they shut out all sounds but their own sighs of pleasure and whispered words of love.

They did not part until just before dawn, when fear of discovery made them cautious. He folded the blankets and led her to the bower. There he kissed her long and vigorously. She scolded him though both knew she had enjoyed it.

Sleep overcame her the moment she crept in beside Sigrid.

Baptisms, like weddings, were a time of great rejoicing in the household of Gunnar Trygulfsson. Knowing no such feast would greet Raff at home, where his father had not accepted the Christian faith, Gunnar offered a lavish celebration. It began at midday after the ceremony. They ate and drank, planning to rest before returning home later in the day.

The warriors welcomed more festivity, even for a Christian purpose. And Ella was greatly pleased that such rejoicing was held in her son's honor. Only Raff seemed withdrawn.

He said nothing, strove to betray nothing, but as the gala went on he felt Ambyre's eyes on him, eyes that showed the concern he could not deny she should feel. It was coming upon him.

A whisper to Ella brought the feast to an end. Raff should be at home. All his men knew why.

Gunnar, being a most congenial host, was concerned when they took their leave early. He was ignorant of Raff's condition, for Ella had not wanted known the fact of treachery within her household. But Gunnar could see that Raff was ill and was not offended.

The journey home held none of the lightness of yesterday. Before long Raff was slumping upon his horse; his pallor worsened, and though the winter air had warmed from previous days, he sweated and trembled with cold in the same instant.

When their village home came in view Ambyre wondered if he would be put back into the tent. Thinking what argument she would give Olaf if this was his order she hardly noticed Ella directing several slaves to prepare a bed for Raff in the hall. With relief she saw him being taken into the longhouse.

Fauntley greeted her. Seeing the furrow on her brow he said no more.

She shared the vigil with Ella and Sigrid. Raff's body heat was high yet he said he felt cold, so she suggested they take him to her room. Small, it was easier to keep warm, and certainly her bed was more comfortable than the pallet laid for him near the hearth. The thought of where she was to spend the night did not enter her mind.

Ella had knowledge of special herbs to bring the fever down and ease the pain in his stomach. She brewed teas, strong and potent, administering them herself while the girls looked on. From time to time Ambyre would press a cool cloth soaked in lavender oil against his brow to ease the pain he confessed was there. Sigrid stayed nearby with fresh water. Though Ella gave him generous amounts of herbal teas cooled to help bring down the fever, he complained of such great thirst that they wondered if he could hold all he consumed, for he passed almost nothing.

Before long Ella sponged the rest of his body with the cool water, wiping the skin briskly after each application. She said this would help the blood flow easier for his skin seemed to have no color at all.

Day and night they stayed at his side. When Ella rested Ambyre assumed her ministrations. Sigrid carried on when Ambyre had no strength left, then Ella would begin again. Raff slept as though dead and Ambyre found herself checking to see that he still breathed.

The second day was more trying than the first. He seemed to be awake, speaking and flailing his still powerful arms. At times he imagined himself in battle giving orders to his men and fighting with his sword *Kappi* at his side. And often he spoke of AElfwyn, as he knew her, saying such things that brought color to Ambyre's cheeks to have Ella and Sigrid hear. He spoke of her loveliness, of the skin he found so fair, of what was hidden beneath her clothes; he spoke of her kiss, her touch, as if she lay beside him and he was making love to her. But her embarrassment was not as great as her joy that he thought of her even in the grip of fever. Love was as much a part of him now as the glory of leading his men into the imaginary battles of his delirium.

Ambyre soon stopped counting the days. The three of them took turns sleeping at the hearthside while one of them remained at Raff's side. Meals were brought to them but they ate little. Ella tired first paying no heed to their admonitions to rest.

Ambyre could not remember if it was the fourth or fifth day when he opened his eyes, looked straight at her, and smiled. So amazed was she that she popped from her seat with a startled gasp, awakening Ella and Sigrid.

The fever had left him and some color had returned to his cheeks. He had no strength but for the first time in days he had his wits, and that was cause enough for celebration.

He said he could take a milk-porridge rather than the thin broth they had been giving him betwixt the teas. Sigrid hurried to fetch it. His only other request was a washing. A serving wench brought a bowl of water and lye soap, cleansing his hair as he asked. That whole day passed with Raff awake and alert. News spread through the village that he was recovering.

But with the night came the fever. Once again he saw strange images and spoke with fever-madness. The three who tended him, already overtired and tormented by his tenacious illness, fell into despair. Though they had not let their hopes soar too high by thinking he was cured, they had not expected him to sink so deeply back into the fever.

Twice this happened in the next two days; he would appear recovered only to be taken again by the fever. And the three remained by his side.

Ambyre hadn't set foot outside the room. Cuthbert, she knew, was delighted to stay with these Danes for as long as he could, amid the companionship of Alf and the other warriors who had taught him so much of what he yearned to know.

It was Fauntley who would feel the delay, he

who had suffered from the first in this captivity. Ambyre had barely a moment to think of him but when she did it was with sorrow. He had expected to be home by now. And again Raff was to blame for the postponement.

As the days passed, her desolation began to share space in her heart with hope. Surely, since so much time had already passed, this poison could not be as strong as Raff. His brief remissions strengthened that belief.

But mixed with that was a dread she could not deny. His recovery was first and foremost in her heart. Yet with it would come an unavoidable confrontation with the truth. She could not lie to him forever.

She put these thoughts aside whenever they arose. It shamed her that she could dread the day when he would be well. She loved him more than life and often wished it was she upon that bed suffering in his place. Perhaps then he could have found forgiveness for her.

The villagers had grown wary of those mornings when word came that Raff was well. The following day would bring the unpleasant news that the illness lingered. Their vexation grew that it clung so tenaciously to him. But this was the second consecutive morning he had awakened with his wits. He was weak as expected but the fever plaguing him had broken. Still, they prepared themselves for contrary work on the next day.

When the fever had been absent for almost a week, Ella herself made the announcement that her son would live. Cheers rang through the hall, loud shouts, hails that Raff could hear and know of the joy.

Tears came to Ambyre when she became convinced of his recovery. She sat on the edge of the wood-frame bed looking at him and finding no words for what she felt in her heart.

He remained weak for many days, forcing himself too soon to take on even the simple task of rising from the bed. When Ella cautioned him he chided her that she should be more eager to see him up. And to Ambyre he said the sooner he regained his bearings the sooner they would be off to Wessex. And the sooner they would be wed.

She was not about to blurt out the truth when that hope aided him so well in his recovery. He was set upon his own healing, with only one reason to hurry. She could not take that reason away.

XX

The day came much later than anticipated when they set sail for Wessex. Raff, except for a thinned, almost gaunt face, had regained much of his vigor. As to his loss of weight, he told his men that a few good drinking bouts would set things aright. He wagered he would outdrink them all, since he had been dry for so many days. But the challenges would have to wait—until after their arrival, after his wedding.

The same ship was fitted out with provisions, the same men to sail her. There was a feast to send them off and by early dawn they were ready to leave.

Alf bid a sorrowful farewell to Cuthbert, who promised to return when he was of age and had the means. To that Alf replied he need not worry. When both were older he would come for Cuthbert himself in one of his own longships. Then they would go in search of treasure among the Turks and Moors and buy fine

Arabian horses the other warriors would envy. They had imagined enough adventures together to take them well into old age.

Fauntley's farewells were brief and only to a few: Olaf and Ella, Kirsten, and finally Sigrid, whom he had grown quite fond of.

But Ambyre's parting seemed strange. She was to be gone only as long as it took her to be wed, yet she bade farewell to Ella, Kirsten and Sigrid as though the separation would be long indeed.

She boarded the longship with undiluted sadness. She was going home. Shouldn't she be happy about that? But as she turned her gaze in the direction of the Danish village one last time, knowing she would never again set eyes on the sight, her heart wrenched painfully and tears welled in her eyes.

"What is it, my love?" Raff whispered in her ear. He stood close behind her, his body touching hers, his hands coming to rest gently on her shoulders.

His presence was almost too much to bear. How could she leave, knowing she was not destined to return with him, her only love?

Suddenly she turned round and flung herself into his embrace. Feigning happiness, she said, "I dream of the day I return as your wife."

She hoped he would believe the tears in her eyes were of happy eagerness, not of the true desolation she felt to the very core of her being. But he kissed her and neither gave any thought to the reasons behind those tears.

As on that first voyage from Wessex, they never strayed far from the coast of England. The farther south they went, the heavier her heart grew.

During the day, Raff spent his time with her and his men, directing the ship from the side steering rail, laughing, singing or jesting with those at the oars. Wulfstan was aboard, and Raff as always enjoyed his company. Cuthbert, too, spent his time with the men, especially Wulfstan, making the most of the few days he had left with them.

And that was what Ambyre sought to do: enjoy and relish each moment with Raff. They shared their meals, sat for hours side by side watching the coast of their homeland pass by, often laughing at the reactions of villagers to the sight of a Danish longship. More than once they watched people scamper like startled rabbits, seeking the shelter of their cottages against the enemy. It had been many years since the Danes had done any coastline marauding, yet their reputation lived on.

At night the two were inseparable. They shared a fur sleeping bag not for warmth but for intimacy. Because of lack of privacy he did not make love to her yet nonetheless stifled more than one amorous laugh with a kiss after having caressed her beneath the fur covering in just such a way as to bring out her reaction. He did not tease her for long however. He found it too hard to overcome his own reactions to the touch of her.

Fauntley heard their midnight banter. More than once his envy was accompanied by true concern for her future welfare. Surely this behavior could only bring more pain for her in the end. He resolved to talk to her on the second morning, knowing their destination would soon be at hand.

He stole a few moments at the earliest possibility. There was little privacy but he spoke in such low tones that only she could hear. Not even Cuthbert, who sat beside Wulfstan not far away, could hear what words passed between them.

"You must tell him soon, milady," Fauntley said, his eyes on Raff across from them at the steering rail. "Have you thought about this while you flaunt your relationship before his men?"

She reddened under the harsh words. But because they were honest she did not retort.

"I see that you love him," he went on, his tone softening, "and I care naught for his pride when his men learn he has been fooled. But *you* love him. Do you not care that this behavior will only make the truth harder to bear?"

"Please . . . please," she softly begged him. "I long for these last moments . . . this last day for him to look at me with love. I know 'twill be forever lost to me come tomorrow, but today I shall savor it. 'Tis selfish, I know, but spare me this, Fauntley!"

He patted her hand, his face full of compassion. "I can act only with love toward you, Ambyre. I spoke only to remind you of reality. 'Tis a fantasy you live upon this boat, pretending nothing will change."

Though kindness prompted his words, they left a frown upon her brow. He was right, she knew. Shouldn't she stop this very moment? But she couldn't! She was weak, she knew. She couldn't help herself.

Edward's fleet came into view long before Wessex itself. Raff raised a banner of peace, and they were hailed by a huge English vessel not so swift as theirs. It escorted the longship to the shores of Wessex where several men disembarked to take them to the palace grounds.

When Ambyre's gaze took in the familiar surroundings a strangeness came upon her. It no longer seemed like home. But she looked forward to seeing Edward and AElfwyn at least.

There seemed to be few people about save for several sentries scattered here and there in an order known only to them. She resisted the impulse to wave fearing one of them would call to her by her rightful name. For Raff to be undeceived in such a manner would not do.

He whispered to her to remember the night so long ago when he stole her away. They had walked this very pathway. Neither had guessed then what lay ahead. She nodded in response but the thoughts that went on behind were miserable. Fauntley's words haunted her; no more than a fantasy.

The escorts led them to the Great Hall. Ambyre thought as she entered how nothing had changed except perhaps herself. Upon the walls were tapestries she herself had helped stitch or mend. This was the Hall in which she had shared so many meals with Edward and his family. Huge tables formed a square with a large hearth in the center. Dogs forever stayed near here waiting for the next meal. Open, unshuttered windows let in light—and cold—and let out the inevitable smoke from the hearth. It was all so familiar to her; every shadow, every scent, every sound. Yet it was no longer home.

Queen Eadgifu, Edward's wife, greeted them in the Hall attended only by her serving maids. The Great Hall was strangely empty despite the fact that both King and Queen were in residence. But Ambyre, in unabashed happiness at seeing the Queen, hardly noticed as she stepped forward. Eadgifu held out both her hands in greeting.

"AElfwyn! how very glad I am to see you safe, home at last," Eadgifu was saying, much to Ambyre's surprise. Had she called her AElfwyn?

She said that Edward was in the chapel but would come forth as soon as word was brought to him. When he prayed most were loath to disturb him, even Eadgifu herself.

She ordered refreshments, cool wine and buttered bread, as well as every kind of confection Ambyre had so fondly remembered of Edward's chefs.

Raff and his men restricted themselves to

wine and were taking their second hornful when Edward entered. Ambyre's face lit up at the sight of his tall, thin body, a look that Raff did not miss. But he was not surprised. How could he be? He ignored the slight turning of his heart. He'd known from the beginning that his love, his bride-to-be, cared greatly for this greedy monarch, her uncle. How he wished it were different! How he wished she'd longed to regain her own kingdom of Mercia and let this man before them rot in the confines of Wessex.

But none of these thoughts showed on his face. He watched silently as she approached Edward.

"AElfwyn," was Edward's greeting, laced with love, relief and concern. He took her shoulders in his hands and kissed her cheek fondly. Ambyre noticed the sobriety in his eyes as they caught hers. "My own dear niece. At last I am assured of your safety."

"They were most kind, Edward . . . uncle," she added, not knowing what else to say. With a glance toward Fauntley and Cuthbert she saw that they, too, strove to hide their confusion.

"You will want to rest and freshen yourself before we discuss all that has taken place," Edward said, turning to his wife's maids standing nearby. "See that AElfwyn's bower is prepared."

It seemed she was ushered off before a slip could be made, and so were Fauntley and Cuthbert. She cast a last glance at Raff before being escorted away. He watched her go, at first sullen, but encouraged her with a smile before she turned her eyes away.

Ambyre did not have to wait long for an explanation. She had been taken to her own bower, not AElfwyn's, where a bath and fresh clothes awaited. She was barely prepared when a servant called her to Edward's presence.

He was in the chancery, a building near the chapel on the opposite side of the palace grounds. He waited alone in the polished wood room. It was cool and dark though several candles lit the table at which he sat.

Upon hearing her enter he stood, leaving the drawings he occupied himself with. He greeted her with a compassionate smile and a kiss on her cheek. Ambyre felt as she had when her father used to greet her with such affection . . . only this had a certain reverence added to it. Edward was the King. Her King.

She returned the smile upon that narrow face of his. He was a comely man for being near fifty, she thought, moustached, bearded, eyes always kind. Yet she could not summon that infatuation she had once felt for him.

"You are as beloved by me as if you were my own daughter," Edward was saying, reflecting Ambyre's own thoughts about their relationship. "I grieved for you each day of your captivity."

" 'Twas not harsh, my lord. These Danes are kind and fair. They are not a gentle people," she added, thinking of Kirsten's baby, "but they are generous and friendly. I did not suffer."

They sat not far apart upon a covered bench along the wall beside a case of gold-embossed volumes.

"Do you wonder why I did not reveal your identity?" he asked.

She nodded.

"There are things you must know before you will understand. Will you listen?"

The rhetorical question was only to remind her of his good will toward her. No one refused to listen to King Edward, least of all Ambyre.

"It has always been my goal, as it was the goal of my father, to unite this island of England. My reign has seen this more closely fulfilled than that of any other Wessex King, and I pray my son's reign will continue in this manner. It hasn't been my goal to expel the Danes you speak of with such kindness. We've fought many a battle and lost many a life but I have always welcomed the settler who will abide among us peacefully. If these Danes had done so by accepting our true God as their own there would have been no bloodshed. But they have accepted neither our God nor our rule; the heathens who seek to dominate their own portion of England would turn back the progress Christianity has made in our land for the past three hundred years. No true king could allow his people to fall back on the pagan, barbarian customs a heathen ruler would revive. For this reason we have fought to keep the heathen out.

"Can you understand this, Ambyre? I have no grudge against these Danes nor prejudice. They have brought with them the strength and stamina to live honorably. They possess a quickness of valor. Our people welcome this new blood; it is a fresh infusion to mix with our own. And these Danes could have conquered, heathens though they be, had there been a united effort among them. Christianity would have united them. So now I strive to bring them to our holy family to merge with us and fight no more."

"Many have already accepted our God," she offered, thinking of Raff's recent baptism.

" 'Tis good and right if they choose to live here," he replied. " 'Tis my duty to see that all, Christian and pagan alike, will seek only the good of this land. We cannot war."

"Peace must be the goal of both sides, milord."

"Then will you understand why I have kept your identity secret? For my niece, AElfwyn, to wed would mean war."

"But you have agreed to the wedding," she said meekly.

"And there shall be one to the woman this Dane believes to be AElfwyn."

She could not stay seated as the words sank in. She paced with sudden anxiety though it meant turning her back to the king.

"It would mean war," she said then, facing

him. "You do not know this man as I do, my lord. His pride outweighs all else. He'll not take well to more deceit."

Edward's smile was compassionate. "I believe I do know him, my dear. I have been raised with his race breathing fire down my back. No man takes well to deceit but this is the price we must pay. Once he is wed the Church will not grant him a divorce. You shall be his wife until he dies."

"The Church will hardly be enough to stop him."

"It will stop him from marrying AElfwyn. At this point that is all that is necessary."

"But *why?*" she pleaded. "All along you've said you wanted peace, that you would welcome an alliance between your kingdom and the Danes. Why risk war?"

"There can be no peace through marriage with AElfwyn. She is Mercia. Were she to wed 'twould invite loyalists to look to her and her husband for leadership."

"Then you . . . you would fight to keep Mercia?"

"From heathens, I must," he told her. " 'Tis more than these Danes can do, my dear. What will happen when this man Rathulfr learns he has been duped? I see the question upon your face and you need not worry about the answer. 'Tis an alliance whether he weds my niece or my beloved ward. True, he might be angry, tempted to war, but then he would be back where he was before. He has no forces, no Mercians, to strenghten his army against me. He will come to understand that he has an affiliation with my kingdom's strength through you, a partnership with me rather than with Mercia. As I rule that land, 'twould mean a general association among all."

She knew this meant Edward's overlordship —a position proposed once before. Raff had not taken well to it then and would not now. Not when Edward had removed the one factor that gave Raff strength of his own: AElfwyn.

"I'll not force you against your will," Edward told her gently. " 'Tis a political arrangement I know but I ask your consent."

A request seemed strange coming from a king who commanded thousands. She knew what her answer must be. Had she not longed to be Raff's wife? But she knew love would die once he learned the truth.

She nodded her consent, eyes downcast.

"You have always been most loyal, Ambyre," the king said softly. " 'Tis an important thing you do for me; you will save my Mercian kingdom from heathen rule and provide a confederation with the Northern lands the Danes now hold. I will remember this always."

She wanted to leave but the King had not dismissed her. Instead of doing so he spoke again.

"I am sorry if this makes you unhappy." His compassion brought tears to her eyes. It wasn't right for him to comfort her. Her duty was to obey. "I can see you care a great deal in this matter," he went on. "Has your time with these Danes made you fond of them?"

"Aye, my lord," she replied. Her voice quavered.

"Then this is for the best," he said. "If Rathulfr loves his people he will see it as so."

"He does . . . love his people."

"Then he will come around. He schemed to marry AElfwyn at my expense; his tactics deserve little better than those I use on him."

These words, perhaps truthful from Edward's point of view, were nonetheless painful for Ambyre to hear. She knew Raff's pride too well to underestimate the blow this would be.

"I believe 'tis more than Danes in general you have come to care for," Edward said. "Else you would not be so sad. Do you worry over him alone?"

She could only nod tacitly.

He approached, lifting her chin to look at her face.

"Perhaps with the love you have you will make it possible for him to find happiness in your marriage. 'Tis more than he might have found with AElfwyn."

She shook her head, looking away. She would lose his love, never again have his trust.

"The wedding cannot be dissolved. Will that give any comfort?"

She could not answer. Edward saw the pain it caused her to speak of these things. He was about to let her go in the long pause that followed but with a frown he detained her once more.

"I think it best you do not see this man again until the ceremony. 'Twill be a small gathering; we shall have it done quickly which would suit him and avoid anything elaborate that carries the danger of revealing your identity. I have commanded the court to Cheddar which is why the palace must seem so quiet to you. My family will be in attendance as well as Rathulfr's men. The nuptials will be celebrated in two days' time lest we have to wait out the Lenten fasts. We cannot delay that long and keep your identity hidden."

She nodded yet again as Edward dismissed her. When she reached the door she turned to the king who had gone back to his sketches.

"May I see AElfwyn?" she asked timidly, remembering their friendship and longing for its comfort.

Edward frowned, shaking his head as if sad to disappoint her.

"AElfwyn is not here."

"You have . . . hidden her for fear of discovery by the Danes?"

Edward sighed. "It seems Rathulfr is not the only one to come up with a plan to wed my niece. Have you heard of a Norwegian called Ragnold?"

Her nod was eager with curiosity.

"I have heard rumors from Wales, perhaps untrue, that Ragnold too wishes for an alliance through AElfwyn."

"Ragnold!" she repeated. He was Raff's enemy, therefore hers as well. "Raff should be told this when he comes to know of my identity. His foremost wish is for his people to remain free of Ragnold who looks to York for victory."

"He need have no such fear," Edward told her, and she found some comfort in the words.

Later she learned AElfwyn had been taken to a convent where marriage could not touch her. Ambyre thought her friend would be content there.

XXI

The wedding plans were simple and brief; Eadgifu herself took care of the arrangements. The ceremony was to be performed in the presence of those few the king had named. A feast would follow, lavish in content if small in number of guests.

As to Ambyre's dowry, Edward made arrangements with her husband-to-be to have her goods sent after they departed. He gave no indication of the many doubts he had regarding that departure, doubts the bride knew only too well. Edward expected anger from this proud Dane whom he knew had no resources for war. While the marriage would be binding he did not believe Rathulfr would hold to it, cementing as it did Edward's overlordship.

Raff did not insist on a large, stately wedding as befitted the king's niece. It might have served his purpose to hold such a feast for political reasons, to invite the Mercian noblemen and show them that Edward himself approved the match, but the argument of time won out. If the wedding was not held within the next two days they would have to wait through forty days of Lent during which no feasts or weddings ever took place. Indeed, once wedded, bride and groom were expected to consummate their vows on the wedding night alone, then keep the marital fast which bound all married folk until the time of Easter.

Ambyre stayed in her bower seeing few people. Eadgifu came often along with several serving maids and seamstresses to fit her for her wedding gown. She would have been overwhelmed with joy had her wedding to Raff been held under any other circumstances.

Instead she walked about her room as if in a daze. She spoke little, ate little. Eadgifu tried to comfort her but Ambyre did not respond. She could think only of the day Raff would learn the truth. She could see his face, hurt, betrayed, sorrowful.

The day of her wedding came and she dressed in all her finery. Her gunna was a pale yellow satin fitted close to her body with kirtle showing underneath of pure white. A girdle of white silk bound her at the waist. Atop her head was a gold satin headrail whose circlet was a gift from King Edward. It was gold and silver with dark smoky jewels that matched the color of her eyes. On her fingers sparkled rings of silver, gold, and amber, one of which Olaf had given her before they left. She was a vision of fresh loveliness, a hint of spring that had come upon the land.

Fauntley and Cuthbert attended the ceremony. Edward's daughters, Edith, Ealhild and Aelfgifu served as Ambyre's bridesmaids, dressed in lavender, pale green, and rose. A rainbow of pastel spring shades entered the chapel that morning with bright yellow sunshine beaming down upon the altar through the windows high above.

Ambyre saw Raff for the first time since the day they arrived and her heart leapt for him. She had never seen him in such resplendence. His hair, always a sheen of yellow silk, was combed and smooth. He wore a red satin tunic embroidered along its edge with images of soaring falcons. His belt was a stark black, as were his breeches, bound by crimson leather cross-garterings from just below the knee down to black leather shoes. At each hip were his weapons, the sword *Kappi* on one side, his jeweled dagger, the very one she had tried to kill him with, on the other. She thought she had never seen a more comely man than he, nor would she ever for the rest of her days.

He greeted her with a tender smile. As they took the last few steps toward the altar together he whispered that he had never seen a vision as lovely as she.

They received the sacrament of marriage on bent knee with bowed heads. Ambyre was glad not to face Raff; she had longed for this moment but not with a secret still between them.

… NORTHWARD THE HEART

After the wedding mass she was ushered to her bower and Raff sent off with his men to await their reunion at the evening feast. It began as the sun set, the Danes surprisingly sober, as if they had been counseled beforehand to act in a seemly manner. There were no wrestling bouts or bold challenges or outrageous boasting. Ambyre found she missed that lively spirit. There was laughter for it was a wedding, but not the wholehearted laughter she knew these Danes could enjoy.

Had there been more people her depression might have gone unnoticed. But Raff watched closely as she moved the food about on her platter; he saw she had not taken a bite.

Placing his hand over hers, he said, "I hope your withdrawal is only due to thoughts of our wedding night—pleasant thoughts of what is to come."

She managed a tremulous smile but said nothing.

Not entirely satisfied but eager to enliven her mood, he teased her. "Tomorrow brings the Christian Lenten fasts. If 'tis true I can't touch you after tonight I must offer a prayer that tonight might last forever. But then we have already broken the laws of your Church. Do I have any hope for the next forty nights?"

How she wanted to give him that hope! How she wished she could look forward to their nights together—for the rest of their lives! But she knew better than to hope for something so obviously beyond her reach.

Still, in order to placate him, she whispered with what might have appeared as demurely downcast eyes, "Aye, milord. We have already proven weak regarding Church laws."

It was not a definite answer. One part of him wanted to demand a declaration however unchaste it might be. But another part of him knew her too well to doubt anything could keep them apart. He clung to that.

Her gloom increased. She longed for his embrace, his touch, his kiss. She longed for him to fill her being with himself. But she knew what was in store. She knew tonight's embraces would be far different from all others. While she longed for him as any loving bride would, she dreaded what lay ahead.

That morning Edward had tried to approach the subject delicately but he was a pious man who did not like to speak of such things to a young girl. Yet Ambyre understood. She was to consummate this marriage to preclude any question of annulment. It was not the act itself she now thought of with shame; it was that she would go to Raff this time not solely out of love as before but out of duty and deceit. It was now proper and legal yet tonight she would feel shame.

During the feast he presented her with wedding gifts. Two gold brooches for her gown, one trefoil brooch for her cloak, with two golden rings, one to remind her of his love, the other of his fidelity. But the gift that made even Edward lift a brow was ownership of one-third of all his land holdings, not only in Yorkshire but Northman's Land as well, Ambyre to do with it as she pleased.

The gift was undeniably generous, one that should have warmed her heart with such a great proof of love. But though she smiled that heart grew heavy with shame. These gifts, announced before witnesses upon their wedding day, were hers forevermore. No matter what he would feel for her on the morrow, they were irrevocable. Such generosity only heightened her remorse.

At midnight the bridesmaids escorted her to the bridal chamber. It was AElfwyn's bower, private and spacious. She remembered it well, her thoughts straying back to the night she was there last. It had been the first time she saw Raff.

He entered after her attendants departed, signaling that the bride was ready for her groom. He gazed at her bowed head and lowered eyes thinking she looked like a shy virgin coming to her husband for the first time. But he knew she had no fear so her mood disturbed him. He placed a hand gently on each of her shoulders and spoke, though she could not raise her eyes to him.

"You are my wife, now AElfwyn," he said. "Is this not what both of us longed for?"

"Aye," she told him.

"Then why do you look as you do?" he asked, adding with a grin, "Do I no longer appeal to you now that I am your husband and 'tis lawful?"

At those words she threw her arms around him, wanting him to believe, if only for a short time longer, in her love. She kissed him as boldly as Northern wenches kiss their warriors.

He accepted it, relieved more than he could admit that her downcast mood had lightened enough to let through the love he had come to treasure in her.

He treated her as was fit for a maiden on her wedding night, taking her to the bed slowly with an arm about her waist. Fully clothed, they sat down as he leaned closer for another kiss. One hand rested on her breast. For a long while they sat this way, kissing, touching, slowly easing their way along, for once not restricted to the darkened, secret hours. Tonight they could use what time they needed, draw out each moment to make it last.

"I am going to make love to you," he whispered sensuously into her ear. "To my wife, my love, my life's desire."

His words sent a shiver of pure anticipation through her body. They were still fully clothed —indeed, he'd barely touched her—and yet she felt such intense longing it seemed that desire had been building forever.

Unwanted thoughts rose stubbornly at the back of her mind. How could she let him make love to her knowing it was, on her part, half affection, half obligation. And what was worse, the obligation was to Edward.

Yet how could she resist Raff? His tongue teased hers making her whole body more aware, more sensitive than ever before. Her clothes slipped away under his touch. She longed to feel his skin. She knew she should stop, confess who she was and have done with it. But she was piteously weak. How she needed him! How she needed this one last time with him. Its memory would have to endure a lifetime.

Boldly she undressed him as deftly as he had undressed her. His body—so perfectly molded, so smooth and hard and rapturously fitted to her own—should have been familiar by now. But the sight of it thrilled her anew. His broad shoulders, his chest, firmly muscled beneath a fine layer of hair, his belly flat and hard. And below... such vivid evidence that her body was just as pleasing for him to look upon.

Gently he pressed her into the softly scented mattress beneath them, kissing her all the while. Entwined in each other's arms, they let their kisses begin to roam. His tongue sent a tingling wave of pleasure through her from head to toe.

With a boldness he had taught her, she let her fingers travel where they wished. Across his strong shoulders, down his muscled back, along his hips and then, with ageless desire ruling her, to his manhood. With pleasure she heard his indrawn breath, as if he couldn't bear the sensation.

She, too, felt her own unsteady breathing as his caress knew the length of her. Her body felt afire, her breasts taut with want, her loins desperate with longing—longing for him to join his body to hers.

Instinctively she thrust her hips against his, demanding. But instead of filling her he prolonged the pleasure. With a longing ache she let him have his way. She thrilled to the touch of his fingers at her white-hot core, writhing beneath him and moaning his name.

"I want you. . ." she said, her breathing deep. "All of you."

"Soon, my love," he whispered back.

Then as if fulfilling her wish, he shifted himself above her. But rather than entering her, though she invited him by opening her thighs, he stroked her with his masculine hardness, only teasing the entrance.

It drove Ambyre wild with wanting. Her eyes, glazed with desire, sought his and found that he, too, seemed on the brink of giving in to the satisfaction so close at hand. How long? she thought. How long could they bear it, this drawn-out pleasure almost too great to sustain? Already she felt their bodies bathed in perspiration smoothly sliding against one another.

She almost thrust her hips upward forcing that bond she knew he'd be unable to resist. But when his eyes stayed locked to hers, she held back. She waited.

His caress against her went on, slowly, rhythmically. They stared at one another as if it were a test of endurance. His eyes, too, seemed to say, how long? And she lost herself in him.

But at last her gaze faltered. It was her undoing for once that trance was broken she could not withhold what they'd put off. Just as she thrust upward, so did he plunge downward, and ecstasy followed. The rhythm between them was quick, hard, almost desperate. Her deep breathing matched his. Their bodies, more damp than ever, slid caressingly against each other as they approached that pinnacle of satisfaction.

She was barely aware of the frenzied rapidity of their movements, of the way he thrust deeper and deeper into her, for she, too, felt only a mad need for this desperate coupling. It had turned almost violent in its intensity, so long, it seemed, had they waited for it. But the delay had brought more pleasure than ever before.

At last they reached mutual climax, for the moment too exhausted even for speech. He lay above her, half supporting himself on his elbows, still one with her. Slowly, lazily, his gaze traveled to hers. He smiled.

"It seems our pleasure has only increased for being husband and wife."

But too soon, only moments after everything else had ceased to exist, reality returned to Ambyre. Husband and wife. The sound echoed in her ears. *For how long?*

Release had come in body only. She could not feel unburdened; she could not forget what lay ahead. Only at the height of desire and satisfaction had those thoughts truly been cast aside. Now, though the rest of the night was theirs and could have brought repetition after repetition of what they had given each other, her tension returned. It was nothing his caress could ease nor his words of love abate. They only made it worse, until she lay under his touch with tears upon her face.

"AElfwyn..." he inquired, gently brushing one of her tears with a fingertip. Both hands came to her face and she could look only at him. "Why do you cry?"

Now that he had seen her tears she seemed unable to control them. He kissed her, then frowned with concern.

"What's happened? You are not happy to be my wife?"

"Nay, Raff! I am happy... in that alone. My love is real."

"And so is mine. Then why do you cry?"

She left his side, standing by the bed and retrieving the crimson satin robe laid out for her use. She covered her nakedness, unable to look upon him any longer. It was good that she could not see her own face; it registered only shame.

"I—I must go... I must speak with Edward—" she stammered, but before she could reach the door, he rose from the bed and, unconcerned with his own nakedness, stood between her and it.

"You'll not leave without explaining what this means, AElfwyn. Why must you see Edward?"

He spoke the name with ill-concealed scorn and took her shoulders firmly in his grip.

"Tell me, AElfwyn," he pleaded. "Have you lost your love for me since returning here to Edward?"

"Nay!" she almost screamed, high-pitched and emotional. "Edward is my king—no more."

"Then why must you go to him on our wedding night? Have I not just moments ago given you pleasure enough?"

"Do not speak so, Raff! I need only to talk with my sovereign, nothing more than that."

"Talk with me," he whispered. "Tell me what has ailed you on our wedding night. If your love is true you should be as happy as I to be wed."

"I . . . I cannot," she said at last. "I have not been true to you, Raff."

His hands dropped as if they lost all strength to hold her. His eyes did not conceal the pain, looking at her with intermingled confusion.

"Is it . . . Edward?"

She shook her head, turning from him. "I cannot go on as I have, Raff. I cannot lie to you any longer. My heart is true to you and my body has been as well. But I have lied. I wished to see Edward to ask his permission for what I must tell you."

"Why must you gain his permission if it has to do with our marriage?"

"Because it also has to do with his niece . . . AElfwyn."

"*You* are his niece," he insisted.

She did not look upon him. "Remember the

night you came here to this very room, stealing me away?"

"Aye," he answered, listening intently.

"There was another maid with me here . . . do you remember?"

He nodded.

" 'Twas AElfwyn," she said in a toneless, wooden voice.

He was silent and she allowed a moment for the words to take meaning. But when the silence continued she thought he had not understood.

" 'Twas AElfwyn I was *with*," she said.

"I understand." His voice was so quietly harsh that she knew a moment of fear. "And you?"

"I am Ambyre of Athelney, ward of King Edward."

"His ward?" he scoffed. "His personal ward to see to his *personal* needs?"

"Unworthy! You know as well as I that I was a virgin before you. . ."

"Aye, I know it. Perhaps I plucked the king's fruit?"

"Raff." Her voice trembled. "You have reason to loathe me but do not believe this. Edward is an honorable, God-fearing man. I have given myself only to you."

"You seem more concerned for his pious reputation than your own, AElfwyn—nay, Ambyre is it?"

"Raff," she said with new urgency, knowing words were all she had to convince him. "I have

NORTHWARD THE HEART

loved you all along. I never *wanted* to deceive you, not about marriage to Fauntley nor about my identity. There have been many times—"

"Spare me, milady," he said callously. "You have been nothing but deceitful to me. Do you think I will believe any words from your guileful mouth again? I should have trusted my initial anger with you. Anger that bade me never trust you again. This time I will not be so naive."

He pulled on his clothes. She wanted to beg him to listen but knew it would only awaken further disdain. He had always admired her pride; let her remain with some intact.

"I do love you, Raff," she told him quietly. "I have never been guileful in that."

His laugh came through a twisted, scornful smile. "Nay, milady. You love Edward. Mayhap 'tis true you have never given him your body but you have given him all else. You have no loyalty left for anyone else. He has had his way in this so that he rules all, is that not so? He wishes no challenge to any part of his land and for that he has made sure the Mercians stay his without alliance to any other kingdom. His powerful hand is on the reins. I see it well, milady." He laughed again bitterly. "I should have known this plan worked too easily. Edward seemed too willing when I knew well it would cost him to have his niece wed to me or to any Danish leader. But I was so damnably in love with you that I became stupid, easily fooled. All I thought of was having you for my wife."

Fully dressed, he went to the door. "Remember this, milady. You may in truth be my wife but I shall never forget this night when you gave yourself to me out of duty to Edward. I shall be no husband to you. Not for all the days of my life."

Word came from Cuthbert who had slept among the warriors that Raff sailed before dawn with his men, only an hour after he had left his marriage bed.

XXII

From her perch at the unshuttered window Ambyre could see all the king's land and beyond. Before her stretched acres of his hunting forests, almost as full of deer and wild boar as trees. Beyond lay the villagers' homes, colorful little huts dotting neat rows of farmland. Signs of spring were everywhere; birds and butterflies, flowers and new grasses. Everything seemed young and fresh. The northward hills looked grey-blue in the morning light, blending with a sky punctuated only with fair-weather white clouds as contrast.

But the burden upon her did not allow appreciation of such beauty. Her gaze went toward the north, not seeing the hills along the horizon nor the pattern of the farmers' fields nor even the puffy white clouds that floated like weightless sculptures. Northward was the direction of her heart, where Raff had gone almost fourteen nights ago.

NORTHWARD THE HEART

Since he left she had only one hope. Her prayers had been that she carried his child. Having no sign to the contrary she had let her hopes rise. If she were to give him a child... a part of him to love and to raise... perhaps an heir, would he not come to her at least once, just to see what she had borne him? And if he did come that once she would try with all her might to dispel his anger. She would force him to remember the love they had shared which brought the child they created together.

Whatever hope she had was cast out the morning her moon cycle came. There was no child within her to bring him back... to have as her own remembrance of how he once loved her.

Mid-morning found her still in her bower. The hours went slowly but she wanted only to be alone. In recent days not even the frequent visits of Cuthbert and Fauntley helped to dispel loneliness.

Of the two, Fauntley was most persistent. He'd come every day since Raff left. At first he'd made polite conversation, trying to force her to respond. But eventually he was satisfied just to be with her, to sit quietly beside her, or to read.

Therefore when he tapped at her door that day, she was not surprised to see him. Ruth, her maid, let him in and resumed her needlework silently in the corner.

Ambyre sat in her accustomed chair by the open window. When Fauntley pulled another chair beside hers, she gave him a vacant smile and turned her gaze northward again.

But today, unlike yesterday and the days before, he had no book or wax tablet with him for diversion while she gazed the afternoon away. He'd come empty handed, which, distantly, she noted. Perhaps he was growing tired of her dull company and would not stay long.

They sat in total silence. Several times she thought he might speak but he did not. She wished he had brought his book. She wished he would say whatever he wanted to say. She wished he would leave.

But he did nothing. At last, with a combination of curiosity and irritation, she spoke.

"Is there something you wanted to say? Something weighing on your mind today?"

His fair cheeks darkened. "No... I... Yes, Ambyre."

But then he lowered his eyes and paused so long she was forced to say, "Well? We've been through so much, Fauntley. Surely you're no longer shy in front of me?"

He looked at her, his brown eyes uncertain, as if he still did not know how to express what he wanted to say. He started to speak once, then, remembering the presence of the maid, glanced her way.

"Would you like me to send Ruth away?" Ambyre asked.

He breathed deeply. "Aye. Perhaps that would be best."

The maid left unobtrusively, taking her needlework with her.

Then she faced him again. He did not look much better.

"What is it, Fauntley?" she prodded gently.

Suddenly he stood, squared his shoulders and looked down at her. He spoke forthrightly. " 'Tis you, Ambyre." Once he began he could not be stopped even when her brows lifted in surprise at his personal attack. "I cannot bear to see you this way any longer. You're wasting your life away for that man. You cannot let yourself do that. When I see Cuddy riding or playing about with the weapons the Northmen gave him, I think of you—how *you* used to spend your days riding in the forest, teaching him things your father taught you—enjoying any outdoor activity you could. Now here you sit, day after day, staring out from this self-imposed cage of yours. Your cheeks are pale, you're painfully thin, you lack any of that passion life once filled you with."

Instead of defending herself or reminding him her life and what she did with it were no concern of his, she smiled wanly.

"You used to scold me for all that, Fauntley. Don't you remember? You used to say, 'tis not proper for a genteel woman to go about on horseback or teach a young boy to wield a sword."

His shoulders drooped just a little and he took his seat again. When he spoke it was earnestly. "But it's all part of you, Ambyre. I was a fool to think I could love you any other way."

"And have you stopped loving me?" she asked. She hoped he had. Love only brought pain. How well she knew!

"Nay, Ambyre! I love the person you truly are, with the enthusiasm to enjoy everything from a half-wild romp on a horse to reading the scriptures. Not this shell of a person you've become. I can no longer stand to see you this way. That is why," his voice faltered slightly, "I want to take you away."

For a moment she wasn't sure she heard correctly. "Take me away?"

"Aye, away from Winchester, away from this palace where you last saw . . . him. I'll take you back to Athelney or to London if you wish. Anywhere would be better than here."

It was, of course, a ludicrous idea, she thought. Why didn't he see that? The ache she felt would go with her anywhere; her surroundings had nothing to do with it.

And what would they do wherever they went? Athelney was no longer her home; when her father died the home and lands where she'd grown up had been handed over to another family. She, being a woman, could not inherit Saxon land, and Cuthbert, who was illegitimate, had been given nothing but his father's love.

"Fauntley, if my home cannot be with my husband, then it must be here, with . . .

Edward." Why, she wondered, had his name been so hard to say? He was her king!

"But you're unhappy here."

"Would I be happier anywhere else? How would we live? You are commissioned by the king to tutor the children of the palace. You cannot just leave."

"If he knew I took you away for your own good he would approve."

"Would he? Who could accept a married woman going off with another man?"

Fauntley flushed scarlet, not able to look into her eyes as he spoke. "It wouldn't be that way, Ambyre. I know now that you could never be mine."

"Perhaps not but it would *seem* that way to the Court. You cannot want that."

"I want what is best for you."

She took one of his hands in hers. Her heart wrenched at this unselfish love that would drive him to do anything to make her happy. She knew that kind of love.

"You've been too good to me already. You've forgiven me so much, you've tried to help me through all my sins. I only wish I could repay you."

"You can," he said, "by being happy."

But she knew there was only way for her to find happiness. And that way had been closed to her forever.

The following day a maidservant brought news that Edward wished to see her. She knew he was displeased at her solitude day after day. He had all but commanded her to dinner two nights ago but she had not returned since. He no doubt wished to see her at this evening's table.

He was in the chancery, sitting at the table with what appeared to be the same sketches he had pored over the last time she had stepped inside this room. When she entered he smiled, remaining seated as she approached. He held up a parchment sketched with several circled designs. All had the same theme, a flying dove bearing an olive branch. She recognized this as the design on the coins he minted.

"I am considering adding new detail to my coins," he said to her. "Tell me, Ambyre, do you know what this picture means?"

"A dove has always meant peace."

"Aye, and this is Noah's dove, for peace in our land."

She lowered her eyes with reddened cheeks. Edward saw her frown and stood, walking round the desk, leading her to sit beside him on the couch.

"The peace is at the expense of the Danes, is that what you are thinking? Because they must settle for overlordship of a Wessex king? But in your pity for them you forget that they—aye, Rathulfr's people, his father and his father's father, have wreaked havoc and scourged this land. They have plundered and harried, stolen, raped, murdered and made shells of Saxon lives. 'Tis the way of the barbaric heathen. But now this era is at an end. My reign will bring peace. For that I count myself proud and glad."

Ambyre did not raise her eyes to him. She could not, for she did not believe the warriors she had known had done such things. Those deeds of their forefathers they spoke of—and she could not deny they spoke of them proudly—were not for the sake of barbarian cruelty. They had plundered and stolen, it was true, but used that money to buy land they desperately needed. Their ally was strength, and they used it to the fullest. She did not reply to Edward's words.

He was about to speak to her again but urgent voices and a pounding at the door deterred him. He stood and bade his soldiers enter. They were so agitated they did not see the king was not alone. Or perhaps they thought her presence did not matter.

"Word comes from York, my lord," the sentry announced in a breathless voice. "Ragnold has marched and ousted the Danish leaders. It is said he proclaims himself King of York, as his forebear Ragnar gave him right."

A frown twisted Edward's face. Ambyre went ashen with the news. For a brief moment, so many thoughts—horrible visions, terrifying sights—went through her mind. She felt dizzy. But no! She *must* be strong. Raff was still alive. He was! Stepping forward she stood before the soldiers and spoke boldly.

"Ragnold has won?" Her heart pounded so

loudly in her ears she could barely hear her own words. "He has conquered the Danes?"

The soldier looked from her to King Edward as if for approval to answer. Edward nodded for him to continue.

"Aye—and hardly more than a skirmish. Ragnold did not have much trouble once he reached York. Even the old Roman wall did not keep him out."

Ambyre gripped the back of the couch she had vacated. York taken by Ragnold, just as Raff had feared. Again, dizziness assailed her. It was her fault this had happened—*her* fault his plan for strength had failed. How could she bear it? Surely he—and all his people—suffered because of her. And how they must hate her for this, with whatever energy they had left!

Edward sent the messenger to bring those he took council with, the Chamberlain and others of trust in the Court. He remained standing, stroking his beard in troubled preoccupation, seeming to forget Ambyre's presence.

This was the king she admired and loved, to whom she had always given her loyalty. But suddenly before her was a man, a rather sad man who had betrayed her and midjudged his enemies. Wasn't it his fault? Wasn't he to blame? He had doomed the plan to marry AElfwyn. He'd said the Danes had nothing to fear from Ragnold. Yet all of Raff's dire predictions had come true.

"You! It was *you* Raff depended upon to keep this from happening! You took away any hope of Mercian help; *you* were to be his ally instead. Yet what has happened? He and his people die at the hands of Ragnold!"

Edward stood before her, stiffening at words no other human being would dare speak against him.

When he kept silent, she came to herself. This was *Edward* she spoke to, not her father, not some kindly mentor. This was the king. In horror at what had happened she fled the room, tears unchecked.

Now she could think only of Raff. Surely he would have fought Ragnold. Was he alive at this moment? Or wounded? And what's more, would he want to survive a battle he could not win? Survive to watch his enemy rule? Nay, this battle would surely mean his death. His pride would not allow it otherwise.

She longed to find him even if he hated her. York was already Ragnold's. Did that mean he had conquered the outlying Danish holds as well? She had no choice but to go and see for herself.

A black grouse rested from its flight taking cover in a thickly-leafed birch. His lyre-shaped tail fluttered before he settled into an instant state of half-slumber. His black, shiny eyes closed below stark red brows. He thought he chose a peaceful glen in which to rest before returning to his moorland.

Not far away, however, horsemen headed for that very glen. Pounding hooves warned the grouse of their approach. Before they came into view he had already decided there would be no rest between here and home.

At the forefront of these intruders was a satiny-blond-haired warrior, shield flung over one shoulder, sword and dagger at each hip, axe in hand. There was no softness in his face nor any of the pain which had been so clearly present for the past fortnight. His expression was one of cold determination, of hardness that spoke no mercy for the enemy.

Behind him rode his father, his retainers, his brother and a score of others who had been gathered from nearby provinces. What unity they had left would be used to the fullest advantage against Ragnold.

But the enemy was not taken by surprise. Ragnold, victor at York just days ago, knew better than to think his new reign was welcome. And so, before Raff and his war party had neared the city wall they knew the enemy lay in wait for them. Some fell into hay-covered horse-traps and were thrown from their mounts into the arms of concealed warriors. Orm's horse went down, sending him under the dagger of a waiting Norwegian.

That was the first of Ragnold's strategies. Those of Raff's men who made it through quickly dismounted their travel-beaten horses. They headed for a slight incline beyond those warriors lurking near the traps. Raff called his instructions and his men, with speed and agility, followed his orders to form a line.

Together they created a shield-wall behind which archers and spear-throwers could initiate the first attack. Weapons were pitched from both sides as Ragnold's men drew near. Arrows flew, some with such strength they passed through shields into the men behind them, to be imbedded deep in the flesh. But the shield-wall held, deflecting attacks until Raff shouted the final war-cry and they advanced upon the enemy.

They were sorely outnumbered, but many of the enemy had been seen to fall before he gave the yell. He knew his men were of like mind; they would not hide behind the comparative safety of the shield-wall when they could go forth into close combat. They longed to use their swords and axes, to strike blows against the skulls of the enemy, drawing the blood of those who threatened their homes and farms, freedom and honor. This was the enemy who made death preferable to living under tyranny.

Shields and helmets were no match for the wrath of the Danes who defended their land. War-cries were shouted, massive growls heard as an axe was swung with all one's might. The smell of blood and sweat grew rank in the air. Fear was not present in these outnumbered warriors; indeed, some even smiled upon meeting their death.

Fury drove Raff, fury not only against the enemy before him. He possessed a rage that had been concealed for more than two weeks, days before Ragnold had marched upon York. With this rage he swung left and right, his shield long since discarded to better use the axe. Never once did he reach for *Kappi*; his axe seemed forever fastened to his hands, glued by the blood that dripped upon them from the enemy. If he took any injury himself he was unaware of it; the white rage gave no quarter to pain. He didn't care if his own blood was upon another's hands; he thought only of the enemy's, at last giving vent to all the anger he carried within.

The cry of victory came before Raff had fallen but he knew which side had won. Under the searing pain of an arrow imbedded in his flesh, he knew the victory was not his. And he wished this wound to be his last.

Ella had tended many battle injuries in her day. These, while numerous, were no different. She expected the worst and so when a few dozen men returned alive she had rejoiced. There was no victory but there was life.

Though her eyes searched for her husband and sons, she hurried to the tasks before her. Soon blood-soaked clothes cluttered the hall; slaves gathered lamb's wool and spiders' webs to mix with oozing blood and stop its flow from sword and dagger slashes; onion soup was boiled for stomach wounds. Cow's urine simmered till it grew dense and thick, stinging the very nostrils breathing its scent. But there was no better cleanser than that.

Bodies lined the benches along the hall. Every able-bodied person, man or woman, slave or free, scurried about to save whom they could. Some died but there was no time to mourn. There was always another to tend.

Ella paused only once when she saw Olaf being carried inside. In all the years she had taken care of him, never before had the sight of his wound so frightened her. But had she not expected this? Had not he himself expected it as well? He was no young warrior to be going off to battle. Both knew the facts when he had left early that morning.

She knelt at his side knowing there was naught to do. The wound he suffered ran from chest to stomach. The hand she took into hers was already cold and bloodless. She cleansed his face hoping to bring what comfort she could.

"My Ella," he whispered in a raspy voice. "Do you see? I shall have a warrior's death ... after all."

XXIII

Ambyre lay still; was she aboard King Edward's ship or was she in a grassy meadow shrouded in a fog that distorted sight and sound? She had heard the whistle of an arrow—or was it just the wind? She had seen it all so clearly—men in combat with swords and daggers, axes and spears. She saw green, dew-covered grass become spattered with blood. She heard groans as men were wounded. It had all been vivid, to the moment she heard the scream.

But who had screamed? Certainly it wasn't a battle cry; and just as certainly no warrior would cry out from pain or fear. It had been a woman's scream, a woeful cry of grief.

Then she remembered. The cry had been her own; she had seen Raff fall. His blood, more precious to her than anyone's, was spilling onto that bespattered grass. She ran desperately, breathing as fiercely as a warrior in battle, but to no avail. Her legs carried her no closer to him. He remained too far away.

And then they came; golden-haired women, dressed in mail that clung to their heavenly bodies. They came from the sky upon horses as black as Odin's raven. They carried shields and swords, these warrior-maidens of the Norse gods, and they came to take heroes who died to the battlefield of Odin.

The first of these Valkyries came toward Raff, lifted him upon her horse, carried him upward until the clouds and the mist hid him from view. It was then that Ambyre's cry awakened her.

It was not a new dream; these same images had haunted her every night since learning of the battle. The ending never changed.

She sat up; the others on board were still asleep. Cuthbert, lying closest to her, clutched his dagger which was safely sheathed. She smiled. He was so like a Dane himself. It was no surprise when he insisted on coming along.

But his was the only familiar face. The others were soldiers of King Edward commissioned by him to see Ambyre safely to her destination. They were aboard Edward's favorite ship, the very one he and his family used to cross the Channel or, now, to sail up the coast of England.

By her own calculations they would reach Yorkshire by midday. As the soldiers roused and made sail she could not hide her anxiety. Eager as she was to return to Yorkshire she feared what she might find. Her nightmare seemed so real; had Raff truly been carried up to heaven? She could not rid herself of the horrible vision.

Yet what if he lived? she asked herself. Would he accept her return? Could she hope for a reconciliation after all that had passed between them? But one-third of all his land was hers, she reminded herself, by right of his bride-gift. She could stay in Yorkshire even if he were alive and spurned her; she had a home there which no one—Saxon or Dane, could take away. Not even he could force her to leave.

As the ship neared the familiar Yorkshire coast, Ambyre forced away her unpleasant thoughts. She watched as the soldiers unloaded the household articles, cloth and gold that comprised her dowry. After she was helped ashore she stood beside the heavily-laden carts and spoke firmly.

"I want only two men to accompany me to Rathulfr Olafsson's province," she said. "One to pull each cart."

A seasoned soldier stepped forward, his face a vision of protest. "My lady, we are to see you safely through the completion of this journey. How can we trust you'll be warmly received by the barbarians?"

She squared her shoulders and rebuked his harsh words. "My husband's people are *not* barbarians. I assure you, my safety is not in question." She spoke with much more confidence than she felt.

"But, milady—"

NORTHWARD THE HEART

"Do not argue," she said. "How do you think these people will take to a Saxon army falling upon their village after having fought a battle they could not win against Norwegians?"

"Our concern is not to spare their pride, but to insure your welfare, as King Edward commissioned us."

"There may be few Danes left but their pride outweighs your caution. I'll have no skirmish fought simply because I wish to return to my husband. I repeat, my safety is not in question. So choose whomever you wish to pull my carts. No one else may come."

The old soldier bent to her command seeing it would be fruitless to debate any further. He chose the two burliest among them and soon Ambyre, Cuthbert and the pair of soldiers were on their way.

She no longer wondered what would happen once she reached the village. She had no idea whether or not she would be warmly received—by Raff or his people. She only knew that this place, his village, was more home to her than Winchester Palace had ever been.

At the outskirts of the familiar province she sent Edward's men back to the ship. Neither gave her argument. She watched them disappear before turning her attention to Cuthbert.

"I want no resistance from you," she began. "You will stay here with the carts until I return. I wish to see Raff and his people alone first."

"But why, Ambyre? Are you afraid they'll turn you away?"

"Do not argue," she said. With that she left his side, giving him no further chance to speak.

It was just past midday but the village was strangely quiet. The huts she passed appeared empty. No voices or sounds reached her ears. Horses were stabled here and there so she knew the village had not been deserted. When at last she came to Olaf's longhouse, she found it, too, oddly empty, though personal articles were abundantly present, tossed carelessly about.

She felt her heart beat wildly, fearing the fate of the villagers. What had become of them? What had become of Raff?

She left the longhouse to rejoin Cuthbert when she heard voices from the trees just outside the village. She rushed toward the sound, anxious and hopeful, her heart still pounding.

She saw the women first, conversing in subdued tones. Behind them were the slaves carrying what looked to be the leavings of a feast. Some distance away, the warriors followed. They were fewer in number than before and some needed assistance in walking. But they still proudly displayed their polished weaponry.

Her eyes searched the crowd anxiously for Raff but could not find him. Then she knew the dream of the Valkyries had been prophetic. He was dead.

She kept watching, frozen with grief, until

one last man emerged from the grove.

Her heart leapt joyfully inside her breast. It was he, walking tall and straight but with obvious stiffness in one leg. She longed to run to him, to cry out her relief that he still lived. But the women stepped in front of her, obscuring her view. The look upon their faces made her pause.

She had chosen to wear the garments Sigrid had give her long ago. Dressed as a Danishwoman, she might have been one of them but for the darkness of her hair. If she hoped this would tell them where her loyalties lay, she saw in their eyes the attempt had failed. There was not one friendly gaze, except perhaps from Kirsten who looked upon her with pity.

Suddenly angry shouts came from the warriors. She shouldn't be surprised, she realized. Hadn't the Danish women just now warned her with their silent animosity?

In a moment she had been surrounded. Yet she was not afraid for Raff filled her eyes. He stepped before her, blotting out the sight of the warrior's angry faces. Love surged within her at the sight of him, though his face looked hard as stone.

When he spoke the mood of his people became painfully clear. "We have just come from burying the warriors your deceit has killed. You are not welcome here, witch."

" 'Twas not my doing—" she tried to defend herself but her voice was no more than a whisper as she stared into the coldness of his eyes.

His words were bleak. "Do you expect me to believe you now? After all your lies?"

"I did what you would have done if kidnapped by the enemy. In the beginning, you *were* my enemy."

"We still are your enemies!" another warrior interjected.

"Nay!" she cried, at last looking around to see Raff's bitterness mirrored on the faces of those nearby. Fear filled her but she spoke again. "How could a weak and helpless woman be a worthy enemy? I had to deceive you—I feared for my life and the lives of my brother and Fauntley. But that makes no difference now—if I *had* been AElfwyn, Edward would never have agreed to a marriage. He would not have risked losing Mercia to AElfwyn's husband!"

"Perhaps that is so," Raff spoke up, "but he would have had little choice had you truly been AElfwyn and we gave you back your throne. The Mercians would have been with us."

"Edward would have kiled the lot of you!"

"Not with Mercian forces combined with our own."

"You still would have lost York! You would have been too busy fighting off Edward to pay heed to what Ragnold was doing. But now Edward wants peace with you! Though I'm not AElfwyn, he recognizes our marriage as an alliance between our people. He promises to contain Ragnold in York where he cannot touch you. He wants us all to live in peace."

"Then he should have recognized that alliance before York was taken."

"But he didn't know Ragnold's objectives! Now, what is done is done. Edward wants no more bloodshed. Ragnold will not be allowed to spread his tyranny beyond the walls of York."

Her words made sense but her plea failed.

"None of that makes any difference," one warrior shouted. "Not where your deceit is concerned! *You* are the one to blame for our humiliation, for Ragnold to have gained York as he did."

Two warriors grabbed her by the arms and dragged her away—away from Raff who stood stock-still. He alone as chieftain could save her. But he did not move. The warriors led her toward the wood, jeering at her as they went.

No amount of premonition on Ambyre's part could have prepared her for this. *They will kill me*, she thought, and for a moment stunned amazement kept her silent.

But then, from some deep recess, the instinct for survival emerged. She struggled wildly against her captors, all the while not knowing why. Why should she live, when Raff hated her as much as these warriors did? But her body fought in spite of her thoughts. In the struggle one sleeve ripped away from her gown. No one seemed to care. Murder and vengeance filled the air.

Would Raff allow this? her mind cried out.

Would he let them go through with this lust for her blood? The answer made her struggle seem fruitless. What did it matter? she thought again. Why live now?

One warrior's words reflected the uselessness of her attempts at freedom. "You cannot escape us, Saxon witch. We will send the demon who inhabits you back to hell where you both belong."

Their vengeance would be satisfied only with her blood . . . but hers was innocent blood! she cried to herself.

But was it? Wasn't she, at least in part to blame? Three people were responsible for the loss of York: Ragnold, Edward, and she. Since the Danes could not wreak their vengeance upon Ragnold or Edward, they would settle for her. Perhaps she deserved it, she thought with desolation so fierce she felt on the verge of giving up her soul before they had a chance to send it on its way. Perhaps Raff was right to let her die.

They neared the forest from which they had come. Through the bodies of those pressing closer she caught a glimpse of Wulfstan and Torquil. They stood next to Sigrid and Kirsten, near a few other warriors she remembered. Pity was on their faces. But when she caught Raff's eyes there was no pity at all. He had not moved from where he stood, watching as she was led to her death. He *would* allow his warriors to do as they wished.

Still shouting, they tied coarse rope to her

wrists. Her arms pulled outward and the rope tore into her flesh, spilling blood down her arms. She did not flinch at the pain or cry out, not even when one warrior ripped the bodice of her gown to shame her before the others. She stood tall, unable to cover herself, crushing down her urge to survive in order to retain her pride. She would struggle no longer. She did not know what sort of death they had planned for her but as she stared at Raff's emotionless face she realized it did not matter. Death could be no worse than life without his love.

She bent her head in sorrow—sorrow not that she would die, but at the bitter turn his love had taken. Did his hatred go so deep? Couldn't he remember a hint of the passion they'd given one another?

She accepted her death, anticipating the release it would bring.

But then he spoke. "Free her," he commanded. With those two soft but firmly-spoken words all movement stopped. Though the strength of his voice carried above the din, its tone did not allow her any hope of forgiveness.

The warriors, too, must have sensed it. They did not hasten to carry out his command but merely stared at him in disbelief. He, of all present, should most desire her death. She'd tricked him, shamed him, fooled him into a marriage that would never see an heir. No offspring to take his place as chieftain. Surely he wished to be free of her so that he could take another woman to wife, one pure of spirit, innocent of the lies that would make their marriage a farce.

"Free her," he repeated. "She is no longer a threat to us. She is to be returned to her king."

But the Danes, caught up in the blood-lust like hungry sharks, boldly challenged Raff despite the fact that he was their chieftain.

"Let us free you of this marriage!" one warrior shouted.

"Let us send her corpse to the king!" another yelled, and more voices rose in agreement. "We'll show him what we think of his loyal subject!"

Raff stood firm against his people. "And have his army finish what Ragnold tried to do? Nay—I said free her. She means nothing to us dead or alive. She will be free to return home."

Ambyre heard his words but they brought no comfort. So he would spare her life after all. But what difference did it make if he banished her from his sight?

The warriors argued again. "If she lives you will have no heirs to give our people! No son to be named chieftain in your stead."

"I have brothers to carry on," Raff said without emotion. "She shall be returned."

"Nay."

The single word, spoken softly, silenced all others. For it had come from the victim herself.

Ambyre spoke again, this time boldly. "I do not care to return to Wessex." She found the barest pleasure in seeing his surprise. "Let me stay or kill me, Raff. I'll not willingly leave your side. I am your wife and have the right to follow you anywhere—even if it means my death."

After her declaration the silence continued. Raff stared but his eyes were still distrustful. She could see the doubt like a deadly disease. Then he turned his back on her once again.

"You may do as you please," he said to his men. "I no longer care."

He spoke the words over his shoulder. As Ambyre heard them she knew death could be no more painful. She stood still, willing them to proceed.

Several warriors backed away, joining those who had played no part in it from the beginning. But those who remained did not seem mollified by her display of loyalty. They led her to a fallen tree and forced her to kneel, facing it. Her arms were bound around its wide perimeter. The bark chafed her exposed flesh bloodying her tender arms and chest.

But that was the least of her pain. One warrior pushed her face roughly against the bark and pulled her hair to uncover the back of her neck. She could guess what was to be the method of her execution judging from the size of the man who approached her with his heavy sword. No doubt her head would be severed cleanly from her body. She looked up at him, bruised and spotted with blood, bound to the trunk, unable to move. Her one hope was that death would be swift.

The warrior, seeing her eyes follow him, stopped as he reached her side. She displayed no tears no hatred, no fear. She merely watched. He was not reluctant to kill a woman—aye, in his raids he had done so before. But never had the eyes of his victim looked at him so calmly, as if Valhalla itself waited just beyond. He wondered if the spirits beckoned this woman.

His hesitation became apparent. Other warriors urged him on.

"Kill her!" they yelled.

"Send the Saxon to hell!"

"Remember our fallen warriors!"

He took the last step toward her and grabbed his sword in both hands. Raising it slowly, he felt a chill down his back as he gazed at the serene face of the woman he was to kill. Unable to bear looking at her a moment longer he closed his eyes, clutching his sword tighter.

"No! Stop—I command it!"

Had the warrior kept his eyes open, he would have seen Raff hold up a hand to halt the execution. Had not the other warriors shouted their blood-lust, he would have heard Raff's command.

Ambyre heard the deadly whistle of the sword and knew the end had come. Her eyes remained open, one mad thought behind them. She wished her last sight could be of Raff instead of this burly warrior with his eyes closed.

Stunned, she heard the axe hit the trunk with a thud, imbedding itself barely clear of her face. Had the warrior lost his aim because of his closed eyes? Would she have to face that raised sword again? The horror threatened to snap any sensible thought from her mind.

Raff stepped forward, pushing aside the shame-faced warrior, wrenching the sword from the tree. He cut the ropes which bound her wrists.

She stared at him blankly, still prepared for death. Was this another torture for her to endure, to feel his gentle touch before he carried out her execution himself? She was beyond caring, exhausted by terror, too weak to stand.

He picked her up, pausing to look at the bewildered faces around him. "I reclaim this woman as my wife," he said. "Henceforth, she will be treated as such."

He turned away from them, carrying her to the darkened longhouse. It wasn't until he laid her upon the familiar bed that she realized where they were.

He left her side only long enough to bring some cool water and a soft cloth. Tenderly he bathed her wounds, covering her with the torn remnants of her shift. She watched him, feeling his soothing fingers, wishing he would lift his eyes to hers. When at last he did, she wasn't sure of if she could believe the love she saw there.

"I'm sorry," he whispered, one hand stroking the bruise on her face.

"*You*. . . ?" she began, baffled. " 'Tis I who have transgressed. Can you ever forgive the things I have done?"

His voice was husky with emotion. "You talk of my forgiving after what I've just put you through? I tried to stop him... he didn't hear me. By Odin I swear I tried to stop him! If he hadn't purposely shifted his sword... part of me would have died with you. I'd not have wanted to live on alone."

"Then—you can forgive me for everything?"

He smiled at her difficulty in believing him. "I was stupid, Ambyre. You spoke the truth today. 'Twas not your doing that caused us to lose York. And, if Edward sees that Ragnold is contained there—not to interfere with my province or others—perhaps we can live in peace."

She turned wide, wondering eyes to him. "Raff... do you... love me?"

He laughed at the question, holding her face between his large hands. "The moment I saw you had returned... the moment you said you wanted to stay... I knew I still loved you, no matter what had gone before."

"But the others—you wanted them to—"

"I was blinded by my own bitterness. I didn't know if I could believe you—you said you didn't want to live without me but you'd said other things I should not have believed. I didn't want your love to be a lie as well."

"Would I have returned if it were? I love you, Raff Olafsson—that you can believe no matter what else has passed between us."

"I wouldn't let myself believe it—not until..."

"Then I'm glad for what happened if it made you believe me. I would go through it all again if necessary to convince you."

"Oh, no!" he protested. "I've boasted about my bravery but I admit today has tried my wits as never before."

She smiled. He met her lips with a kiss.

"I've come to stay, Raff," she whispered. "Cuthbert is here and—"

"Not Fauntley!" he exclaimed, thinking she was about to name the tutor as well.

She laughed. "Nay, I doubt he would return very willingly. He was quite happy to remain in Wessex. I've brought my brother and my dowry. I will call no place my home except at your side."

"Then you are home, my love," he said, and underlined his words with another kiss.

BE SWEPT AWAY ON A TIDE OF PASSION BY LEISURE'S THRILLING HISTORICAL ROMANCES!

2048-3	**SECRETS OF MY HEART** Cassie Edwards	$3.75 US, $4.25 Can.
2094-7	**DESIRE ON THE DUNES** Nancy Bruff	$3.50 US, $3.95 Can.
2095-5	**THE PASSION STONE** Harriette de Jarnette	$3.50
2141-2	**DYNASTY OF DESIRE** Carol Carmichael	$3.95 US, $4.75 Can.
2173-0	**TENDER FURY** Connie Mason	$3.75 US, $4.50 Can.
2184-6	**EMERALD DESIRE** Lynette Vinet	$3.75 US, $4.50 Can.
2194-3	**THORN OF LOVE** Robin Lee Hatcher	$3.95 US, $4.95 Can.
2205-2	**LEGACY OF HONOR** Linda Hilton	$3.95 US, $4.95 Can.
2216-8	**THE HEART OF THE ROSE** Kathryn Meyer Griffith	$3.95 US, $4.95 Can.
2255-9	**RECKLESS HEART** Madeline Baker	$3.95 US, $4.95 Can.

UNDER CRIMSON SAILS

Lynna Lawton

Beautiful, spirited Janielle Patterson had heard of the reckless way pirate Ryan Deverel treated his women. He seduced them with the same abandon with which he plundered ships. To the handsome pirate, women were prizes to be won, used, and tossed away.

Ryan intrigued and repelled Janielle—and when they finally met, she was shocked to discover that her own nature was as passionate as the pirate's!

But while he was driven by desire, she was driven by a fierce hatred. Yet she knew neither of them would rest until she had surrendered to him fully.

LEISURE BOOKS

THRILLING HISTORICAL ROMANCE BY LEISURE'S LEADING LADY OF LOVE, CATHERINE HART

2131-5	FIRE AND ICE	$3.95 US, $4.50 Can.
2226-5	SILKEN SAVAGE	$3.95 US, $4.95 Can.
2287-7	ASHES AND ECSTASY	$3.95 US, $4.95 Can.

FORBIDDEN LOVE
Karen Robards

PASSION, TENDERNESS AND WIT

Justin Brant, Earl of Weston, had prided himself on meticulously fulfilling his obligations as guardian to his dead brother's adopted daughter, though he regarded the rebellious child as a nuisance. On her part, Megan considered him a stern figure, cold and distant.

Now, at seventeen, Megan had blossomed into a breathtaking beauty. For Justin, Megan was forbidden fruit dangling temptingly within his grasp. But Megan knew that in spite of everything, she must give herself to the one man in the world whose bride she could never be.

LEISURE BOOKS

PRICE: $3.50 US/$3.95 CAN
0-8439-2024-6

SIZZLING, SENSUAL HISTORICAL ROMANCE BY SANDRA DUBAY

2245-1	WHERE PASSION DWELLS	$3.95 US, $4.95 Can.
2164-1	IN PASSION'S SHADOW	$3.95 US, $4.95 Can.
2153-6	CRIMSON CONQUEST	$3.50
2101-3	WHISPERS OF PASSION	$3.75 US, $4.50 Can.
2031-9	FIDELITY'S FLIGHT	$3.75 US, $4.25 Can.

STORMY SURRENDER

Robin Lee Hatcher

WAR AND LOVE

At sixteen, lovely Taylor Bellman finds her gentle and elegant world crumbling around her with the death of her father. Forced by her half brother to marry a man over forty years her senior in order to keep their beloved home, Spring Haven, in the Bellman family, Taylor's platonic marriage becomes a source of strength and contentment to both herself and her husband. But Civil War threatens her peace— and a gallant Yankee visitor awakens her sleeping heart to the thrill of illicit love.

Though their passion cannot be denied, Brent and Taylor know they must part. So begins a saga of war and tragedy, and of burning love that will never die, no matter what obstacles fate has placed between them.

LEISURE BOOKS

PRICE: $3.75/$4.25 CAN
0-8439-2073-4

Make the Most of Your Leisure Time with
LEISURE BOOKS

Please send me the following titles:

Quantity	Book Number	Price

If out of stock on any of the above titles, please send me the alternate title(s) listed below:

                                       Postage & Handling _____
                                       Total Enclosed $_____

☐ Please send me a free catalog.

NAME _____
(please print)

ADDRESS _____

_____ STATE _____ ZIP _____

Please include $1.00 shipping and handling for the first book ordered and 25¢ for each book thereafter in the same order. All orders are shipped within approximately 4 weeks via postal service book rate. PAYMENT MUST ACCOMPANY ALL ORDERS.*

*Canadian orders must be paid in US dollars payable through a New York banking facility.

Mail coupon to: **Dorchester Publishing Co., Inc.**
6 East 39 Street, Suite 900
New York, NY 10016
Att: ORDER DEPT.